Sign up for our newsletter to hear
about new and upcoming releases.

www.ylva-publishing.com

OTHER BOOKS BY
ELLEN SIMPSON

The Light of the World

ELLEN SIMPSON

A HEIST STORY

PRELUDE

Wei, at the moment when it all began

THE FIRST DROP FELL QUIETLY, then another, and another. Falling from long-pregnant clouds, bursting forth into downpour in the gray of dawn. Through a crack in the window, the steady fall of rain filled the room, only to be drowned out by the shrill beep of a phone. In the quiet, dark space that existed between the waking and the dream worlds, two figures lay curled together in a bed too small for their togetherness. Bodies nestled under thick blankets against the just-spring chill and the ever-present edges of the bed. The window looked out over a mist-laden haze of rooftops toward the center of London.

Wei Topeté woke with a headache. Sleep clung to her like mud. The lull of the rain pulled her back to dozing just as strongly as the shrill beeping of her phone had her grinding her teeth in irritation. Who could possibly want to speak to her at this hour? Speaking of...what even was the hour? Wei rolled over and tugged her phone from its charger. She ran a hand over her face, exhaustion pressing into her on all sides. It had been a long night already. Too long. Sitting up late. Obsessing over uncontrollable details.

The screen's glow hurt her eyes in the darkness of the not-yet-dawn. LePage was calling. Wei scowled at the screen. He was in the States; it was the middle of the night there. Had something happened? Had LePage finally gone off the deep end and forgotten everything she'd told him about how this was *supposed* to work? There were rules in the game they played, levels of secrecy set up to provide plausible deniability should anyone try to dig deeper than the surface of their investigation. They had one chance, *one*, and if LePage screwed it up by harassing her at stupid o'clock in the morning—Wei stopped herself.

Kat would wake up if Wei didn't answer the phone. She was a heavy sleeper, but her waking was, at this juncture, the last thing Wei wanted. She sat up, hissing in displeasure as her feet hit the icy floor. Her sleepshirt was short, barely skirting the tops of her thighs. Gooseflesh rolled up her legs in a steady wave that left her wanting for the warm bed. With a quiet curse, she pulled the throw blanket from the end of the bed around her. She did not want to talk to LePage.

"This'd better be good."

Rain was pooling on the windowsill, the sheer white curtains blowing back into the room, ghostlike in in the cold spring breeze.

"He's dead, Topeté." LePage's voice drifted through the fog, full of static as it came across the ocean. He sounded rough, like a night on the town was only just ending for him, echoing in the tiredness of his voice and the fearful, almost apologetic way he spoke. "Yesterday at noon. I only just heard."

Wei frowned, her fingers twitching at her side. She'd chased him for months, knowing full well that it was only a matter of time until his terminal prognosis took hold and the answers Wei needed fell into her lap. She'd meticulously planned each detail of this moment, down to the final coup de grâce, when he would be dead, and his secrets would be the property of the American government and set to be graciously loaned to her. The pieces were moving now, the plan starting to come together.

"And his estate?"

LePage heaved a weary sigh. "Gone."

A chill shot up Wei's spine, settling at the back of her neck. She rubbed at it and exhaled. This wasn't good. She glanced over to the bed, looking for confirmation, but her companion slept on. Could she have known and simply not mentioned it? Was this the moment their fragile truce finally fell apart?

"Gone? What do you mean, gone?" Her accent grew more pronounced, the French vowels coming fully into her voice as her displeasure mounted. It couldn't be gone, not when they'd worked so hard for so long to find it and ensure the circumstances of its resurfacing ended up in their favor. "That was all that we asked of you."

"I know."

"You were supposed to watch him. He wasn't meant to get to a lawyer."

"I know."

The repetition was grating.

It was raining harder now. Wei pushed the window closed, and the wind lashed heavy droplets against the pane. Wei choked down her disappointment. What were they going to do now? What could they do but start again, tracking down the lawyer and the—it didn't do to think of it now, not before a few more hours of sleep or a large cup of coffee. She pressed her fingers to the cool glass, staring out at the bleak dawn. "Where is Mock's estate?" She leaned against the damp windowsill, phone cradled between her shoulder and ear. She could see Kat this way. She could watch for warning signs.

Kat stirred as LePage spoke. A fond smile drifted across Wei's face as Kat pulled a pillow over her head and grumbled about the early hour. This was how Wei liked Kat, when the masks fell away and there was nothing left but the ease of sleepy touches. Kat was not often like this, which made this conversation a risk Wei could not afford to take. Especially not now, when they were so close to the end of Wei's next play.

"Do you have an address for the lawyer?" LePage grunted the affirmative. Wei stared at Kat's still form, deciding. Could she risk this move so soon? Would it be safe? Would Kat see through the flimsy excuses already tasting sour on Wei's tongue? She could not afford a slip, not on an investigation of this magnitude. LePage coughed. Wei bit her lip, coming to a decision. "Call the office."

"You're going in? It's five-thirty in the morning."

"Did she assign you to me so that you could question my decisions?"

"Well," LePage started. "No, I don't suppose she did."

"Exactly."

"Okay, fine, I'll send it in."

When she hung up, Wei turned to see Kat sitting up in the middle of the bed. Words filtered forward, statements of mourning and grief, words that should be said when one loses a dear friend and mentor. But the secrets living between them were such that those words stuck to the roof of Wei's mouth. All she could do was crawl back into bed and pull Kat's sleep-warm

3

body back under the blankets and pretend the world they carved for each other in this apartment was enough.

They clung to each other, no words were spoken. Wei felt sick, her stomach roiling when Kat kissed the skin where her neck met her shoulder. Kat's touch was gentle, her eyes full of warmth. Wei could not look at her. This could be the last time.

PART ONE

The Mastermind, at Conception

CHAPTER 1

Marcey, Going Visiting

FROM WHERE IT SAT, HALF-FORGOTTEN beside her mouse, Marcey's phone buzzed. She glanced down at it out of habit before her eyes flicked back up to her computer, only to have her attention instantly drawn back down again, surprised by the name flashing across the screen.

New Facebook message from: Rebecca Johnson.

"Becks?" she muttered. Disbelief washed over her. She hadn't heard from Rebecca in years—not since her high school graduation when Rebecca had been allowed to walk despite finishing the school year in treatment for a pill habit. A pill habit that Marcey might have enabled. A lot. It had been a particularly miserable time for Marcey: facing down the failure that could have decided her future and the acute loss of her best friend, absent from the proceedings when Rebecca was allowed to be present.

Marcey slid her finger over the screen, taking in the messaging app and the note that followed. Rebecca Johnson had grown into a looker, still rail thin and looking as though sleep was an elusive thing for her. But it wasn't her picture, or her arms wrapped around some girl who wasn't Marcey, that caught Marcey's attention. It was the content of her message.

Rebecca: Hey Marcey—long time no talk! I can't believe where the years have gone. I looked you up the other day, curious as to what happened to you. Imagine my surprise to find you working for your mom. I would have assumed you'd be off saving the world or something…

Marcey stopped reading. The "or something" had a particular bite. She knew where Rebecca thought she should be. Marcey wasn't going to bother responding. It wasn't worth it. The "you should be dead," was implied. Or, she supposed, the message could have read: "You could be locked away for getting someone killed" that Rebecca wasn't saying. Well, it was a timeworn hypothesis. Marcey'd heard it for years. She'd gotten out of that life. Too smart to run with a gang, too stupid and green to run her own crew.

The screen of her phone, gone black with Marcey staring off into space and being pissed off at the girl she'd fucked in high school for a while, lit up once more.

New Facebook message from: Rebecca Johnson.

"Christ." Marcey exhaled. "Fucking leave me alone." She drew her finger across the screen again and forced herself to keep reading. The rest of the first message was just nostalgia about college. Shit Marcey couldn't care less about. But the new message...

> **Rebecca:** I know I'm the last person you want to hear from after what happened in high school, but I couldn't...not tell you. My mom's running for district attorney in November. She's got this new ad, it's up on her campaign YouTube channel. You should see it.

> **Rebecca:** I told her...I told her not to, Marcey. I hope you'll believe me.

Marcey, perhaps out of spite, or perhaps out of a broken heart never quite healed from injuries close to a decade old now, didn't respond to the message. She glanced over her shoulder at the cubicle that housed her manager's desk, but the woman's back was turned and she appeared to be on the phone. Emboldened, Marcey navigated to the campaign YouTube channel.

"Johnson for DA," the autoplay ad began, before going into all of the many accomplishments of Assistant District Attorney Linda Johnson. She put criminals and would-be terrorists behind bars, kept criminal syndicates out of the local schools, and fought for better protection for police in officer-involved shooting incidents. It was a typical, run-of-the-mill political advertisement, Republican and abhorrent to Marcey, save for one detail: in the middle of all of it were two crude artist renderings—crude and cartoonish, but obvious to anyone who knew Marcey—of the twin mugshots of Marcey and her best friend, Darius, the day they'd gotten arrested. Their faces were superimposed over a headline from the *New York Post* declaring a prescription drug ring had been brought down by solid investigative work at a local charter school. It was a lie. A lie that pushed Marcey to the edge of her seat, disgust pulling her lips away from her teeth in a snarl.

Rebecca hadn't been lying—this was bad. *Shit.* She had to call Darius. *Shit*, she had to call Darius's lawyer. Marcey's mind raced, but she struggled to see the end of this train of thought. It was too awful. In that moment, the moment when everything horrible running through her mind came to an end, she would know what to do. She had to envision all the possibilities, all the horrible endings, until they were spun into something—something that Marcey could work with.

Her vision blurred and her anger built. The rage of all of this. The audacity of that woman to try again. To try and take Darius's life from him again. And to do it in the court of public opinion.

Linda Johnson—Rebecca's horrible mother—was back. And she was set to ruin Marcey's life in new and exciting ways.

"Fuck her." Marcey's voice was barely more than a growl. She pulled her phone toward her and opened the messaging app. There was something in her that wanted to yell at Rebecca. To cuss her out for the strife this was going to cause, but it didn't seem worth it somehow. Marcey sighed, her teeth grinding and jaw working as she tried to get her reaction under control. She set her phone down, her resolve shaking. "Just...fuuuuuuck her."

"Hmm?" Her cube mate pulled a headphone out of his ear. The low din of conversation was never enough to drown out the unrelenting hum of the office's piped-in white noise. No one was saying anything.

"Nothing." Marcey rolled her chair forward and replayed the advertisement, phone forgotten. Rebecca wasn't worth it. Her mother, however, was a different story. That came with a whole lot more baggage Marcey was more than willing to unpack. "It isn't worth getting into."

"Ohhhh-kay?" Her cube mate shrugged and turned back to his work.

Marcey exhaled. She couldn't tell him, not when these walls had ears. She clicked back into the Johnson for DA campaign's YouTube profile and watched the other advertisements. None of the others mentioned her or Darius, but a few made reference to the case.

It was the case that had made ADA Johnson's career: her redemption after the terrible Mock trial, where she couldn't prove the guilt of a man so obviously guilty it was almost comical. Her failure and the subsequent acquittal had been all over the papers when Marcey and Darius were arrested. Marcey got off because of an exceptionally talented lawyer and a technicality. It was that, more than Rebecca's OD and subsequent rehab, which had landed Marcey forever on ADA Johnson's shit list. Darius hadn't been so lucky. He'd had a good lawyer too, Devon Austin Jackson—a guy Marcey'd been meaning to see, actually, about something else. Devon needed to know about this sooner rather than later. The lawyer'd been decent, but it hadn't been enough to make a jury of Upper West Side shitheads look past the color of Darius's skin and the nature of the crime. He had to do the maximum. He was lucky he'd been only sixteen at the time.

She opened her email and started typing. She could tell him this way, in e-mail, and avoid so many of the complicated feelings that came with articulating the emotions of this in person. But it wouldn't be enough. It was going to have to come out. She was going to have to go into his office and sit across his desk from him and tell him that her goddamn ex's mom was set to fuck up Darius's upcoming parole hearing by running for public office.

Marcey frowned, her lips pursing. Wasn't this slander? Her record wasn't sealed, and it was only by the good grace of nepotism that she'd landed this job at all. But Johnson shouldn't be able to use her picture—even a crude likeness. Not without Marcey's explicit consent.

Her face stared back at her from the paused video. She looked haunted, eyes sunken and hollow. Her hair was sticking up from her school braid, her scowl deep and unflinching in the artist's rendering.

Marcey closed the e-mail window and sat back, fingers knitting together in a bridge over her stomach. This was a nightmare scenario. What the fuck was she going to do? The picture was all wrong. She'd been crying that day. Not scowling. It had been a nightmare. She, just sixteen, was saved serious jail time, while Darius, her best friend and confidant, was sent away for eight years. The look on Darius's face as the verdict had come down was one Marcey would never forget as long as she lived. She'd begged ADA Johnson in a private meeting room to save Darius before the verdict was read. She'd told the truth: Darius was the only one she'd come out to.

"You came out to my daughter."

"That's different," Marcey had insisted. "She's...she and I understand each other."

"I don't understand her preoccupation with you. Or your continued presence in her life."

"Don't out me," Marcey had begged. She couldn't beg not to be punished for her crimes, that wouldn't have been right—she'd been caught fair and square—but this, this was different. This she couldn't stomach. "He's the only one who knows—outside of Becca." Darius was the only person who had accepted her without question no matter what she told him. He was good people like that. The mess with Becca and the OD and Johnson deciding to gun for Marcey and Darius both—that had been her fault. She'd enabled Becca. She'd let it become a thing when she should have stopped it. Darius just happened to be with her at the time; they shouldn't send him away for something that was all Marcey's fault. She couldn't do that to him. She couldn't.

Johnson had looked down her nose at Marcey and asked her why she had allowed Darius to confess to the crime if he was the only one who loved and supported her. The condescension, and the powerlessness of that moment, still haunted Marcey. Johnson wasn't going to change her recommendation to the judge just because Marcey was a lost little lesbian. She had just wanted to hear Marcey beg for leniency. She'd relished it. Darius was sent away, and Marcey had been left to deal with a homophobic mother and a pseudo-private school that saw her as a problem because of her association with Darius and because of her sexuality.

Marcey was alone then. Truly alone, trapped in a hostile environment at every turn. It had never gotten any easier.

When Marcey was young, she used to fantasize about what sort of person she would become later in life. Her pediatrician had asked her every year, in his kind way, what she wanted to be when she grew up. The answers varied. For a while, she'd wanted to be a mermaid, and then a skateboarder. There was a brief period at around six years old when she wanted, more than anything else, to be Mulan. As she grew older, Marcey had stopped having easy answers for her doctor. She would look away, mutter some sullen teenage excuse about not wanting to box herself in, and find herself wanting.

She went to school for statistics, because she was good at numbers and liked the probabilities and how easily data could be manipulated. She took the numbers like her mind took possibilities and weighed them to see the best possible choice. Marcey told herself she went to school for statistics so she would never become one, but it wasn't quite true. She already was one, and not one trending in the positive. She wanted to get better at weighing odds, to avoid the bad choices that had gotten her into the situations that plagued her still.

What did she want with her life? What did any kid with a fairly public—though ostensibly sealed—juvenile record want? What did any kid who'd suffered through high school because their best friend was ripped away from them want out of life? Anonymity. To be left in that vacuum of alone they'd dumped her in.

In a single thirty-second sound bite, Linda Johnson's ad tore down the rickety framework of lies and half-truths she'd told her coworkers about her past and her childhood. Marcey never outright lied to her peers—she just had no compunction about omitting the truth. If they really wanted to know, they could use Google as well as anyone else.

By the time the ad finished playing for the third time, Marcey's mind was made up. She picked up her phone and shot a message back to Rebecca.

Marcey: Thanks for telling me. It's good to hear from you. If you're smart you'll lose my number.

There was no way she could continue to allow this to stand. She had to get the ad off the air. By any means necessary. And if she couldn't, she was going to destroy Assistant District Attorney Linda Johnson's career before the election in a very public way. Rebecca and whatever feelings Marcey still had for her be damned.

Rebecca: What are you going to do?

Marcey Daniels has successfully blocked Rebecca Johnson.

Marcey set down her phone and sat back. The sigh on her lips tasted wrong, like the ill-fitting clothes she wore and the curling idea of revenge in her stomach.

Only...she had no idea how to exact a revenge like that. She wasn't a criminal, thanks to her mother putting herself into debt to pay for the lawyer that had gotten her off. She wasn't even a lawyer; she was a kid with a degree in math who saw patterns in things.

She minimized the internet window and exhaled quietly. Her computer wallpaper, a photograph of herself a handful of years younger than her twenty-five years, alongside her best friend, winked into view. They were standing in front of a Starbucks, heads thrown back to catch snowflakes on their tongues. Darius was clad in all black, a cream-colored hat perched awkwardly on top of his just-trimmed fade. Marcey's bright red scarf matched her cheeks. She was wearing Darius's heavy winter jacket. It was one of the last photographs of them happy and together. Rebecca and everything that had come after that awful party...was all a bad memory now. But this—this moment was *pure*.

Marcey stared at it for a long time, heart warm with the memory of that day. His monthly visitation was soon. The first Friday in March. Marcey was going up to visit him again then. Maybe he'd have an answer about Johnson, the mysterious package she'd received a few weeks before, or what to do about the fact that they couldn't talk to each other but in code. Marcey hated the slog of going in and out of a high-security prison once a month. She hated the never-ending guilt.

In a way, she was grateful for the forward thrust of the early stages of revenge.

Anything was better than dwelling in the past.

Marcey didn't get the chance to drive much. It came with living in New York, squatting in the spare bedroom of her mother's already too-small apartment. She relished the opportunity to get behind the wheel and out on the open road, driving up I-90 toward Albany and then on to Canada. Driving was freedom, divorcing herself from the concrete jungle of the city and pulling her into the rolling Adirondack foothills north of the capitol.

Nestled deep amid the forested mountains was a tiny village that played host to the prison where Darius was locked away. Called Dannemora, it hardly evoked the hardened home of some of the worst criminals from the state of New York, picturesque as it gathered at the edge of a national forest that shared the village's name.

ADA Johnson had made sure to send him to the scariest prison she could arrange: Clinton Correctional. The name meant nothing if you weren't from New York, but if you were, and you had any passing brushes with the law, you feared the place. It was where they sent the worst of the worst criminals, where they locked them away and tossed the key into the Hudson.

Or whatever dramatic shit they say on Law & Order, Marcey mused pensively.

Marcey had spent the past few weeks stewing about ADA Johnson's political ad while in meetings with Darius's lawyer. He had to figure out if the ad was illegal, and they'd spent hours debating what to do with the strange package that had arrived on her doorstep. She gripped the steering wheel of her rented Hyundai, trying to focus on the drive. On the seat next to her, sticking out of her purse, was a small black Moleskine notebook. Marcey glanced at it before training her eyes back on the road. *That* was another mess that would only serve to distract her. She and Devon weren't in agreement about the best course of action. It was starting to snow; the road was slick and the prison was fast approaching. Her mind couldn't wander now.

When she sat down across from Darius thirty minutes later, she barely took the time to take in his gaunt appearance and the dark circles under his eyes. His skin was dry when he grasped her hand and pulled her in for the one hug she was allowed at the beginning of the visit. They'd kept him in here longer than they should have—some technicality his previous parole hearing had invalidated the whole process. Marcey didn't want it to happen again. What Johnson wanted to do could change that, somehow keep Darius locked away forever. She couldn't look at him, not without telling him the awful truth. He had to know—it would impact him too.

Marcey swallowed, looking at her hands to avoid Darius's serious brown eyes, and spoke quickly. "Linda Johnson's using our mugshots in a campaign ad. Devon says it's legal and we can't really do shit about it, and now the entire world knows that I was involved in your arrest and that you're about to come up for parole again."

He stared at her. "You're joking."

"Nope." Marcey paused, forcing herself to look up. She sighed, pushing her hair out of her eyes. "Well, that's stretching it a little. They're cartoonish renderings, but they're very obviously based on our mugshots. I didn't want to ask anyone, but I think if your ma or mine saw it they'd know. Same with anyone who knows us. That's what worries me."

"Man." Darius scrubbed at his face. "You got off for this bullshit."

"I shouldn't have," Marcey said, spitting it out quickly. She always did. He resented her freedom enough as it was. There was nothing she could do about it either, other than be quicker to the punch of her white guilt.

He glared at her. "Don't start." He sat back. "Devon doesn't think it's libel or something?"

"Not as far as any research can figure. I've spent the past couple weeks stewing about it. Talking at him about it. He's looked into it, off the clock. Basically, Devon says it's a matter of public record. And apparently the Super PAC who paid for it isn't known for their scruples. I'm sure they think I'm locked up somewhere too." Marcey pressed her hand flat on the table before them. "I'm not sure what this means for your parole hearing."

"Probably means I'm fucked." Darius's first appearance before the parole board was scheduled for May, when the campaign would be really heating up prior to the summer campaign season. Marcey'd checked those dates too. There was no way to get the ad pulled without a lengthy court battle. Darius rubbed at the back of his head and looked away. "Fuck, man." He looked like he was on the verge of crying.

All Marcey wanted to do was reach out, draw him into a hug, and not let him go. He was her best friend; he knew her secrets and she his. She looked down at her hands, useless on the table. They weren't allowed to touch. The distance opened like a great gash across the space between them. "I'm sorry."

It never sounded like enough.

"Devon's pretty convinced she wouldn't show up in person, I guess because of the campaign. He called me and told me that. This musta been why. Said we'd get some green-eared kid who'd recommend parole and I'd be out in June." Darius seemed to crumple in his tan scrubs. His gaze met

Marcey's. "Man. If she's using this case as a cornerstone for her campaign, she's gotta show up. My ma's gonna have a fit." There were tears in his eyes, borne, Marcey suspected, of frustration. "She wanted me to come home last June. It's been more than eight years."

"What if there was, say, a way we could get back at her?"

"We'd be stupid." His tone was sharp. "There's no way we can do that, Mar. The most you could do is get that group in trouble for using your picture in an advertisement. I got no rights. And it won't fly. If they've done it, it means it's probably legal, no matter how dubious."

"True." Marcey bit her lip and glanced over her shoulder. The guard at the far end of the room was distracted by a young mother's squalling child and not paying her much attention. Marcey leaned forward, her tone dropping and growing urgent. These visits were monitored. She had to be careful. "But I think I might have found something that could help."

He tilted his head, skeptical. "What?"

"I got this book in the mail. I can't show it to you. I left it in the car. But I think it might be the key." Marcey glanced over her shoulder. "You know that guy, the one that Johnson wasn't able to convict right before our case, when the papers were calling for her to be fired and sanctioned by the New York State Bar because of how it ended? The book belonged to him." Marcey prayed Darius remembered. It was so long ago, and she couldn't tell him much else about the strange encounter and series of disagreements she'd had with Devon Austin Jackson about what to do with the book. Darius's lawyer evidently knew the man. He knew everything about him and about the contents of the book before Marcey could even ask about it. He knew and he'd sat there and smiled at her and told her that Linda Johnson was well within her rights about the ad and had asked what she was going to do about it before implying other people were looking for the book as well.

"Are you sure, Mar?"

"There's a story here, Dar. A connection. I just have to pick at it..." She leaned forward, her fingers gripping the edges of the table. "I want to know what it is."

It was a lie. Marcey knew what it was, but she couldn't say it here and they both knew it.

At first, Darius didn't say much at all, sitting hunched over in his tan scrubs. Frowning, Marcey took him in then, saw how the years in this place had shaped him into someone far different from the baby-faced kid she'd cared so much about as a teen. His hair was getting longer, which Marcey liked, and his face was hollow now—it bore the weight of all he'd been through.

"I don't want you doing anything that'd mess up the parole hearing." Darius's eyes took on a resigned look. "Everyone knew there wasn't a snowball's chance in hell to get out a few years early. Then that bullshit happened last year and I got stuck for another year. If you go and fuck it up for me, Mar, I don't think—" He trailed off, but the implication was clear. It wasn't Marcey's place to do this for him. "Don't follow up with this."

"But—"

His expression hardened. "Take your guilt and shove it. Don't. Fuck up your own life."

"It could ruin her, if she's connected to someone like that."

"Is it worth my freedom?" Darius slammed his hand on the table. A guard looked over at them, one hand on his belt. "Everyone knows she wanted you more than she wanted me. Because of Rebecca. She offered me immunity. She offered me *freedom*, Marcey, if I gave you up. I never said shit. Now she's making us look like cartoon villains to make her career."

"Career..." Marcey snatched her hand away from the table, getting to her feet.

"Where are you going?" he demanded, half rising. "We still have fifteen minutes."

"I just thought of something, something that I think will help you when you get paroled."

"Marcey, I told you no! If you look into that guy—that case—you'll poke the bear, and she'll come for you. Then what will you do?"

"Fight back, I suppose." Marcey sat back down. "I want to do this for you."

"I don't need your fucking savior complex." From across the room, the guard gave Darius a stern look, and he scowled at the guard before nodding to Marcey. "You don't need to save me. I can save myself, convince the parole board I should be let out. The ad is damaging, yes, but it will be a hell of a lot worse if you poke the *freaking* bear."

17

Marcey hung her head. She'd known he wouldn't want her help. Her mind was already back on the book, thinking hard about the contents and the thin threads of connection between its author and the letter he'd sent, and how it all could be tied back to ADA Johnson. That connection couldn't be ignored, no matter how risky it was to Darius. If this was the same guy, as Devon claimed he was, then the risk of possibly turning over some stones to rattle Johnson's campaign wasn't such a bad idea, even if it would make Darius angry.

"I won't," she promised. It was a lie that slid easily from her tongue. She had to do this. For him more than for herself. If it hurt him to get to a better outcome, so be it. The drive to act anyway, and do what she felt was right, it hit her hard and settled in her stomach. Darius would understand. "It's snowing like crazy outside and the eastern half of the state's under some sort of winter storm watch. I want to get on the road before we get upgraded to a blizzard."

He nodded, clearly not quite following. His confusion showed in the furrowing of his eyebrows and the way his lips pitched downward into a frown. Marcey mouthed *I'll tell you later* and said her good-byes. She had a lot to think about on her way back to the city.

CHAPTER 2

Marcey, Stumbling into Something

SIX AND A HALF HOURS into an early-March snowstorm that only seemed to get worse the closer she got to New York City, Marcey's eyes were stinging with the effort of keeping them open. She had three texts from her mother, demanding to know when she'd be home, that she couldn't answer. She didn't dare take her hands off the wheel to text her mother until she'd pulled into the parking lot of a twenty-four-hour storage facility in the Bronx.

> I'll be home soon, I still have one more errand to run before I return the car. I got you that syrup from Albany you wanted.
>
> It's snowing. Roads are a mess.

Marcey shoved the phone into her back pocket and tugged on the beanie she'd thrown into the back seat with her coat. Her straight, mousy-brown hair was full of static. Marcey cursed quietly and attempted to smooth it down before leaning into the back seat to retrieve her jacket.

It was humid outside. Snow still fell, and Marcey was grateful for her LL Bean boots as she stepped down into a puddle easily three inches deep of slushy, disgusting water. She wrinkled her nose and scowled as she shook her boot off before hopping through the slush over to the kiosk at the front of the facility.

Her feet were wet. She squelched her way up to the office. The man sitting inside was overweight and dozing, listening to the Knicks on the radio. He eyed Marcey as she pulled the Moleskine notebook out of her purse.

"Can I help you?" he asked. His shirt read "Ted."

Marcey nodded. "I need to see"—she flipped to a page toward the back, where the details were copied down in a precise, masculine hand—"unit number five-four-three-three."

"Ya got a key?"

"There's a combo-lock."

Ted grunted and pushed himself slowly to his feet. He flipped the "OPEN" sign hanging from a suction cup on the window over to read "BACK IN FIVE MINUTES" and passed Marcey a clipboard. "Gonna need to see some I.D."

Marcey frowned. "Why? I thought the whole point of these places was to be anonymous." She jotted down her name in the messiest handwriting possible.

"Got something to hide?"

It was a lie, but Marcey shook her head. "Nah. Just hate my license picture." She dug it out of her wallet and passed it to him.

"Don't we all?" Ted took the license. He glanced at it, and then at Marcey's face, before passing it back. He picked up a set of keys. "Five-four-three-three is toward the back. Come with me."

Ted was a lot taller than Marcey had anticipated. He towered over Marcey's slight frame when he stepped down from the office and shuffled toward the back of the facility. He moved with the grace of someone fifty pounds lighter as well, even if he wasn't doing much to pick up his feet as he walked. He led Marcey to the back row of bright red doors and pointed. "Down at the end. If you're not out in an hour, I'll come check on you."

"That won't be necessary," Marcey answered just a bit too quickly.

He stared at her for a moment. "Suit yourself. Hit the red button beside the unit if you start to panic or anyone back here gives you a hard time. This place gives me the creeps late at night." He turned and started to shuffle back toward the office.

Marcey glanced out the window at the swirling snow. It was just past seven o'clock, not even that late. "Thanks." Her words echoed strangely in the corridor. A tremor of excitement shot down Marcey's spine. She had no idea what she was meant to find here, but if she was right, it was the first piece of a puzzle left behind as a clue to something bigger.

Unit 5433 did not belong to Marcey, or anyone she knew personally. The number and address were written in the book and its purpose explained to Marcey in a letter from a man who claimed to know her, given to her by Darius's lawyer. How Devon had even had it was beyond Marcey at this point. He'd said it'd been left with him. Marcey wasn't so sure now if it wasn't all part of some elaborate plot.

When the book arrived on her doorstep, Marcey didn't think much of it beyond a passing annoyance at the courier, who'd left it without bothering to knock. Obviously, this book had some value, or it would not have been delivered by one of the city's elite private messaging companies.

"Everything happens for a reason, Mar," Devon explained, offering it to her between two fingers. "This might give you a better idea of why this is happening."

"For me?" She frowned, reading the address in the same slanted handwriting. "I don't even know the guy."

Devon smiled his mysterious smile and retreated behind his desk, leaving Marcey to read. It was...something else. The ramblings of an old man who had mistaken her for someone else. It claimed the writer was her father, and that he was leaving Marcey his legacy as she was an honest woman.

"An honest woman?" Marcey raised an eyebrow. "Sure."

"Well, you are, after a sense." Devon pursed his lips, the corners of his eyes crinkled with amusement. "No jail time on your record."

Marcey actually laughed, flabbergasted and yet not that surprised by what Devon had said. "I wouldn't be here if I didn't have to make an inquiry about that damn ad," she said. "Darius wanted me to stop bothering you when you were prepping for his parole hearing. The book would be in the trash and I'd be going about my life."

Devon put his hands in his pockets and sat back. "That so?"

Marcey scowled at him. He knew her pretty well by this point, and he wasn't exactly wrong in thinking that she was intrigued. Marcey let out a heavier sigh than she'd perhaps intended. "Well...what's this about a job he didn't get to pull off?" She flipped to the second page. "And what's this about him being my father?"

Devon told her all he knew. It wasn't much. He flipped through the book with her and found the storage unit address and number. "You should go there, see what Charlie had cookin'."

The unit belonged to Charles Mock. The same man that ADA Johnson had failed to convict in a very public, very messy trial, not long before she'd taken Marcey and Darius's case. The man who was apparently Marcey's father. There wasn't much proof of that in his note, just a few scant details on an affair when Marcey's mother was in graduate school at NYU, struggling to support herself. The details were written with such care, though, as though the memories contained in the letter were fond and treasured. Her mother's backstory was something Marcey knew like the back of her hand. For most of her life, Marcey had been told stories to encourage her to work harder, to be a better person. But her mother had apparently lied about everything for twenty-five years.

Marcey wanted to hate Devon when he showed her a photograph, because it made this whole thing real. The person who did this to her was real, an honest-to-god person. Not some sort of joke she could dismiss as Devon being a dick and trying to pull a fast one on her.

"This is Charlie." Devon tapped a man in the center. "He asked me to show you this."

Marcey took the photograph from him. Her eyes narrowed and then went wide with recognition. This was the guy who'd made Linda Johnson look like a goddamn fool right before Darius's trial. There were pictures of him walking out of the courtroom following the abrupt acquittal and near accusation of Linda Johnson's office fabricating evidence all over the newspapers. His head was held high and a wicked smirk danced across his lips. Even though she was in high school at the time, Marcey remembered those pictures. They'd felt like a victory for the little guy and a mockery of all that was corrupt and wrong about the criminal justice system. He looked younger in those photographs than in this picture. *No way...*

She scowled. No matter how cool or badass it was to get off like he had, this man's antics had fucking ruined her best friend's life. This was the guy who sent her this book? This was the guy who was supposed to be her father? She stared at the older man with a head of hair the same color as her own, curling at the top of his head. He was wearing sunglasses, but his nose was unmistakable. Marcey saw the same nose in the mirror every day. She'd seen that nose before too, on an old man down in the park she'd played chess with on the weekends sometimes, back when she'd still had time for that—back before her entire life had gone to shit.

In the photo, Charlie Mock stood on a beach somewhere, flanked by two women. One was black, taller than Charlie by a good three inches, and smiling broadly behind blood-red lipstick. She was stunning, her arm draped around Charlie's shoulder and her hair damp from the ocean. Beside them, grinning lopsidedly at the camera, was a blonde woman with pretty green eyes clad in a man's oversized white shirt and a long, flowing skirt. She was shorter than the others; Charlie's arm was wrapped around her waist. Her eyes were alive, bright with emotion. Marcey's breath caught in her throat. She was beautiful. Both of the women were.

On the back of the photograph was a carefully printed note in the same masculine hand that filled the Moleskine notebook. *Charlie, Shelly and Kat, Rio, 2013*

The photograph was tucked inside the Moleskine, along with the letter from Charlie Mock to Devon explaining the conditions of Marcey's inheritance. The letter was full of emotions, things she wasn't meant to hear. They were for some image of a child Charlie Mock had in his head, a child Charlie thought would be clever and whip-smart—a child with ambition. Marcey had ambition, yes, but she didn't want it ascribed to her by a stranger she hardly knew, asserting he had some claim on her life.

The papers weren't the only place Marcey had seen him before. The realization hit her hard. She looked up, stunned. "He played chess with me," she said. "When I was just starting high school—before that trial that ruined Linda Johnson's career. Like when I was a freshmen or whatever. He would come to the park and play chess."

Devon's face was impassive. "He was always a coward about interpersonal relationships. Amazing he and Shelly hit it off at all, given how she is about commitment. But whatever. He told me that he couldn't face the idea of ruining your life by telling you these things that your mother wasn't able to bring herself to admit. I'm sorry you had to find out this way."

"Why does he want to lay claim to me like this? I'm not a possession he can just say is his."

"Do you think that's what he's saying?"

"I don't know."

The conversation died after that. Later, when Marcey returned home, she went through every photograph her mother kept in the apartment. She devoured old address books and diaries, desperate to find a trace of Charlie Mock. The diaries were empty, and the address books held no more answers than the photographs. Marcey was convinced that this was all an elaborate prank by someone who knew her history with Darius and wanted to mess with her. It was a dick move. She went to bed fuming.

In the morning, she called Devon back. "How did he know it was me?"

"You should probably come back into the office."

So Marcey took the train and walked the ten blocks to Devon's office filled with a feeling of not quite dread not quite something else entirely. Devon waited until the pleasantries were done before he pulled a file from his desk drawer and paged through it. "The reason he knew is because he had you tested." He held out a single piece of paper from the file, his brow furrowed and his lips pursed into a thin, disapproving line. "Not that I thought it was a good idea, but that's white folks for you."

"Tested?" Marcey took the paper from him. It was a DNA test, establishing a paternal match.

"Charlie told me that he and your mother saw each other on and off for a few years while she was at NYU. He never knew that she'd gotten pregnant until he happened to see a picture of you in the newspaper with her a few years back." At Marcey's blank stare, Devon passed her a second sheet of paper, covered in the same spider-like handwriting of the letter and book she received—Charlie's handwriting. Marcey didn't like that she recognized it now, and the creeping sense of violation from the idea of being *tested* was taking all of her mental energy to hold back. She'd deal with that later, when Devon wasn't around to witness her disgust and horror.

Attached to the page was a newspaper clipping from the *Times*, a small black-and-white photo of her mother and Marcey, holding a giant pair of scissors, about to cut the ribbon on the firm's new offices.

She must have been fifteen in the photo. "This is more than a few years ago." Swallowing, Marcey leveled her gaze at Devon. Her hand was shaking. She bit the inside of her cheek to keep her expression neutral. She could not—would not—let him see that this bothered her. The idea of this strange man seeing her in the paper and then jumping to all kinds of conclusions about her. She glanced back down at the date on the picture, thinking back. She'd met Charlie not long after that in the park for the first time. "Kinda creepy if you ask me." It was dismissive, but it did somewhat reflect how she felt.

Devon laughed. "I suppose you're right. But I don't—*didn't*—put much past Charlie. He was always doing questionable things. And hey, time flies."

Marcey set the clipping aside to cover the disgust that swept over her face. "This doesn't prove anything."

"No." Devon shook his head. "But this will." He tapped the paternity test with his pen. "I don't know how he did it, I didn't ask, but somehow he got hold of your DNA, got you tested. I think he used a private investigator friend of his."

That was it. Marcey pushed away from the desk, the chair she'd been sitting on rolling away to slam into a bookshelf full of legal reference books. The terrible revulsion she'd only just been keeping in check boiling over and spewing forth from her lips. "How could someone who wrote such beautiful words—" She'd thrown down the results and stalked over to the window in disgust. "How could he just *do* that without my consent?"

The violation, the creeping sense of knowing *exactly* when Charlie Mock had gotten her DNA—during one of their chess games, he'd pulled a hair from her jacket and flicked it away as though it had been nothing... That must have been it; he must have kept it.

"He was a criminal, Marcey," Devon said, his expression resigned. "Not a good person."

<hr />

Charles Mock died in a prison.

Marcey thought of Darius, her stomach clenching. She couldn't imagine losing him while he was stuck behind those impermeable walls up at Clinton Correctional. ADA Johnson had her plan: she wanted to keep Darius locked away and she wanted to drag Marcey's name through the mud despite her acquittal. This was a revenge, and a petty one. Marcey wasn't sure why Johnson wanted it, or why it was so important to do it now, when Darius was set to be released in two months. Provided he won the parole request.

Marcey wanted to know why, and if that why was here, in this run-down twenty-four-hour storage facility in the south Bronx, then so be it. She was going to follow the leads and Charles Mock's paper trail until it went cold. She wanted to know if this was all connected to Charles, or if it was truly just about herself and Darius.

Ted's heavy footfalls soon fell silent with his retreat and Marcey was alone. She shivered in the cold air and set her jaw. There was no telling what she would find hidden behind the unit door. Devon hadn't been able to tell her much about what Charles Mock had locked away here.

Her boots were slippery on the concrete floor of the unit. Marcey hummed, thinking back to the meetings with Devon. The whole situation was a mess, and she didn't like anything about how Charlie had confirmed her relation to him. Devon's answer, that he was a criminal, wasn't enough. Marcey hoped there was something in this storage unit that justified why Marcey had to handle the violation of a strange man snooping into her paternity—into her fucking DNA.

No answer would be good enough for Marcey. Just as the crawling feeling at the pit of her stomach of violation. Marcey didn't like being lied to. She didn't like that Charlie Mock had never even bothered to say anything. All she felt was anger. He'd just taken his proof and dumped his last job in her lap. She'd left Devon's office confused and upset. There were no other answers, and the feelings she had were difficult to articulate. She'd thrown herself into researching the book and to making sure she had time to come to explore this storage unit.

The lock in her hand warmed quickly in her palm, sweaty despite the chill at the back of the storage facility. Marcey twisted the knob to the combination she'd memorized almost upon seeing it. Memory was Marcey's greatest asset: she could recall the ebb and flow of numbers across the page, and recognize patterns where seemingly there were none. She put her tongue between her teeth and pulled down on the lock. It didn't budge. She tried again. 15-2-34. After another moment of resistance, the lock clicked open and the rusted bolt of it fell loose. Marcey tugged it away from the latch and tucked it into her jacket pocket. It jangled against her keys.

The door rose about an inch or two from the ground, a small puff of dusty, disused air escaping from underneath it. Marcey bent and grabbed the handle, using her shoulder to throw the door into the ceiling storage space beyond. It rattled, echoing loudly in the empty hall, almost covering up the click-click-click of approaching footsteps.

Marcey froze. The bright light of the hallway streamed into the unit, but she couldn't look, not with someone close. She jumped up, grabbing at the handle. She had to close it. Charlie Mock's secrets were closely guarded, the sort that could not be shared with even a passerby. Marcey was certain of this. What if this person was investigating Charlie, looking to see if his death was faked? What if this person knew of Johnson's vendetta and wanted to come after her? What if this was one of Devon's people, following her to make sure that she'd stay out of trouble?

Click-click-click-stop.

Marcey peered up the hallway, her knees bent to try and jump up in order to grab the door handle.

A woman approached. She was broad shouldered, her hair impeccable despite the cold humidity of the weather outside. Her long jacket was coal gray and set off against her dark skin in a way that Marcey found fascinating. Most of all, she was beautiful. Her eyes were sharp, but not unkind, and her lips painted a bright red that stood out starkly against the dark color of her dress beneath the jacket and the warm brown of her skin.

When she spoke, it was in an affected voice. It took Marcey a minute to figure out why, before the realization slowly slotted into place. "If you're looking for Charlie," she called, stopping well away from Marcey, her hands in her pockets. "He's gone."

Marcey straightened. "I wasn't."

"This is his unit, you're trespassing." The woman's gaze flicked from Marcey to the open storage unit, narrowing as she took in Marcey's face. "I've been waiting for three weeks now for someone to show up. How did you find it?"

"Er—there's a book," Marcey hedged. "With the combination written inside." She pulled the lock from her pocket and held it up so it caught the light. "And I unlocked the door. Are you a guard or something?"

There was a smile evident in the woman's tone, even if it did not translate to her face. "Or something."

CHAPTER 3

Marcey, Following

THE STORAGE FACILITY WAS QUIET, save for the gentle buzz of the overhead fluorescent lights and the creak of ancient baseboard radiators. Marcey shivered, wrapping her arms around herself. Her jacket was too thin to linger in a place like this. She hadn't meant to linger at all. She wanted to get in, see whatever it was that Charlie had put here, and then go home to figure out her next move.

He'd left her instructions in that letter. Devon had feigned ignorance, but Marcey knew he was intent on making sure Marcey followed through. Was this woman's presence meant to confirm that?

She had to tread carefully. If she didn't, she was bound to run into more situations like this: a standoff that left her naked, unable to act for fear of blowing everything before she had a chance to get started.

Her purse swung from her shoulder, passing into the void of open space behind her—all of Charlie's secrets were back there, and all she wanted to do was slam the door shut and run. Darius was right. She shouldn't be here, digging into something that could make her life worse before it ever got better.

"Who are you?" Marcey was surprised her voice didn't shake. She squared her shoulders, a muscle working in her jaw. She could run away from this woman, duck back out to the rental, and go home. No one would have to know she was ever here. Except this woman. With her full lips and mocking grin. Why was she so damn amused? What was so funny about this? There was nothing funny about her scaring Marcey half to death.

"Aren't you going to go inside?"

Of course she wanted to go inside. How could she not? This woman was an unknown variable. She did not factor into Marcey's plans. Marcey bit her tongue, her gaze never leaving the woman's hard eyes.

"Who are you?" Marcey asked again.

The woman's body was fluid in her movements, despite her large frame. Marcey wondered if she'd been an athlete—maybe a dancer—when she was younger. She moved with the grace of one used to being nimble on one's feet. Marcey stepped back, the heel of her boot catching on the edge of the unit. She didn't stumble, not quite, but it was close. Her foot ached as she straightened, and the woman was there, looking down at her from her great height.

"My name is Shelly Orietti." She held out a hand. That was why her face was familiar. She was the Shelly from the photograph. "And you are?"

Marcey hesitated before politeness overruled her anxiety about intimidating strangers. "Marcey Daniels."

"This storage unit does not belong to you, Marcey Daniels, so why are you here?"

Marcey shrugged. "Like I said, there's a book. Arrived in my mail a few weeks back."

Stupid, stupid. Why had she brought up the book *again?*

Shelly let out a low curse. "That man." There was a smile in her voice, even if it didn't reach her lips. Her tone was rueful. She stepped back from Marcey to plunge her hands into her pockets. "He probably saw something in you then, I'd guess."

"Weird…because I've never met him in any official capacity." It wasn't quite the truth, but she didn't think she wanted to air her dirty laundry about Charlie Mock and the chess sessions where he'd been too chickenshit to tell her who he was.

If this shocked Shelly, she gave little sign, a genuine-seeming smile blossoming at her lips. Marcey tilted her head to one side, watching Shelly. In a moment of relaxation, her entire demeanor changed, and she seemed far friendlier than before, her hands emerging from her pocket, casually falling to her sides. People could not be trusted by their body language alone. The lesson of the lying smile was one Marcey had learned when Linda Johnson nodded at her testimony, a smile at her lips, only to turn around and use her words to divest Darius of his freedom. Linda Johnson's eyes were hard when she'd listened to Marcey's testimony in that courtroom and later listened to her beg for mercy and leniency, but Shelly's eyes were soft. Kindness seeped into their warm brown, and crow's feet creased at the corners of her eyes.

"So, you're not the heir."

"According to his lawyer, he's my father."

Shelly's eyebrows shot up. "Your father? But that's—"

"Yeah." Marcey rubbed at the back of her neck. "I didn't even know."

Shelly stepped forward, moving almost reflexively. Marcey took another step backward into the unit, and Shelly's fingers twitched, as though she wanted to reach out and hug Marcey. Marcey swallowed. She didn't want a hug from a strange woman in the middle of the Bronx as night fell.

"Oh, child," Shelly said at length. "I am so sorry. Charlie was a piece of work, but he wasn't stupid, at least not stupid like this. I wish I could undo what he did. You don't deserve that." She inclined her head. "But you're here, at his unit, which means he left you the details."

"The details?"

"Of his life. Or at least his last job." Shelly pushed past Marcey, heels clicking on the floor. She crossed to a work bench and began opening the drawers of a small utility storage chest sitting in one corner. "Could you get the light?"

Marcey reached over and fumbled for a moment before her fingers connected with the plastic-and-metal plating. The room flooded with light, and Marcey felt the breath leave her chest. This was it. Somewhere, locked away in this trove of a single man's history, there was the groundwork of a job. And maybe, if Marcey was creative about it, she could use that job to humiliate Linda Johnson. She'd have to look at it. Charlie Mock had beaten Johnson once before. Maybe the way he'd done it was locked away in here. Marcey refused to sit idly by while that woman used her and Darius as a tool for career enhancement.

Charlie Mock had been meticulously organized in life. Just looking at this room where everything had its place spoke volumes about the man. Marcey was no master at understanding body language, but she'd always been able to read a room. Under a layer of dust, there were carefully rolled-up schematics, stacks of notebooks, binders of photographs, and, in the middle of the far wall of the room, a single photocopy of a painting tacked to the center of a corkboard. It was nothing more than a face. A face contorted in a silent scream.

"That's some picture." Marcey leaned forward to get a better look. "Makes the place seem real homey."

Shelly let out a little snort of laughter, glancing up at the picture. She shook her head before going back to her rummaging. Half muttering to herself, she said, "Kat truly thinks she can reproduce *that?*" She said it like "fat chance" and Marcey frowned.

"Who's Kat?"

The girl in the picture, the other one, her name was Kat.

"No one." Shelly answered. She held up a pack of cards. "Got what I came for. You take care now." She brushed past Marcey and out of the storage unit.

That was…it? She was just going to walk away? No. She could have the answers Marcey wanted about Charlie. Devon hadn't been able, or was unwilling, to tell her much about Charlie. Marcey lunged for the light switch and flicked it off. She pulled the unit's door shut and clicked the lock into place. Breathless, she ran after Shelly.

"Wait!" she called, her boots squeaking on the concrete floor. "Shelly, wait!"

Shelly was already nearly out of the building by the time Marcey caught up to her. She cast an annoyed look at Marcey before buttoning her coat up and heading out into the snow. Marcey followed, zipping up her jacket and frowning as the snow thickened. Ted, from his place in the facility window, watched them go with narrowed eyes.

The city was awash with the warm yellow glow of streetlights against freshly fallen snow. Their feet crunched in the two-inch accumulation. The city fell silent when it snowed, and Marcey hardly dared speak for fear of breaking that quiet serenity.

"You know about Charlie."

"I do."

"Can you tell me about him, what he did, why he was in prison? How he managed to get off when Johnson had him dead to rights?" Marcey babbled, half a step behind Shelly's long strides.

Ignoring her, Shelly kept closer to the buildings, turning down several side streets and then up an alley lined with garbage cans. At the far end was a set of stairs and a glowing neon sign advertising a pool hall and Pabst Blue Ribbon beer. Shelly stepped gingerly around a half-empty Chinese take-out container and popped her collar against the wind. The outline of the pack of cards was gone from Shelly's pocket, vanished up a sleeve or into her purse, Marcey wasn't sure.

"Will you at least talk to me?" Marcey begged. She followed Shelly down into the bar. It was smoke-filled—even though smoking indoors was illegal—and dark. Very dark. Marcey peered around owlishly at the slouching old men at the bar who watched a grainy television feed of the Knicks game and nursed their drinks. A well-muscled man at the far side of the bar jerked his chin to Shelly, who nodded back politely. The guy looked like The Rock, but far scarier. Still, Shelly didn't seem bothered by him, sliding off her coat and then hanging it on the rack beside the door.

Should I just leave? Marcey wondered, as Shelly headed toward the Not-The-Rock. She glanced over her shoulder at the door. She could always wait. Hang out until whatever business Shelly had with these guys was done, have a beer, watch the Knicks lose.

"Marcey?" Shelly called. Marcey whipped around. "Leave your coat out here and come on."

Not needing to be bid twice, Marcey tugged off her coat and hung it beside Shelly's. No one in the bar paid her any mind when she crossed the room.

"Hold out your arms," Muscles said. Marcey did so, and he patted her down. "There's a one-hundred-buck buy-in, kid. You got that?"

There was no time to look to Shelly. Muscles was looking at her with the intensity of a guy who wanted nothing more than to beat the shit out of someone. It didn't matter if she was a tiny girl or not. Marcey nodded mutely and tugged her wallet out of her back pocket. She'd gotten money for the trip and hadn't spent any of it. There were six crisp twenty-dollar bills there for Muscles to see. He grunted his approval and ushered them through the back door.

Beyond the door was a storage room for the bar. Kegs lined the walls. Cleaning supplies were cluttered together with bottles of Budweiser and Miller Lite, dull with dust, on wire structures shoved toward the back. At the center of the room was a low table, with a handful of older women sitting around it. A few raised their hands in greeting to Shelly, and the only man in the place chewed moodily on an unlit cigar.

"We don't take newbies," he grunted.

"She's fine, Earl," Shelly answered. She nudged Marcey. "Sit over there." She pointed to a spot across the table from a woman with blue-gray hair and thin lips. "That's Candy. Next to her is Latoya." Latoya had a cherry-red wig. Her velour jump suit was shabby, though, the color faded and stained. She gave a little wave.

"What is this?" Marcey hissed, her voice barely above a whisper.

Shelly just winked and took her seat next to Earl. Marcey sat down between Candy and Latoya, confused. This was some sort of underground gambling ring for old folks. Or something.

"Where's Tony?" Shelly asked, leaning back and selecting a dusty Miller Lite for herself from the rack. "He said he was gonna be here." She popped the top off her beer and set the cap aside.

"You just wanna see his face when you wipe the floor with him again," Candy groused. She lit a cigarette and blew smoke all over Marcey. "It's unusual for you to bring a friend to our weekly get-togethers, Shelly."

"What can I say, sometimes I get sick of y'all's faces."

"Fat chance." Candy laughed. Latoya slapped her on the shoulder.

From her pocket, Shelly produced the deck of cards. She cut them neatly, shuffling them with the skill of a casino dealer, the many rings on her fingers flashing in the low light. When she did the bridge, she made sure to leave all the cards face up for a moment. Earl, Candy, and Latoya all leaned forward and squinted at the cards, scrutinizing them.

"Is this a new deck?" Earl asked.

"Yes." Shelly said. "Bought 'em at the Duane Reed this morning."

That was a *lie*. Under the table, Marcey's knee started to bounce. She chewed the inside of her cheek to keep herself from saying anything. Why was Shelly lying? What was this game? Her mind raced as Shelly explained the typical rules of Texas Hold 'Em to Marcey and everyone put their money on the table. *As if they didn't know.* Marcey's crisp twenties were small compared to the stacks the others had. Shelly produced a roll of twenties from her pocket the size of Marcey's fist.

The door opened once more, and Muscles came in with a tray full of empty glasses, a bucket for ice, and a bottle of Jack. Behind him trailed another guy, this one far meaner-looking than the old-timers gathered around the table. He had tattoos running up his arms and was well-muscled despite his age. He looked over the table as Muscles passed out glasses to everyone and set the bottle and ice on the wire rack next to some scouring powder.

"The fuck is this?" His voice was rough—a smoker too, evidently. "We don't take outsiders."

"This is Marcey, Tony," Shelly said calmly. She sipped her beer. "She's good for it."

Tony turned his chair backward and sat down heavily, eyeing Marcey from across the table. "She better be."

Swallowing back a retort, Marcey glanced to Shelly. Tony set her on edge. She wanted to beat him. Shelly was lying about the deck of cards and where they came from. This was a game. She was being tested.

CHAPTER 4

Marcey, Just Escaping

SHELLY WAS A SHARP DEALER. She played the river well but never seemed to bet more than Marcey thought was reasonable for these old-timers. Tony watched Marcey like a hawk, knocking back first one, then two, then three fingers of whiskey before the first round was fully completed. Marcey folded the first time, stuck with a two and a seven and shit on the river. Shelly won, her fingers twitching as she scooped up the handfuls of fives and ones that Earl and Latoya threw down on the table. Candy also folded.

The second round was similar. Tony drank another two fingers of whiskey. Marcey sipped on hers and threw more ice into it than she would have liked normally. What Shelly was doing required her full attention, and alcohol never helped her concentration. This time Marcey had a queen and there was another on the table. She bet cautiously, watching Tony from behind her glass, her cards on the edge of the table. He was watching her too, his eyes a little owlish with booze.

"You look familiar," he said.

Marcey set another dollar in the pot and then added two more. "Call. Raise you two." She tilted her head to Tony. "Must have one of those faces."

Tony shook his head. "Nah, you look like someone. Some rat bastard who swindled—"

"Marcey has nothing to do with that life, Tony," Latoya cut him off. She tossed a twenty into the pot. Marcey's eyes grew wide. What was she sitting on? Marcey's gaze slid to Shelly, who pursed her lips slightly, looking at the pot. Latoya tapped her fingers on the table. Her nails were long and painted matte periwinkle blue. "Look at 'er, for fuck's sake. She's dressed like she's still in college."

"It's Friday night," Marcey pointed out.

"You're dressed like you're nineteen and off to your first party," Candy answered. She gestured to Marcey's ratty T-shirt and the holes in the knees of her jeans. "And not even one where you're fixin' to get laid. Boys don't like girls who dress like that, hon."

"Who says I care about what boys think?" Marcey drained the rest of her drink. She added another twenty to the pot, and then threw in another on top. "Raise."

"I'm out." Candy folded. "Isn't my night."

Marcey reached for the bottle of whiskey, only to find it gone before her fingers could close around it. Tony snatched it away. "I bought this bottle, kid. It's for me, not you."

"Fine," Marcey retorted. She sat back, checked her cards again, and let them lie. She wouldn't bet again. A competitive streak in her was waking up, throwing off the dust of years removed from high school soccer games. She leaned forward, the small pile of her winnings from the previous hands between her elbows, watching Shelly watch Tony. He was the mark Shelly was after, but why? He didn't bring more than two hundred bucks to this game. Shelly didn't have more than five hundred. There was no point in risking something like this for such a low reward. Crime was always high risk; it should have high rewards.

Shelly flipped over another card, this one a king, and glanced around. Everyone nodded. They all called the bet. Marcey's leg was bouncing again. Tony's eyes were bulging, bloodshot with booze. Marcey held her breath. The final card was a ten, the same suit as the others. She'd won. A small smile pulled at Shelly's lips.

"Awesome." Marcey pulled her winnings toward her.

"Lucky draw," Tony grumbled, but it was almost affectionate. "Beginner's luck, maybe."

"Just admit you lost, Ton'." Shelly bridged the deck and started to deal once more. Tony won that round, and the round after that. His smug smile grew wider with each passing hand. Earl lit his cigar and blew blue smoke all over the table, making the game seem as though it was inside a cloud.

After four more quick rounds, confusion overtook Marcey's thoughts of bad luck. Tony was winning, every single hand. Latoya and Candy had good hands, but Tony always seemed to win on the final river card. He played recklessly, until he'd amassed much of the available cash to win.

Latoya got to her feet unsteadily. "I'm out. Shelly, we still on for lunch Tuesday?"

"Uh-huh. Got an endo appointment, but I should be free by one."

"Got it."

Shelly dealt again. That time Earl won, but it wasn't on a great hand. Marcey started to watch Shelly's hands as she dealt the cards. Mostly Shelly folded, losing dollars here and there. She won a hand two rounds later, recouping her losses. Candy bowed out then, and then Earl, retreating to the bar to wait out the snow.

Alone at the table with Shelly and Tony, Marcey felt the temperature drop by degrees. Shelly dealt the next round and they played in silence, seeing bets and raising. Tony's expression darkened when Shelly kept raising the bet. Marcey was running out of cash. She didn't have a bad hand: a pair of twos, and the river would give her a pair of nines as well. But it wasn't a winning hand in this game. No one had much of anything last hand, and this hand wasn't much better.

There was no reading Shelly's face, but Tony's expression grew more and more smug with every passing moment. Marcey threw her last twenty into the pile, not really caring anymore. She just wanted to get out of there before the stakes grew too high and she ended up screwed. She wasn't trying to make a fool of herself. Shelly wouldn't tell her any more about Charlie if she thought Marcey was an idiot.

A thought struck her then. Would Shelly think she was stupid for wanting to dig into Charlie's past when Darius's parole hearing relied on Marcey keeping her head down and her nose clean? Would her want for revenge be seen as noble in Shelly's eyes? Marcey glanced at Shelly. Her cheekbones glinted in the light and her throat bobbed as she hummed and called Marcey's bet. Would she think Marcey was justified, or just carrying around the guilt her privilege afforded her?

"Why don't we play for something real then?" Tony asked. His voice pulled Marcey from her thoughts. He pulled a small bundle from his pocket and unloaded it in the middle of the table, on top of the already full pot. Marcey's breath caught. Inside the bundle were three small, rough stones. They looked like quartz, but Marcey guessed by the way Shelly was eyeing them that they were anything but quartz. "She has to keep playing. Keep you honest, Shelly."

Marcey didn't want anything to do with this. "I don't think—"

Shelly cut Marcey off. "That's fine, Tony. Marcey can play."

Marcey stared at Shelly, open mouthed. "I don't have any more cash."

"You'll play," Shelly snapped. Her eyes were narrowed, a warning.

"What are you afraid of, girly?" Tony held out his hand. "I'm sure you're good for it."

Marcey swallowed and glanced at her cards. There was no way she could afford to stay in this game. She had to get out—had to leave. This wasn't what she wanted.

Shelly called Tony's bet, her expression steely. Marcey rummaged in her pocket and found the rental's keys. It was the only thing she had. Those stones were probably worth as much as a Hyundai. *Fuck*, fear was coiling like a snake preparing to strike in her belly. She had no choice. Her fingers shook, gripping the keys. She looked to Shelly, but Shelly wasn't looking at her. This was the only way to stay in that she had. Marcey swallowed, tossed the keys onto the pile, and sat back. "That's collateral," she said.

Tony scowled, drunkenly picking up the keys and squinting at the tag on them before throwing them back down in the pot. "That's a rental."

"As I said, collateral. I'm good for it." Though she'd always been a proficient liar, this didn't sit right. It was probably all over her face. Feeling sick to her stomach, Marcey checked her cards. Her two pair was not going to cut it. No way. Shelly or Tony was sitting on something big. She wondered if this would empty her savings account.

"Shelly, where did you dig this bumpkin up? Who the fuck bets a car they don't even own?" Tony got to his feet, drunkenly swaying as he walked. Marcey pressed her cards flat to the table. Tony poured himself another two fingers of whiskey. "You're up to something, I know you are. She's here because you're afraid I'll see what you're doing."

"Add some ice to that, Tony. You've had a few too many." Shelly's answer was curt. "Marcey's an old friend's kid. She's good for the money, even if she is a bit stupid for betting her *rental* car."

"You caught me off-guard." Marcey held up her hands. Her heart hammered away, somewhere around her throat. She could scarcely hear the music of the bar over the rush of her blood, coloring her face and making her terrified she would give whatever game Shelly was playing away in her ignorance. "I thought this was a friendly game between old-timers. I brought cash, didn't I? Didn't think this was some high-stakes bet-your-uncut-diamonds bullshit." She stuck her chin out defiantly. It too was a gamble.

Shelly inhaled sharply. Tony squinted at Marcey through eyes heavy with drink.

"You have balls," he said. "For a shrimp."

The room seemed to relax. The tension in Shelly's forearms subsided.

"I'm good for it," Marcey insisted again. Tony sat back down, throwing a few ice cubes into his glass before he knocked the whole thing back.

Marcey showed her hand, indicating her two pair with the river. Shelly hummed politely and tutted quietly, looking to Tony. He, perhaps smugly, turned over triple nines. A good hand, for sure, but not with all the fuss over high-stakes betting.

"Sorry, kid," Tony said. He reached for the keys once more. "Hope you're good for it."

Shelly paused and flying out to grab his wrist. "We're not done." She turned over her carts. "Full house, threes and sevens."

Tony's eyes bugged out wide, and he got to his feet so quickly the chair tipped over. Marcey pushed away as well, her back hitting the storage rack of cheap beer. "You—you cheated!" he shouted.

"I don't think she did," Marcey said. "Tony, it's all right, everyone loses sometimes." It was too late. He lunged for the table, gathering his tiny precious stones and trying to shove them back into their little bag. Shelly took a step back, allowing the guy with the muscles, who'd appeared when the chair fell to the floor, to grab Tony and wrench the winnings from his hands. Muscles tossed them back on the pile and hauled Tony, cursing up a storm at Shelly, out of the room.

Shelly leaned forward and collected the stones, sitting back and exhaling. "Take your money and your keys back," she said. She picked up Tony's bottle and took a long swig directly from it. Marcey took her six twenties and her keys and put them into her pocket. Candy, Earl, and Latoya came back into the room and collected their money as well. They split the remainder between themselves, leaving a small pile on the table. Shelly gave each of them one of the three little stones. "Don't spend it all in one place."

Candy blew Shelly an air kiss and Shelly smiled prettily at her. Marcey just watched, dumbfounded.

"What just happened?"

"You won yourself a couple hundred bucks." Shelly ducked out of the room, leaving Marcey alone with the small pile of additional cash before her. She gathered it up, another two hundred bucks, and shoved it into her back pocket. Shelly returned with both their jackets and gestured toward a door half-hidden behind a pyramid of kegs. "We're going out this way."

Marcey put her coat on and followed Shelly up a narrow flight of service steps and out onto the avenue above. Shelly looked around nervously, her breath fogging and the new-fallen snow making her look even more exhilarated than before.

"Those were trick cards," Marcey said.

"Maybe."

Shelly hailed a cab. It slowed to a crawl, the driver leaning over to open the door. Marcey settled in beside Shelly. "That was...amazing," she said. "I've never felt like that before."

"You almost ruined it, with the stunt you pulled with your keys. It's a goddamn *rental!* You can't just give that shit away."

Marcey bit her lip, feeling petulant. "I would'a stopped at an ATM if you'd *told* me that was where you were going or what you were doing."

"The whole point was that you didn't know." Shelly reached into her pocket and produced the deck. "These are Charlie's. Put them back in the locker next time you're in there, if you don't mind."

Marcey stared at the backs of the cards for a long time, trying to figure out how they were rigged. "What was he like?"

"Who?"

"Charlie. What was he like?" Marcey sat back, tucking the cards into her jacket pocket. She wouldn't put them back until she figured out their trick. "I never met him...not really."

"Not really?" Shelly frowned. "How do you mean?"

"Do you know Devon Austin Jackson?"

"Charlie's lawyer, sure." Shelly gave Marcey a searching look. "What's he got to do with this?"

"He showed me a picture. Of you. Of Charlie. And this other girl."

"Kat."

"Yeah." Marcey nodded. "Is she his girlfriend?"

Shelly laughed. "That would be me, Marcey."

"Oh." Marcey faltered. Maybe there was more to Charlie than just a petty criminal. She didn't think just any guy would date a woman like Shelly. She shook her head, catching herself before her mind raced too far away from the current subject. "Well, when he showed me that picture, I realized that I'd seen Charlie before. When I was in high school, he'd come and play chess in the park with me."

"So that's why you said you'd never met him in any official capacity." Shelly frowned. "That was smart, to hedge it like that."

Marcey tilted her head to one side. Snow was still falling outside the cab window. "How do you mean?"

"Charlie was a good man, a kind man—"

"He was in prison." Marcey tried to keep her tone flat.

"Well, yes, but I think you know that there are good people who are put away all the time." Shelly inclined her chin to the side of a bus they passed, Marcey and Darius's cartoonish mugshots there as clear as day for the world to see with the scripted "Johnson for DA—Taking Gangs Out of Our Schools" written beside them. "That's some mess. Johnson's always been a piece of work, but that's somethin' else right there."

"She tried to do Charlie, right before we fucked up." Marcey sighed. "You read the papers back then at all?"

"Sure did. They were calling for her to be fired, maybe disbarred, for how poorly she handled that case. He certainly made her look like an ass, on top of walking free as a bird outta that courtroom when he was guilty as sin. Kat was in stitches."

There it was, that name again. Marcey frowned. She reached into her bag and pulled out Charlie Mock's book. Shelly's eyes went wide, but Marcey pretended not to notice. She flipped through the pages until she found the photograph Devon had given her. "This Kat?" Marcey held out the photograph. Kathryn wasn't an uncommon name, after all; it could be just a coincidence. She had to be sure.

Shelly turned on the flashlight in her phone to see the picture just as the cab slowed to a halt. The rental was still parked outside the storage facility, the sole car in the small parking lot. "Wait a sec," Shelly told the driver. She got out of the car, Marcey following her. "That Kat, yes. But you should stay away from her. She's bad news."

"I hadn't—"

"Well, *don't*. You're too green to be messing with Kat Barber." Shelly handed Marcey the photograph back. "What were you expecting to find in there, anyway?" She jerked her thumb toward the storage unit.

Marcey sighed. "Charlie's last job. Devon told me about it, and he mentioned it in the letter he wrote to me explaining everything. He wants to steal some ugly painting. I was…" Marcey looked down at her hands, grasping for the words. "I was hoping maybe I could find something to use to get back at Johnson for her public smear campaign."

"Why does she hate you so much?" Shelly's expression was steely. "Is it because she knows about your connection to Charlie? Because it if is, you should stay far, far away from this. Your friend's been locked up for what? Eight, nine years now? Isn't he eligible for release soon?"

Marcey looked down at her hands. "Yes, in May."

"Then why you gonna mess with his chances of getting out?" Shelly scowled. "That should be the most important thing for you, not some sort of revenge."

"It isn't *revenge*—how can it be? She's the one who went after me *first*." She sounded petulant. She didn't care. "I dated her daughter when her daughter was struggling with a pretty bad pill problem. Linda blames me for Becca's spiral. She couldn't get me. My mom basically bankrupted herself to ensure that I had the best lawyer I could get. Darius wasn't so lucky."

Shelly grabbed Marcey's arm. "He did time for you. Don't do him like this."

"He can't fight her in there. I can." Marcey scowled.

"That's fucked up." Shelly said. "You need to let the system do its job. Devon's a good lawyer—"

"You know him?"

"Of course I do. He's Charlie's lawyer." She still hadn't let go of Marcey's arm. The moment dragged on. Snow fell. Shelly looked pensive. "You could always bring a lawsuit against her."

"Can't. Devon says it won't work. He's already worried that Darius won't get past the parole board because of this."

"It would be less messy than whatever Charlie was planning."

Nodding, Marcey put the photograph away and tucked the book into her messenger bag. "It could. Devon told me a bit about Charlie's case with Johnson, and then when I heard he had this job in the works I wondered…"

"Wondered what?"

"If there was maybe a way to salvage my reputation and catch Johnson with her pants around her ankles in the process." Marcey smiled up at Shelly. "Would you be interested in getting involved with something like that?"

Shelly reached into her pocket and pulled out a cigarette. Cupping her hand against the wind, she lit it. There was snow in her hair now. The cabbie tapped on the window. Shelly glared at him, rubbing her forefinger and thumb together—there was money in it for him, if he waited.

"I don't think that's a good idea." Shelly shook her head. "And I don't think you should get involved with this either. Revenge is a lonely road, Marcey, and you're already playing with more lives than just your own. You'll have to walk it alone if you want to be beat Johnson at her own game." She exhaled smoke. "Do you want that?"

The answer did not come immediately. Marcey unlocked the Hyundai and relocked it, hands anxious for something to do. "I'm not sure," she said honestly. "I'm not sure I want to sink to her level. But what she's done to me...what she's doing to Darius. She tried to do that to Charlie as well. She's using my best friend as a political punch line, calling him a thug and a dangerous drug dealer, making it so that no matter what happens, when he gets out, he can't have a future. I want to right that wrong."

The warm glow of the lit end of the cigarette stood out against the inky blackness of the snowy night. Shelly exhaled smoke; it curled fog-like around her head. "You shouldn't do something like this for a man. Your friend. Charlie. Don't do it for them. If you're going to do it at all, do it for yourself. That's the only way these things work out."

She turned and got back into the cab, leaving Marcey alone in the gently falling snow.

CHAPTER 5

Wei, Looking for the Missing Pieces

IT DID NOT OCCUR TO Wei until the Monday morning she was summoned into Linda Johnson's office that the girl she'd seen in Charlie Mock's lawyer's office was the same girl whose face featured so prominently in all of Johnson's campaign ads. Was it a sign she was slipping? Or that the girl had a face so unremarkable that Wei hadn't paid her much mind, too busy sparring with Devon Austin Jackson over Charlie Mock's missing estate? Either way, Wei was tired. She'd barely managed to get any sleep on the red eye from London. Now, sitting across from the woman herself, framed as she was by the campaign ad behind her, Wei saw the connection effortlessly. Why did Johnson hate that girl? How had that girl allowed her face to be used in an ad when she clearly was *not* in prison like the other guy?

The phone rang. Johnson, a diminutive old white woman, answered with her lips pursed in annoyance. "I'm in a meeting, Gladys." A pause, and then, "Oh, all right, give me a second to go into the other room." She got up and put the call on hold. "I have to take this. Shouldn't be long."

Wei nodded. "Of course."

Johnson ducked out of the room.

LePage sat beside Wei, his fingers twitching. There was dirt under his nails and his suit was wrinkled. He looked bedraggled, like he'd slept in his clothes. Wei squinted at his fashionable haircut and exhaled. When would Macklemore hair go out of fashion? LePage was pushing forty, as was she. It wasn't exactly a good look for a man his age to be sporting a hairstyle better suited for a twenty-something. Still, somehow, with his square jaw and olive skin, it worked.

"So, how've you been?" LePage asked. He started to pick at the lint on his suit pants.

"Fine," Wei answered.

"How'd it go with the lawyer?" LePage knew the answer. He was filling the silence with small talk because he was a nervous talker. Wei hated that about him. She opened the folder in her lap and passed him her notes on the meeting with Devon Austin Jackson. He scanned them and passed them back. "So you met her?" He jerked his thumb toward the campaign poster behind Johnson's desk.

"Yeah."

"Does she have the book?"

Wei shrugged. "I was hoping that Linda might have had that detail for us. Can't see any other reason why she'd smear some kid's good name like this otherwise."

LePage tilted his head, contemplating the poster. "Maybe she isn't a good kid. Maybe she's just one of those ones who looks clean on the outside, but is rotten to the core once you crack the surface." He tapped his fingers on the desk, picked up one of Johnson's paperweights, and fiddled with it. Wei wanted to slap his nervousness out of him. "She's got a record, you know. Sold drugs at a high school."

Of course LePage had thought to look her up. Wei closed her eyes so she didn't have to see that girl's face anymore. "Did Johnson choose to prosecute?"

"She got off. Devon Austin Jackson got served, though. He defended her friend. Think after the Mock debacle, Johnson was itching to destroy *someone's* reputation to make herself feel better about how her own was beyond jacked."

Ah, Wei thought darkly. *There's the Linda Johnson I know.* Johnson was vindictive to the core. Wei should have guessed that there was some past involvement between the two of them; otherwise it was just a poor political move. Johnson did not like to lose. Her failure to convict Charles Mock—a defeat so improbable there had to have been external help (or at least jury tampering)—was the reason they were both here after all.

LePage leaned back in his chair, looking just a little smug and just a little smarmy. Wei wanted to scoot away from him. The clock on the wall ticked loudly. "Heard you've been running back to London whenever your masters allow you to come and go."

"Did you?" Wei kept her tone mild, wishing Johnson would hurry up. "What makes you think I have any business in London?"

"Oh, a little bird may have mentioned that you're still seeing her."

Wei's eyes narrowed. "Does this bird have a name?"

"It's slipped my mind," LePage answered airily.

The door banged open. Johnson returned, dumping a stack of folders on her desk. Wei shifted back to avoid one that fell off the front end of the desk. LePage reached out and caught it, setting it back on the top of the tilting stack.

"Who would like to explain to me why Charlie Mock's book is not currently in my hand?" Johnson stood behind her desk, leaning on the stack of folders. The light from the window cast her face in harsh shadows, sinking into her wrinkles and making her look skeletal. "I completed all that paperwork to have you on permanent loan, Agent Topeté, for what? You had the inside track to where that book would end up, and it's not in London where you said it would be."

LePage raised his eyebrows at Wei. Wei wanted to sink into the floor. She had hoped, perhaps foolishly, that the details of her affairs would not be broadcast so publicly to the tune of her humiliation before a man she already despised for what had happened in Rio some five years ago now. Johnson loved to get people under her thumb and push though. Wei didn't know why she'd expected any different.

"All my research indicated that Barber was the heir apparent to Charlie Mock's empire," Wei answered. She shifted forward. "Devon Austin Jackson—"

"Who is a *blight* on my good profession," Johnson put in.

Wei inclined her head. She'd never much cared for lawyers who defended criminals willingly, seeming not to be bothered by their crimes. Charlie Mock's lawyer was among them, and he wielded the shield of attorney–client privilege like a weapon.

"Indeed," Wei continued. "Devon Austin Jackson did not give me much, only that the estate in question, which I can only assume means

46

the book, was sent by courier upon him receiving notification of Charlie Mock's death."

"And you were with the individual who should have received it at the time you found out?" Johnson sat down and wheeled her chair forward to get a better look at the paperwork Wei had laid out on in the small space of desk not overtaken by leaning towers of case folders.

Very carefully avoiding looking at LePage, Wei nodded. "I was with Kathryn that morning. I left briefly, to go into the office to receive the confirmation from William."

"There's no chance she got it while you were out?" LePage asked.

Wei shook her head. "I can't see how. Devon Austin Jackson said he sent it by courier. He wouldn't have been able to send an in-person delivery on an international flight that quickly. I checked the flight manifests that evening. Any courier would have missed the 10:00 p.m. flight bank on account of Charles Mock dying at 9:15 that evening. There simply wasn't time." Wei indicated her notes. "I attached that to the back of the second page, Linda. My theory is that it was delivered to someone in the city."

"Really?" LePage scratched at his already growing shadow. Corsicans. Wei wrinkled her nose. "That would make sense. Would we need to run down the regular courier services to see if we could locate a delivery around that time?"

Johnson closed the folder. "I don't care how you do it. I just need you to *find the book*. It was supposed to be in my hands by now. The election is coming up, and with it the window of my ability to prosecute this case to the fullest is closing. I will not miss out on a chance to right a wrong just because of my own ambition."

Frowning, Wei took her notes back and tucked them into her folio. She didn't say so, but she did think pushing so hard for Charlie Mock's book was only going to get them more trouble. The investigation was falling apart already. Wei's one chance to make things right between herself and Kat hung in the balance. They were dismissed, Johnson turning her attention to her files enough to drive that point home to Wei. She followed LePage out of the office and out into the cluttered bullpen.

"Want to get a coffee?" LePage asked.

Wei didn't want a coffee. She wanted to go back to her hotel room and sleep. Decorum and partnership forced her to nod, head dipping jerkily.

Americans couldn't make a decent cup of coffee if their lives depended on it, and LePage was not the type to seek out the un-American parts of the city to find a place that understood how to appropriately brew.

She followed him outside, dug a cigarette from her pocket, and lit it. The nicotine hit took down her anxiety over Johnson's edict.

"You're still sleeping with Kat Barber, then?" LePage asked, lighting his own. He exhaled smoke up into the gray sky above them.

The city was caving in on Wei. To admit the truth was to subject herself, and her methods for controlling a volatile situation, to a man she loathed, but to lie was not an option. She walked slowly, shivering in the cold. Her thick leggings beneath her professional dress and wool overcoat did her little favor. Did she want to tell LePage the truth? Was that worth the humiliation of it?

Was she even humiliated by it?

"Yes," she said.

The end of LePage's cigarette burned bright. He led her north to the subway stop, taking the J train toward Brooklyn. Wei did not want to venture that far away from the office just yet, but it seemed that to earn whatever modicum of respect she could claim back from LePage, she was going to have to grit her teeth and bear it. At least the train would be warm.

"Why still do it? After Rio, I'd assumed you'd stopped. Is she making you?"

"William, there is very little about my personal life that I am willing to discuss with you, let alone Linda Johnson. My work on the Mock case, and in conjunction the Barber case, is a matter of public record in this country. Anyone from you to Johnson to Kathryn is able to look at that record." Wei glared at him. "My personal life, however, is just that: private."

The train arrived. They got on and sat down. LePage got up to allow a pregnant woman to sit down. He loomed over Wei, grinning down at her. "Barber's a looker. I don't blame ya."

"You're a pig," Wei muttered in bitter French. She wrapped her arms around herself, thinking back to a moment long before this had become so complicated.

Kat, sun-kissed and freckling in the heat. Her knees skinned, splattered in mud from a puddle on the roof of the world. A snow-capped mountain rose behind them, giant and menacing. Its crown was almost a cragged, sleeping man against the backdrop of an icy blue sky. Kat's hair had been frizzing out of its braid and her lips had been warm against Wei's, kissing her in the shadow of that terrible mountain. This had been a future, a past, and a present, all rolled into one, this moment of adoration, of falling in love. This moment had been the breaking of the surface, twenty days in Nepal, walking counterclockwise and ever upward. That had been the Kat Wei fell in love with. The one before the mess in Rio and the Mock trial. Johnson had chosen to exploit that relationship, encouraging Wei to let it grow when her better instinct upon discovering Kat's true nature had been to cut all ties.

"Love's complicated." LePage was still talking, rambling on about love like he had some sort of experience. "People come and go, but the ones who are true, they stay forever."

"Do they?" Wei asked mildly. They were racing under the river.

LePage nodded. "There was this girl, once, Gwen. Beautiful as can be. She and I got involved about seven years ago now." He still had that nostalgic air about him when they got off a few stops into Brooklyn. They emerged in Williamsburg, and Wei relaxed immediately. There was something about being in a neighborhood that could remind her so strongly of home that put her at ease. She let LePage lead her to a small shop in the basement of a house; the place smelled of roasting beans, smoky and soothing. Wei looked around. Kat would love this place. If this worked, and Wei was able to secure her freedom, they'd have to come here.

Over surprisingly tolerable coffee, Wei listened to LePage's theories about Charlie Mock's book and shared a few of her own. They didn't have much to go on, but the investigation would have to progress quickly if they wanted to catch the new owner before they realized how valuable a resource they now had in their possession. Wei wanted to look up that girl from Johnson's campaign poster and Devon Austin Jackson's office.

"Why?" LePage asked. "What does Interpol care about some drug dealer's reputation?"

Wei looked away. She'd seen the girl in person. She saw the resemblance. That nose. She'd know it anywhere. "Call it a hunch, as you Americans say." She sipped her coffee, worry gnawing at her gut. Would she be able to pull off the ultimate coup?

CHAPTER 6

Marcey, Starting Things

WHEN MARCEY WAS A CHILD, her mother had put up constellations that danced across the sky at midwinter on her bedroom ceiling. Ursa Major dipped just at the edge of the crown molding, Orion at full prominence, Cancer and Gemini glowing stark against the blank canvas of her cracked eggshell-white ceiling. When Marcey was little, it had been a gateway to another world. Now it was just another place, fleeting in its prominence. Her bedroom was like everything else in the apartment: neat, square, and suffocating.

Late on Wednesday night, Marcey lay awake, turning over the events of last Friday. This was the first time she'd allowed herself to think about it. She'd gone to work on Monday and tried to ignore the itch to return to the Bronx and dig through Charlie Mock's files until she found something she could use. She'd pushed Shelly's accusations and Darius's warnings to the side. They would understand—they had to understand. She had to find something that would allow her to define herself beyond the bitter knot of feelings that settled at the pit of her stomach whenever she thought about Charlie.

She wanted to track down Shelly, to take the woman's love of the man who'd passed and find a way to use it to her advantage. Shelly would be key, Marcey was sure of it, in understanding what Charlie was planning. The letter was scant on the details. Marcey heaved a frustrated sigh. Shelly had made it clear: she had no interest in having any further involvement with Marcey. If Marcey wanted the answers to her questions about Charlie, she had to find them somewhere else.

Work had been a wash on Tuesday, and again on Wednesday. Now, Marcey couldn't sleep. She wanted to know more about Charlie Mock, about this job. She hated that she couldn't just come right out and ask someone for all the details.

That wasn't how the game worked. Marcey'd been in and out of it enough to know that much. The game was played in a series of moves within moves.

Marcey got the book from her bag where it lay by the apartment door. The picture was tucked into the inside cover. Marcey had caught herself looking at it more than once over the past few days. Just seeing it was enough to make her heart race again, the euphoria of Shelly's game still fresh in her mind.

There was only one Kat Barber in the book. A Kathryn, actually. A Google search of her phone number indicated she lived in the UK, more specifically London. Five hours ahead. It was seven in the morning there.

Marcey took the book and retreated to her bedroom. Her mother was asleep. Screwing up her courage, Marcey typed the number into her phone. Her fingers trembled as she hit send and raised the phone to her ear. She didn't know what she wanted. Or rather, she did, just not how to ask for it.

How do you ask for someone to tell you all their secrets on the off chance they want to be involved in a dead man's last stand?

The static of an international call faded into the pulse of the phone connecting. Marcey's stomach churned, and her tongue felt sandpapery in her mouth. She wished she'd brought the glass of water with her.

The phone rang three times before a sleepy voice picked it up.

"It's awfully rude to call people at this hour." Though a little hoarse from disuse, Kat Barber's voice filled Marcey's stomach with a deep warmth. It dragged, low in tone, over Marcey's mind, touching, tasting, sampling the wares in the sort of accent Marcey would find dismissive and polished in any other setting. Thick with sleep, it was merely intriguing.

Glancing at the digital clock by her bedside, Marcey forced herself to speak. "I'm sorry. I thought…the time." She gestured lamely in the dark.

"It's two in the morning. What do you want?"

Marcey inhaled sharply. "You're in New York?"

"Where the bloody hell else would I be? I have work in the morning." There was a rustle of blankets, and another voice, accented in a way Marcey did not recognize, murmured sleepily.

"I'm sorry," Marcey said quickly, her cheeks burning with embarrassment. "With the number, I just assumed you'd be in the UK somewhere. Where it's seven in the morning."

"Who is this?" There was a shuffling on the other line and the sound of a door closing gently.

"My name is M—"

"*Christ*, you are new at this. Don't share your name, it'll make it easier for one of us to come and find you."

Sticking her chin out defiantly, Marcey countered, "Then how can I tell you who I am?"

Chuckling with a still-sleepy warmth that set Marcey off-balance, the woman laughed. "You know who I am because you're the new point of contact. The heir to that massive fortune. I don't give this number out to just anyone, you know—certainly not to strange women without enough sense to call at a decent hour. You're the new Charlie. You must have his book. How else would you get my number?" She drew out the word like she was savoring a fine wine.

"Then we understand each other," Marcey answered. "You're Kat Barber. I have a picture of you. In Rio. With Charlie."

Kat hummed as if nostalgic. "That was a good day. Are you offering me a job, Young Charlie? Or is this purely a call to reminisce?" She paused, creating a tension Marcey felt thrum in her chest. Marcey's heart raced, waiting for her to continue. "Because, if it is, bugger off so I can get some sleep."

"This isn't a social call," Marcey said quickly. "But it isn't to offer you a job either. I..." She ran a hand through her bangs, staring out into her bedroom, at an absolute loss for words. Marcey had no idea what to do. She couldn't just ask Kat Barber for help, could she? "I'm not sure I fully understand what Charlie intended. He left me the plans for his final job, the one he meant to pull up in the mountains." Marcey swallowed but pressed on, anxiety making her heart race and her voice move just as fast. "I met Shelly Orietti Friday night and she pulled me into some card game and I helped her play this guy outta at least fifteen grand in cash and diamonds at a poker table with a hundred-buck buy in." Marcey sucked in a deep breath. "I didn't ask to be brought along, she just did it, let me feel what it's like to be on a con with her like that. Told me afterward she doesn't work with others. I—"

"You're *green*." Kat said the word like it was dirty. She exhaled, a long sigh. "Why would you send *her* the book, Charlie?"

The comment wasn't for Marcey. She bit her lip, before flopping back on her bed. "I'm sorry for waking you."

"I would've gotten up soon enough. Jet lag goes both ways, you know." A smile, or at least a hint of warmth, crept into Kat's voice. "What do you want from me? I'm not in the business of offering to engage in enterprise with total strangers."

"I don't want that."

"Then tell me, what do you want?"

Marcey stared up at the constellations on her ceiling. What did she want? "Do you know what happened when Charlie was arrested, right after that picture was taken, in Rio?"

"I know of it, yes."

"The woman who represented the state of New York on that case is no friend of mine. I know what she did to Charlie. And I know what she did to me and mine. Shelly hinted at how angry she was that Charlie did not end up in prison under her watch. I handled the aftermath of that in my dealings with her." Marcey exhaled; she hated putting on airs to make herself sound smarter. "I want to take this job of his, this last idea he had, and use it to see her *hanged* on a rope woven of her own hubris."

"That's an awfully large request of a total stranger, Young Charlie."

"My name is Marcey." She didn't like being called Young Charlie. The name stripped away who Marcey was and replaced her with the name of an old dead guy. And while they might be kin, he was nothing more than a sperm donor. One Marcey still wasn't sure she wanted.

"So, your name is Marcey." Kat hummed thoughtfully. "A little girl who wants revenge and to carry out a dead man's last request."

A small bark of laughter escaped Marcey's lips. "Oh, this isn't for Charlie. I don't give a shit about him."

"You'll find that a great many of us do." Kat's tone was curt. Marcey mentally cursed; that wasn't what she meant. A silence drew out. Marcey wondered if she'd gone and put her foot into it, but Kat finally continued. "My experience with revenge is that it sours with time. The vindictive desire fades and you're left with the pieces of a job you'd never attempt, had you not been pushed the point where you decided to get comeuppance. It never ends well."

"Shelly said the same thing."

"Shelly would know better than most."

"Why?"

"Oh, my dear Marcey, that isn't my story to tell. If you want anything from Shelly, you need to approach her with a plan. She's rubbish at planning, logistics, and such, you know?"

Marcey frowned. "That's hardly fair." Shelly seemed to have her wits about her.

"Shelly's skills at planning have gotten me into some uncomfortable situations in the past, sorry to say." With a yawn, Kat continued, "Why don't you come find me tomorrow? I can show you something that you might like to try."

"I don't think that's a good idea."

"Why is that? I don't bite." Kat's tone of mock hurt was transparent.

"As you said. You don't know me, and I don't know you, Kat Barber. Why would I willingly walk into a potential set-up? Give me something to *do*, let me prove to you what I can do, and then maybe we can meet in person."

"Mutually assured destruction. Smart."

Marcey sat back, biting down on her curiosity. Would Kat agree to tell her what to do without a face-to-face meeting? Was that a faux pas? All she could do was listen to Kat's quiet breathing and wait. Discomfort made Marcey shift. Navigating on a minefield when she was so tired was leaving her drained.

The sounds of the city at night filled the phone line. Kat had gone outside. A siren wailed in the distance. Marcey imagined her, the beautiful woman from the picture, standing in a nightgown and robe on the roof of some high-rise hotel, her hair blowing in a stiff breeze. She was clean, pure, a white splash of paint high above the smell and grimy grays of the city.

"But…" Kat spoke in a low voice, barely audible over the wind. "There's a way to go about doing this, Marcey, and this isn't it." Whatever she said next was lost on the wind. Marcey strained to hear, but there was nothing but static. She frowned. Had Kat hung up on her? She was about to hang up too, when Kat continued. "There's a painting. On display at the Perôt in SoHo. I'm meant to appraise it later today. It'll be kept there over the weekend, and then returned to its owner on Monday."

"Okay." Marcey wasn't sure what else she was supposed to say.

"Show me what you can do on short notice. Get in there. Take a gander at the painting." The line went dead. Marcey pulled the phone from her ear and stared at the screen as it glowed a jumbled collection of apps that dimmed and then fell into blackness. It was only when she was in darkness, the glowing constellations of the night sky above her, that Marcey allowed herself to exhale.

It was a challenge.

One she would relish.

CHAPTER 7

A Heist, at Its Impetus

MARCEY AWOKE, DROOLING, TO A knock at her door. Her head was fuzzy, and she sat up too fast. "Yeah?" she called. Wincing, she rubbed at the back of her head.

Her mother stuck her head around the door. She was dressed casually but professionally. Tax season was upon them. She was going in to the office. "Hey Mar," she said. "I wanted to catch you before I left for the day and give you this." She stepped into the room and held out an envelope. "This was taped to the door this morning."

Marcey took the envelope and flipped it over. The penmanship was beautiful, her name like a work of priceless art in spindly black handwriting. "Huh. Any idea who left it?"

"No." Her mother frowned at the clock. "Shouldn't you be up? Aren't you going to work?"

A swell of panic surged in Marcey before the calm of understanding came as she woke up. "No," she answered. "Got stuff to do today."

"What's gotten into you? You run off like you do every month to go see your criminal boyfriend only—"

Marcey set the letter aside and looked up at her mother. She looked harassed, the lines on her face were drawn, and the black circles under her eyes could not be covered up with makeup.

"I'm gay, Mom. No boyfriend."

"Whatever."

Marcey wasn't awake enough to bristle at the dismissive way her mother spoke of her sexuality. It was a battle that wasn't worth fighting.

"You always come back on Mars," her mother continued, "but this time it's worse. You're walking in a cloud, so far removed from reality that I'm starting to worry about you—staying out to all hours of the day and night, not telling me where you're going or what you're doing."

"I didn't realize I had to tell you everything I do with my time."

"You do when your supervisor calls me and demands to know where the hell you are."

Marcey frowned. "I was in the office all week."

"Maybe in body, but definitely not in spirit. I got you that job because I wanted you to be *respectable,* not some low-life drug dealer's girlfriend. You've spent entirely too much of your life invested in this boy, and he's done nothing for you. He's a black hole. Like his cousins and his fool of a mother. You need to make a decision." Her mother turned to leave. "Whatever he's got you mixed up in, it isn't worth it. You saw your face on those posters. That's what comes from associating with people like him."

"It's libel," Marcey answered shortly.

"Then sue, but go to work and actually be there, Marcey. I won't stick my neck out for you if you get fired. Both of us have a lot to lose if you screw this up." Her mother rested her on the doorframe, seguing away from their tense conversation. "Will you be back tonight?"

"I'll be out."

"Well, don't come back too late. The weather's awful." With that, her mother was gone, vanished off down the hallway. Marcey tossed the letter onto the floor and rolled over, pulling her blankets over her head. She was exhausted and had too much to think about. She needed a few more hours of sleep before she'd be able to function.

Sleep was an elusive foe. Twenty minutes later, Marcey was sitting up in bed, blankets gathered around her waist, reading the letter. Her hand shook. How—

M

You should take better care with your personal information. It was a scarce challenge to locate you. As the guardian of Charlie's legacy, take heed: people want what you have come to possess.

After our conversation last night, I felt the need to apologize. I do not wish to impose my agenda upon you. The job is open, should you choose to take it.

Impress me,
K

The paper smelled of spice and flowers, a gentle scent. Marcey thought it was almost sweet, touched by the smudge of lipstick on the corner of the page, until the fear set in. Her hands were still shaking. How…how?

Marcey reached for her phone and fumbled for Charlie's book. Finding Shelly's number was easy enough; Charlie kept a neat ledger. She dialed, screwed up the numbers and had to start again. The phone rang and rang. "Pick up, pick up, pick up."

Finally, Shelly picked up. Marcey swallowed, knowing that this was out of the blue.

"You're using Charlie's book," Shelly said in lieu of greeting. "You figured out how to read it."

"It's written in plain English." Shelly snorted. Marcey glared at the wall, feeling petulant. "How the hell did Kat Barber find out where I live?"

"She's smarter than she looks. Also, you probably told her by using your damn cell phone to call her." Marcey looked down at her hands guiltily. Shelly hummed thoughtfully. "But a better question would be what the hell are you doing talking to a woman like Kat Barber when I specifically told you to stay away from her?" A lighter clicked. Shelly exhaled. "She's dangerous, especially for a kid like you."

"I had to do something. You wouldn't help me."

"There was nothing I could help you with."

"Well, I think you can now. Can you meet me at Charlie's storage unit?"

"Some of us have day jobs. Crime doesn't pay."

"You pulled in God knows how much with that diamond a week ago," Marcey pointed out. "Look, it won't be for very long. Maybe just the lunch hour. I want to get a better understanding of what Charlie had in mind with this job and see if maybe what Kat's proposing—"

"And what is Kathryn proposing?"

"A job. No details." Marcey shrugged.

"I told you, Marcey. I don't work with others." Shelly sighed. "There are too many variables. People get hurt. I don't want you involved in something like this. You're supposed to be the caretaker of Charlie's legacy, you're not supposed to go running headlong into the first job offered by some floozy."

Marcey frowned. "I thought my goal was just to keep the book safe and take care of Charlie's last job. You didn't read his letter. You don't know what he asked of me."

"No, but I knew Charlie better than anyone. I know what he was about. This is exactly his game. This web of confusion and lies. You're a fool if you think you can pull a fast one over on me, or on his memory. Kathryn is too." Shelly's tone was curt.

"Then tell me, Shelly. Help me understand why Kat Barber is telling me people are after this book. Tell me why Charlie's last job is set to be so dangerous."

A long-suffering sigh, resigned and definitely annoyed at the resignation, escaped Shelly's lips. "When do you want to meet?"

"Two o'clock. I'll text you the address."

"You're stupid if you think that's a good idea."

"Fine, I'll Snapchat you the damn address. That shit's encrypted and disappears. What's your username?"

Marcey pulled a pen from her purse and wrote it on the back of Kat's note. Shelly was right. She was being careless. The book had risk. Marcey wanted to know what the risk was.

The Perôt was an upscale gallery off Broadway with a reputation for moving harder-to-find pieces from lesser masters and more obscure European artists. It was tucked into two floors of a 1920s relic of a building. Marcey stared up at it from under the awning of the Banana Republic across the street. The building was made of a gray stone, dirty with age. It clung to a carefully maintained shabbiness that did not fit with the high-end retailers buttressing it on either side. The building was done up Deco style, with a flair for Greek revival, mock columns running up its narrow face with wide windows open at the front. Shorter than the other buildings around it by a good four or five stories, it appeared the upper floors were either studio space or apartments.

Marcey put her hands in her pockets and tugged her baseball cap low across her forehead, picking her way around a puddle to go peer into the window of the gallery. Shoppers and tourists jostled behind her, but Marcey couldn't see them. She stared into the empty gallery space. There was only one painting visible, on the far wall, but it was one Marcey recognized. Charlie had a picture of it hanging up in his storage unit. A face, contorted in a scream.

A blonde woman stood with another woman with black hair, their backs to the window. The blonde gestured at the painting, leaning in to hear her companion speak at some length. Marcey stepped away from the window. This was not how she wanted to meet Kat Barber. She still wasn't sure she wanted to meet Kat Barber at all. She retreated to the subway station and took a train uptown, lost in thought.

Pieces—a few of them, anyway—were slowly clicking into place. Kat had always been aware of Charlie's plan. Shelly had implied it from the first time she mentioned Kat's name. So why propose that Marcey steal it, if that was Charlie's original intent? There had to be a reason. Marcey sat on the train, headphones jammed into her ears and listening to chill wave. The pulsing beat calmed the swirl of questions.

Marcey transferred to a bus for the final ten blocks and got off to find herself on an abandoned street. She bent her head against the wind and hurried up to the storage facility.

There was no one at the front desk, so she didn't bother signing in. The place was busier during the day. Marcey saw a handful of people moving in and out of units, pushing carts up and down the hall. She moved quickly, her mind on the painting. She couldn't get it out of her head. The screaming face, the horrifying, grotesque nature of the way it contorted, lips pulled away from teeth that appeared to be chipping, shouting in anguish.

It wasn't long until Shelly appeared in the doorway, her arms folded across her chest. Today she was wearing a long tunic and leggings underneath her thick wool overcoat.

"I didn't think you'd come," Marcey said. "I was rude. I'm sorry." She grabbed the lock and entered the combination. It clicked open, and Marcey pulled the door up just high enough for herself and Shelly to slip inside before she closed it once more. It was dark inside. The air was stale. Marcey flicked on the light.

"You're not sorry at all." Shelly grinned. "But maybe you surprised me."

"Good to know." Marcey gave a little mock salute. From her back pocket, she pulled Kat's note and passed it to Shelly. "That's what she left me. Taped it to the door."

"That *is* brazen, even for her." Shelly skimmed the letter. "What'd she want you to steal?"

Marcey pulled down the photocopied image from the book from where it was tacked to an exposed piece of wood. She turned and held it out to Shelly. "This."

"That?"

"It's at the Perôt, in SoHo. Kat said she was in town to appraise it and that it would be returned to its owner on Monday." Marcey turned back to Charlie's workbench. "Clearly it's Charlie's last big job—stealing this painting. So why…ask me to steal it when I could offer her a way to get it more easily?"

Shelly set the paper down carefully, as though it was a precious thing and she was afraid it would break. She exhaled, looking around the storage unit. The single lightbulb overhead cast everything in long shadows. Shelly's eyes were lost in the darkness. "Kat wants you to fail, Marcey. She wants you to get arrested doing this job, because she's pretty sure she can use that moment to get Charlie's book. The letter's a threat."

"And a challenge," Marcey interjected. "She wants me to impress her, prove that I'm cut out for this. Why not do it? Why not prove that I can?" She was pretty sure she could, at any rate. She'd need a day or two to have a look at the place and really understand what was happening there, but she was pretty sure she could pull it off.

"Marcey, even with the best team available, you'd need more *time*. This is insane." Shelly bent and blew dust from one of the notebooks that lined the table. It floated, hazy, in the air between them. Marcey's nose itched. "Kat Barber is the first person anyone would look to for that job. She's setting you up, leaving clues that will lead straight back to her, and then she'll be able to flounce in and be all"—Shelly affected a terrible rendition of Kat's posh accent—"Oh, no, officer, it couldn't've been me, see? I was off fucking one of your officers in front of a crowd of fifteen people."

The thrill of the chase was a fleeting thing. It was already slipping through Marcey's fingers. She couldn't grab it for fear of losing everything. "You say this like it's a thing that happened."

"Charlie was caught in Rio, by a man we thought was a friend. Kat was…otherwise occupied at the time with an agent by the name of Topeté."

"Otherwise occupied?"

Shelly raised a single eyebrow. "Use your imagination."

"That's cold," Marcey replied.

"Kat's cold. She knew Charlie was going to get caught and she knew when it would happen and made sure there was *no way* she could be connected to it." Shelly looked at the paper. "I don't want to work with her. You shouldn't want to work with her. She'll do the same to you."

Marcey bit her lip. Danger curled around the image she had of Kat Barber in her mind, but it was the sort of danger Marcey wanted. She wanted to walk into the Perôt and take that painting off the wall, just to see if she could do it without the disaster scenario Shelly was proposing. Marcey sat on the rickety stool she'd pulled out from under the work bench and watched as Shelly leafed through one of Charlie's notebooks.

"You saw my face on those advertisements, right?"

Shelly hummed, noncommittal.

"There's a meeting on Monday at my job. My real job. I'm probably going to get fired and sort of want to quit to save them the trouble."

"Why?"

"Because of the fucking pictures. Because everyone knows I fucked Linda Johnson's kid in high school and now she's exacting revenge fucking two-point-oh on me. Linda Johnson's got her Super PAC going after me while she hides behind the protection of Citizens United. She's letting them fight dirty because her daughter—as far as I can tell on Facebook—is about to marry another woman. I'm the one who made her gay."

"You can't make people gay."

"I know!" Marcey threw up her hands. "I want to fight back. I think Kat Barber can help me do that."

"You don't know her from Adam, Marcey. You were buggin' out when she found your place." Shelly swept across the room, drawing herself to her full height and staring down her nose at Marcey. Her lip curled. "That tells me you're afraid. Afraid of what might happen if you step wrong. You're not looking ahead, not thinking like this is a game. You're not ready for this life. Too risky, 'specially when you're as green as you are. You're going to get caught. I won't go to prison. I can't."

Marcey shook her head. "I have to *try*. I have to fight back. Teach me, Shelly. Show me what I'm doing wrong if it's that awful, but help me, or get out." She pulled another notebook from the shelf and flipped through it. She sneezed in the dust and rubbed at her nose. She squinted, looking up through the cloud of dust with stinging eyes.

Shelly was staring at her with a closed-off expression, her lips pursed into a thin line. Her arms folded over her chest and shoulders hunched, she looked smaller than Marcey had ever seen her. "If the gallery is the Perôt and Kat's already been there, you have bigger problems."

"*We*, you mean."

"I never said I was getting involved, but the Perôt's not the easiest place to just get into, Marcey. For Kat to be there...she had to have had an escort."

"Kat said she was appraising the piece. She was there with another woman. I saw her, right before I came here."

"What'd this other woman look like?"

Marcey shrugged. "Didn't get a good look at her. Dark hair, about the same height? Looked like she could've been Asian, but that also could've been the light..."

"Topeté."

"The one from Rio?"

"Yes. That Topeté. Oh, that does complicate things." Shelly reached for Marcey's bag and pulled out Charlie's book without asking. Marcey let her, watching warily as Shelly flipped back a few pages from her own entry. Shelly settled on a page and handed the book back to Marcey. On the page she indicated there was a short entry, written in smudged ink—as though it were written quickly. Marcey took the book and read the entry with a frown.

Topeté, Wei Lin—Belgian, Interpol
Est. contact Algiers, 1999. Berlin, Moscow 2000-2004.
Moved Lyon, 2005, London 2009. Assigned KB 09-1283YJ.

"She's with Interpol?" She didn't know Charlie's shorthand. The entry seemed to indicate that the woman either went legit or was still at least passively involved in petty crime, despite her Interpol credential. "That's bad, right. Because this is an art job?"

"Very." Shelly's tone brooked no argument. "Charlie's worked with her in passing… The sort of mutual back-scratching thing that crooks and cops get into. I don't know how amiable their relationship was after she got scooped up to work directly with Interpol. Before then she bounced around investigative agencies, mostly for insurance, I think. She worked with him then somewhat. Usually on the odd job where they shared a common enemy." Shelly sat down on the stool and took the book back from Marcey. "There are at least five people in this book that I know of who are behind bars because of Wei Topeté. She did Charlie too, got him back to the States and put him away with the first thing that stuck. She succeeded where your girl Linda Johnson failed."

"Then why is she with Kat?" Marcey frowned, thinking back to the Perôt's pristine white gallery walls. Was she witnessing the calm before bloody fallout of some arrest years in the making? "Shouldn't she want to lock Kat up?"

Frowning, Shelly nodded. "I'll go with you to look at this painting, Marcey, but I won't help you steal it. If you want that, you'll have to ask Kat Barber for help. There's too much risk here. I don't want you getting into this life only to have it ripped away from you by someone like Topeté." She didn't meet Marcey's gaze as she spoke, gathering her things. Slinging her purse over her shoulder, Shelly inclined her head to the door. "We should go."

Marcey locked up before they fell into step together. Marcey was wrapped in her own thoughts, and a quick glance at Shelly told her that the other woman was as well. She was lost in the possibilities of taking the job, and she wondered if Shelly was thinking the same.

"I'm not going to ask Kat Barber for help."

"Then you're not going to get away with stealing this painting." Shelly raised her hand to hail a cab. "Sorry, kid, them's the breaks."

Sticking her jaw out, a little more determined than ever before, Marcey shrugged. "We'll see."

CHAPTER 8

Wei, Rekindling Friendships

WEI WOVE THROUGH THRONGS OF pedestrians, heads bare and faces shining. The mood was infectious when the weather was like this. The clouds broke and faded into sunlight, and the sun-starved people of the city basked in its warmth. It was just spring, a moment of renewal.

Her destination was a small bar on the Lower East Side, a place she knew well enough but hadn't been to in years. She never called New York home. She never stayed long enough to put down roots. That chaos, the constant movement and hard-won sense of place, was learned when she was a child—her father had been in the Belgian foreign service, her mother the daughter of Chinese émigrés had come to the West just after the second World War. He'd never been posted at one place long enough for Wei to feel as though she belonged. Shanghai, Algiers, Moscow, Berlin—the cities had been stopping-off points, nothing more. It wasn't until London that Wei had settled enough to start tentatively putting down roots, and the roots were largely because of Kat.

The nomadic lifestyle suited Wei. It kept her life simple.

Simple, though, would be the last word to describe her life of late.

The bar was small and homey, brightly lit by wide windows. At night tea-lights dotted the ceiling to look like the stars the city swallowed in itsfluorescent glow. Wei glanced around. There were a few happy-hour patrons lingering into the dinner hour, but the floor was quiet.

A woman sat at the back, tall and broad shouldered. Her fingers splayed out over the lip of her wineglass. It was a red, the same deep color as her nails. It had been some time since Wei had seen this woman, and it took a moment to recognize her. Time had been kind to her. Transition had too.

Wei approached the bartender and ordered the house whiskey neat. She took her time ambling over to the woman at the back, watching, and waiting. She wanted to see if she'd be noticed. She set the glass down on the table before sliding into the seat opposite, a smile pulling at her lips. "Hello, Shelly."

She did so enjoy these moments where she pounced.

Shelly looked up, her eyes going wide and her hand jerking before she stilled it. "Wei." She cursed. Wei wished people would learn to say her name properly, to let it roll off their tongue in a breath the way Kat did.

"I almost didn't recognize you," Wei confessed. She smiled, the small, polite smile of one reminiscing with an old friend. "Time has been kind to you."

The compliment—and it was one truly, for Shelly was a beautiful woman and Wei was not without eyes—seemed to take Shelly aback. She glanced down at her hands, fidgeting with her wine glass. "It hasn't been easy."

"Such things never are."

"Especially in my line of work."

"You could always get out of it, you know." Wei sipped her whiskey. "Do something more interesting—like youth advocacy."

Shelly picked up her wine and raised an eyebrow. "Ah, yes, the transgender woman, exactly the sort of person parents would want mentoring their kids." She sighed and sipped her wine. Setting her glass down, her expression grew more serious. "I'll take the compliment for what it is, Wei. It's been a long road. One I've had to walk alone for a while now, thanks to you."

The intensity of Shelly's words bit into Wei's psyche, and she felt guilty again. Shelly's transition was a joke in some of the circles, but Wei admired her for doing it despite the implications for her career. The game was hard enough without the added complication of gender politics. "I'm sorry for your loss." Wei did not feel sorry, but it was better, sometimes, to give the lip service required. "Charlie was…well, a good man."

"Why are you here?"

"I thought I'd look you up," Wei answered. "Offer my condolences."

"Did Kat send you?"

"I'm not her messenger, Shelly. Never have been. We don't work like that. If anything, you could say Linda sent me." Wei tipped her drink and smiled smugly. She sipped, feeling the warmth of the whiskey filter down her throat and settle in her stomach. "You know what she's after."

"She won't find it if she's having you look me up." Shelly took a large swallow of her wine. Wei watched the way her throat worked around the wine. It was a larger swallow than Shelly must've intended; it took her a moment to continue. "I haven't the slightest idea who Charlie sent it to. I would've *thought*"—she paused, eyeing Wei thoughtfully—"that it would have gone to Kat. She was the heir apparent, after all."

That was why Linda had called Wei away from London, from her actual investigation. Kat owed Interpol that book, and she'd bargained far more than her freedom for it. Wei was here to make sure it ended up in Kat's hands, rather than Linda Johnson's mess of an archive room. It would never see the light of day again if it were left there, especially not if it contained everything Wei suspected it did. Charlie Mock's career had spanned decades, and he'd documented everything. Wei couldn't even begin to think of the power Johnson would hold with that document in her hands.

Wei drained the rest of her drink and motioned to the bartender that she wanted another.

Shelly ran a finger along the edge of the table. "Say it were to resurface. What would you want from it?"

The bartender brought a second glass over. Wei almost asked him to leave the bottle, but this was a game of cat and mouse she couldn't play drunk.

"You know Kat, how she is." Wei shrugged, deliberately evasive. "You know what's in the book."

"Ah, that dirty secret of yours."

"Too right."

The wine in Shelly's glass cast a ruby-colored shadow on the table. It almost matched the color of Shelly's lipstick. "Kat's in town."

"Appraising a painting, yes."

"She's not trying to steal it?"

Wei glared. The hobbies of her lover were not something Wei discussed in the company of anyone, let alone fellow criminals. "The lesser nature of it doesn't carry much weight—even if it's suspected to have been an influence for *The Scream*."

"Is it now?"

"Of course it isn't, but Kat can talk a pretty game and there are some similarities."

"Why'd she appraise it for two mil then?" Shelly raised an eyebrow. "You and I both know that's a price tag reserved for lesser great works. That smells like Kat's on the job. Which isn't a good look for the collar you've effectively slapped around her neck for your bosses in Lyon."

"She can't be—" Wei thought back over the past week. There'd been nothing to indicate... *The phone call.* She'd pretended not to notice Kat stealing away in the night. She'd pretended because that's what they did around each other when their lives butted against the truth. It was a relationship founded on lies. Unhealthy, perhaps, but it was what allowed them to work as one.

"It's enough for Johnson to hang you out to dry, Topeté." Shelly reached across the table, a heavy hand on Wei's shoulder. "And if she ever gets the book she'll find out about Berlin and Algiers, and your career'll be ruined."

Wei ground her teeth. She needed something stronger than this weak whiskey. She couldn't acknowledge the accusation. She pulled her arm away from Shelly's superficially kind touch. "I don't know what you're talking about." She drained the rest of her glass. This conversation was not going the way she wanted it to go. "Be careful, Shelly. One word and I could have you arrested."

"You've got no jurisdiction here. Interpol's gotta be invited in," Shelly shot back. "And besides, with both your feet firmly planted on this sinking ship, you've got no place to judge."

Frowning, Wei asked, "Did you come here thinking I would come by?" This was an old haunt of Shelly's, her turf, a place where Shelly felt safe. Wei had come here knowing there were only a few places in the city where she could "bump into" one of Charlie's old crew regulars.

Shelly smiled the elusive smile of a con artist. "See, that's the problem with you, Wei. Once, you had this all figured out. You played both sides like a fiddle and used them to propel yourself forward. Now, with too much time on the side of angels, the devils are getting the jump on you." She took a sip of wine, savoring it before setting the glass down. There was a smudge of lipstick on the glass. Shelly swiped it away, smearing it with her thumb. "Johnson can't get her hands on the book for obvious reasons, and you've made promises, clearly, for Kat's future. Why not work together?"

"And what?"

"Stop Kat from recruiting someone new into the fold. Stop Johnson from getting her hands on the book. All that foolishness. I know what you'd do for her. What you're doing for her now."

They stared at each other, Wei steely and Shelly smug.

Wei got up, tossing a crumpled twenty down onto the table. "I'll be in touch."

She left in a hurry, walking aimlessly in the growing twilight. She went north, and then west, before getting turned around and heading down to the subway platform to find her way back to the hotel. She couldn't get the thought of what Shelly had said out of her mind. Kat didn't bring people in. That was the job of the leader. It was what Charlie Mock had done before he died. He'd brought people of unique skillsets together for work, and he'd allowed them to thrive before turning them loose onto the world. That was what had made him dangerous as a criminal—he was able to draw people in and have those people commit the crimes for him. He was the facilitator. The liaison. He wasn't the man who did the work, most of the time.

Another player was on the board.

Emerging from the subway station in a part of the city she did recognize, Wei headed up to the crosswalk that would allow her to walk the two blocks to the hotel. She drew her cellphone from her purse and called LePage.

He answered on the second ring. "What?"

"Get down to the Perôt. It's a gallery in SoHo. Broadway and something. I think someone's going to make a play at that painting."

"I'm on it."

It was a lead. A lead Johnson would jump on.

CHAPTER 9

A Heist, Considered

THE PERÔT HAD A TOP-NOTCH security system. Marcey typed the name she saw printed on the side of the small box affixed to the wall into Google on her phone. Her eyebrows shot up, reading the rave reviews from newspapers as far-flung as Moscow and Shanghai. *Christ*, she was fucked. This was, despite it not being Marcey's first rodeo with the law, the first time she'd ever come face-to-face with something so daunting. She'd never stolen anything so valuable either. She didn't know if it could be done.

It was Sunday afternoon, and Marcey was inspecting the mostly empty gallery. A security guard drifted around the space with his smart haircut and ill-fitting uniform, leaving Marcey alone with the grotesque painting that dominated the far wall. There were other pictures in the gallery, but it was consuming, drawing Marcey into it.

She stared up at the painting, trying to figure out how the hell she was going to get it off the wall and out of the building. Kat Barber had said to impress her. Marcey *wanted* to impress her. But this was a far more daunting task than she'd initially imagined.

"It's creepy, isn't it?"

Marcey started. Shelly was standing beside her, hands in the back pockets of her jeans, her shoulders squared back, defiant.

"I thought you weren't coming."

Shelly tilted her head back as though taking in the painting. "Call it a change of heart. Or a want to not see Charlie's only kin end up in jail at the hands of an ally." She didn't meet Marcey's eyes, and the dishonesty of the statement hung heavy. Why was she lying?

It didn't take much to knit the implication of Shelly's presence together with her previous reluctance to be involved. The truth was there, drifting like a half-imagined slight. Marcey looked away from Shelly. "You're here to babysit me."

"You asked me for help. This is me helping you, hon."

"Did she send you?"

"Who? Kat?" Shelly shook her head. She glanced toward the doorway and jerked her head, indicating Marcey should follow her outside. The temperature had turned chilly overnight, and Marcey shivered as she stood under the gallery's awning. Shelly stared down at Marcey, her expression unreadable. Her hair drifted in the slight breeze. "Kat doesn't even know you've involved anyone else, if I'm right about this." From the back pocket of her jeans, she produced a single sheet of white paper. "I thought you should see this."

Marcey took the paper and unfolded it. In the shadow of the screaming man was the same printout of the painting from Charlie's storage unit, only with significantly more information filled in than a simple Google image search. There was an appraised value and a signature that began with a sharp downward stroke before slashing back across the line with a relish. Kathryn Barber's signature was cutting. "Two mil?" Marcey read the number in disbelief. "This isn't even that good a painting. Or that important of one."

"What do you know about art?"

"Admittedly very little, but that is a ton of zeroes."

Shelly took the paper back from Marcey and folded it carefully. "You don't know anything about this world and yet you want to live in it. Come with me." There was still a tension on Shelly's shoulders. She headed up the block. Marcey hesitated, glancing back at the painting one last time through the Perôt's window. The screaming face stared back at her, sending a shiver up Marcey's spine. She exhaled and hurried after Shelly.

Once out of view of the outdoor security cameras, Shelly visibly relaxed. Her expression became less pinched and worried. It was still early on Sunday, but already the street was crowded with shoppers. "You can't just walk into a place and look like you're casing it. The guard noticed you. He could describe you to a cop."

"He wasn't even paying attention." Marcey scrunched up her nose. "How could you tell he was paying that much attention?"

"Because I know how to *look* in a room and see things you don't even know exist." Shelly folded her arms over her chest, scowling. "How many security cameras were in the room?"

Marcey thought back. There were two outside, plus one that she'd noticed, mounted in a corner. It was static—pointing solidly in the direction of the door. There had to be others. She closed her eyes, picturing the gallery: a wide bright space full of natural light. There were no walls to break up the visual, just white space. It was logical that there would be others, and she could guess where they were. "There were five," she answered. "Two out front. One at the back that was static, and two on two-eighty-degree rotations in the front corner. There's no large blind spot that I can think of. The coverage is uniform."

Shelly nodded approvingly. "And the rest of the security?"

A shopper bumped into Marcey. She stumbled slightly. "There's something on the back of the painting. I couldn't see what. Regardless it will need to be cut directly from the frame for transport."

"Very good." Shelly started to walk once more. "That was a motion detector, rigged to a pretty low-end security system, by this gallery's standards, but you missed the motion detection at the door and two secondary cameras trained on the painting. That two-million-dollar price tag will make even the most miserly of gallery owners take extra precautions." Shelly shook her head. "Even with an elite crew and plenty of planning time, this would be a risky job."

They reached the corner. Marcey chewed on the inside of her cheek, thinking hard. Was Shelly just trying to scare her away from trying to take the painting? "What if we were to approach this differently? Like, I don't know, waylay the transport crew that's set to move the painting tonight and take it then?"

Shelly laughed and paused at a street corner, waiting for the light to change. "Now you're thinking."

They sat in a Starbucks and watched the crowd for a while, not speaking. Shelly bought Marcey a coffee. Marcey sipped it, the worn leather of her jacket creaking as she moved. "This isn't going to work, is it?" The thought, like the coffee, was bitter.

"Probably not." Shelly was shredding a napkin slowly. "You're rushing, and rushing is dangerous. You have to be careful with these things. The more you hurry, the more the moving pieces come apart. You're playing into a larger hand now too. Kat Barber wants something from you. I think you know what it is."

"Charlie's book."

"Yes." Shelly plucked Marcey's coffee away from her and took a sip. "Kat always has an agenda. You have to understand that going into anything with her."

"You make her sound like some sort of cartoon villain."

"I'm being serious, Marcey. If you want to do this, you can't just rush in and do a smash-and-grab. This isn't the best place to do this job, despite everything Kat's hinted at. You don't back down from dares, that much is obvious, but take this from someone who's been around the block with Kat a few times: this isn't a dare you want to get involved with. If you're caught—arrested and locked away—they'll have grounds to seize your shit."

"I thought that was illegal."

"It isn't if they think it will be used in the commission of a crime. It's called civil forfeiture." Shelly tapped her nails on the table. "Charlie's book is a guide to his entire life. It's got everything you'd need to put together a crew to steal anything. If they arrest you, they'll get it."

"How do you know they want it?"

Shelly smiled sadly. "Because Kat Barber doesn't have it. If she did, I doubt we'd be having this conversation."

Marcey didn't follow. "I'm sorry?"

"Look, kid, I know that you're new to this, and that you think you've got it all figured out, but I'm here to tell you, you don't have a fucking clue." Shelly met Marcey's gaze evenly. "Your beef with Linda Johnson? Over her daughter? That's fucking cute, but it's nothing compared to what went down between her, Charlie, and Wei Topeté. Linda Johnson is Wei Topeté's contact here in the US. She's worked with Johnson before, when Charlie was arrested and eventually tried and sentenced for a securities scam he ran in 2007. If Topeté is after the book, she could get it from Kat, sure, but she'd want it for different reasons than Johnson would. If Johnson gets it, it stays here, in the US. If Topeté gets it first, it ends up feeding into decades of Interpol investigations and probably Kat Barber never ever getting arrested for the crimes she has committed." Shelly shook her head. "Basically—with Charlie dead, everyone is scrambling to find his estate."

"So, we need to screw Linda Johnson," Marcey said firmly. "Because through her we can get to Topeté and through Topeté comes Kat."

Shelly gave Marcey a long, searching look. "Why go after Kat?"

"I'm not *going after her*," Marcey answered. "I'm just leveling the playing field. Charlie was meant to leave that book for Kat, wasn't he?"

"As far as anyone knew."

"Then there's got to be a reason it's in my hands now, rather than hers." Marcey shook her head. Shelly was angling for something, that much was obvious, but what, Marcey couldn't figure it out. Talking about Kat was safe until she could figure out what Shelly's motivation was for coming back. She couldn't just ask. Asking was too easy; it begged the question of why she was thinking about it at all, and that just planted seeds of doubt in people's minds.

Shelly looked thoughtful. "Charlie… He did things his own way, you know. After a while I just sort of stopped being in awe that this wonderful man was willing to be with me, despite—well. And I just went with it. He never cared about the details like that, I think because he was always ten moves ahead of everyone else. He could predict behavior, to an extent. It's what burned him in the end—he couldn't predict Kat."

"She screwed him." It wasn't a question.

"Royally."

"Then I want to screw her. And Linda Johnson, because let's be real, Linda's the one who stands the most to gain by this."

"I wouldn't be so sure of that, Mar."

"How do you mean?"

"Think about it. If Kat gets this book, if you get your ass arrested because you're too proud to admit that you're *in over your head* with Charlie's half-baked plan—"

Marcey swallowed and met Shelly's gaze evenly. "It isn't half-baked, though. The whole thing's written down in his storage unit. Every single thing we'd need to do." She didn't mention that Charlie's plan was about this painting as well, and that Marcey's willingness to look into it was far more of a professional curiosity about Kat Barber than it was about wanting to steal it.

"And you want to use it to somehow turn the tables on Linda Johnson?"

Marcey's head dipped a nod. She couldn't meet Shelly's eyes. "That's what I want. I want to use Charlie's book—and whatever Kat Barber is up to with this painting—to ruin her." She exhaled, slow. "Is that possible?"

Shelly hummed. "Perhaps. The first move is always the hardest."

<hr>

It was close to eleven when Marcey left her mother's apartment and walked the two blocks north to the subway station. Shelly was back at home, in some far-flung part of Queens, having left Marcey at the subway hours ago with instructions to do the same. They'd each come at this from a different way.

Shelly was right. This was a game, and someone had to make the first move. Kat had made her gambit, but it wouldn't be until all the players were on the board that Kat would know what she had to work with. Charlie had the sketches of a crew, a plan up in New Hampshire. It could be done. Marcey could do it. And she wasn't about to let Linda Johnson or her pet Interpol agent, or even Kat Barber, make any moves until this was in place. There was falling on her sword, and then there was seeing what would happen if she did.

Marcey hummed to herself. That part of the plan was still at its beginning stages. What would happen if she did get caught? Would she even be arrested? Would she allow herself to go far enough to try?

What if she did succeed? Would she cut the painting from its frame and irreparably damage it? And what would happen then? They couldn't sell it through legal channels. Marcey bit her lip. But what if they could find a way? Charlie's notes mentioned something about a fake. Maybe that was the key. And the funds to buy the painting would have to come from Johnson. That was the ticket. That was what they had to do to expose Johnson as power hungry and corrupt.

The subway station was abandoned, which wasn't all that odd at this hour. The 6 train was equally empty: a few sleepy tourists headed back to their expensive Midtown hotels and a few drunk kids headed back after a night of the basketball tournament. It filled up, the closer they got to Midtown, but it was nowhere near the levels Marcey was used to.

Marcey got off the train ten blocks up from the Perôt, her heart was already racing Even when she and Darius were younger, this was never something she'd done. Shelly hadn't listened when Marcey tried to tell her that maybe they could stage something to distract the police. She didn't listen to any of Marcey's ideas, shooting them down and telling Marcey to go home and call Kat Barber in the morning. There was no point in any of this—they were just going to get arrested.

That's when the idea struck Marcey, and the plan jumped, fully realized, into her head. It was quick, simple, easy.

The painting could not be stolen tonight.

However, it could be made to look as though an attempt was made. Marcey could get caught, or come close to being caught. Charlie's connection wouldn't be seen at first, except to the small handful who knew he was planning this job. If Marcey was careful. If Marcey was careful, maybe left some evidence behind, maybe Linda Johnson would start to grow suspicious too. And that was good. Suspicious people were less careful. They'd fuck up.

Perhaps that was what Kat Barber desired to see as well. Maybe it would force her to come clean about what had happened with Charlie in Rio and why she was after Charlie's book now. Marcey wanted to know why Kat hadn't been forthright from the beginning, and why Rio was such a mess for everyone involved.

Marcey kicked a pebble and hurried along, occasionally glancing over her shoulder and pulling her hoodie down low over her eyes. Shelly would never agree to this part of the plan; Marcey had a gut feeling about that.

Darkness was never true in New York City. Especially not so close to Midtown. Still, if one stayed off the main avenues and walked east to west instead of north to south, it was fairly easy to find oneself in total darkness. This was a residential part of the city, not quite transitioning back into skyscrapers and offices. Marcey sloshed through puddles and ducked her head to avoid the streetlights. She was a shadow, stealing her way down the street.

She was far too full of herself and overdramatic to boot.

Chuckling at her overdramatic mind, Marcey pressed on.

When she reached the well-lit part of Broadway that played host to the shuttered businesses and sleepy galleries, Marcey was largely alone on the street. She didn't pull her hood down. She kept it, and the snapback holding it firmly in place, pulled low and walked with her gaze trained on the ground in front of her.

The Perôt itself was silent, empty at the late hour. Marcey stole into a shadow on the far side of the building before deciding to walk around the block and check it from behind. The back half of the building, a filthy alley buttressed by dumpsters and the tell-tale squeak of rats, was ugly compared to the ornateness of the front. Windows crammed with AC units became one with the night sky above.

The back door to the gallery was surprisingly unguarded. Usually the first level of any building in the city had some sort of anti-theft device—Marcey had learned that the hard way with Darius's cousins back in college. Marcey tugged her jacket sleeve over her fingers and tried the door handle. It was locked. She stepped back and pulled out her wallet, taking out a Panera card and trying to jiggle the handle and force the door open with her card. Darius had taught her how to do this when they were kids, but she couldn't remember it now.

The card slipped, and Marcey dropped it. She bent, scrabbling on the dirty ground. Her fingernails came away black. She wiped them on her jeans and shoved the card away into her pocket. When she got up, her shoulder bumped against the door.

Perfect.

A shrill beeping rang out. Marcey stumbled backward, and the alarm grew louder and louder. She turned, her feet slipping on the wet trash in the alleyway. Marcey ran. She ran as fast as she could, circling the block and heading out into the brightly lit sidewalk. Already there were two police cruisers parked in front of the Perôt. How had they gotten there so quickly?

Breathless, Marcey dodged around a taxi and crossed the street to where there was a growing gathering of onlookers. She looked like shit, dressed all in black, covered in mud and smelling like a dumpster. She should just get out of there, but Marcey wanted to see *why* there was already a crowd of gawkers outside. She frowned, eyes narrowed. Something wasn't adding up.

"What happened?" she asked a guy filming the scene with his phone. There was a live Periscope feed opened. "Did someone get hurt?"

"Look." The guy stepped aside, allowing Marcey's shorter frame to step into the red and blue flashing light of the police cars. The windows of the

Perôt were smashed in. "Said they saw someone…with a hood and a ball cap." He glanced at Marcey, eyeing her suspiciously.

Marcey shifted away from him, trying to slip back into the crowd, only to find herself making eye contact with one of the beat cops corralling the line. He stepped forward and gestured for her to come closer. Marcey couldn't run. If she ran, she'd look guilty. Maybe she could talk herself out of this?

All she'd tried to do was jostle a lock, after all. They couldn't prove anything else. She was careful. This? She hadn't done this.

"Can I help you, officer?" Marcey asked.

He glanced at her clothes, her hoodie under her leather jacket, the Jets snapback she wore. The mud and grime staining the knees of Marcey's jeans was obvious now. As was the dirt on her fingernails, she'd been somewhere dirty recently, and the alarm in the alley went off. "Do you know what's happened here?"

"Someone broke the window," Marcey answered. "It's a shame. There was a pretty cool painting in there. Did someone steal it?"

"Why would you think someone stole a painting?"

Stupid. Marcey feigned self-flagellation and closed her eyes, as though preparing for the inevitable. "I just assumed, it's a gallery, ya know?"

The cop stared at Marcey for a moment. "You're that kid from the posters. The one who sold those drugs in that school."

Marcey opened her mouth, actually flabbergasted and no longer acting. "What the fuck, man."

"I'm afraid you're going to have to come with me and answer a few questions to clear up what's happened here." The man's face was a twisted contortion of smugness and cruelty. He pulled a pair of handcuffs from a pouch on his belt.

"What?" Marcey took half a step backward. This time the instinct to run felt real, the crushing, defeated sense of resignation that she would not be able to pull this off as cleanly as she would have liked. "I didn't do anything."

"You match the suspect description."

"But I—"

"Don't resist."

Marcey put her hands up. She wasn't resisting. Marcey let herself be led away. She scanned the gathering crowd for Shelly only to find the tall woman missing from the gaggle of onlookers.

Marcey started to speak as she was manhandled to the car. The cop banged her head, shoving her into the back seat of his cruiser. Little bursts of color filled Marcey's vision, fusing with the blue and red of the lights overhead.

When she got out of this, her first phone call would be to Kat. That bitch had called this in. She was the only one who could have known when Marcey was there and what Marcey might be planning to do.

PART TWO

A Heist, Unraveling

CHAPTER 10

Marcey, Leaping

Security camera footage exonerated Marcey in the end. The detective, LePage, pulled it from the Banana Republic across the street and reviewed it for *hours* before he was willing to let Marcey leave. He showed her the footage before cutting her loose, apologizing for the mistake. "We took a look, and you can see that the guy who broke the window is a lot taller than you. I'm sorry for the mix-up."

Marcey fumed, watching the footage. The person in the video was obviously large, easily a foot taller than her five two. And heavy too, judging by the way his feet fell onto the pavement as he ran away once the window was smashed. "That's it?"

LePage frowned. "What?"

"That's all I get? An apology? You locked me up for hours. You didn't let me call my mom—or a lawyer."

"Innocent people don't call lawyers, Ms. Daniels."

"They do when they sue your ass for wrongful imprisonment." Marcey snatched her things from the bin the clerk passed her and tugged her jacket on. Indignation she could do; it was a face she wore easily. She could channel the idea that she had never been treated this way before. She knew it was because she looked guilty as sin, because she was in the wrong place at the wrong time, but that shouldn't've mattered. For all they knew, she wasn't doing anything that any other kid out on a night of the NCAA tourney wouldn't do.

No, she'd looked good for it, and they'd hauled her in, no questions asked.

It'd help if LePage didn't look so fucking disappointed about the whole thing. He rubbed at the back of his awful haircut. "Look, I'm sorry. You're the kid from those posters, okay? I just saw you and thought…"

"Maybe I'll sue Linda Johnson and her sleazy Super PAC too. That shit's illegal and you know it." Marcey tugged her collar out from where it was twisted under her jacket. She gathered her hair in a sloppy bun. She wanted a shower. If she was going to get arrested, she wanted it to be on her terms, and not so clearly orchestrated to prove a point. "Just…let me go, okay? I didn't do this. Let me go." She stormed out of the precinct office and nearly walked straight in to Shelly and— "Devon?"

He waved a hand at her, looking a little sheepish.

Shelly threw her arms around Marcey's shoulders. There was weight to her actions. Marcey didn't know how to take it. It felt so maternal. "Are you all right?" Shelly asked, stepping back and squeezing Marcey's shoulders in a reassuring gesture. "We were just coming to get you out. I came as soon as I heard."

How Shelly knew was not exactly the first question on Marcey's mind. She just assumed that this was all a part of some lesson she was meant to learn but hadn't quite seen the truth of yet. The actual truth wouldn't be until later, when the pieces slid into place. Marcey was more preoccupied with how Shelly was fussing over her, steering her away from the precinct door and settling her on a bench at the bus stop, tutting at the mess on her jeans and how dirty she looked.

"They just locked me up. Didn't ask questions, didn't bother to get a statement, just shoved me into some black hole in the basement of the precinct for *hours*." Marcey's fingers trembled. "I can't—I don't know—" Darius. She couldn't get the image of him behind bars like that out of her mind. When they were kids—they hadn't been locked up, just dumped back with their parents. This was different. This was terrifying. "I can't go back in there."

Shelly smoothed Marcey's dirty bangs from her forehead, before pulling her close. She exchanged a look with Devon over Marcey's head, one that Marcey was pretty sure Shelly hadn't meant for Marcey to see. It spoke volumes and drove home Marcey's true fear. This was deliberate. "No one's going to throw you in jail, Marcey. You're free to go…"

The trailing end of the sentence made Marcey push Shelly away and get to her feet. "You were right." Hot tears stung at the corners of her eyes. "I didn't realize it, didn't want to hear it, but you were right. I'm too fucking *green* for this shit. I needed to be careful and I wasn't. Look where it got me."

Devon frowned. "It's just a night in jail, Mar. Wouldn't be your first..."

Fuck, he knew her well. Marcey glared at him. She swiped the tears from her eyes. Eyeliner and mud smeared in the wake of her hand. She needed to wash her hands. "Kat Barber set me up, Shelly. You saw right through that. She set me up knowing that there would be cops all over that place. She wanted me to get caught. For what purpose, I have no fucking clue, but this was what she wanted." She pushed past them. "I'm going to go call Kat Barber."

"The fuck would you do that for?" Shelly hurried after her. She grabbed Marcey's shoulder and turned her around. Her expression was hard. "She *wanted* this, Marcey. She wanted you there, on that street, at that time, looking at that painting. Did you ever stop and think of why?"

Marcey jerked her shoulder away from Shelly. "She wanted me to impress her. She wanted me to prove myself and then she went and made it as hard as she possibly could for me to do that. I'm going to call her, and I'm going to ask *why.*"

Shelly softened. "And what if she tells you an answer you don't like?"

"Without something on Johnson, I'm just going to be that face on the campaign posters, a criminal forever. I think she can help with that. This painting... There's something here, something she wasn't telling us. Charlie's job was about that damn painting. I want to know what it is before I end up some fucking statistic locked away because that idiot, Officer LePage, in there saw my poster and just assume I was good for it."

"Wait a minute," Devon cut in. "LePage? What's his first name?"

"Uh, I'm not sure. He never said. Or if he did, I was too distracted by his terrible Macklemore hair." She dug in her pocket. "Hang on, I stole a business card from his desk." She produced the crumpled card and passed it to Shelly.

Shelly stared at it, her lips pinched into a tight frown. "That man wasn't an officer."

"Then who the fuck was he?"

"Trouble," Devon answered. He stepped into the street and hailed a cab, waiting until they had all clambered into it and were headed toward Marcey's home address before he spoke again. "He's Johnson's investigator. One of those detectives permanently assigned to the DA's office to do further investigation of anything the cops don't have the manpower to get to, or anything supplemental." He frowned. "I mentioned him when you first came to visit me about this."

Marcey nodded. "Yeah, the guy who got the jump on Charlie with Topeté in Rio and ended up getting him arrested."

"Oh, there's more to it than that." Shelly sat back. "Rio was a hot mess. I'm not sure whose side everyone was on, what with Gwen and LePage bringing their personal drama into an already heated situation because of Topeté." She glanced at Devon. Marcey felt squished in between them. "That was about the time she stopped walking the line, right?"

"Thereabouts, yeah," he agreed. "If LePage was the one who arrested you, it's because someone's given Johnson a tip. And if Johnson's involved, then Topeté can't be far behind."

"I thought that Topeté was Johnson's pet?" Marcey turned to Shelly. "Wasn't that what you said?"

Shelly was silent for a long time, tapping a red-tipped finger against the cab door. "If you go running to Kat Barber, you're playing into whatever game Johnson's setting up. She wants what you have, Marcey."

"You've said that."

"I'm *serious*," Shelly said sharply. "Be pissed at Kat if you want. Hell, I know I would be, but LePage arrested you. He was playing at beat cop because he wasn't sure you were a threat. Next time, you won't be so lucky."

"And if Kat set me up?"

"Then she's switched sides and you don't want any part in it." Devon pulled a ten from his wallet and passed it to the cabbie. They were at Marcey's place. "Don't be pissed, Marcey. Just be careful." He didn't get out of the cab. Shelly did, following Marcey and pulling her into a tight hug.

"If you do call Kat, get the fucking details of whatever job she was planning with Charlie. It's no coincidence that that painting was the one she asked you to find. It's up in his storage unit for a reason. I, for one, am mighty curious what sort of game she wants to play."

Marcey nodded, waved her good-bye, and went inside. She wanted a shower. She wanted sleep. She wanted to figure out what the hell she was doing.

An envelope was taped to the apartment door. Marcey pulled it away, glancing over her shoulder, back to the stairs. If she hurried, maybe Shelly and Devon wouldn't have left yet. But at the same time, she didn't want them to see it. Not just yet, at any rate. There was something to be said for holding back on details. Especially when Shelly's reaction and her willingness to go running to Devon said that she knew more about what was going on than she let on.

The note was from Kat Barber, written in the same hand, on the same stationary as the other one. Marcey jammed her key into the lock and let herself into the apartment.

M

When I said impress me, did you mistake my meaning for an edict to do everything at once? Your arrest was not my intention, but I could not have the painting stolen just yet. I believe it's time we talk.

K

"That bitch," Marcey muttered, throwing the letter down in disgust. Kat had set her up because she wasn't playing into Kat's hand. Annoyed, Marcey stripped off her dirty jeans and headed to the shower. She'd figure out what to do after she was free of alleyway grime and jail cell dirt.

⬥

It was much later before Marcey figured out what she wanted to do. Kat was an enigma, but there were pieces missing here. Why that painting? Shelly was right; it was just a lesser work, not worth the value Kat had assigned. It wasn't worth the effort, or arrest under false pretenses.

Somehow, in the process of saving the painting from Marcey's aborted attempt at stealing it, Kat had inadvertently put Marcey back onto Johnson's radar. It was ammo for Johnson's continued crusade and vendetta. It'd get funneled through backchannels to that Super PAC, the one that was so determined to smear Marcey's name by any means necessary.

After she showered, Marcey took an Uber up to Charlie's storage unit and found as many papers as she could on the painting at the Perôt. If he was looking into it, there was something bigger at play here. Marcey just had to put it together before she called Kat and let her anger fly. If she could be angry but have proof enough to pull one over on Kat, she'd be golden.

She returned home and took up residence of the couch, which was where her mother found her hours later, papers spread out over the coffee table.

"Where were you last night?" Her mom asked, toeing off her shoes. "I was worried."

"I was out, sorry. Passed out on a friend's couch." Marcey exhaled, rubbing at her eyes. The words were starting to blur together, and she hadn't made heads or tails of Charlie's plans.

"Where did you get all of that dusty junk?"

"Storage unit." Marcey grunted, not looking up.

Her mother wrinkled her nose as she peered down at the mess of papers covered in Charlie's spindly handwriting. Marcey saw it like a slow-moving accident. The photograph sticking out of the top of Charlie's book in her mother's hand before Marcey could reach up and stop her. This wasn't good. No, no. Oh *no*...

"This is..." Her mother's tone took on a far-off tone, as though the memory evoked in her was long-denied. She stared at it for a long time before tucking the photograph back into the notebook and disappearing down the hall. Marcey swallowed. Should she go after her mother and demand to know the truth about what had happened between her and Charlie all those years ago? Marcey didn't move. She didn't want to have that conversation. Not now. Not ever. Her mother was a liar, and Marcey couldn't bear the idea of her admitting it to her face.

She gathered her things and retreated into her bedroom, where she locked the door and slid down to sit on the floor. The emotions of the day flowed off her in tears. Relief, gratitude, and fear all massed into a messy series of sobs as she stared, blurry-eyed, at the photograph of Shelly, Kat, and Charlie. What was she going to do? Her mother had seen.

It was only a matter of time before other people did too. Johnson, Shelly, even Kat Barber would see through her. See that she was in over her head. She picked her phone up and dialed Kat's number, putting it to her ear and listening to the crackle-pulse tone of the line. It wasn't that late, and she was still in the city.

"I see that you continue to have no concept of when is an unacceptable time to call."

"Coming from someone with no respect for a person's privacy, you're one to talk." Marcey closed her eyes. She could push back, even with nothing, right? "Aren't you still in New York if you're leaving messages on my door?"

"No," Kat said shortly. She yawned. It was four in the morning in the UK. Marcey decided she didn't care that she'd woken Kat up. "You'll finally allow yourself in my presence then, Marcey Daniels?"

"I got caught. You made sure I did. Why?"

"You're three steps behind, Marcey. This isn't about you."

"William LePage was the arresting officer."

That got Kat's attention. The sharp inhalation and click of her tongue told Marcey Kat was surprised. Good.

"Ah," she said. "That changes things."

"Does it?"

"Come and see me, Marcey. I believe it's time we discussed the elephant in the room." It was spoken like a dare, a challenge. A crooked finger beckoning her back into darkness. A siren's call.

CHAPTER 11

Kat, Away

MARCEY SLUNG HER CARRY-ON BAG over her shoulder, her body aching and her mind muddled. Her seat was at the middle of the center row of the transatlantic flight. She was tired, jet lagged, and desperately wanted to be away from *people*. Grudgingly, she followed the signs for domestic baggage claim and arrivals, hating all the noise. Anxiety sat like a knot in her stomach. She'd never done anything like this before, flying halfway around the world to meet someone. Someone who terrified and intrigued Marcey, her presence a blinding light looming large on the horizon.

Unfamiliar accents and a cacophonous multitude of languages surrounded her. She'd never been to Heathrow Airport before, or England for that matter. At least she'd cleared customs. A shrill beeping cut through the buzz of conversation like a gunshot. Marcey fumbled in her pocket. A few other people did the same, but it was Marcey's phone ringing. Marcey slid her finger over the phone's screen. The number was restricted. Only the caller's location, *Dannemora, NY* was visible.

Marcey grinned. Darius. A politely disinterested operator's voice came onto the line. "This is a collect call from an inmate at a New York State penitentiary. Would you like to accept the charges for this call?"

"Yes." A pause. Marcey bit back a huff of annoyance. There was a very specific script for this, and the operators, she had learned, were trained to listen for a certain line and nothing else. "Yes, I will accept the charges," she clarified.

There was a moment of static before Darius's drawling voice came over the line. "Hey, Mar."

She missed him. Missed his voice and his letters. They didn't talk nearly as much as they'd used to, but the communication was always constant. She'd been too caught up in Charlie's book, and Darius had retreated into preparations for his appearance before the parole board. He was too busy using his limited phone availability to speak to Devon or his ma to have any time for Marcey. A little twitch of dread appeared in Marcey's stomach. Did he know what she was up to?

This call was a pleasant surprise, one that Marcey couldn't quite contain her joy over receiving. "Darius," she said breathlessly. "It's good to hear your voice."

He chuckled. "Yours too."

She paused under a sign indicating that arrivals and domestic baggage claim were down a set of stairs. "Is everything okay, Dar?"

"Been hearin' the craziest things. Devon won't shut up about you."

"Oh?"

"Yeah. Wasn't sure what to make of his awful attempt at small talk. I figured you'd tell me better."

"They monitor these calls," Marcey said, her voice flat. "I can't exactly tell you anything."

"Tell me why Devon's being so weird about this parole board hearing then." The phone receiver rattled in Marcey's ear. "I heard your name today, from some dude in here for white-collar stuff. Not Devon." He let the implication of all that he wasn't saying sink in for a moment. He shouldn't have overheard at all. "He said he heard from a buddy of his that you were the heir apparent, whatever that means."

A cold knife of fear cut through Marcey's resolve. She sucked her lower lip into her mouth, chewing nervously on chapped skin. "I know exactly what it means," she answered. "And even if you didn't, you probably already asked Devon to tell you all about it, didn't you?"

"Never said that," Darius shot back. "You aren't getting involved in something, are you, Mar? We *talked* about this."

A hot flash of anger surged in Marcey's stomach. It was a familiar companion, the same rage Marcey had felt when she'd realized she'd been set up at the Perôt. This wasn't acting though, pushing more hurt and fear into a situation to see what would happen. No, this was genuine, hatred that tasted coppery in her mouth as the retort rose to her lips without warning.

"You're not my protector anymore, Darius. What I do is my business, not yours, and certainly not Devon Austin Jackson's."

He exhaled. He knew her tells as well as she knew his. This was the moment when Darius rolled over and died, allowing Marcey's rage to build. He never participated in the rage—in allowing Marcey to let the creatures that lurked beneath the surface of her calm exterior loose into the wild. No. Instead Darius preferred to completely disengage with Marcey when she reached these moments of emotion. Sometimes she wondered if it was because he did not want to experience her emotion, or if it was because he was simply unable to relate.

It cut into her, a knife sinking into her skin and reminding Marcey, yet again, that she was shouldering the guilt of what happened to Darius for no reason. He hated that about her. Hated how she blamed herself for what happened to him.

"I'm not some prop for your guilt complex," Darius shot back. "If you go through with this, Mar, we're done."

"Done?" Marcey scowled. "For what? For me caring about you and wanting to make sure that your life isn't fucking shit when you get out of that hellhole?"

"Linda isn't going to let me out and we both know it. I have two years left on this sentence. I can't count on it being a sure thing that my good behavior gets me an appearance before the parole board, let alone a chance. She's gonna fucking show up and tell them about how those EMTs had to give her daughter a damn Narcan shot because she'd taken too many of those pills."

Air escaped Marcey's nose sharply. "You don't think she would actually do that, do you?"

"I wouldn't put it past her if you fucking piss her off." His glare was evident in his tone. Marcey worked her jaw, stewing. "You're not just fucking with your own life when you do shit like this. You gotta fucking remember that when you do this impulsive bullshit."

"I'm not—"

The airport intercom chose that moment to announce, in plain English, that Marcey was welcome to and should enjoy her stay in London. Marcey's eyes fluttered closed. "I can't really talk now, Dar. I have no idea how expensive calling collect is internationally."

"Where the hell are you?"

"Can't say." It was pretty fucking obvious, and Darius wasn't stupid, but Marcey didn't want Darius to repeat the location in case anyone could overhear. That wouldn't work for the plan.

There were eyes on her. Marcey looked down the stairs at a blonde woman standing with her hands plunged deep into the pockets of her long khaki rain jacket. Marcey's breath left her. Kat Barber was shorter than Marcey had expected, standing in dark brown boots up to her knees, an expectant look on her face.

"Why not?"

Kat Barber was smiling up at her, her lips curling into a crooked smile that dimpled her cheek. Marcey raised a hand tentatively and waved. Kat Barber pulled her hand from her pocket and waved back. There was cheekiness about her smile, like she'd just gotten away with something, like she was plotting the end of the world. Marcey took in Kat's dirty-blonde hair pulled back into a messy bun. She looked amazing, a dream come alive only to realize that such dreams never came without some trepidation.

"Seriously, Marcey, where the hell are you?"

"Tell you later, Dar." She hung up on him and headed down to the final security checkpoint. She'd cleared customs in two countries without incident. This was an accomplishment, a victory to be savored.

"I thought you'd be taller, Marcey Daniels." Kat Barber's voice was far richer in person, full of warmth and humor. On the floor beside Kat was Marcey's checked bag.

Kat Barber's eyes were green, and her makeup was soft but absolutely perfect despite the late afternoon hour. Marcey felt rumpled, standing next to her, but she had been on a plane for the better part of seven hours and Marcey felt she was allowed.

"I thought you'd be…" Marcey cast around for an appropriate response to Kat's barb, but nothing came. Her preconceived notions of Kathryn Barber were not entirely unfounded—they came from the picture of her and Shelly with Charlie on the beach in Rio. Kat, sun-kissed, the highlights in her hair shining in the sun. She settled on, "More blonde." In the picture, Kat's hair was the color of straw just harvested. It was faded now, dull with the winter. Marcey liked it better this way.

It won her a quirk of pretty lips stained dark with lipstick and a polite, but dismissive, nod. "We're going to have to work on that."

"What?" Marcey asked.

"Your sparring ability, Ms. Daniels," Kat Barber answered. She bent to pick up Marcey's bag and slung it over her shoulder. Marcey swallowed, feeling herself start to relax just a little. She took Kat's arm when it was offered. "If you're going to get into this line of work," Kat continued, "you're going to need to know how to murder someone with words alone."

<hr />

"Is it okay to call you Kat?"

Kat didn't look at her, eyes trained on the city as it flew by them outside the car window. Kat had a driver. Or at least had thought to hire a car service for this trip. "Most people do. Kathryn's a mouthful and I'm not eighty-five." Kat rested a finger on her chin and hummed, pensive. "Who were you talking to, earlier? I can't imagine you thought to buy yourself a SIM card. Must have been expensive."

It was a foolish thing, to want to trust someone like Kat Barber, and all Marcey's better angels were against the truth. It tumbled out of Marcey's lips like a benediction. "A friend."

Kat sat back. "Tell me about your friend?"

Marcey shook her head. "No."

"Why not?"

"Because I'm not here to make nice. You had me arrested."

Wordlessly, Kat leaned over and raised the privacy screen to cut the driver off from eavesdropping. When it was raised fully, she spoke in carefully measured words. "You don't want to make small talk with me, Marcey?"

The contempt in Kat's voice was enough to make Marcey want to lash out. Her fingers twisted around the hem of her oversized sweater, her attention on the traffic outside. The annoyance at Darius came creeping back, dark and oil-like in her mind's eye. Her attraction to Kat, the thrill of this game, everything seemed to fall away. This place was backward—everything about this was backward. She'd gone about this all wrong. Shelly was right about that. Shelly was right about a lot of things, and Marcey felt like she was drowning in Kat's expectant stare.

"No, I don't," Marcey answered.

"Why be so standoffish?" Kat asked. "You want to know about me, I want to know about you. You didn't strike me as the type to have many friends." She turned to look at Marcey. Her eyes were warm and the bright green of the wide-open spaces Marcey had longed for as a child growing up in a concrete jungle. "Maybe I could be one."

"I have friends," she clarified. Pride was a foolish thing. So much time was wasted on feeling frustrated, annoyed by the limitations of communication between two people who had never spent any amount of time together. "Friends who are honest enough to tell me the full details of their plans before *someone ends up in jail.*"

"What's done is done, Marcey. I can no more change the past then I can predict the future. It was an unfortunate, but necessary thing." Kat smiled wanly. "Could we perhaps start anew, try and see if a friendship can be forged between us?"

To have a beautiful, terrifying woman propose such a thing was too much. Marcey shifted, uncomfortable in Kat's scrutiny. What did she want from Kat Barber? A line from an old movie about people much like themselves came to mind. "First, we should try it before we can come to trust each other."

"Been watching old Connery movies, have you?"

"I wasn't watching for *him.*" Marcey grimaced.

The coded conversation there, the implication of it, lingered. Kat's lips turned upward into a slow smile. They were kindred spirits in that regard at least. The city fell in beside them, rows of houses slotting into buildings crowding out the sky. Marcey relaxed as they loomed higher and higher overhead. It felt like home.

"I'm sorry, for what happened." Kat picked at a speck of invisible lint on her jacket. "It was not my intention to see you in distress, but the time wasn't right. I couldn't have you—"

"The time wasn't right?" Marcey retorted. "You told me where the painting was, you told me to *impress* you. What the hell was I supposed to take that as, if not an invitation to try and steal it?"

"I would have hoped," Kat said forcefully. "That your association with Shelly Orietti would have made you more cautious."

"How did you—"

"You met her at Charlie's storage unit, didn't you? Don't give me that look—people in these circles *talk*. Even if they don't particularly care for each other. Word gets around quick. A fresh face and a good liar helping Shelly out on a con? That's *news*, especially when she was using Charlie's trick cards."

Feigning ignorance was never Marcey's style. Still, she frowned. "They were trick?" She tried to keep her voice full of the wonder that she felt it would be deemed appropriate for such a revelation. It felt hollow, but it did the job.

"How else do you think she won so easily?" Kat sat back in the car seat, her attention no longer fully focused on Marcey. "You'll want to be more observant."

Marcey sat back, staring up at the roof of the car. She was observant, thank you very much. The dome light was chipped and the covering was drooping in places. "You know Charlie left me the whole plan, right?"

"Did he now?"

"He did. Told me everything there was to know about that painting, and about where it's supposed to be kept, too. It being at the Perôt was merely for its appraisal, wasn't it? It wasn't meant to be there."

Kat's lips pursed into a thin line. Marcey watched her face, watched the way the muscles in her neck moved as she swallowed and then focused herself once more. "You should tread carefully, Marcey Daniels."

"I don't think I need to be careful. I think I need to follow Charlie's plan—"

"My plan."

"Sorry?"

Marcey turned to look at Kat as she spoke, taking in how she sat sprawled back on her seat, a queen looking down upon her worshipful subjects. She looked at Marcey as though she were the most fascinating person on the planet. "It's my plan. My way of making up to Charlie for Rio."

"From what I heard you sold him out."

"Shelly would say that, yes." Something flashed, resentful and dangerous, in Kat's eyes.

"Is that not what really happened?"

"There's more to every story, Marcey. I'm sure you've learned this by now. These things come not in the black and white of American justice, but in shades of gray. I was in a difficult position, yes, but Rio went sideways because of LePage and Gwen's breakup, nothing more."

"Wait…LePage? The guy who arrested me LePage?"

"I'm afraid they're one and the same." Kat didn't sound particularly troubled. "People talk, Marcey, in these circles. You need to be more careful."

"If people are talking, then I want to know why they're talking. I want to know why you couldn't just tell me all of this over the phone. I want to know why you made me fly halfway around the goddamn world to have a conversation with you. Skype is a thing."

"You were a bit put out when you called me. Perhaps I merely wanted to make it up to you. I did, after all, put you through an awful ordeal."

"Don't pretend you know me."

"I think you'll find that I do know you. Girls like you are common as muck. Your friend on the phone is the one you got locked up, the one whose freedom is being threatened by that witch you Americans like to call an Assistant District Attorney. You feel guilty over his imprisonment and more so now that it's campaign season and Linda Johnson has eyes larger than her station. You want to do something about that, don't you? You want her crushed, her reputation squandered, for what she did to your friend." Kat's gaze hardened. "Am I close, Ms. Daniels?"

Marcey glared at Kat. Who the hell was she to think she knew Marcey? She was right though. Right about all of it. And the shame burned Marcey's cheeks. She looked away, to the pulling fabric of her leggings. "That is…a good summation of things, but…" Marcey reached into her bag and rifled through her paperwork until she found a crumpled "Johnson for DA" poster. She'd torn it off a wall in a subway station on her way to the airport. "You're forgetting the most important piece." She passed the paper on to Kat. "From what I've been able to surmise, the group funding this isn't connected to Johnson, but she's consulted on the messaging. That's me, if you couldn't guess."

"Awful likeness." Kat held up the paper, her expression thoughtful. "Doesn't really capture you at all."

"It's supposed to be an artist's rendering of a 'generic criminal' but to me it looks as though they ran it through a Photoshop filter and called it a day."

"I would assume there is legal recourse for something like this?"

"There is, if it's Johnson who's behind it. But I'm pretty sure it's not her camp putting these out. It's some law and order parent watchgroup against drugs in schools." She couldn't mention the other angle. She didn't want to have to explain Rebecca to Kat Barber of all damn people.

"Ah." Kat folded the poster and tucked it away in her jacket pocket. "You'd know all about that, wouldn't you?"

"Don't pretend to know me, Kat," Marcey repeated.

"Don't push me away then. I want to know you, Marcey. You're interesting." Her face was perfectly still, a wispy strand of hair falling into her eyes. There was nothing to betray what she was thinking. "If you're still talking to the friend you got locked away, you're better than most in this line of work." She raised an eyebrow. "Get caught, get dropped." Her accent grew more pronounced, crasser as she spoke. "You can't afford a slip-up like what happened to him again, can you?"

Marcey shook her head. "I can't. No one can." Kat's lips twisted up, the barest hint of a smile. It was all teeth and insincerity. "So then you know what I want."

"I do." Outside, a car sped past, weaving in and out of traffic at breakneck speed. Marcey recoiled, almost on instinct. Kat's hand moved, coming to rest on hers, lying almost forgotten on the seat between them. "I think we may be able to help each other."

"I'm glad you think so." Marcey should've put it together that this was how the conversation was going to go between herself and Kat. This black cloud of a woman was looming on the horizon, just waiting to strike. Shelly'd seen it. Why hadn't Marcey? "I want her ruined for what she did to Darius. What she's trying to do to me now. She's getting her petty revenge. I want mine." Kat's hand was so warm. Marcey wondered how she could be so furnace-like, her skin burning Marcey's fingers. And there, Kat's long nails, capped with painted tips of a green that matched Kat's eyes, lingered. But there was other paint, not polish, around the edges of Kat's nails, bright yellows and dull ochre browns.

"That's his name? Darius?" His name on Kat's lips felt like a betrayal.

"Yeah."

They lapsed into silence.

Kat lived outside of London. Her address in Charlie's book was listed as way out in the countryside, in a tiny little village that housed about three hundred people. Marcey had spent a good hour plugging it into Google Maps on the plane, tracking the roads in and out, making sure that there was a good route out if things went south with Kat. It had been worth the twenty bucks she'd spent on Wi-Fi for that alone.

"Where are we going?" Marcey asked. "Charlie's book said..." She stopped herself before she spoke further. The driver turned off the main road and was now driving through bustling city streets, taking them into the heart of the city. The car finally stopped down a quiet street, already cloaked in the gloom of twilight, coming to rest before a nondescript building. Marcey swallowed nervously.

"Charlie's book says many things," Kat answered. "Not all of them paint a full picture." She moved to get out of the car, motioning for Marcey to do the same. Marcey grabbed her bag. Kat's eyes were on her through the back dash of the car.

Kat stood on the curb, speaking to the driver through his window for a moment before straightening up. When he pulled away, Kat headed up a short flight of stairs to a set of double doors. Marcey followed her, curious. From her pocket, Kat produced a ring of keys, one of which was large and iron, old fashioned. She slipped it into the lock and turned it, then leaned over and punched a code into a keypad half-hidden by the ornate molding framing the doorway. She glanced over her shoulder, her crooked smile broadening. She pushed the door open and stepped aside, allowing Marcey passage into the building.

The foyer inside had high, arching ceilings that went up three stories and were lined with windows. The entire space was lit in a strange blue light, the color of twilight filtering in from the wide, multi-paned industrial windows half cast in shadow as the sun set behind the swirling mass of gray clouds overhead.

An ancient-looking elevator, cast in copper and steel, dominated the far wall. A staircase spiraled around it. Marcey was grateful when Kat headed for the elevator, pulling open the cage and not so much as blinking when the entire thing groaned and creaked.

"What is this place?" Marcey asked. The floor fell away beneath them as the elevator creaked its way upward, pipes hissing and groaning as it rose through the floors of the old building.

Kat turned to regard Marcey, her expression solemn. "Studio space. It doubles as a city residence when I need to be in town for business." She tapped Marcey's bag, slung over Marcey's shoulder. "I'd thought we could stay here, to save us the drive from the country in the morning."

"That seems wise," Marcey answered. "Are you sure you're okay with my staying here? I'm really okay to get a hotel if you'd rather me not be in your hair."

When she'd told Shelly that she was going to see Kat, Shelly hadn't been particularly surprised. She'd warned caution, as she had before, but told Marcey to go if that was what she wanted. "Just be careful," Shelly had urged. "Find out what game she's playing with Johnson before you drag both of us in so far that we can't get out." It was a good warning, one Marcey could take to heart.

Kat's eyes were on her, a panther on the prowl. Marcey shifted uncomfortably, moving ever so slightly away from Kat. She was drawn to Kat. Kat's personality filled up all the empty places Marcey tried to ignore within herself. Being drawn to Kat wasn't a good idea.

The elevator ground to a halt. Marcey shifted, uncomfortable in her oversized sweater and leggings next to the sleek lines of Kat Barber and her very ornate, if rickety, elevator. This was Kat's domain. And she was willingly walking into it.

"Come in, come in," said the spider to the fly.

CHAPTER 12

Kat, Storytelling

"You haven't answered my question," Marcey said. "I really can stay somewhere else. It's no trouble."

Following a complete stranger, never mind one she knew to be dangerous, to a foreign country was not Marcey's brightest move. She didn't think that Kat Barber wanted to hurt her, but the there was so much tucked away into the pretty little rich girl façade that didn't break the surface of calm that Kat clearly worked so hard to put on.

Kat Barber leaned in close enough for Marcey to catch a whiff of her perfume and the scent of something fruity in her hair. Marcey couldn't breathe, her mind completely taken up by the image of this beautiful, charming woman. She swallowed once, and then again, as Kat spoke. "Why on earth would I ever send you away, Marcey Daniels?"

The silence between them was heavy. Kat was standing far too close to Marcey, the air full of things left unsaid. Implication was everywhere, and Kat's intentions could not have been clearer. Marcey swallowed, looking down at her feet. She had to look anywhere but Kat, or else she would be ensnared.

She's involved with someone else, Marcey reminded herself. She still inhaled deeply; she still took in the scent of Kat's perfume and committed the spicy, floral scent to memory. She couldn't help herself.

"This place has plenty room for two," Kat added, turning and walking away into the great open space before Marcey could think of anything to say. They were on the top floor. The great spiraling staircase narrowed into a thin line, but the ceilings remained far higher than Marcey would have ever expected.

"I'll say," Marcey muttered. The room had an open floorplan, cast in the same gray light as the foyer below. There was a kind of sadness clinging to these walls, but it was a sadness that Marcey found oddly welcoming. A melancholy—a lack of understanding with pure-white walls and large windows.

Marcey turned and pulled the elevator gate shut. She followed Kat and the click, click, click of her spiked heels across the hardwood floor. They were venturing further into the flat, into the great belly of the beast that was Kat Barber.

"How did you end up with a place like this?" Marcey asked.

Kat gestured airily. "Oh, I own the building. Or my father does. An investment, if you will."

The apartment spoke nothing of this wealth. It was a Spartan space, all raw wood in the eaves. The floors were the color of warm mud, scrubbed bare and varnished to a dull, scuffed sheen. A few rugs decorated the floor, threadbare in places, as though they were cast-offs from a household long in the habit of acquiring new things when the old ones no longer looked the part. They had once been beautiful marvels of work and patterning, all in black and white faded to gray with time and use.

A kitchen lined one wall, against a bank of windows. The stove and refrigerator were enclosed by a half-wall that gave the illusion of a separate room. Marcey was drawn to the windows. Outside, telephone lines reached out from above the corner window like strands of a great spider's web. A flock of small black birds were perched on the wires, their cries silent through the cool glass. Marcey rested her fingers on the windowpane.

She was walking in a dream. This place, this city, it was shrouded in a thick fog as twilight fell. Marcey's head felt fuzzy with the jet lag and the late-earliness of the hour. It was early evening yet to her mind it was only lunchtime. Her focus was elusive, slipping like smoke through her fingers. All she saw was Kat's bewitching smile. It was enough to make her lose herself, to drive her to utter distraction.

The birds sat adrift above a sea of foggy clouds. Despite the beauty, the place was cold, soulless. Marcey didn't like its emptiness, the hollow feeling as her feet fell on the scuffed floors. The echo reminded her of how much she'd lost, in a way, and how much she wanted to go back on everything and try again. Marcey leaned forward, her forehead pressing on the cool glass. Her breath fogged before her.

Somewhere behind her, a kettle whistled. Through the reflection in the glass, Marcey watched Kat. She'd rolled up the crisp white sleeves of her blouse and was in the process of getting down mugs and a box of tea. When she stretched, the sliver of skin that appeared at her stomach was enough to make Marcey's mouth go dry. She had birthmarks, little moles. God, she was beautiful.

The ritual of tea was easy: boil water, steep, flavor, enjoy. Marcey took solace in it when very little else seemed familiar. Kat stood before a stove, her sleeves rolled up. Her hair was curling at her neck in the steam, a frizzy halo.

"Do you take sugar?" she asked, not looking at Marcey.

Marcey didn't look away from the window, staring at Kat's reflection, warm and inviting in the pale-yellow glow of the kitchen light. "One," Marcey answered. Tea was a universal language. "Thank you."

A mug, handmade of gray clay and beautifully glazed in blue and green, was presented to her. Marcey cupped it to her chest as Kat came to stand beside her at the window. Her mug was blue, the handle chipped, red clay showing the fleshy inside of the pretty exterior. "Why so quiet, Marcey? Surely you have things to ask me."

"I do. I'm just picking what I want to ask first." Marcey hid behind the mug. The tea was still too hot to drink.

"Why not start with the painting?" Kat's prompt came with a wicked smile. "Since that's what had you storming across the Atlantic to give me a piece of your mind."

Marcey set her tea down and met Kat's smug gaze. She was enjoying this. Marcey itched to do...something to her to make her stop looking so damn happy about this development. "No. Your stunt with LePage was what got me here."

"William's presence was...unintentional on my part, but it opens up a bigger playing field."

Exhaling, Marcey steadied herself before speaking. "With LePage comes Linda Johnson, and with Linda Johnson, apparently, comes your Interpol agent."

"What of my Interpol agent?" Kat asked. Her expression was unnervingly blank. Marcey chanced a glance at her, only to look away hurriedly, cheeks coloring. Kat seemed as though she could outwit death. "What happens between us has very little to do with any of this." She gestured at the space between them, hand moving as if it were caught on a wave.

Marcey let out a quiet breath of air. "Well," she began, forcing herself to look at Kat's politely disinterested smile and carefully measured blinking. "You tell me. I find myself in possession of an artifact belonging to Charlie Mock, one that Shelly tells me your Interpol agent was very keen to get her hands on. And then, less than a week later, I'm hauled off to jail by one of her known associates."

Kat was silent, her lips pursed. Thinking. Marcey wondered if she was trying to decide how much to disclose. Marcey wished she'd just say everything. Secrets were a currency in this line of work, and Marcey was only just starting to learn how they could change the conversation effortlessly, depending on how they were applied.

"Wei works for Interpol. Not the New York District Attorney's office. I see no reason why you should assume the two are connected other than a healthy case of paranoia." She looked down at the mug in her hands for a moment, her cheeks puffed out slightly, as if deep in thought. Marcey followed her movement, the way her hands splayed, long nimble fingers stark white against the blue. Some deeply buried and oft-ignored part of Marcey—the romantic in her, perhaps—found the way Kat gripped the mug to be desperate and angry, but really, her grip was like her face: artfully arranged into a perfectly friendly expression. Marcey's throat went dry. "But…I'd imagine that you'll want assurances that Wei won't be a problem?"

"I want more than assurances. You might dismiss this as nothing more than a coincidence, but I don't think it is." Marcey frowned, remembering the woman in Devon Austin Jackson's office the first time she was there. The one looking for *the estate*. "She was after Charlie, wasn't she?"

"Many people were after Charlie. That goes with the job description."

"But many people aren't also fucking you."

Kat tilted her head to one side. "There's no need to be crude, Marcey. I don't get involved with just any old girl off the street." Kat's lips pulled into a smug smile.

People with *old money* are not deviant. They're eccentric, but they do what's right in the end. Kat positively oozed old money. Marcey watched her with narrowed eyes, watched the realization grow and watched the sadness creep in. People like Kat, like Marcey, they were touched with that sadness, because it's so easy to recognize in each other's eyes. The touch of hidden identities and masks worn in public. "I've shocked you," she said.

"No." Marcey shook her head. "Not really."

"Well, that's something, isn't it?"

"People should be free about stuff like that."

"If we're being free, Marcey, then you should know that I had no idea William was skulking around the gallery. If he was, it changes things."

"But Wei won't be a problem?" Marcey raised her eyebrows. "Sounds to me like she's already involved in this"—she gestured to the space between them—"*whatever.*"

"Do you want to see it?"

"What?"

"The painting."

"I saw it in the gallery."

Kat's smile broadened. "You saw the original, yes, but mine's much better." She moved across the room to where the apartment turned cluttered. A long table was shoved against the far wall, covered in what looked to be bookbinding supplies. Paint splatter covered everything. A drop cloth formed a sort of rug, secured with little hooks that came up from the floor. "There's a mat underneath it, so don't worry about slipping," Kat explained as she stepped onto the drop cloth. Kat didn't seem bothered as her bare feet traversed a sea of splotches—the paint was dry. She crossed to the far wall, where canvas after canvas leaned. Kat bent, reaching behind a large, partially finished large-scale reproduction of a fresco Marcey was pretty sure she'd seen on a trip to Italy as a kid, and pulled out a smaller canvas.

It was maybe two feet by eighteen inches, but when Kat flipped it over, showing it to Marcey, her breath caught at the back of her throat. Her first instinct was to turn away, revulsion welling in her stomach.

Marcey had known when she'd drawn the comparison to *The Scream* that it wasn't the closest painting that she could think of. It was far darker than that. Less of an impression and more of a grotesque romantic horror. It reminded Marcey of those Baroque paintings... The ones depicting beheadings and crucifixions in all their bloody gore. Maybe Kat had been right and this work was an inspiration to Munch's piece, but it lacked the bright swirls of colors that made that piece so intriguing to look at. It was far more realistic, there was none of the impressionist flair that characterized Munch's work. The tiny thumbnails on Charlie's printouts did not do it justice.

Kat's open palms cast odd shadows down the deep brown of the background. The face itself was stark white. The skin was stretched tightly in places, as though the model was bone-thin and starving. His face was contorted, wrapped around something unseen, caught in a horrible yell that echoed through the empty space of the loft. *That's the remarkable thing about it,* Marcey thought as she stepped onto the drop cloth. *The scream reverberates without making any noise at all.*

"You forged it?"

Kat made at tutting sound. "Forge is such a loaded term. Perhaps I'd hang it in a child's room, remind them to behave." Kat bent forward to take in the horrible, yellowing teeth of her reproduction and shook her head. "Perhaps I copied it because Charlie and I were going to steal the original, the one you saw at the gallery, before he got locked away."

Charlie had written of Kat as though she possessed all the secrets of the universe at times, but this was the first time Marcey'd seen the plot through to the end. She exhaled, her hands slipping into her pockets, thoughtful. "Is that why LePage and Topeté are so set on keeping tabs on it?" *Is that why you asked me to try and steal it even when you didn't want it gone?*

Kat set the canvas aside, carefully turning it around and leaning it against the other canvases. She came to stand before Marcey, her eyes a little hooded and her fingers twisting in the soft knit of Marcey's sweater. "Perhaps I was hasty in my assessment of the safety of this enterprise, when Charlie and I first hatched this scheme. Perhaps it came from a place of guilt, rather than mutual appreciation of the job at hand. It's complicated. Everything we do is complicated."

"No such thing as an easy job."

"No," Kat agreed. "Never." Her fingers burned through two layers of Marcey's clothing. "I think you'll find, Marcey," Kat continued, "that there is a great deal you can get away with without your bedfellows finding out." Her voice was honey. The lying smile that went with it set Marcey's teeth on edge. But the touch at her shoulder was an invitation. A confusing, messy invitation.

Marcey didn't move away. She stayed there, close, perhaps too close. Kat Barber was offering something Marcey had never thought possible. "What do you want me to do?"

"Nothing." Kat's voice was breathy, hot on Marcey's cheek. "Just yet. We can talk about those plans in the morning."

"Why not now?" Marcey's fingers twitched. She was seized in the moment of decision. She had two options: continue, or allow this to dissipate and lose whatever chance she had at understanding. She reached out, her fingers slipping on the soft fabric of Kat's shirt. "Why not lay it all bare for me to see?"

The smile Kat offered then wasn't lying. It wasn't anything at all, but an easy sidling closer into Marcey's personal space and nails gentle as Kat wove her fingers into Marcey's hair. "You catch on quickly, Marcey Daniels, but even you deserve a little distraction…time to process these things. No sense dumping this on you all at once."

She was close. So close. Marcey swallowed. Kat was involved with someone else, and this—this was clearly manipulation. But she smelled so good and she was there and real and warm. Heat radiated off Kat, and Marcey grabbed her, pulled her closer still. Their lips met briefly, and the triumphant gleam in the blown black-green of Kat's pupils was the last thing Marcey saw before she closed her eyes.

It was quick, heated. The sort of kiss that could start something far, far bigger. She saw it for what it was, like the scattered remnants of bookbindings and leather journals stacked on a paint-covered table. It was just a piece of a larger puzzle. Kat had a plan, and Marcey was a part of it. If this was a distraction for a few hours, Marcey would take it.

"Now." Kat's lips brushed against Marcey's cheek. "Why don't I take you out? I can show you parts of this town a tourist will never see."

Marcey smiled, just a little shyly. She leaned in, her fingers tangling in the soft fabric of Kat's sweater. Kat came closer, willingly, breathlessly. Marcey kissed her again. When she pulled away, her fingers were on the hem of the sweater, pushing it up, touching warm skin. "What if we just stayed in?"

Kat's laugh was wicked.

CHAPTER 13

Wei, Shattered

KAT'S PHONE WENT STRAIGHT TO voicemail. Wei frowned, perplexed, looking up at the building. There were lights on, and Kat hadn't mentioned returning to the country for the weekend. A sick, anxious feeling crept over Wei. The knowledge of what she'd been denying, the printout of the details of Marcey Daniel's flight—thanks to a flag on her passport—were sitting in her pocket. Kat wouldn't...

Except that Kat would, and that was exactly the problem. Shelly Orietti was many things, but Wei would never outright call her a liar. No, that was reserved for other cutthroat villains in Wei's acquaintance. Shelly, though, Shelly's heart was in the right place.

"Kathryn, it's me. Where are you?" Wei hung up and made sure her ringer was on before shoving the phone into her pocket. "*Merde.*" Wei's breath fogged in the cold rain. She stood under an awning, staring up at Kat's building. She didn't dare go up, not without a reason. There were rules to their arrangement. Rules that made this work. Wei didn't like them, but they were what she knew. Kat's space was her sanctuary. Wei wasn't about to push past that protective barrier. Not without cause. And Kat hadn't given her any. Yet.

That was the problem with Kat. There were so many unknowns: variables that hurt Wei's head and heart to think too much about. She couldn't be trusted. Kat could never be trusted. She went and told tales and sold her soul for the six pieces of silver that Wei could not get back.

Long ago, before Wei had met Kat, she was warned by her mentor about women like Kat. "Anyone who is bored is a threat. Fonts of endless creativity, they are."

"What do you mean?"

"Thrill seeking is a matter of pride for some of these people. They've never hungered for it. It makes them dangerous, risky people. Wildcards."

It was a damn shame Wei had been so bad at listening when she was younger. That lesson never took. Which was for the best, because without it, Wei would be alone. There would be no Kat to feel heartbroken over; there would be no ghost of Charlie Mock to chase. There would be nothing but the bitterness that radiated out of Wei's heart. Kat had changed all that, on a road around an incredible mountain that stole Wei's breath away. She'd taken Wei's hand and led her down a path that was full of secrets and lies. The lies were the easy sort; they betrayed everything with a bewitching smile and the passing, if not fully cognizant, acknowledgment of the roles each of them played. Nepal was a different place, but they'd gone there for the same reasons. Two people wanting to walk a circuit and know themselves. Maybe that was too much to expect from a place like Nepal.

But vacations and their absurd ideas had happened, and Wei was ready to embrace it as it was presented. There was nothing that stopped her from finding herself, or Kat Barber, along the dusty path. And find both she did. That was the curse of Kat, the memory that would not go away. Wei chased her, because that was what her job told her to do. She chased her because she loved Kat, and Kat was pulled apart and made whole again by her love of Wei.

Were they wrecked by this? Even now, years later, Wei couldn't say. Kat destroyed her effortlessly, fraying her in ways that Wei could scarcely articulate. Wei would do anything for her, and Kat would do what she could to make their situation better. Away from those beautiful weeks in Nepal, they couldn't be together. Their love affair was problematic for them both—doubly so when they found themselves on competing sides of legality.

With a last, forlorn look, Wei turned and headed up the street. She was drawn to Kat's favorite haunts, only to find them devoid of any sign of her. She wandered from bar to gallery to bar again, sticking her head inside to find many familiar faces but not the one she was looking for. The last pub was on the corner, not far from the apartment. Wei stuck her head into the dingy space. It was a Friday night, and the place was packed.

"Wei!"

She started, turned, surprised. Not far from where she stood at the doorway, a friend of both her and Kat was smoking a cigarette, his beer hanging loosely between the fingers of the other hand.

"Nev!" she said. His cheeks were rosy with drink, but she was glad to see him. "Have you seen Kat?"

"Kat? No." Nev frowned, drunken logic taking an extra moment to process. "Haven't seen her in ages. Have you locked her up finally?"

"Locked her up for what?"

"Stealing my Wi-Fi."

Wei threw her head back and laughed, just a little hysterical. "She's *not.*"

Nev nodded. "She is. Thinks I don't know either. I'm watching her, though. Got that network monitoring in place."

An idea took Wei—a bad one, if the paper weighing in her pocket rang true. "I could come up," she offered. "Take a look." She forced her smile to look mischievous. It was hard when she felt anything but. Where was Kat? What was she doing? And, perhaps more importantly, where was Marcey Daniels?

Nev contemplated this for a moment before he threw his cigarette down on the street. "Maybe we could mess with her a bit. She's stealing all of my daytime bandwidth. How else am I going to watch *Game of Thrones* if I can't torrent it?"

Wei wrinkled her nose. She understood that they were friends and technically she had no jurisdiction to cite him for the crime, but it was still a blatant undermining of her authority. Kat did that too; it drove Wei to grind her teeth and huff dismissively. She did that now, scowling at Nev. "You've been downloading things illegally."

"Whatever. The Americans like it. They keep track of the numbers."

Wei folded her arms across her chest, scowling.

"Don't be an arse, Wei." What he didn't say was that she could not, in fact, do that. Wei was grateful he didn't hit her with the sting of honesty about how neutered she really was. At least in America she had the clout of the New York DA's office behind her. She could force issues where here she had to liaise with local police to get anything done.

"Sorry." Wei wasn't sorry.

Nev drained his beer and ducked inside to return the glass. Rain was spitting from the heavy clouds overhead. Wei tugged the hood of her rain jacket over her head and shivered. The night had taken on a bitter chill during her search, late winter still clinging to the harsh cold that came from northerly winds gusting arctic air southward. Nev emerged from the queue of people by the door a moment later, pulling his collar up against the wind, and together they walked back to his place in silence.

When Nev let her into his apartment, Wei shivered and glanced around. "Where's your router?"

"Over by the window." Nev answered. His hands were in his pockets, rummaging for something. "Shite. Forgot I'm out of cigarettes."

Wei stuck her hand in her pocket. "I've got—"

"Something bloody awful and continental, or worse, *American*, I'm sure. I'll go and get some of my own, thanks." He paused. "There's no password on the computer, so feel free to boot it up. Network pass is on the router." He bent to tie his shoe.

"Did you ever wonder if maybe that's how Kat got it?"

Nev looked sheepish. "Would, but I don't think she's ever been up here."

A short huff of laughter escaped Wei's lips. She walked to the window. It was a wide bay that she'd always been envious of. The windows in Kat's flat were tall, but they weren't the wide, narrow-paned things that lead to slanting light in the midafternoons. They gave Kat fits, making it hard for her to paint in natural light. Wei never minded the windows until she was up in Nev's flat, staring out his wide, repurposed-industrial window and hating that Kat had picked the wrong building when she'd decided to take advantage of her trust fund and get into the real estate business.

At least that's where Wei pretended the money came from.

Nev was a friend of Kat's more than Wei's anyway. He was some sort of math genius who worked in the financial sector. Wei had never bothered to have him checked out, but now that she thought about it, it might not be a bad idea. Kat's and his friendship seemed to be born of being neighbors and frequenting the same pubs on the weekend.

Wei couldn't believe Kat had never been up to Nev's apartment. "Really?" Wei turned, raising an eyebrow at her friend.

He grunted. "Not for lack of tryin' either. She's just private, your Kat."

"I'm aware." Wei shook her head. "I'll still be here when you get back, go."

He gave a mock salute and tipped an imaginary cap. "Cheers." Wei waved at his retreating back and set about inspecting his router. She couldn't bring herself to draw up the blinds and stare across the street into Kat's flat. It didn't take long for Wei to find the wireless repeater tucked behind a flower pot on the window sill. She sighed and logged on to Nev's computer to change his Wi-Fi password, hunting for a pen before sending the new password to him in a text along with a note to buy some pens.

It was then that Wei reached for the cord and drew up the blinds. And there, though the misty haze and half-open windows, she saw them. The flat's floorplan was open, but Wei knew the layout well. She stared, her hand pressing to the glass. Two silhouettes moved in an age-old dance. Bodies touching, pushing against each other.

Wei's hand shook. Kat, pressed against the window, her face a blur and her head tilted back. Her eyes opened then, and even across the impossible divide, they bore a hole straight into Wei's heart. There was no way Kat could see her, was there? Wei's stomach clenched. Kat threw her head back, lips parted and eyes fluttering closed and fingers curling around her companion's neck, drawing her closer.

This was a show. It was meant to send a message: they would always hurt each other most of all.

The girl, a little waif of a girl, was blinded and dwarfed by the presence of Kat in the room. She moved slowly, deliberately, walking Kat back to the bed and pushing her down. Kissing her and touching what did not belong to her in ways that made Wei's blood boil in her veins.

This was not the agreement.

Heartbreak was never part of the bargain. They loved each other. Love was a hard concept in their line of work; it meant the destruction of a long-held belief system. It meant that moments like this weren't meant to happen. Wei should not be forced into the role of the voyeur, watching, waiting, anger coiling, hot and acidic in her stomach.

She would destroy this child. William had accused her of playing games with the life of her lover, but this girl's life had been forfeit the moment Wei saw her in Devon Austin Jackson's office. Wei would skewer her, take away her freedom in exchange for Kat's, and she wouldn't think twice. This girl knew what she was doing, and she did it anyway. This girl was a fool.

It was only later, when Wei was able to wrench her gaze away, that she realized that she'd slowly, steadily, shredded half of her paperwork describing Marcey Daniels's flight details, her fingers trembling with the effort to keep from screaming out the betrayal.

If that was the way this would be played... Wei swallowed. Made a few calls. The line crackled into life. "You were right," she said.

"I was?" William sounded surprised, and just a little smug. Brittle, a breath of wind could shatter Wei and William was threatening to push her over the edge. She couldn't stand him as it was. He was not allowed to be smug about this. Never about this.

"You were. I want you to strengthen the flag on Marcey Daniels's passport. I don't want her stopped at customs, but I want to know as soon as it's scanned, no matter what. She's got the book, I'm certain now."

"Johnson's not going to like this. You know she'll try and get Mock posthumously if she can." Wei wondered if Johnson knew their connection, or if that detail hadn't been brought to her attention just yet. She wondered if maybe that was something that would come later, when it would hurt the most.

"That's ridiculous. His heir is wandering around London fucking..." Wei choked on the word. She couldn't go on.

William, for once, was silent, allowing Wei's near-silent tears turn into a growing rage without comment.

"The plan was so simple. We would get Kat to give up the book, she'd turn evidence, get her to give up the rest of Charlie's cronies. Now it's fucked and I can't fix it without taking this girl and skewering her." Wei ran a hand through her hair. "I want her fucking obliterated."

"We don't kill people, Wei. Just lock 'em up for crimes they actually committed." William exhaled. "She hasn't done anything illegal, yet."

"We watch her. We get that damn book and we go back to the plan. I want Johnson happy and Kat safe. As soon as Daniels is back in the States, she has a tail. Twenty-four seven."

If William had anything to say about Wei's tactics, he did not voice his opinion. "I'll get back to you when I know more." Wei was grateful he did not ask why she was crying when he hung up.

The final call Wei made was to a little village in upstate New York. She flagged one visitor, and then another. She stripped the young man, still locked away, of all his privileges, using the authority of the office Linda Johnson aspired to possess. Maybe it was petty, something she should not have been capable of doing. He'd never done anything to warrant the treatment he was about to be subjected to upon waking in the morning—by all accounts he was a model prisoner.

But Kat had made promises she couldn't keep, and Linda Johnson's bitterness over losing the Mock trial was easily manipulated into Wei's endgame. The other pain, the pain over her daughter, that was something Wei wasn't supposed to be aware of, but a truth that burned into her like icy resolution. Johnson wouldn't know what hit her. She'd be too busy being blinded by her hatred of the girl who had corrupted her daughter.

She pulled a cigarette from her pocket and hesitated. Nev wouldn't want her to smoke in his apartment without cracking a window. There was an ashtray on the sill for just that reason. Wei's hands were shaking. She didn't think she could open the window without Nev's help, not with them shaking like this. She needed the cigarette. She glanced around. He was long gone. Wei cupped the lighter in her hand and lit the cigarette, staring out at the low-lit illumination of Kat's betrayal, nude and dozing, in her bed. She told herself she didn't care, but the wound in her heart festered all the same. Blackness threatened to overtake her love, corrupt it into hatred. She pushed at it, but it slipped past her fingers, like she was trying to hold back the sea. Anger, that was understandable, but what was she going to do about it?

Kat had picked her side. It was time for Wei to do the same.

Smoke billowed from her nostrils, curling around her head.

This was the moment when everything changed.

CHAPTER 14

Marcey, Upon Return

Amid the mess of bookbinding supplies and paint-splattered canvases, Kat came undone for Marcey. What was offered was freely taken, with no thought to the consequences. That came later. The morning after their first encounter, Marcey woke to find Kat on the telephone, speaking in a placating voice. The conversation went in and out. Dozing and sated, Marcey tried to focus. Kat wanted the caller to be reasonable, to know that the ends justified the means. The black void of sleep gripped Marcey not long after. She fell into a world of dreams, twisted and fraying, stories where beautiful women became deadly beasts.

She was suspicious when Kat woke her, returning to bed with two mugs of strong black tea and a distant expression.

"Who was that?" Marcey asked, her voice still thick with sleep. "On the phone, earlier?"

"No one," Kat lied. Marcey didn't press. Instead, she told Kat of Charlie's plan, and Kat told her of her role in all of it. A simple switch and sell. Nothing too fancy. The only problem was that Kat wanted to run the show, and Marcey wanted no part of that.

The compromise came in the form of a proposal. "Why not work together?" Kat asked. "I know some of what Charlie was intending and you certainly can't pull this job by yourself, green as you are."

So they would work together. Marcey had no problem with that. Kat could help her find a way to get Linda Johnson off Marcey's back. Maybe even expose her. Kat perked up at that suggestion. It was an even exchange, and a satisfaction of both of their desires. From the way her body moved, humming with a sort of manic energy that set Marcey to jitters, Kat seemed taken with the idea of revenge.

"For a job like that, I know just who you should call," she added as Marcey flipped through Charlie's book looking for potential crew members. Kat paid rapt attention, making sure Marcey paused on certain pages. She studied her own entry—one of the longest in the book—and then Topeté's like a scientist examines a fresh specimen. "There's a woman, Gwen Lane-Wright. She was involved with William before the whole messy business of his chosen career path came to light."

"Messy business?" Marcey asked. This was what Shelly warned her about—the lie that would go into the job in Rio. Kat's justification for what she did. Marcey closed her eyes, and braced for it, knowing what was about to be said would be categorically untrue.

Kat nodded. "When we found out, we were knee deep in a job in Rio, one we couldn't untangle ourselves from very easily. Charlie got caught because of it. Gwen lost her engagement. I wonder if she'd be interested in some comeuppance. She's ace at jobs like this. Good at getting into places she shouldn't be allowed into."

What went unsaid was that Kat manipulated the whole situation from start to finish and Marcey was pretty sure that Kat was aware Marcey knew the truth. She was like Marcey—she knew her role and that she had to play it. Without that clear boundary, there was no chance of this enterprise ever coming to fruition.

They didn't speak of it. It was a known thing. Marcey didn't want to have to tell Kat, and Kat certainly had no interest in telling Marcey. Silence suited both of their purposes just fine. Betrayal could come later.

———————⋘⋙———————

Marcey returned to New York three days later pleasantly sore and utterly exhausted. Kat had seen her off with kiss on each cheek and a promise that they'd meet again soon. It was all very poetic, if a bit dramatic. Marcey caught herself in the moment before the unclean feeling set in and the fleeting desperation of the weekend faded away into nothingness. She felt dirty, walking away from Kat. They were a volatile combination, Kat's needling quickly sparking into something Marcey never wanted to let go of, should she only manage to catch it in her hand. Kat was electricity. She was the wind. She was something intangible. Something powerful.

Something terrifying.

So Marcey went back home with a list of names and the beginnings of a plan, in Kat's eyes. Kat's recommendations aligned pretty closely with what Charlie had wanted already, but Marcey was still hesitant to deviate from his plan at all without a lot of contemplation. She'd spent the flight across the Atlantic running through the list of names and comparing their previous work with Charlie and with each other. Rio. It all came back to Rio, with the exception of the question mark next to tech support Charlie'd left behind. Kat had thoughts about that as well, but she'd left it up to Marcey to figure it out.

Marcey had a short list. She wanted to run them by Shelly before she made her selection.

And there was one name...

"Next!" Pulled from her thoughts, Marcey hurried up to the customs agent and handed over her passport. He looked it over, looked her over, asked what was going on in England, and stamped her back into the country. It was a relief to step through customs and realize that nothing bad was going to happen. Marcey had spent the entirety of the flight over dreading the moment when her passport was scanned and the customs officer made her take her hair out of its ponytail because her hair "wasn't like her picture."

But there was nothing like that at all. The man didn't even bat an eye before glancing at his computer screen and giving a small grunt that could have been interest or approval. Marcey swallowed nervously but kept her expression neutral.

"Welcome home," the agent eventually said. He held out Marcey's passport.

"Thanks," Marcey answered.

Just beyond the door, Shelly was waiting for her, leaning against the wall by baggage claim. Her arms were folded over her chest, a scowl etched across her lips. She took one look at Marcey and the consternation on her face turned into a huff of annoyance. She moved to Marcey, her hand streaking out faster than Marcey could see it coming, and smacked her at the back of the head. "Are you stupid?"

Marcey rubbed at the back of her head, wincing. "What was that for?"

Glaring, Shelly gestured to the fading bruise on Marcey's neck where Kat had kissed too hard for too long. "You slept with her. You stupid girl, you walked right into her web and let her have you. Oh, I could just—" Shelly let out an annoyed little grunt and threw her hands up in the air.

"Just what?"

Shelly said nothing, her nostrils flaring and her eyes concerned.

Marcey shrugged, wanting the conversation to end. Maybe she didn't care that it was a bad idea. She didn't like talking about things like this with other people. Especially not in the middle of a busy airport.

"God, Marcey. Kat has a very complicated relationship with law enforcement. Agent Topeté isn't exactly the type to share. You're an idiot." Shelly stepped away from Marcey. She was already a good foot taller than Marcey, and the height difference, aided by heels, was enough to look comical—especially when Shelly was glaring down at her like Marcey was a misbehaving child. "I don't know how you got through customs."

If Marcey was being truly honest, she didn't know either. "I didn't do anything illegal," she pointed out. "They have no reason to stop me, and if they did they'd have a lawsuit on their hands."

"But they'd have an excuse to search your person. And Charlie's book, I'm sure, is on your person." Shelly shook her head.

"Trust me," Marcey said, eager to talk about *anything* other than what she and Kat had done. "I'm surprised I got through as well, but I'm not stupid. The book is safe, Shelly. I brought it with me, yes, but I know how to keep it safe."

"Do you though?" Shelly scratched at her forearm. "Well, you're here at least. And Kat didn't utterly destroy you. That's something. Why the hell did you let her fuck you?"

Marcey bit her lip, hesitating only for a second. "I did it because I wanted to, not because she…I don't know…forced me into it, or tricked me. She pushed and I pushed back. Somehow the combination worked."

"You want to know the reason why Charlie worked so well with all of these people? Because he didn't get fucking attached."

"He got attached to you," Marcey pointed out.

"That's *different*," Shelly snapped. "What we shared, what we went through? Most straight men don't stick around once they find out. Most straight men walk away. Some would attack. Some would commit violence against me."

Marcey had no idea—how could she? Sure, Shelly was taller than your average woman, and her shoulders were *great*, but it wasn't the sort of thing that Marcey thought of as unusual. Women came in all shapes and sizes. Everyone's journey to owning their womanhood was different. She wasn't one to judge. There was nothing in Shelly's face or language that hinted to Marcey of that struggle. Now, confronted with it, the bitterness of the grim truth of that experience crept into Shelly's voice. Was Marcey naïve to not even think of such a thing? Was it ignorant of her to just take all of Charlie's compatriots for what they appeared to be? In truth, Marcey had no idea. It did make her see a few things differently.

"Shelly—"

"What that was... I don't know if he ever anticipated it. And sure, people like Kat, they got attached to him, but he didn't give a damn about us. Objectivity, Marcey. With her, you no longer have it. I hope it was worth it." Shelly exhaled. "That girl does whatever the hell she wants. She'll leave you to die and won't think twice about it. She has her own agenda."

"I know," Marcey said dejectedly. "She doesn't seem too keen on you," she added.

Shelly sucked her teeth. "She wouldn't, I don't think. She knew me too early in my transition for that. She didn't like how Charlie loved me, thinks I stick out like a sore thumb and that it puts any operation I get involved with at risk. Never mind that I'm far better on the grift than she's ever been."

Marcey smiled weakly up at Shelly. "She's agreed to come on, and she wants to gather a crew."

"Did you tell her that Charlie already suggested one?"

Marcey stared at her.

"Oh, don't give me that look, Marcey. I'm not stupid. Charlie wouldn't have sent you, a rank amateur, in without a plan. And even if he hadn't, I *sincerely* doubt that he intended for you to ask Kat fucking Barber's opinion on anything."

"No, he didn't, but I didn't tell Kat that I had the thing all laid out either." Marcey shrugged. "You're right, Shelly, she's got her own agenda. I want to know what it is."

Shelly's eyes narrowed. "So you're what? Feeling her out?"

"She wants to get a crew together to do Charlie's job as well. She wants to run the show, but that's not happening, so I agreed to compromise and take both of our points of view into account, provided that it still follows Charlie's plan."

"For your little revenge quest."

Marcey shook her head. "No, for something bigger, but it does involve that too. Kat filled in some of the details that Charlie's notes were scant on. The ones that Charlie didn't think were necessary to convey, but that required a lot of faith."

"Oh, right." Shelly frowned, her voice cutting. "The ones that basically all end in all of us getting arrested."

"Yes." Marcey shook her head. "Those." She grew silent and glanced around. They were alone, but Marcey didn't like talking about such things in so public a space. Their footsteps rang out on the linoleum of the airport floor. "There's an auction. On Memorial Day. And a lot with our name on it. Kill two birds with one stone, ya know?"

Shelly looked pensive. "So you trust her?"

The question made Marcey pause. "I'm not..."

"I don't trust anyone, Marcey. Least of all you. You've made some shit choices already. Why should I go along with you when you haven't proven to me that you can make the smart choice?"

Marcey looked down at her feet. "Because I need someone like you," she said earnestly. "I need someone like you to tell me when I'm fucking up."

"I'm not some sort of angel on your shoulder. I don't play like that."

They boarded the train, circling back to the station in Queens where Marcey would take a train into the city and Shelly would walk out onto the street to hail a cab. They were alone in their car. "Would it be so bad?" Marcey asked. "To work with someone else for a change?"

Shelly sighed heavily. "Who else did Charlie want?"

"Will you work with me?"

"Who else, Marcey?"

"Gwen Lane-Wright...maybe someone for tech. Kat had a few suggestions. Charlie had nothing but a question mark."

"Try Montou. I think her first name is Kimiko." Shelly tapped her chin in thought. "Charlie worked with her, but I'm not sure if she's out of the game—"

"Wait, Kim Montou?" Marcey's brow furrowed, trying to place the name. She knew the name very well, but it couldn't be... "Japanese, parents came here and now run that bookstore in the West Village where all those anime nerds like to hang out...about yea tall?" Marcey indicated her own height. "That Kimiko Montou?"

"Yeah, got arrested a while back. Your girl Johnson if I remember right. Something about a two-millisecond delay on some eBay thing. Why? Do you know her?" Shelly asked, expression open and genuinely curious.

"Yeah," Marcey answered, shifting her bag to her other shoulder. "I went to high school with her."

Shelly left Marcey to the nearly two-hour journey alone with her thoughts on the train without a concrete answer as to whether she'd get involved. When she emerged at her stop, night had fallen, casting the city in a haunting shadow of misty rain.

Her mother was still up, sitting behind her desk in the home office, illuminated by a pool of light from a cheap IKEA lamp, her face drawn in shadow, deep, dark circles under her eyes. "You're back." Her mother tugged her glasses from her face and rubbed a tired hand at the corner of her eyes. Eyeliner smeared out like errant brush strokes in the wake of her fingers.

Marcey let her duffle drop to the floor and bent to remove her shoes. "Yeah," she answered. "Guess I am."

"Do you have *any* idea how worried I was?"

Marcey could not image her mother worrying that much during the tax season. From February to the middle of April, Marcey didn't so much as *see* her mother, let alone interact with her. She was too busy hiding herself away at work and shirking her parental responsibilities.

"Sorry." Marcey shrugged. "I had a thing I had to go to."

"A *thing* is not a two-thousand-dollar last-minute ticket to London, Marcey. A thing is a weekend in the Poconos, or taking off to Montreal for a weekend. It isn't running away to another continent." Her voice was rising now, angry, hurt—all the buried emotions they never talked about and just left simmering, waiting for the next big fight. The pressure of trying to be perfect, trying to hold it all together to make up for the sins of her past, they pressed at Marcey's will. She gritted her teeth and met her mother's accusatory gaze evenly, waiting for the next admonishment.

"What the hell were you thinking?"

"I'll pay for the ticket," Marcey mumbled. God, her entire body *hurt*. The memory of Kat Barber was still present everywhere. Beneath the canned smell of airport and subway air, there was still a hint of her that made Marcey's cheeks burn. Marcey pushed her bangs back off her forehead. "I just...I couldn't take it anymore. I had to get away."

"You have to learn to live with what you did. Everyone knows that criminals have to pay their dues to society. Even if they're coming back to haunt you, you gotta own up to them."

"I have paid my dues!" Her mother flinched at the force of Marcey's rebuke. "I've paid them over and over again. Now, everywhere I look, I see my face turned into a cartoon representing what's wrong with this city." Her mother's lips parted, but Marcey blundered on. She couldn't stop now. "I never said anything about it. Never complained. I did that for you, for this family. I'm not a criminal. I wanted to be the *good* daughter. I had to *get away*." Marcey's chest rose and fell with the effort of spitting out the truth.

"And you walked away from everything, because you couldn't handle the pressure of being better than your reputation." Her mother drew air in sharply through her nose. It made her look birdlike, all narrow face and flyaway graying hair.

"I can handle the pressure," Marcey answered petulantly.

"You walked away from your job. You walked away from everything I've given you, thumbing your nose at it because it wasn't good enough. Let me tell you something, Marcey. Nothing is good enough in this world. Life, the job that you flat-out dismissed, it won't ever be enough for you. For anyone. You just have to deal with it, suck it up, and take the good with the bad."

"You're no better." The words were out of Marcey's mouth before she could stop them.

"How dare you!" Her mother was positively shaking. "How *dare* you say something like that? How dare you imply—"

"Imply? There's no implying. I tried my damnedest to make people see that I was no better than Darius back then, but you know what? They saw my skin and my address and they just assumed I was along for the ride, that he was my boyfriend, the scary black man who led me astray. And you know what? You told them that. You let them believe that. You sold a story to those reporters who came to the school, telling them that your perfect daughter could never, ever be involved with that, and it must have been because of bad influences. Do you know how many kids lost their scholarships at school that year because of that? Do you know how many lives you destroyed because of that one remark? Darius is in prison, Mom, and not just a nice prison like you see on TV. He's stuck in there with people who've murdered, who've stolen cars with guns, who've raped. And you know what he did? He let me talk him into helping me steal some prescription pills so we could buy booze for parties."

Marcey inhaled deeply. "Now you know what's happening? Linda Johnson is using that story to get herself elected. She's not telling the truth, that she was pissed off that I'd kissed her daughter. She's putting my face—*his* face on her campaign posters as a criminal not worthy of anything other than a snap judgment. And you know what? It was all my idea in the first place. I wanted to fit in with the cool kids, so we sold the pain pills I got after getting my wisdom teeth out, and Darius's leftover Vicodin from when he'd messed up his knee. We took stuff that wasn't going to be used and we sold it to kids who wanted to get high. We did it over and over and we got caught. We should both be in jail."

Her mother looked flabbergasted. "I couldn't let you go to jail! What would people say?"

"Maybe they'd say that I'd done my time." Suddenly tired, Marcey sighed. "Look, I'm exhausted. I've been on a plane for hours, and then the commute from JFK…"

"Where did you go in England?"

Marcey swallowed, looking away, her fingers gripping the strap of her bag tightly. "I…" Marcey felt like she was choking. "I was in London, like the ticket said. I was with a friend."

"Does your friend have a name?" her mother demanded. "Or are they just another lie like everything else that comes out of that mouth of yours?"

She didn't want to have this conversation. There was no way to weave the truth around the lie she struggled to keep from bubbling forth. Marcey turned and stalked down the hallway to her bedroom. Her body thrummed with tension. She wanted to hit something. She wanted to scream. She was stupid. Stupid. Her mother would go off and blab to Johnson at the earliest instance, if she was ever asked. The last thing Marcey wanted was her mother asking questions about Kat. There was no finesse in the way her mother handled herself when she was angry. Marcey was afraid of the carelessness.

"Don't walk away from me!" her mother shouted.

Marcey slammed her bedroom door and tossed her keys onto her desk. From her travel bag, she pulled Charlie's book out and flipped through it. The entry for Kim Montou was toward the back, nestled in between two complicated-looking Indian names Marcey wasn't going to even attempt to pronounce.

Montou, K. - NYC - 917-555-0745
IT, TECH, 1st int, 2006, Tehran.
Arr. 2012-2 yr. WC

In 2006, Marcey and Kim Montou were eighteen, still in high school. Marcey got unsteadily to her feet. The book was open in her hands, and she closed her eyes. She tried to remember if there had been any indication Kim even had the aptitude for something like this, let alone the wherewithal. *Something illegal, something that would have involved Charlie in Iran in 2006...*

Marcey pulled her phone from her pocket and thumbed down in her contacts to the letter K. There, between a Kailyee and a Lena Marcey barely remembered. Kim's number hadn't changed since they were in high school. Interesting. She closed the book and dialed Kat's number.

"I trust you made it back in one piece." Fondness crept into her voice. Marcey could almost see her crooked little half-smile. "No trouble at the border?"

"None, thank goodness." A chuckle tumbled easily from Marcey's lips, warm and familiar. This was too fast—too much, even. She should know better. Kat was involved with someone else... Not that it had made much difference when she took Marcey to bed, but still. "That actually isn't why

I called. Shelly suggested that we get Kim Montou. I wondered if you'd ever worked with her?"

A shuffling sound filled the phone, and then the sound of a door opening and closing again. Its hinges creaked something fierce. Marcey guessed it was the squeaky door to Kat's bedroom. "I have," she answered. "She's about your age, I think. Helped Charlie with that bit of insanity in Iran back in…well, I don't quite recall the date, but it was about a decade ago now."

"What happened in there?"

"This isn't exactly the sort of conversation to be had over the phone…" Kat trailed off; the pause was heavy with realization. "Oh, you *know* her, don't you, Marcey?"

"I could know her," Marcey said, trying not to give anything away. She was grateful that they were doing this over the phone when she caught sight of her reflection in the mirror over her dresser. Her cheeks were bright red, infatuated. "Is she any good?"

"Oh, she's very good, or she was, until she disappeared a few years back. I always wondered what happened to her."

"Shelly says she got arrested. Something about eBay."

"Huh."

They lapsed into silence. It was the comfortable sort of companionship that had Marcey wondering how come she wasn't upset, or even angry that Kat had a lover. Another wrench in this machine that could ruin everything.

"How did Shelly take it?"

"She thinks I'm an idiot."

"You are," Kat agreed. "I have a piece of you now, and you me…but it was a foolish risk. It can't happen again."

She hung up a second later, before Marcey could say good-bye. Marcey stared down at her phone, the +44 country code winking out into blackness.

Marcey fell back onto her bed and stared up at the ceiling, lists and names and ugly paintings drifting lazily across her mind's eye as she slipped off to sleep.

CHAPTER 15

Marcey, Rekindling Friendships

MARCEY SPENT THE WEEKEND LURKING around the West Village. She passed the time easily, standing on street corners and perched on a stool at the counter of a bar, watching and waiting. She'd gone to the library and logged on to one of the public computers to look up Kim Montou's name, only to find that she'd been sent to prison for two years in 2012 for some sort of phishing scheme on eBay. It explained her disappearance, to say the least. It also explained why she was back here, under her parents' supervision.

She eyed the bookstore belonging to Kim Montou's family, caught on the memory of the place. It used to be a gathering place for the arty offbeat kids who didn't fit in with the more popular and affluent students who attended Marcey's high school. If memory served, Kim had worked the register on the weekends. Marcey hoped she could catch a glimpse of her.

There was very little about Kim written in Charlie's book beyond the basic description of who she was and what she did. Marcey's attempts to look up any details about the job in Tehran turned up next to nothing. Sitting across the street, stirring her coffee, Marcey scowled. Going to prison would put anyone off their game, especially in Kim's ever-changing field. How the hell was Marcey supposed to tell if Kim was still in the game?

Christ, she was just getting her feet wet with this, but already the frustration was mounting. She wanted to go up to Dannemora and see Darius, not spend the weekend watching high school wannabe goths and pimply nerds go in and out of a Japanese-language bookstore.

Her instinct to just walk in and see Kim was powerful. They'd known each other back then. It wasn't that long ago. Marcey had always liked her. She wasn't sure what was stopping her, but after spending Friday and Saturday sitting on the same stool scowling out across a street at the same elderly Japanese men and women coming in to pick up the newspaper, Marcey was ready to crack. She was sick of watching the patrons of the store, young and old, American and Japanese alike, stop and chat in a language she didn't know.

On Sunday, Marcey checked Facebook from her phone. There was nothing interesting in Kim's feed, save a shared post from *Hon-Ya*—the bookstore's—page in both English and Japanese announcing that the store would be celebrating Golden Week with a series of events aimed at families. Marcey put her phone away. The burner was unfamiliar still and uncomfortable to use. At least there was free Wi-Fi here.

In the papers before her, Marcey had all she could find on Kim's case. It sounded as though she'd gotten caught through a sheer stroke of luck on the part of the NYPD. There had been a power spike on account of her computers, and they'd thought she was growing weed in the basement of the bookstore. The carelessness bothered Marcey. Should she bring in someone with such evident disregard for something as easy to correct as an overloaded power grid?

Marcey read through the transcript of the quick, no-contest trial, and a name caught her eye. The prosecuting attorney for the state was listed on the court record as Linda Johnson. A smile broadened on Marcey's face. Maybe this was a good idea after all. Anyone with an axe to grind against Johnson was a potential ally, especially if things went off the rails with Kat.

It was especially warm. Marcey discarded her jacket and leaned forward, her jeans stiff from drying after the morning rain. Her ratty Green Day T-shirt gaped at the neck. Marcey picked at a thread, lost in thought. It was as though her world contracted again into this single island, suffocating her after it expanded in a burst of vibrant color and the taste of Kat Barber's skin on her lips. Marcey pulled at the thread harder, watching as her sleeve grew looser and the thread tightened. Marcey jerked her hand down, snapping the thread.

"—payment comes on delivery. Not the other way around. Don't— Okafor, I don't have the time to sort out all of your orders right now, I'm sorry."

Marcey looked up, surprised. She hadn't heard that voice in years.

Kim Montou was standing at the register, squinting up at the board. The guy behind the counter had his eyebrows raised. "Not you," Kim added hurriedly to him, pressing the phone to her shoulder. "Americano black. Small, please." She looked messier than Marcey remembered her from high school. Her hair was cut at her shoulders and tugged into a low-effort ponytail. She was wearing a sweater and leggings. She looked like any other post-college twenty-something; the roundness of her cheeks had fallen away to sharp cheekbones and a small nose that still turned upward as though she'd smelled something terrible. Her face was different—it made Marcey look twice. Her eyes were sunken, like she was haunted by something and slept very little because of it.

Marcey picked up her coffee and sipped it. The guy at the register shook his head and went to get Kim's coffee. Kim stepped back, her eyes narrowing, glancing over at Marcey. They went wide, and she hung up quickly.

Marcey set her coffee down. Her fingers trembled. Had she been discovered? How would she play this?

"Americano small?"

Kim took the to-go cup from the barista and flashed him one of those disingenuous smiles—the look all girls perfect sometime in their mid-teens. She turned toward Marcey, a slow smile easing onto her lips. Marcey fumbled with her coffee, sloshing it all over the saucer and bar.

"You haven't changed a bit, Marcey Daniels," Kim said. She sidled over to where Marcey sat, her coffee steaming. "What are you doing in this neck of the woods?"

"I could ask you the same thing," Marcey answered, gathering up her papers as quickly as could seem casual. "I thought your goal was to get as far away from that store as you could possibly arrange."

Kim's lips pursed into a thin line. "That was a long time ago. A lot's changed since then."

Marcey hurried to put her papers away in her bag and then straightened. "I'll say. Where did you end up going to school? I know you had an offer from MIT."

Sitting down opposite Marcey, Kim fiddled with her coffee cup. "Didn't go," she answered. "Wasn't worth it. I had a better-paying gig." .

"What? Really?" Marcey grinned. "That's awesome. Who you working for now, then? I'm still stuck at my mom's. Went to Binghamton, studied statistics." This conversation, stilted thought it was, was a familiar thing for Marcey. She'd lost touch with most of her classmates after high school. These occasional run-ins were filled with nearly a decade of catching up and remembering why she'd resolved, at eighteen, to never speak to any of these people again.

Oddly, she'd never thought about Kim that way. Kim was different, a friend but not a friend. Now she just looked exhausted. Her phone buzzed. She ignored the call, fixing Marcey with her hollow stare. "That sounds boring as fuck."

"Eh, it's not so bad. I get to enjoy the nepotism of it all, I guess. I was thinking about quitting. New gig's come up."

"Oh?"

"Yeah." Marcey nodded. "Working with some new folks on a project that could net a good bit of cash. I just have to pick the right people."

"Sounds like you're in my line of work," Kim commented, just a little tentatively. "Gigs are great, until you end up stuck at your parents' because of the lingering problems of a government-mandated dry spell."

"Yikes."

"Well, I don't really mind it. My mom was sick until recently. She died about a year and a half ago."

"Christ, I'm sorry," Marcey said. She knew when Kim had been in prison. That was right around the middle of her sentence. "Were you, um…able to be there?"

"*No*," Kim said sharply. "Some bitch lawyer made sure I couldn't. It's water under the bridge now, I suppose. Helping out my dad keeps the cops off my back and makes me look good, I suppose. But, oh my God, I am so sick of bookstores and their dumb bookstore bullshit." Kim sipped her coffee. She gestured to her phone. "This guy? He's doing some sort of aid work with a bunch of Japanese ex-pats in northern Nigeria and wants Japanese language books shipped directly to Lagos, despite the fact that he can't afford the shipping and the NGO won't pony up for the cash to ship that and their other supplies in." Her phone buzzed again. "Now he won't stop calling me."

"That's…damn, Kim, that's horrible."

"Yeah, talk about needing a change of scenery. Too bad I'm stuck here."

Marcey dug in her pocket and produced a crumpled receipt. This was a casual in, a way to tell Kim to start digging. "I heard you had a run-in with Linda Johnson." She dropped her voice low. "My mom saw it in the paper a few years back. I kept meaning to come down here and offer to buy you a drink so we can commiserate about that awful woman." She wrote her number down on the paper and passed it over to Kim. "I can come by, maybe some other time?"

"Is this you trying to pick me up?" Kim winked.

"No." Marcey shook her head. "This is just me trying to be friendly."

Kim pocketed the number. "I just may take you up on that offer." She checked the time on her phone. "But I need to go back. The papers will be arriving soon and I have to get them out." Kim got to her feet. "It was nice seeing you, Marcey."

"You too," Marcey answered. She held out her hand, and Kim took it. "Be seeing you."

Kim turned and left, and Marcey was left staring after her, utterly confused. Was she still in the game? Was she not?

What had happened to her?

<hr>

The next morning Marcey slept in until nine-thirty. She had always been an early riser, and sleeping in was unheard of for her. She woke alone, her mother having left for work several hours before. Marcey's job was more transient. Marcey stared up at the ceiling, thinking about her job. Fuck that place, she decided. There was no point in staying there.

There was a text on her phone from a blocked number. Marcey read it, her brow furrowed.

You weren't telling me everything. We need to talk. 11:45. HY.

A small smile tugged at Marcey's lips. Kim had gotten curious then. Good.

She got up and dressed, taking care to look professional but not too remarkable. She wore jeans and a button-up, tucked in and accessorized with a belt. The look was preppy, and it was fun to sweep on a trench coat against the cold and rainy early April morning outside. Marcey stood in the mirror, tugging at her hair and debating a fedora, like it was the forties and she was some sort of Bogartian private eye. She settled on a beanie, tugging it on slouchy, its warm, cream wool gentle against her hair.

Marcey took the local over to the West Village, switching trains twice to get across the river. The creeping, uncomfortable paranoia of being out in the open had her fidgeting, looking over her shoulder. It was a miserable feeling. She didn't think Johnson would go so far as to have her followed, but Johnson's people had already implied she had. The last thing Marcey wanted to do was to get arrested again.

Hon-Ya stood in the middle of a block that bustled even early on a Monday morning. Marcey approached it, munching on a bagel, unable to quell the anxious flutter of her stomach. The store wasn't open yet, but the door was unlocked. Marcey swallowed, drew in a deep breath, and ambled over to the counter and an extremely bored-looking Kim Montou.

Kim wore a black apron with the store's logo done in stylized calligraphy printed in white across the front. She was slouched forward on a stool behind the counter, distractedly moving her finger across the surface of her tablet. Her other hand dug into her cheek, making it look lopsided and misshapen. Her jeans were ripped at the knees and the blue hooded sweatshirt she wore beneath the apron made her look like she did back when they were in high school, some eight years before. She did not look like a threat, or the best in the business when it came to hacking. Marcey wondered if the look was intentional and was about to say hello when Kim looked up. Her pupils were blown. She was high.

"Hi." Marcey said. "You wanted to see me?"

Kim narrowed her eyes. "You didn't tell me everything."

"I...I couldn't just blurt out what I wanted to know, now could I?"

An amused grunt of laughter escaped Kim's lips. "You weren't just in the neighborhood yesterday, were you?" Kim leaned forward and hit one of the function keys on her tablet's detachable keyboard. The screen flickered black, the onscreen cursor flashing green. "You've been in the neighborhood for the better part of a week. If I didn't know better, I'd say you were casing the shop to rob it. Or stalking me."

"Who says that I'm not?" Marcey leaned forward and gripped the edges of the counter, a wry grin pulling at her lips. "Maybe I wanted to offer you a job."

"You sold drugs. You were never a thief," Kim replied dully. "You don't happen to have any more of them, do you?"

"'Fraid I'm out of that business."

"Shame." Kim hummed. "I called around, looked you up. You've been seeing some interesting people recently, Marcey. People that would make our mutual friend at the DA's office very keen to talk to you."

"What'd she get you for?"

"Not selling drugs at a school party, I assure you." Kim's smile was twisted. "But then again, I went and did my time for better or for worse. Missed my mom dying. Couldn't go to the fucking funeral because Johnson was on some power trip about me learning my lesson. It's a fucked up, bullshitty world, Marcey. We just live in it."

"I'm sorry."

Kim pressed on. "You, though…you got out of it. And now she's using you as an example. That PAC of hers isn't exactly the cleanest thing out there." She shook her head. "That ruling's a mess. Fucking with the whole country."

"I don't want to talk politics, Kim," Marcey said shortly. "That isn't a safe topic these days."

"Far safer than whatever it is you're mixed up in now. Kat Barber? Really, Marcey?"

Marcey feigned ignorance for all of two seconds before Kim's don't-bullshit-me stare got the better of her. Was one of the people she'd called Shelly? Or maybe Kat? Or was Kim, like Kat, surprised that it was Marcey who'd ended up with Charlie's book? "Sounds like you know her."

Kim tapped her fingers on the back of her tablet. "She was in town recently, looking at a painting."

"Do you guys, like, all keep tabs on each other?"

Kim raised an eyebrow. "It's a hobby." She paused. "I don't work with people like Kat."

"Like Kat?"

"Bad track record of getting people she works with arrested. Like she did to Charlie." She shook her head. "Or for making sure that people do time when they had no reason to."

"Ah. Then you know about what happened in Rio." Marcey fought back a laugh. "I actually got your name from Shelly Orietti. I, um, wasn't expecting you to dig in so quickly."

"Shelly's involved too? Oh, I'll bet she and Kat are fighting like, well… cats." Kim let out a low whistle and looked somewhat horrified at her bad joke. Marcey just wanted to laugh at it.

"Kim, that was awful."

"It was pretty bad, wasn't it?"

"It really was," Marcey agreed. "How do you know Shelly?"

"Well, I met her…I guess you'd still say her, she was still pretty early in her transition, our junior year. She was working with Charlie on some sort of complicated-ass double cross where she had to be about five different women before the end of it. I was so mad at her, Mar. Almost walked away from the job. I couldn't believe that she was going to risk exposing us all like that. I couldn't look past it, until I saw her in action."

"How do you mean?"

"She's fantastic on the grift. Fucking amazing at it. Charm your socks right off and you'll thank her for it. Can't say I was particularly mad when she showed how good she was." Kim pursed her lips. "But if you're running into this with her…and Kat—"

"This is more for me than for Kat Barber. Darius is set to have a parole hearing soon, but his chances of getting out look awful."

"So you bring Kat Barber into it?"

Marcey nodded.

"Art, right? It's never anything else with Barber." She tapped a few keys. "Why are you involved? You never seemed like you had the stuff for job like this."

From her bag, Marcey produced the same poster she'd shown Kat. She smoothed it flat on the counter. "Because of this."

Kim leaned forward, let out a low whistle. "Isn't that libel?"

"No, because it's an artist's rendering. It's only obvious it's me if you know me."

"Shit, Mar, I'm sorry. That's just Johnson's style though, isn't it? She pushes into these little places in people and makes them feel small. You're lucky she hasn't come to try and arrest you again."

"I know."

"So you want to do this? With Kat Barber."

"And you," Marcey said hopefully. "If you're willing."

Kim frowned. "What's the take?"

"Eighteen percent, even split for all involved," Marcey answered.

"Why not twenty?"

"There's a percentage for overhead as well. Kat had to buy some sort of oven…and bookbinding supplies."

"Bookbinding?"

Marcey shrugged. "Search me."

"Where's this gig at? I can't exactly leave the area. Not with this." She pulled her foot out from under the counter and showed Marcey the monitoring anklet she wore. "It'll be a few more weeks until it's off. When does this need to happen?"

"Up in the White Mountains, some rich guy's estate by Mount Washington." Marcey pulled out her phone. "I think sometime in May. Is that too soon?"

Kim nodded. "It is, but I think I can try and make it work. I've been trying to find some way to get back into the game. Been stuck here working my ass off to keep the shop open since we got up to our eyeballs in debt with Mom's medical bills. Fat lotta good that life insurance policy did when the medical folks decided to get cute and use some backdoor loophole from Obamacare to deny our claims for all of that worthless treatment."

"I'm sorry."

"Don't worry about it." She rubbed at the back of her head. "Just…Kat Barber, Marcey? Seriously?"

Marcey looked down at her fingernails. "I don't have much more of a choice, do I? I gotta at least pretend that I like her."

"You were always the best at pretending, but you need an ally," Kim agreed. "I'll do what I can."

CHAPTER 16

Marcey, Forcing the Issue

THE STORAGE-UNIT DOOR OPENED WITH a groan and Kim wheeled her go-kit inside. She glanced around, taking in the place, as Marcey flipped on the light and pulled the door halfway shut behind them. Kim settled, bouncing on the balls of her feet for a moment. Marcey's hair was caught in the static from the beanie in her hand. She patted it down. "Never imagined Charlie would keep a place like this tucked away."

Marcey shrugged. "I never really knew him, so I can't tell you much about what he did or didn't do."

"And yet he left you with this mess to sort through." Kim shook her head. "Typical man."

"You're the only one who's said that." Marcey blinked in the semi-darkness of the storage facility. "Most everyone else's been all *lucky you inheriting all that* or *I can't believe Charlie left* you *in charge* or *oh, I just miss him so much.*" Exhaling a breath that felt like she'd been holding it for weeks now, Marcey met Kim's gaze evenly. "I didn't ask for this."

"Then why are you doing it? Jobs like this, jobs where people are invested for more than just the endgame, people get hurt when not everyone's bought in."

"Oh, I've bought in." Marcey toed a dust bunny. It puffed up and stuck to her shoelace. "Just not to the bullshit about how he was such a good person. Or that everyone loved him. People wouldn't be so damn dedicated to ensuring that they possess his legacy if they cared about him. They want it more than they care about him."

Kim pressed her lips into a thin line, her eyes narrowing. "Did you ever wonder *why* people want it so bad?"

Marcey hadn't, but she would not allow Kim to see her admit it. She turned away.

"Every single person Charlie Mock ever knew trusted him with their secrets. He never, ever, trusted them with his. Only person who ever got close was Shelly, but that's different. They loved each other. We came in, we did what he needed, we got paid. It was to *prevent* things like what happened in Rio."

"With Kat?"

"With everyone. Everything about that job was a mess, from what I heard, and that was just whispers on the inside."

Marcey jammed her hands into her pockets. "I feel angry at him." Kim had known Marcey a long time, but this was a secret she'd kept from Marcey too. This secret life with Charlie Mock. Everyone had a life with this guy who'd been too chickenshit to try to have a life with her.

That anger, the old hurt of a child growing up without a father figure, was a hard one for Marcey to stomach, and it was one that she didn't think she'd get over quickly. Her fingers twitched in her pockets. "He never tried with me."

"I won't make excuses for him," Kim said. "There aren't any excuses for that. Especially if he knew who you were."

Marcey shrugged. "Clearly he did. And clearly I was the best option for this."

"Because of Linda Johnson."

Marcey nodded, her jaw tightening. "Somehow he knew about that."

"Dude, everyone knows about that." Kim frowned. "Just because you thought you'd gotten yourself past it doesn't mean the world forgot. Linda certainly hasn't. I'm sure she's still hung up on Rebecca and that pill problem she had."

"Like that was my fault."

"Well…" Kim sighed. "Look, I'm not here to relieve you of the guilt you feel over Darius. That's on you. Granted, it's white people guilt and something you have to work on. You can't do all of this just because you feel awful about what happened to him. You couldn't help it. Systemic bullshit and all that. But you gotta know that it doesn't…really fly when you talk about your hard past 'n shit when Dar is literally sitting in jail for the same shit while you walk free."

Rubbing her hand at the back of her neck, Marcey looked around the storage unit. "You think I don't know that? Fuck, Kim, I would give anything for it to be fair, for it to be equal. That's what it should have been. Now she's off trying to fuck him again and I'm in a position to do something about it. Let me have this, *Christ.*" The small, enclosed space was claustrophobic, cluttered with the relics of a dead man.

Kim shrugged. "Suit yourself, but remember, this isn't some sort of burden you have to bear. It isn't your fault."

"I wanted to give stuff to Becca. I wanted everyone to have a good time." Marcey whirled to face Kim, her nostrils flaring. "Isn't that fucked up too? That I let it happen?"

"You couldn't predict an OD."

"No, but I could've been responsible for it." Marcey exhaled hard. "I'm a disaster, Kim. People who come near me get hurt."

"Oh, boo hoo, the white girl with the inheritance of a grandmaster. Get back to me when your life is actually hard." She said it gently, but there was an air of finality about her.

Marcey let it drop. She thought of Charlie. Was he really a grandmaster? He hadn't known Marcey beyond the girl he'd sometimes played chess with, and yet that was enough to draw the connection to Linda Johnson, enough to damn Marcey to this life. She stepped forward and took in the painting, the memory of it propped up against Kat Barber's thighs still fresh in her mind.

Kim had stories about Kat Barber. Stories that Kat wasn't willing to share and Shelly was too polite to breathe aloud. Marcey's jaw tightened, and she swallowed. "Tell me about Kat Barber."

"What do you want to know?"

"Charlie was planning this job with her. He's got it all worked out, but she thinks that this is as much her job as it's his."

"You told me this was Charlie's job."

"It *is.*" Marcey gestured to the painting on the wall. "But Kat's the one who forged this."

Kim let out a low whistle. "That has got to be the most terrifying painting I've ever seen in my goddamn life." She pulled the photocopy from the wall, her beat-up, oversized army surplus jacket falling off one of her shoulders, dragged down by her messenger bag. "What the shit is this? Who the fuck does Charlie think he's playing if he thinks that *this* is going to earn us any money at all? *Who* the fuck would buy something like this?"

"Fucking beats me. Kat told me it's a minor work of some unknown painter, but maybe that it inspired *The Scream*."

Kim hummed. "That sounds like some artist bullshit line. The sort of bullshit Kat Barber excels at. It's an ugly painting, Marcey. Everyone knows *The Scream* came about because Munch was dealing with some pretty messy mental illness. And if Kat had Charlie all up in it's shit then maybe we have bigger problems."

"Why?"

"Kat doesn't play well with others. She doesn't like being out of control. You holding all the cards on this job where she's done the leg work? She'll see that as a threat. She'll screw you like she screwed Charlie."

"Did she resent him like that?"

Kim shook her head. "Nah, man, he was like her father."

A white-hot surge of anger laced through Marcey. Her hands, still tucked away in her pockets, twisted into fists. How could he? How could he when Marcey had been *right there*? "Oh," Marcey said.

Kim turned to Marcey. "You weren't really a criminal, Mar, not like Kat. I wouldn't stress about it."

The anger, white hot and cutting, surged forth in Marcey. Her mouth was moving before her mind caught up to what she was saying. "You don't get to say that. No one gets to say that. You don't know what I've been through. You don't know what I've done in my life. Linda Johnson branded me a criminal even if she never succeeded in getting the conviction she wanted."

Kim glared. "She ruined my life too. My mom…Christ, Marcey, my mom was *dying* and the woman wouldn't grant me leave to go to her bedside. She's on a damn power trip and we both know it. You want her ruined. I want her ruined. We're not going to get anywhere unless we can work together."

Marcey put up her hands, placating. Vulnerability was not something she *did* per se, but it was something that she could put on when she needed to achieve an end. The problem was Kim knew her well enough to see that the hurt she felt over Charlie Mock caring for someone like Kat was at least somewhat genuine. She swallowed and then closed her fingers over her thumbs, a gesture she'd learned long ago would make her feel calm. "Charlie's last job is all we're here to do, but I think I know how we can get some comeuppance in the process."

Kim grinned. "That I'd like to hear." She relaxed visibly. Her eyes flicked down to the picture in her hand. "I seriously can't believe that this painting has any value at all."

Marcey chuckled. "Beats me, but Kat says it's valuable."

"Why couldn't it have been pictures of kittens or puppies? Not some gross dude's face screaming. This is horrible, Mar."

"I know." Marcey bent and blew some dust off one of Charlie's work benches. Using a series of short, spitting breaths, she cleared most of it off. This left her coughing, miserable as a mouthful of dust settled in her nose. She rubbed at her nose, straightening up and stepping away for Kim to start to set up her laptop. "Kat Barber sure knows how to pick 'em."

"That's one word for it," Kim said.

"What's another?"

"Manipulative." Kim eyed Marcey. "She's already got her hooks in you."

Marcey frowned. "How do you mean?"

From her pocket, Kim produced a flash drive and dropped it into Marcey's hand. Marcey's frown deepened. "What is this?"

"It's an insurance policy. For you. Everything that I can find out about what happened to Kat in Barcelona."

"What happened there?" Marcey asked. "I thought everyone got nailed in Rio?"

"Oh, Kat got nailed all right, just not in that sense." Kim shook her head. "No, that's what happened afterward. When Interpol caught up with her and no amount of loudly proclaiming she was fucking Wei Topeté would get her out of the charges."

"Then Kat's been to jail." Marcey stared down at the drive in her hand. Kat had never mentioned time spent in prison.

"Didn't say that. She should have, going off of that arrest. But she never did. Makes a person wonder why."

Marcey closed her fist around the drive. It did. Kim's expression was far off and almost deliberately aloof. "Then you're okay with this?" Marcey shot back. She tucked the flash drive into her pocket and checked her watch. Shelly would be arriving soon.

Kim bent down and fiddled with her kit. "It's boring, you know? Working there. I hate every moment of it. Mom's dead, Dad's just wasting away. I lost my chance to say good-bye because of Johnson. She hurt Charlie. She hurt me. She's got the damn cops up my ass every two weeks demanding to inspect my computer and phone as though I'd ever let them find anything on it."

"I'm sorry."

"Getting sent to prison, no matter how shit that was, and everything I missed…it really did put some perspective on things. Being out the game for a while was nice, in a way. Gave me time to breathe."

"Are you okay with my getting you back in?"

Kim nodded. "To take down Linda Johnson? To see Charlie's legacy though to the end? Well." Kim shrugged. "You're an old friend, Marcey. I could do with more of those." She glanced over at the entrance and her whole face lit up. "Speaking of old friends. Shelly!" Marcey stepped out of the way just in time to see Kim launch herself into a comfortable hug from Shelly.

Another pang of longing swept through Marcey. Shelly had been Charlie's lover, and she had the maternal way about her that Marcey didn't feel from her own mother. She wondered if the awe and rush she'd felt back at that bar with Shelly had been something else entirely. Maybe it was the thrill of maternal approval. She shook her head. How silly could she be?

"Hey, Kim." Shelly's voice was low. "How's your dad?"

They talked to each other despite the fact that Kim was "out of the game." Marcey filed that bit of information away carefully, hoping she'd never have cause to use it.

"He's getting there. Mom, well, you know she was his everything."

"That's how it goes." Shelly nodded.

"And how are you? It couldn't've been easy."

"It's day to day. After Rio, everything fell apart anyway." Shelly looked away. "I see Marcey's got you up to speed?"

"Yeah."

"What do you think?"

"I think that there's a lot we still don't know."

"Like if you're going to get involved, Shelly. Or just supervise from afar." Marcey glanced over at Shelly. "Care to weigh in on that?"

"A great deal of my willingness to participate revolves around what, exactly, Kat Barber has planned for this painting and how it fits into Charlie's plan for Johnson." Shelly's eyes narrowed. "And what sort of security this place up in New Hampshire has."

Marcey frowned, thinking back to the conversation she'd had with Shelly at the airport. Had she spoken to Shelly about the details? There'd been so much going on, Marcey couldn't remember. "Okay," she said. "How do we do that?"

Kim pulled her tablet from her bag. "Now, granted, this was only what I was able to uncover based off public records, but this"—she tapped the screen and an image of a clean-cut older man appeared—"is John Unita. He's a collector. Really weird dude, too, from the looks of his collection. He's looking to unload the painting for liquid capital. That means he wants cash on hand, Marcey—"

"I *do* work for an accounting firm."

"Oh." Kim looked sheepish. "Barber's appraised the thing at *way* over its actual value, which means that this job is going to involve an element of the lost heir con. Kat loves those. She enjoys playing princess." Kim made a face. "Anyway, so this painting is going to develop some tangible connection to a great work. Best guess being Munch's *The Scream* based on the similar subject matter, style, and color palette. Though that's risky." Kim paused. "I was able to hack into the security company after you left yesterday. These are the blueprints for the house in New Hampshire." She flipped her finger and the blueprints appeared.

Marcey inhaled sharply. "You did all of this...in like, a night?"

Kim scoffed. "Nah, did it before my shift was over, then went to a rave over in Jersey City." She shook her head at Marcey's baffled look. "You underestimate me, Mar." She bent down and tapped her anklet. "Amazing what you can do once you know how to spoof the GPS on one of these things."

"Guess so."

From where she stood, Shelly was irritatingly stoic. Her expression was blank. "So we know a bit about this property and the system guarding it, but nothing about the man himself."

"Yes, that's the problem," Kim answered. "I need time, and I need capital to do that kind of dig."

"I'm not fronting the cash for this," Shelly said. "I don't have it, and neither do you two."

"Kat's got it covered."

"And then there's *that*."

Marcey rolled her shoulders back and stared at the ceiling. "Must we do this, Shelly?"

Kim set her laptop down heavily. "Look. I get it. Kat Barber's not exactly anyone's favorite after Rio, but if she's going to foot the bill for this, why not let her waste her money?"

"Marcey has a blind spot where Kat's concerned," Shelly answered. "It's something that you need to be aware of as well, Kim. She's not coming into this the cold arbiter of Charlie's last wishes."

Later, Marcey would recall this as the final straw, the moment when she lost her temper at Shelly's judgment. At the time, though, it just felt like more of the same. The anger was still there, a bubbling resentment at anything resembling the people who'd known and were known to Charlie Mock, but it was the fear that settled into Marcey's stomach now. Not knowing if Shelly wanted anything to do with this job and knowing that they would depend on her expertise in all things Charlie was an all-consuming fear.

She stepped toward the workbench, toward Kim's laptop where it'd been set up and was slowly buzzing to life. "We all have our roles to play," she began. It felt like a fool's gambit, a chance that they wouldn't think less of her if she were to speak now. "I don't give a shit about Charlie Mock. I care about Linda Johnson. I care about that revenge. I will have that revenge. Be with me, or be against me. We can earn a lot of money if we work together and take down an absolute bitch at the same time."

Marcey turned back to Shelly and Kim. They looked at her oddly, as though there was nothing more to her than the put-upon bravado of her words. She held her hands out open, welcoming. "Yes, I fucked Kat Barber. Yes, she's probably going to try and screw us all. The only protection against that is awareness. And I do not intend to be caught with my pants down."

The scowl cutting across Kim's face was deep. "You want to play a game with Kat Barber. Kat fucking Barber would eat you for lunch, Marcey. What makes you think that you've got anything that could pull something over on her?"

"I know that she's desperate for Charlie's book. I want to find out why."

Shelly's gaze fell heavy on Marcey. She didn't say anything, but her head dipped just once. "So we're stealing this painting."

"Seems we are."

CHAPTER 17

Wei, at a Crossroad

WEI LAY AWAKE, STARING UP at the crackle board ceiling of her hotel room. She was bone-tired, but sleep was elusive. She'd been on both sides of the Atlantic for just long enough for her internal clock to start adjusting before leaving once more. That was the problem with this work, the problem of her liaising with Linda Johnson, the problem of having to let a crime unfold before going in for the kill: too much travel, never enough time to recover. Her body ached of it.

Blearily, Wei turned over and stared at the glowing blue of the alarm clock. Four in the morning. Kat would be awake, and maybe more willing to have the conversation she'd effectively shut down in London a few days before.

The hotel room was cold. Spartan. Cheap—if cheap was a thing one could have in a city like New York. Wei set the coffee maker to brew and opened her laptop. A few texts to Kat ensured that she would answer.

Wei sat cross-legged in the chair at the room's small desk and waited, staring at a black screen. Pulse. Pulse. Finally, Kat answered, looking sun-kissed and sleepy. She was at her loft, amid her paints, wielding a thin calligrapher's knife and not paying attention to Wei. She glanced up. "You look like shit," she said.

"Jet lag." Wei sipped her coffee, which was scalding hot and black. She made a face. It tasted burnt and weak. "What are you doing?"

"Bookbinding."

"Why?"

"Thought I'd try my hand at something new."

"Ah." Wei sat back. "Are you ready to talk?"

"About what?"

Grinding her teeth, Wei wished she didn't have to spell it out. "Marcey Daniels."

"She has what you want, doesn't she? After last weekend, she'll keep following me until I can get it." Kat set her knife down and turned to give her laptop screen her full attention. The picture went fuzzy, before sharpening to see the dark circles under her eyes. She wasn't sleeping either. The small, petty part of Wei liked that. Let her be haunted by her guilt. "You mustn't be cross with me for it."

Wei took another sip of coffee. This one she had to choke down as it curled into a wave of nausea in her stomach. "I am cross with you for it." Her English was slipping, fading into accented incomprensibility. "You told me you would see what she wanted, see if you could get the book. You didn't tell me you were going to have her."

Kat said nothing. Her pen scratched on the paper in front of her. "Maybe I wanted to have her."

There was a ringing in Wei's ears. This was it. This was the end. "Why, Kat?" Her hand shook. She put her coffee in the hotel's cheap paper cup down on the desk beside her laptop.

Kat set her pen down. "Does it matter?"

They were rubbish at this. Wei and Kat both. "It does to me." Her voice was barely a whisper. "It matters to me, Kat. That's not what people who love each other do."

"Do we?" Kat asked. She leaned forward, setting her book—a small cream-colored thing—aside. "Love each other?"

A question Wei could never ask. *I do.* "Yes," she said. It didn't taste dishonest.

Kat was silent, her expression unreadable. She shifted, picked up a mug of tea, bag still dangling off its side, and sipped it. Set it back down. Wei swallowed, watching her stew on the admission. "I'm sorry."

"I am too."

What Wei wanted to ask was why, but the why stuck in her throat, too big and too damning to speak aloud. This was the lie they told themselves to keep this going because love was a lie they clung to.

"What did you put her on to?"

"Something that will guarantee things," Kat said. "Free us of this yoke around our necks. Allow us to be free. Wouldn't you like that, my love, being free to forget these alliances and the messy business of choosing sides?"

Despite herself, Wei nodded. It was what she wanted more than anything else. "You want me to let this happen?"

Kat shrugged. "William's doing a fair job mucking it up as it is. Let him run it until you have to step in. By then the crumbs will be there and you'll get the book."

"And you, your freedom." That was the end goal of all of this, after all. Kat bartering with things that didn't belong to her was hardly new, but this was meant to belong to her. The girl—the girl who Kat had manipulated into showing her hand—had it now. And it was just a matter of time until she messed up. William had already arrested her once; he just hadn't seen the whole picture.

"Darling, you make it sound so good." Kat smiled, serene and beautiful. "Let me handle the girl."

"Will it happen again?"

Kat pursed her lips. "If it does, will you be terribly cross with me?"

Wei wanted to say yes, because it would be the betrayal all over again, but she couldn't. Kat was right. They had to thread a needle, and controlling as many variables as possible was the only way to ensure that their desired outcome was the one effected. Wei clenched her teeth. "Do what you must," she said through them. She reached up, not wanting to look at Kat's face anymore, hit the space bar, and ended the call.

CHAPTER 18

Marcey, Assembling the Merry Band

MARCEY STOOD ON A TRAIN platform three days later in the middle of Penn Station, waiting for the AMTRAK to arrive from DC, fidgeting. This was supposed to go well. Gwen Lane-Wright was an almost mythical figure within the community; Marcey'd heard of her even before coming into Charlie's book, and she wasn't surprised at all when Shelly had mentioned that they might want her expertise. Gwen was the best safecracker on the eastern seaboard, known for heists down at the Disney resorts in Orlando and for daring ski escapes in Colorado and Vermont after liberating the residents of exclusive ski resorts of their valuables. She was a legend, a DC native, and not someone Marcey had ever even dreamed she'd get a chance to meet.

"The last time I heard tell of her was for that job she pulled in Atlanta. The jewelry store?" She practically vibrated with excitement.

"Stop it," Shelly hissed. Her hand closed heavy on Marcey's shoulder. "She'll see you and get spooked."

"I can't help it, Shelly. The woman is a living legend."

"You tell her that, her ego will get huge and then we'll never be able to use her because she'll want fifty percent of the profit." Shelly's fingers tightened. "Now. Be. Still."

Scowling, Marcey tried to be still. She was fretting, anxious. The call to Gwen hadn't gone exactly how Marcey had planned it. She'd wanted Gwen to just agree to come on board, no questions asked, as Kim had done. Best intentions, however, could be troubling. Marcey had had to explain to her the details of the heist, the fact that Kim was involved, all over an unsecured phone line. It wasn't ideal. If Topeté or LePage was tapping her phone, they were already fucked, but Kim had checked it last night and had said that Marcey, despite her lack of solid encryption software, was blissfully wiretap free.

Gwen hadn't been keen to hear from Kim and was even less keen to be put on the phone with Marcey. They couldn't really hold that against her—Marcey was an unknown. She had Charlie's plan though, and explaining the situation to Gwen, the players involved, hadn't gone well. There was still so much they didn't know, still so much they were struggling to piece together.

"I don't know what more I can tell you right now," Marcey had said, her voice feeling heavy as Kim watched her thoughtfully from the workbench. "Shelly Orietti spoke highly of you and thought you'd be best for this job."

Shelly had been the one who opened the door. Shelly had been the one who'd gotten Gwen to speak for the first time over Marcey's babble about logistics. "There's a train," she'd said. "At Penn Station tomorrow at eight. Come meet me and I'll make my decision."

Bringing Shelly was a security blanket. One that Marcey needed to ensure that this didn't go horribly wrong. Marcey fidgeted.

"Stop," Shelly said again. "She's here."

Gwen was a lot taller than Marcey, though not as tall as Shelly. Her hair was short, cut close to her head, and her eyes stood out like smears of white paint against the darkness of her skin. Alert and attentive, they flicked over Shelly appraisingly, a smile pulling at her lips, before settling on Marcey. Marcey stared right back. Gwen was dressed like this was a business trip: pressed slacks and a blazer over a flowing green top. Marcey was in jeans and a T-shirt, hunched over and just a little cold in her leather jacket that was more stylish than warm. They couldn't be further apart from each other.

She held out a hand. "I'm Marcey."

"Gwen Lane-Wright." Gwen's hand was dry, her fingers rough and callused, incongruous with her polished appearance. "You look like him. Especially in the nose." She moved with the grace of a dancer, but her body was all muscle, stepping away from Marcey to shake Shelly's hand. "Shelly. You look great."

"Gwen." Shelly nodded. "You've gone natural."

Gwen patted her hair, short and tightly curled. "Well, it was too much work otherwise."

"Girl, I feel that."

Marcey rubbed at her nose, scowling.

Gwen smiled thinly at her, hands in her pockets. "So you're the one." The once-over she gave Marcey made Marcey feel naked. "Charlie's heir." Gwen's gaze slid over to Shelly. "You would've thought it'd be her."

Shelly hummed her agreement. "That was what I thought as well. But." She sighed. "For better or for worse, it isn't Kat who's kin. Marcey's his daughter, despite his never mentioning her existence to any of us. She's green."

"I'm *right here*," Marcey ground out.

"I know, honey," Shelly answered. "She's got this bug up her butt about wantin' to go, and well, she wants to finish up Charlie's last job."

"Why?" Gwen frowned. "I thought it went south when the pieces didn't fall right...and when Kat..." Glancing at Marcey, she shrugged. "Okay. Charlie's last job."

This was the tricky part, the part where honesty could not hurt. Marcey plunged her hands into her pockets. "It's an art job, and I know there's some personal baggage with half the team involved, so I'm not going to ask you to betray any loyalties. This job is twofold. I want to finish Charlie's job because there's a lot of money in it for everyone." She exhaled. "But the other part of this is personal. I'm sure you know what landed Charlie in prison? Johnson's hurt me too. Me, people I care about. Kim has business with her as well, and we think we've worked out a way to combine these two jobs. I want her career ruined."

"Lofty goal," Gwen answered. "Why not just kill her?"

"Because I don't do that. Isn't that enough?"

Gwen folded her arms over her chest, hip cocked out to one side. "No. It isn't. Tell me why. You're trying to enlist my services to work with someone I *loathe* and you haven't given me a good enough reason to stick my neck out for you. You're an amateur. You're my arrest wrapped up in a tiny package." Marcey glanced at Shelly. Her expression was stony; there was nothing for Marcey there. Gwen set her bag down. "Give me a good reason."

This question, this question. Rattling around in Marcey's head. She hated it. "I remember sitting in Linda Johnson's office, terrified, alone. I was only sixteen, my mom'd gone and hired this lawyer we could barely afford to get me off and all I could think was that whatever happened, I deserved it. This was my fuck up. My cross to die on." She exhaled. "But it wasn't my cross to die on, not with a lawyer like the one my mom got me. I sat there and listened to that woman steal away my best friend's freedom like he was nothing."

"All criminals are nothing, until they're something." Gwen frowned. "That still isn't a reason."

Marcey let out a frustrated little sigh. "I *want* it, okay? I want the glory. I want to feel the thrill of the game. I know I can do it. In that interview room, when I was sixteen, I was humiliated. Laid bare. They took everything I ever held dear about myself and stripped it from my flesh. They used who I was against me and I cannot ever let that happen again. I want her to pay for what she did to me. The humiliation, the muckraking, the fact that she's brought it up again, years later, as if to salt the wound—I want her to suffer for it. She doesn't deserve the position she covets, and besides, she's *dirty*."

"Dirty?" Shelly looked up quickly. "Are you sure?"

Marcey made an affirmative noise but did not say how she knew. That detail was for later, when they trusted each other more. "I found out some things, when I went to London and spoke to Kat Barber, details that I don't even think she was meant to know. Linda Johnson told William LePage to fall in love with you, Gwen." Gwen bristled at this. Marcey ignored her. "She orchestrated all of Rio, from Kat and Topeté getting caught in the act how they did to the fact that LePage turned just when everything looked like it was going to work out in the end. Kat Barber may have exposed his lie in making sure that your relationship took a hit, but she wasn't the one who made it happen in the first place. LePage is involved in this. I know he hurt you. Why not get some revenge on him and the woman who's ultimately responsible for that? I want her ruined. I can give you the revenge you want." She stepped forward to Gwen, her hand extended. "Isn't that exactly why we do things like this?"

Gwen didn't take her hand. "I don't like your methods. Personal baggage isn't something to be wielded like a weapon."

"But will you do it?"

Gwen's chin dipped just once.

There was little conversation in the cab they took back up to the storage unit. Marcey watched the fare tick up and up and winced when she pulled out her wallet and swiped the credit card Kat Barber had overnighted her for the purposes of this job. "Keep a spreadsheet," she'd said in a note. "I'll need to track expenses."

Marcey'd nearly cut up the card and mailed it back to her, but a quick look at her bank account and the slowly dwindling funds that resided there had made her wince and tuck the card away in her wallet.

She paid the fare and they piled out to slip through the back door into the storage unit. Shelly picked the lock with expert speed and Marcey kept watch. They couldn't all keep going through the front entrance. It was too risky.

"What are we looking at?" Gwen asked. "And where."

"New Hampshire," Shelly said. "In the mountains. It's a painting. Come along and see."

"So, you're not coming?" Gwen tilted her head to one side. "A black trans woman in rural New Hampshire? You'd be shot on sight."

Shelly chuckled. "Depends on the town, there are pockets of reasonable-minded folk, but you've got a point."

Gwen grinned right back at her.

"Gwen's black too, you know." Marcey felt stupid, pointing it out. "I know you're supposed to be the best, Gwen, but if Shelly can't go, how can you?"

"I went to Exeter."

Marcey's eyes went wide. "Oh…oh, so you speak prep school."

Gwen flashed her an uncertain smile. "Something like that. It wasn't fun, being the only person like me there, but whatever. That was years ago. Needless to say, I can walk in those circles well enough to get by. Besides, it's the off season, no matter what this freak weather we're having is doing. Gonna be mud season soon enough."

"True, true," Marcey agreed.

Kim was already waiting for them at the storage unit door, tapping her foot impatiently in time with whatever music was blasting at exceedingly high levels from her ear buds. She brightened when she saw Gwen and stepped away from the doorway to allow Marcey to unlock the door. When it rolled open and they all trooped inside, Marcey flipped on the lights and closed the door once more.

"So," she said, turning to the room. "This is us."

"So it would seem," Gwen answered. "Why don't you tell me what we're looking at, Kim, so I can see if you actually need my help?"

"Oh," Kim said. "We really, really do." From the poster tube she'd tucked up against her side, she produced a series of blueprints. After locating tacks and the wooden accent bar three quarters of the way up the storage unit wall, Kim hung the blueprints.

They examined the plans. They were simple, just a house with standard alarm features. A few motion sensors by the doors, but nothing that Marcey would categorize, even in her limited experience, as a hardcore security system.

Kim glanced at Marcey before her eyes slid over to Shelly. "There's no security apparatus indicated, which means this guy is either mad cocky, or he thinks he's got us figured out."

Gwen trailed her finger down one of the blueprints, tapping on a void. "He has a safe."

"You think."

"I know." Gwen tapped the void again. "There."

"But shouldn't there be something there? From what Kat told me, and my reading of Charlie's notes in here…this place is supposed to be like Fort Knox levels of hard to get into." Marcey didn't understand.

"Fort Knox isn't hard to get into," Gwen murmured distractedly, her eyes fixed on the blueprints. "This though, this could prove challenging."

Shelly leaned around her and trailed a French-tipped nail along a small corridor toward the back of the house. "There it is."

"There's what?"

Gwen and Shelly glanced at each other.

"Christ, you are new at this, aren't you?" Kim unrolled a second image. "Look here." She tacked it above the first. "This is an air shaft to a panic room. And inside the panic room…" Her gaze slid to Gwen. "There's a safe."

"A safe." Gwen nodded. Kim hummed her agreement and passed Gwen her tablet.

Marcey craned her neck to get a better look. Inside the panic room at the back of the house was a safe. A big one, by the looks of it, with a complicated door that was mostly pixelated and blurred in Kim's laptop screen. "One that we won't be able to get into on our own. Safe makers contract with security companies, but they never reveal their secrets. We'd have better luck trying to get a straight answer out of a politician."

"So that's why you need me." Gwen sighed. "That isn't so bad. I'll need time, of course, to plan. And time inside the vault with this beautiful foe."

Relief flooded Marcey. "Then you're in."

"Yes."

"And you're not worried about Topeté at all? Or LePage?" Marcey didn't know why she felt the need to question this, or to even bring up their names, but she wanted to make things as clear as possible as they moved forward. She didn't want there to be any surprises.

It was Kim, not Gwen, who drew a sharp breath at the mention of Wei Topeté. Marcey thought back, trying to recall if she'd mentioned to Kim that Topeté was involved. There'd been so much of a waiting game that she hadn't thought much of it beyond the assumption that Topeté and Kat, for better or for worse, were a matched set.

"No," Gwen said. "If William comes, then he comes. He knows that he'll get his due."

Shelly's eyes narrowed. She had the look on her face of a woman who'd just realized something important that she'd forgotten to do. She turned and gathered her purse. Her fingers flew over her coat buttons. "I've just remembered something. I need to…" She gestured to the door.

"Do you need us to call you a cab?" Marcey asked.

"It isn't like that, hon," Shelly answered.

Gwen shouldered her bag. "Can I split the fare? I need to go back to Midtown anyway. Find a hotel."

"Of course."

They were both gone then, vanished in a swirl of Shelly's gray wool jacket and a proposal of Shelly's *very comfortable* couch as a viable place for sleeping.

Kim watched her go for a moment before turning to pack up her tablet. "Topeté's lurking?"

"Yeah. And LePage arrested me when someone—not me, mind you— tried to break into the gallery where Kat appraised that painting. So yes. Topeté is lurking." Marcey sighed. "I don't know what for... She's got her fingers into this too. Probably because of Kat. Or because of Johnson."

"It's because of Charlie's book."

"What?"

"Everyone wants Charlie's book. Johnson, and probably Topeté too, because it's the key to everything Charlie did with his life. Interpol are waylaid by red tape and bureaucracy, but when they get going, they're unstoppable. While they're stuck in that waiting game, they liaise and work in counterterrorism. But there's one thing they're *damn* good at."

"Catching art thieves," Marcey finished.

"So, are you sure you want to go down *this* particular route to get your revenge on Linda Johnson?"

Marcey through about it for a minute before nodding. "I am."

"Okay. Then I am too." Kim slung her bag over her shoulder. "But if this goes south, don't expect me to back you up." She walked out of the unit and waited for Marcey to lock up and join her. They moved in silence after Shelly, heading out into the cool afternoon toward the train station.

For a while, Marcey couldn't think of anything to say. When the words came to her, she had to shout them over the squeal of the arriving train. "Why wouldn't you?"

"What?"

"Why wouldn't you back me up?"

"I almost ended up in jail the last time I worked with Kat Barber."

Marcey drew in a shocked breath. "Really?"

Kim leaned against a support beam, grinding her palms against each other like someone squishing a bug. "I don't mind working with her on art jobs, though, because she's always distracted by the pretty things." Kim's expression grew darker. "It's the other jobs you have to be worried about. She thinks she's fantastic on the grift, but she's really not. Any time she gets away from art jobs, it goes south. That's why Rio went south in the end, you know?"

"Is she why you didn't work with Charlie for a while?" Kim frowned and opened her mouth to reply, but Marcey pressed on. "He documented each interaction he had with various, erm...subcontractors. I have his docs.

Your entry goes blank for a period between 2008 and 2011. Did Kat have anything to do with that?"

"Nah," she said, waving her hand dismissively. "That was that stupid eBay thing."

"Oh. Then what happened with Kat?"

"The same thing that always happens on the job. Things get out of hand, security guards can't be as easily manipulated as they should be, we have to scatter... Kat and Charlie get into a tight position with a security guard, do a few things, and then suddenly I'm locked in the back of a van, blindfolded and pissing myself I'm so scared. Charlie had to come get me. He was furious. But not with Kat. Never with Kat. That at least wasn't her fault. Not like Rio when she figured out everyone else's game and decided to go with the nuclear option rather than reevaluate with Charlie. I wonder if she saw the writing on the wall with Charlie, about his diagnosis..."

"Why did everyone think that Kat was going to inherit Charlie's legacy if she was forever fucking with people?" Marcey asked. "This is two times she's gotten you into a bad position that you've told me about, and then Rio... You'd think it would've soured people to her entirely. Charlie, especially. I know there's no loyalty amongst thieves."

Kim was quiet for a long time after that. "Charlie loved her, that's the best I can figure. She was the only one of us who he ever allowed closer than Shelly. I think Shelly always resented that to some extent. Kat is *damn good;* you have to remember that. She is, in a lot of ways, the one Charlie trusted with his secrets. She knows more about what's in that book of his than anyone other than you. So, it was just logic. She'd be the heir." Kim shook her head ruefully. "So yeah, I'm not exactly thrilled at the prospect of working with her again. I don't like her knowing my secrets."

"I'll keep her in line."

"Marcey," Kim said very seriously. "You're the *least* likely person to be objective around a pretty blonde. I saw you in high school. I'll keep my own counsel on what to do about Kathryn Barber, thanks."

CHAPTER 19

Wei, Acting

"THE INJUNCTION'S FLIMSY AT BEST." Linda Johnson wrinkled her nose and tossed the paperwork onto her messy desk. "Austin Jackson must know we've got him. Or at least that we're sniffing around."

"He does," Wei pointed out. "He isn't stupid. He was Charlie's lawyer for *years*."

"Then why countersue?" Johnson demanded. Wei's fingers twitched. Johnson knew the answer; she was trying to figure out if they had put it together yet. Wei hated that about her, the constant testing of her abilities. When she'd first started working with Johnson, she'd assumed William was the one being tested, but he was Johnson's golden boy after Rio. Wei was the one who was on a short leash.

"Plausible deniability," William answered. He raked a hand over his two-day-old beard. "He wants to make sure that he saves face before he caves. Attorney–client privilege extends after death."

"But you have him, on that train job in Rio from five years ago." Johnson leaned forward. "What are you waiting for, then? Arrest him and force him to confirm that the girl has the book." She turned to LePage. "You had to cut her loose once already, William. What's to stop you from doing it again?"

LePage flipped back a few pages in his reporter's notebook. "I spoke to her mother about her trip out of the country last weekend. She went to London, as Topeté confirmed." He lowered the notebook, his gaze drifting from Johnson to Wei. "And met with Kathryn Barber, which Topeté failed to mention."

Wei shifted but did not allow her expression to drop. "I only confirmed this morning. Barber was...cagey about the visit when I saw her in London last weekend."

"'Fraid she got caught cheating, was she?" LePage wiggled his eyebrows.

"*T'es un gros porc*," Wei ground out. "Leave that out of this."

"Why, Agent Topeté, when it's relevant? You're obviously compromised." Johnson's smile was slow and smug. "And Barber is with you. You're her handler, or at the very least I expect you to exert some form of control over her. I will not have a wild card. If you can't handle her, LePage should run point on this. He can be objective."

"And when some ghost from his past shows up too?" She had to push, just enough to make it seem as though she wasn't thrilled with the development, though it was the sort of thing that really, she had no control over in the first place. Johnson was harder than William, and she had to believe that Wei was annoyed. Wei crossed her arms and slouched, like a child instead of a woman past forty. Johnson was lazy, distracted. She only needed a few crumbs to jump to a conclusion. "Can he be trusted to be objective?"

"He's doing a better job than you are right now," Johnson answered curtly.

Good.

"Fine." Wei got to her feet. "You'll have my report from Lyon and London this afternoon." She stalked out of the office, counting in her head. Three, two, one.

"Topeté!"

She didn't turn around.

"Wei, *wait*." LePage grabbed her arm and spun her around. Wei clenched her fist. He had no right to touch her, even if he looked immediately apologetic, his hand jerked away and open. "This is your collar, we both know that. You're the one who caught Barber that first time in Barcelona. She had secrets she was willing to sell. Where are the fruits of that investigation?"

"That should have gotten us Charlie Mock's book," Wei hissed. "But it didn't. And now she's pulled it away from me too. How am I supposed to string Barber along if she thinks I don't have the authority to direct this case?"

"Well." LePage rubbed at the back of his neck. They had an audience in the bullpen. He jerked his head to an interview room. Wei followed, silently, full of affected anger. "You don't have any authority here anyway. You're a liaison, assigned to catch an art thief."

"I've caught her."

"Then what's she doing sending some kid into the Perôt?"

Wei shrugged. "I don't know much about the kid beyond what we suspect. She's the one who got the book from Mock's lawyer. I'm curious what she's doing with it, though."

"Don't you have contacts in that world? Contacts who could get you that answer?"

"William, are you asking me to compromise myself and this investigation to get confirmation?" She laughed. "Don't you also have contacts? Why not ring your ex?"

He shifted, uncomfortable with the mention of his time undercover. Wei knew what Kat had done when she'd exposed him for the liar he was. She knew what it had cost his ex-fiancée. "That'd be a bad idea."

"Quite." Wei closed her eyes. She could try Shelly, who was never too keen to work with people anyway. But who was to say that Shelly knew anything about the girl? Shelly had thrown a bone last time. Maybe she'd play ball again. "Give me twenty-four hours. I'll see what I can dig up."

"But your report—"

"The price you have to pay, William." She left the interview room, a smile pulling at her lips.

It was a brilliant spring morning outside. The sun was shining, so much so that Wei's eyes hurt. She hailed a cab and told them the address of a library in Queens. "That's a ways away," the cabbie said. "Got a preference for how I go?"

"No." Wei closed her eyes. Johnson's office would pick up the tab. "Just drive."

An hour later, Wei made her way up the steps of the central branch of the Queens Library. It had been a long time since Wei had been to a library, longer still since she'd been in one that didn't carry the telltale smell of body odor that tended to permeate many of the libraries Wei had frequented in college.

Her quarry sat behind a bank of computers at the library's reference desk. Wei waited until Shelly Orietti's gaze drifted up from her computer screen. She didn't want to show up unannounced. If there was any reaction from Shelly, it did not show on her face. She tapped her candy-red nails idly against the back of her mouse, her chin resting on her free palm.

"You're the last person I expected to see today," Shelly said dryly as Wei approached. "Looking for microfiche? It's downstairs."

Wei scowled. "No. I was looking for you."

Shelly blinked up at her through fake eyelashes. "Why ever would you come traipsing all the way out here just to talk to little ole me?"

"Cut the act, Shelly." Wei's hands were jammed in her pockets, and she clenched them into fists, out of sight of Shelly, though the tension clearly showed on her face. "You know why I'm here."

Sighing the long-suffering sigh of a woman oft put-upon, Shelly got to her feet. She moved quickly, long strides drawing Wei out of the library to a back alleyway where she pulled a cigarette pack and a lighter from her pocket. She offered the pack to Wei. Wei shook her head. Shelly shrugged and lit up, exhaling smoke before speaking. "I told you, I don't have it."

"No, but you know who does. I want to know what they're doing with it." Wei leaned against the building. "There's chatter of a job. The kind she can never turn down."

Shelly pulled the cigarette from her lips. "Barber?" She shook her head. "Honestly, Topeté, if you think Kat isn't the one running this thing already, you're stupider than I thought."

"But she's not alone, is she?" Wei reached out, touching Shelly's arm tentatively. "Once, there was a trust between us. We were able to work together when everything came apart in Rio."

"People ended up in jail because of that," Shelly said shortly. "People I loved. People who had no business dying in prison, *alone*."

"Then you'll understand." Wei wanted that cigarette now but didn't know how to ask for it. These conversations were crushing, terrible things. They tore into Wei's soul mercilessly, shredding the dignity and integrity she never quite managed to cling to. "That the book has no business ending up in Linda Johnson's hands."

Smoke curled around Shelly's head, her expression arranged into a careful blankness that was more deliberate than it was telling. "You're planning something."

"I might be."

"And you want me to do what? Supervise?" Shelly took another drag. "*Christ,* Wei, games like this will get someone killed."

"LePage knows about the girl, Shelly. He arrested her, but had to let her go."

"I know," Shelly spat. "I was there when she was released, or did William fail to mention that detail?"

"That girl is going to screw up again, and I won't be able to protect her, or keep the book from Johnson."

"What do you want with it?"

Wei didn't answer. The truth was so hard to stomach that Wei never wanted to speak the words aloud.

CHAPTER 20

Marcey, Taking Baby Steps

SHELLY CALLED AS MARCEY WAS on her way to Charlie's storage unit two days later. "I'm in, no more doubting that," was all she said before hanging up. Marcey stared down at her phone, puzzled at the shortness, before shrugging and putting it back in her purse.

"Who was that?"

She turned to Gwen, standing beside her on the train platform. "Shelly. She's in."

"I figured she would be," Gwen answered.

"Took her long enough." Kim grunted beside them. "Always dramatic, that woman."

Marcey shook her head, glancing from Gwen to Kim to the tunnel. The train was coming. She exhaled, trying to appear calm. The giddiness that settled into her stomach at the idea of having all these women around her was nothing like anything Marcey'd ever felt before.

On the train, Gwen stood while Marcey and Kim sat; they were alone in the car, for now. Marcey grinned up at Gwen, unable to stop herself from smiling. "So, if Shelly's in, what's our next step?"

"Probably figure out the schematics of the panic room and see if it's got some sort of nasty vault door on it, which I'm sure it does."

"Might be a Monument, one of their round ones." Kim sat back, staring up at the ads overhead. Marcey was surprised there weren't any featuring her face in this car. Maybe it was a sign of good luck. "The opening looks to be something complicated."

"Why's a white dude in New Hampshire going to build a panic room like that anyway?" Gwen frowned. "It's not like he's got anything to be afraid of, except maybe bears."

"These rich eccentrics," Kim answered. "Never had any sense."

"Is it common for there to be this level of security out in the middle of nowhere?" Marcey asked. "It seems so excessive."

"People have their moments of paranoia for a reason, Marcey. This guy could've had something stolen before, or he's just paranoid, you never really can tell, but the moment you start thinking about the why a mark does anything is the moment you're going to get into trouble." Kim's expression was a twist of gleeful smile and admonishment.

Marcey thought about this for a moment. She had her paranoia, this guy had to have it too, but something... She spoke after a few long moments of contemplation, not quite sure if she was right or wrong. "Shouldn't that be everything, though? Like, if this guy has a panic room, and possibly a really complicated safe door on it, shouldn't we ask why he has that? What is there in his past that's making him behave that way? Will it feed into what more he'll do to feel safe?"

Gwen and Kim exchanged a glance, the sort that spoke volumes about what they were thinking without giving anything away. Marcey shrugged. "Like, maybe if he's that paranoid, he's got a guard rotation too, how do we get in if there's humans, not just a locked door, guarding the painting?"

"She sounds like Charlie." Kim raised an eyebrow.

"Yeah, it's uncanny," Gwen agreed.

Sitting back, her legs kicked out, Marcey couldn't help the grin that spread across her face. She was warm, but content. This was what she wanted: a chance to prove herself to these women. Her worth to this job would not just come from her need for petty revenge. No, she could provide a service. And she would.

Thirty minutes later they were at the storage locker, going through Charlie's books. The idea was to locate any of the preliminary research he'd done on the house in New Hampshire to figure out what sort of safe they were looking at. Kim had brought a pocket projector, which she set on an empty milk crate and a series of Charlie's older journals—which Marcey very much wanted to read at some point. She projected the blueprint of the house in New Hampshire, thanks to relatively weak web security of the county planning office. As they searched, anything of relevance was affixed to the long piece of paper Gwen had brought in what Marcey thought, initially, was a yoga mat.

Marcey flipped through pages of one of Charlie's notebooks, looking for anything that might be considered useful. He wrote his notes with no order; one page could be from two decades ago, the next from two years ago. It was hard-to-follow mess. Still, a page at the back of the book seemed recent. Written in blue ballpoint pen was an address in the city. Marcey pulled up her phone to check where it was, only to find it in an office building on the outskirts of the Financial District. Next to the address was a file number and the word Monument.

"Guys, I think I have something."

Gwen and Kim crowded close to Marcey, reading over her shoulder.

"Guess that proves it's a Monument," Kim said at length. "What's that business?"

"Not sure." Gwen pursed her lips. "Never heard of KMT Imports."

Kim typed a few commands into her laptop, her eyes narrowing as she did so. She clicked a link, and then another, and then another. It seemed to go on and on forever. "That's a neat trick," she answered.

"What is?" Marcey asked.

"Look." Kim flipped the tablet around. On the screen was a complicated algorithm that seemed to be kicking back a property address in California. "That's the company that makes the Monument, among others. They've hidden this company under a series of dummy corporations and behind two fake tax loopholes. Yet it's them."

"You were able to figure all that out in just a few minutes?"

Kim gave Marcey a look that said, *What, like it's hard?*

"Think it's their archive?" Gwen sounded eager.

"Archive?" That didn't make any sense.

"Yeah," Gwen said. "The place where they keep all of their old data, schematics and the like. They're usually housed like this, hidden behind dummy corporations and in tax havens. I'm surprised they're not in Switzerland or something, to be honest."

"Those banks can be broken into," Kim pointed out. "This place? It looks to be operating under the guise of an insurance agency. Just hidden in plain sight."

"That's a nifty tactic," Marcey said. "So what? Down in their basement is just a bunch of files?"

"Dunno, but…if you were to go down there and find that—"

"PN-45-A-76 file?" Marcey read the name out of the notebook.

"Yeah, if you were to go and get that file, we could figure out what we're up against and develop a plan." Gwen leaned against the wall. "Shelly would be great at that."

"Really?"

"Yeah, walking right into places and robbing them blind is something of a specialty of hers," Gwen said.

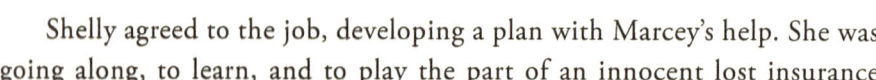

Shelly agreed to the job, developing a plan with Marcey's help. She was going along, to learn, and to play the part of an innocent lost insurance worker, if pressed.

The plan was simple, the sort of game Marcey read about in books and saw in the movies. Like a kid in a candy shop, she planned. They picked Monday, with the weekend for prep. Marcey dug through Charlie's notebooks, finding all the little details he'd provided while casing the joint at the time he'd been arrested. A quick check late on Thursday afternoon and again on Friday morning before work proved that his guard rotation observation held. They could slip in, unnoticed, using a camera blind spot near the men's bathroom. There was a door there with no keycard, just a simple lock.

"You'll need these." Shelly held out a worn leather pouch on Friday afternoon after catching a glimpse of the lock. "I trust you know how to use them."

Marcey did not, but that was what the weekend was for. On Friday, she went to Home Depot and paid cash for a selection of locks, each more daunting and complicated than the next one. That evening, on the tablet Kim had loaned her, she got onto a TOR relay at the local branch of the library and googled instructions on how to pick locks. There were more videos than she could possibly watch, and her eyes soon glazed. She unrolled Shelly's picks and stared at each of them in turn. In places, the polished metal was worn smooth. They had seen a lot, those picks. Marcey stared at the rake pick's wavy end and sighed. Practice, it seemed, was in her future.

By Monday Marcey was at least proficient at getting into all the doors in her apartment. She hadn't dared go out into the corridor to try her neighbor's or the front door, however, she didn't want to give Johnson any excuses, and having lock picks? Definitely could be considered a criminal's tool. Totally cause for arrest in the city.

Shelly met her at the subway at four-forty on Monday afternoon, and they walked together, in silence, to the nondescript office building. In his notes, Charlie had documented the exact route in and out of the building, once they slipped by security.

"Did he do a trial run?" Kim wondered out loud when Marcey showed her the entry toward the front of another journal. All the pieces were there. All they had to do was put them together.

"He could have. This is too well-documented to be anything less than a job a few days away from completion." Shelly ran her fingers down the pages of Charlie's notebook. "There are places here where it looks like he had a false start or two. It isn't like him to work solo either. I think Rio shook him."

"Because he got arrested?" Rio was always this story in the back of everyone's mind when it came to Charlie. Marcey wanted to know more about what had happened then, but everyone was mum on it. There was no sharing that story.

"Everyone gets arrested in this line of work. What happened to Charlie was more than that, you know? It was a culmination of so many things, allies betraying him, the mark getting the jump on him, Kat's turn..." Shelly shook her head. "It was a mess."

"Was that when they found out Kat was involved with the Interpol agent?" Marcey asked.

Gwen shook her head, her expression closed off but conveying a hurt Marcey couldn't ignore. "No, that was when Kat Barber used her connection to Interpol to expose William for what he was. A double agent."

Marcey thought about that conversation now, trailing after Shelly into the office building. It had the musty, damp carpet smell Marcey associated with all old buildings. There was another, more sickly scent underneath it, like something had died in the wall somewhere and no one had bothered to go find the source of the smell. She wrinkled her nose and strode purposefully toward the door. Marcey had been around the block enough to know that half of any good crime was confidence.

Shelly walked into the large atrium like she owned the place. It was a great way to divert attention, but it soon fell sour. Everyone here looked as though this awful building was in the process of digesting them, cooking their insides and slowly killing their will to live. Marcey let that look wash over her and affect her demeanor. Shelly could look authoritative enough to push past the reactions of a woman in charge. Her presence was commanding, but in an understated way that indicated years of practice at being both visible and invisible at the same time. Marcey, however, was content to fade into the background and blend in with all the other harassed twenty-somethings drifting across the atrium.

Shelly stepped to one side of the door. She was blocking the security camera's view of the doorway, speaking to Marcey in a low, reassuring voice. "This is it, kid," she said. "Your moment of truth."

Marcey pulled the lock picks from her back pocket and exhaled. Selecting the snake pick and the slanted diamond wedge, she pushed them into the lock. The tumblers whined in protest but soon opened as easily as a knife sliding through butter. One, two, three. The fourth was tricky. Marcey caught her tongue between her teeth and wiggled the snake pick.

"It's not going."

"You know how to pick locks, don't you?" Shelly raised an eyebrow.

"I practiced all weekend!" Marcey hissed. She shoved the snake pick between her teeth and grabbed another, this one long and narrow, more of a wrench than anything else. She twisted the diamond pick upward, her wrist screaming in protest.

Thunk.

The door swung open to reveal a hallway. Marcey pulled the picks out quickly and used the hem of her shirt to wipe off the door handle before shoving the picks, still loose, into her back pocket. Shelly glanced up the hall before looking back out into the lobby. A quick glance into the open area behind the guard's station revealed that the security guard was absorbed in his iPad. He hadn't even noticed them.

Marcey's heart raced in her chest. This was the moment of truth. Charlie had done the mapping, but he hadn't done a dry run. Marcey hadn't mentioned that to Shelly. She wanted this to go off without a hitch. Telling

Shelly that this was entirely her plan, as opposed to building off of Charlie's preset seemed like a terrible idea. Fear clawed at her throat, choking the air out of her. Marcey jerked her head slightly to clear it.

"We go left." She led Shelly down a long hallway. It was dark, for the most part. Off the hallway were rooms containing bookshelves upon bookshelves of files. Marcey barely saw them. She was counting doorways. PN-45-A-76 was housed in the seventh door to the left, back five rows of shelves on the back side toward the floor.

They ducked into an alcove when a clerk hurried by, a stack of paperwork on a cart pushed before him. He hummed Drake as he worked, selecting files and putting others away. Marcey flattened her back against the wall as he walked by. They went unnoticed. And she exhaled shakily.

Shelly's fingers closed around Marcey's hand and tugged her forward into the seventh door on the left. It stood open, but that was not uncommon. Each of these doors was like that, left partway open. Was it because there was so much crap stored in here that the security system that rented the space wasn't worried that anyone would figure out what was tucked away in their archive? That had to be it. Nothing else made sense.

PN-45-A-76 was a small brown box containing a flash drive on a keychain with a Japanese anime cat's face printed on it. Marcey stared down at it for a moment before tugging it out and attaching it to her keys. She put the box back and grabbed a few other smaller file boxes. "Anything else we need in here?" she asked Shelly.

Shelly had found one of the carts. Marcey dumped the files into it and fell into step beside Shelly. They were silent until the kid with the cart backed out of the room. "Oh," Marcey said. She smiled, not unkindly, at the kid with the headphones. "Haven't seen you down here before..."

"I'm new," he confessed. "I didn't realize there were other clerks."

Shelly laughed. "Oh, there aren't. We're just down here because we're not used to you being here. That vacancy's been a pain in the ass."

He smiled sheepishly. "Ha, they said it was open for a while."

That's how Charlie did his dry run. No one down here to ask any questions. So why not take it then? Marcey frowned but said nothing.

Shelly flipped him a set of keys. "Thanks for keeping an eye on the place. Looks like we won't be down here as much now."

He smiled. Later, Marcey would understand that her reaction, to bristle and ask why Shelly was making herself *memorable* to a person they were actively stealing from, was unfounded. Shelly was a transgender woman. She was memorable in her very presence. It was the act of creating a memory that was not about her face or her voice or her height that dictated her role on the con. This was as foolproof a defense mechanism as anything Marcey had ever seen.

She felt like an asshole, sitting in what had to be one of the last internet cafés in all of New York, waiting for Kim and Gwen to come and meet them.

"Why did you do it?"

"Memory is like a sieve. People look at you, they make a snap judgment. They look at me, they make an entirely different snap judgment. What you have to do is redirect that judgment onto something that, ultimately, makes you forgettable. A sieve can only catch so much, you know."

"So, what would I want to distract from?"

"The fact that you have no idea what you're doing would be a good start." Shelly laughed. "Or the fact that you're a midget."

"Not all of us are fucking giants," Marcey grumbled. The anime cat keychain dangled from her keys. "This isn't going to like, infect the entire city with some virus, is it?"

"Fuck if I know," Shelly answered. "That's Kim's job. If I were to touch a computer it'd blow up. But that's probably why we're here, to see what might happen."

"What could be on here?"

Shelly shrugged. "No idea."

Marcey stared at the smiling cat. "I hope it's nothing bad."

CHAPTER 21

Marcey, Found Out

KIM WASN'T ABLE TO CRACK the flash drive at the internet café, nor was she able to break into it using the desktop computer she'd built from scratch in the basement of her parent's bookshop. Gwen was trying other contacts that might know something about the Monument's design, and Shelly was asking around as well. Everyone was busy with other contacts, the criminal sort of contacts that Marcey didn't really have. It left Marcey with very little to do.

On Friday, Marcey started her monthly pilgrimage up to see Darius. She was halfway between Albany and Saratoga Springs, heading north on Route 9, when Kat called her. There were still patches of snow on the ground, patchy bits of white against the muddy brown of spring starting to set in. Marcey glanced around, looking for cops, before she answered the phone.

"I'm driving." She fiddled with her headphones, jamming them into her ears one handed and then using both hands, resting on top of the steering wheel, to plug the headphones into her phone's jack.

"Are you?" Kat sounded distant, as though filtered through a fog. Marcey's eyes narrowed. It was affected nonchalance. "Well, if talking to me is illegal, I'd best let you go—"

"No, no, it's okay," Marcey interjected. "I'm fine, I have hands-free. What's up?"

"I wanted to check up on you, see how you were doing. I got a call from Kim Montou asking what I knew about encryption keys... Have you gone and found yourself a crew?" There was a pause before Kat added, almost offhandedly, "I wish you'd have told me, Marcey. I could've helped you get them to commit." There was disinterest in Kat's voice. Marcey guessed she didn't want to talk about this.

"She called you?" Marcey let out a short bark of laughter. The Kim Montou Marcey was starting to get to know again was not the sort of person who readily asked people for help. "God, she must be really stumped."

"Or the encryption is based in something other than a computer language. My appreciation of art led me to a different possibility." Kat paused. "She was less than amused when I told her this, though."

"Oh, you appreciate the art of messing with Kim's head now?"

"You think so poorly of me, Marcey." Kat's smile crept into her voice. Marcey could picture her: tapping her finger on her chin, a coy smile on her face. Her eyes though—they would be deathly serious, as they always were. "I wouldn't mess with anyone's head unless they asked."

"Well, in *that* case." Marcey rolled her eyes. "Were you able to help her out at all? The key, we think, will get us into this flash drive that Charlie had identified as a potential aid to getting into the Monument."

"I think I was able to provide her with a good starting point. The cypher, as far as she can tell, is based on something utterly inane. I told her maybe counting brush strokes would help."

"Counting...brush strokes?"

"Quite," Kat agreed. "It's an old form of communication. It would give the key to only one who was in the presence of the work of art in question. It allows a certain level of discretion therefore. And a security measure to boot."

"You think the key is in the painting—"

"Yes, and Kim was able to break in." There was a sound like rustling papers in the background. "I suspect you'll be wanting more of my expertise going forward."

The pronouncement was so innocent, but it was the way Kat said it, casual, as though there was nothing to it, that sent a shock of fear down Marcey's spine. Fear of losing the small modicum of control she had over the situation. Kat could take command and Marcey would follow her without question, but that was not the game. For this game to work, Kat had to be the one doing Marcey's bidding, not the other way around, or else

Marcey would find herself in hot water. No, that was unacceptable. Marcey thought back to the plan, to Charlie's instructions, and steeled herself for what was to come. "No. I'm going to do this in the usual way, Kat. Charlie did it that way, I want to as well. The plot gets too complex if there are too many players."

"I don't know if you've realized, darling, but there are too many players to begin with." Without another word, Kat disconnected the call. Kat's reaction was as predictable as any Marcey had ever encountered.

"Fuck it," Marcey muttered. Her eyes were trained on the road. The forest that lined Route 9 was starting to fade away into the town of Saratoga. She could deal with deciphering the mercurial nature of Kat Barber another day.

An hour and a half later, Marcey pulled into the village of Dannemora. The drive was monotonous, and she barely noticed the side roads with their guards in high towers as she wound around the outer walls of the super-max part of the prison. The part of the prison where Darius spent his days was not here, but rather in the old, brick structure with high, narrow windows topped in a snarl of barbed wire. This was where the prison did group therapy with a set of low-risk inmates. Darius had gotten his GED and bachelor's here, in the shell of an old mental hospital.

Marcey swung into a visitor's parking spot, her front bumper nudging a lingering early April snowbank. Outside, the temperature was chilly, and Marcey hurriedly buttoned her jacket. She made her way inside, up the shallow steps and through the doors.

It always struck her how easy it was to walk into the prison. It looked a bit like an elementary school, a putrid shade of fifties industrial teal flooring and tile rising high up against the wall. The visiting area was off to her right and the guard station to her left. Marcey passed her driver's license over to the guard. He smiled at her. He was always at the guard station when Marcey visited. Always smiling and always watching her every move.

"Ms. Daniels." He typed her name into the antiquated computer that sat yellowing before him. "It's good to see you back." He sucked his teeth and shook his head. "I swear you come up more than anyone else."

"I have to." Marcey rose onto her toes to get a full look into the guard station. They sat at least three feet above the floor in the atrium. She grinned at the guard. "Otherwise I wouldn't get to see you, Herb. Or the lovely scenery."

"Must be nice to get outta the city for a while," Herb replied. He hit a key again and frowned. The computer made a whirring, whining noise and he tried again. "That can't be right... This says you've been taken off the list of approved visitors..." His brow furrowed. He clicked a key, muttering. "Did Johnson...?"

Marcey's stomach dropped, settling somewhere around her knees. Something had happened. That was why Kat had called.

Herb got up. The chair behind him creaked. He picked up her license in one hand and headed toward the back of the room. There was another door at the back, but Marcey didn't know where it went.

She craned her neck to see why she'd been rejected. The bulletproof glass that surrounded the guard station made it impossible to see anything.

All the words of warning about Kat Barber, about her relationship with the law and with Wei Topeté echoed in Marcey's mind. *Fuck*. She was so fucked. Why hadn't Kat warned her?

A balding man that Marcey had never seen before returned with Herb, his expression grave. He leaned over, moused through a few screens, and shook his head. He frowned, then glanced from Marcey to her license to the screen. "Ms. Daniels, have you been out of the country in the past few weeks?"

She nodded, carefully mute. She wasn't giving them anything.

"You've been flagged by ICE."

"What does immigration care where I've been?"

Herb shrugged. "Beats me. I'd get in touch with your local DA's office. Usually these sorts of things sort themselves out pretty quickly. It's probably just precautionary."

His supervisor scowled and clicked a few more keys.

A strange ringing filled Marcey's ears. "Okay." She backed away slowly. "I'll get in touch with the DA's office and try and figure out what's going on."

Herb and his supervisor glanced at each other. "You do that, Ms. Daniels. Don't forget your license, though."

She had to get out of there. Marcey swallowed, hurried back over to the guard station to collect her wallet and walked as briskly as she dared out of the prison. Once she was beyond the heavy exterior doors, she broke into a run and practically threw herself into the car. She sat there, fingers tight on the steering wheel, and exhaled shakily. She was so fucked.

They *knew*.

They knew who she was and what she was doing. They knew that she had Charlie's book. The one secret Marcey'd been desperate to keep from Topeté seemed to be out in the open now. Kat had to have said something. It was the only way. But why? Marcey's thoughts raced. This was retribution for what had happened in London. Marcey wasn't stupid; she knew what she'd done to Topeté. And if Topeté had pulled this, it meant that Johnson's knowledge of this enterprise wasn't far behind Topeté's own. Christ, she was fucked.

Marcey was almost surprised she hadn't been arrested again. Linda always was the petty, vindictive type.

There was nothing left to do. With a final glance up at the prison, Marcey choked down her anger and gunned the engine. She would fix this. She would deal with Johnson and Topeté too. They'd never fuck with anyone like this again.

⊰⧉⊱

It was a five-hour drive back to the city, alone with her thoughts and her seething anger. She was exhausted by the time she pulled off into a small rest area south of Albany to pee and get some coffee. She drove for three hours along back roads through the Adirondack Mountains, stewing. The thick forests killed any chance of cell phone reception. It was for the best; she was too angry to talk at the start of her trip southward anyway.

She called Kat from where she sat in the rest area parking lot. The phone rang three times before a sleepy-sounding Kat answered. "You fucked me," Marcey growled into the phone.

"I did." Kat didn't sound confused at Marcey's accusation. If anything, she sounded amused.

"No, you *fucked* me, Kat. Got me put on some sort of list so now I can't see Darius. I've driven almost nine hours today already for nothing. Now all I can hope for is a phone call that I could just as easily had sitting on my ass in Central Park." Marcey saw red. She wanted to reach through the phone and shake Kat. How was she so calm?

"Darling…"

"Don't you *dare*," Marcey hissed. Her fingers were white around her phone. All around her, families drifted in from the road to use the facilities. A young-looking guy got out of a battered Subaru Outback and tipped his hat at her. Marcey looked away, guilt pulling at her. She was yelling at the woman she'd had a fling with in the privacy of her car. She was pretty sure she looked like a damn fool.

A quiet rustling sound came over the phone. Marcey closed her eyes, drawing her knees up to her chest. She pictured Kat wrapping herself in a sheet, crossing the room and leaving the sleeping form beside her—the true culprit in this crime—behind. "Marcey, I—" Kat fumbled for the words.

Marcey waited. Kat was going to explain this, and her explanation had better be good because Marcey was so close to cutting her loose and forgoing this whole thing. It would be so much easier to not be involved with someone like Kat Barber, who came with a warning label the size of fucking Texas.

"I only just caught wind of it. Wei called me—told me—about twenty minutes ago. There wasn't time to tell you."

The words bit at the back of Marcey's throat, cutting her down and curling around her. Kat knew *exactly* what to say to dispel the blame from herself. Was it even true? Had Kat sent Marcey on a ten-hour trip just to see what would happen? She could, and she would. Whatever trust they'd built fell away. This was intentional. Had to be. Marcey hated her for it. Hated how easily she could make Marcey feel for her. She'd known, when they'd spoken earlier, she'd known and she'd said nothing. "You'd already left… and I wasn't sure until I saw the paperwork." Kat sighed, long and loud, the exhalation of smoke in an already hazy room. "Wei has your name, Marcey. She has your name and she knows what we did together."

"Because you told her?" Marcey's tone was accusatory.

Kat scoffed. "Do you think I'm stupid?"

"Pretty stupid for an art thief to be involved with a woman who *catches art thieves* for a living," Marcey shot back. "What did you do? Get caught somewhere and have to sing like a canary to get out?" She was building into a rant. Kat ignored the barb. Marcey stopped herself, swallowed, and thought of the end goal. "How the hell does she even know who I am if you didn't tell her?"

"You said William arrested you, down at the Perôt, right? They work together, Marcey. People share information. Wei's in New York right now. Surely you'd put this together by now."

Marcey pressed her lips into a thin line. Of course she had. Letting Kat believe her to be stupider than she was, though, that was far more important. Marcey counted to five and then pushed her voice to the brink of annoyance. "I did," she said though gritted teeth. "I did and I hoped—I stupidly hoped that maybe I could go unnoticed. Or that your sense of decency would prevent you from dragging my name into this until we're able to put the full plan in place."

"You dragged your name into this on your own. She was bound to find out. You're not exactly good at being careful."

"Neither are you."

"Humph."

The flippant dismissal, the assumption it was Marcey who had brought this upon herself, rather than Kat, who loved the sound of her own voice, had Marcey wanting to scream at her. To tell her that Charlie never wanted her to have the book in the first place, and that Marcey was only having her along because she wanted access to that painting.

No, that wasn't the tactic. Kat had to be handled differently or she'd run straight into the arms of Topeté, vindictive and hurt. She could ruin *everything.* "You're the one who told her in the first place. This, all of this, it could turn on a dime, Kat, and it's *your* plot."

There was too much resting on this plot to let Kat's fragile ego get in the way. Darius was going to be paroled. Marcey was going to have a future for him where they could be safe, they could be happy. Where Linda Johnson could never touch them again. Kat couldn't influence that goal.

"But in the end, it won't be my glory, will it?" There was a harsh edge to Kat's voice. It set Marcey on edge. That same flintiness she'd seen in person. It was hard, cutting like a knife through the silence of her car. It was black here. Bleak. "Little girl wandering into a world she doesn't understand, basking in the glory of those who came before her."

"No," Marcey answered coldly. "You know my reasons for doing this. You know I don't give a shit about Charlie or his legacy or whatever bullshit you guys have wrapped up in this mythical man. Your girlfriend getting in the way of things was never part of Charlie's plan, was it? It isn't part of mine either. Keep her out of this."

Marcey ran a tired hand through her hair. She wanted to be *home*, not two hours from the city. She didn't like the vast open space of here—the trees and the granite-hearted mountains that surround this rest stop. She was used to the fast pace and endless light of the city. All this green, all this space, was wonderful, but it was not what she wanted.

What do you want?

She hated that she let herself want Kat Barber. Was she driven by lust and revenge? Or did she like this as much as Kat seemed to? Did she like the games and the subterfuge? She wanted to ruin Linda Johnson's career, but fuck, in this moment she wanted Kat Barber. To strangle her or kiss her, Marcey didn't know. But she wanted it so badly that she was willing to do pretty much anything.

"Look," Kat began. "Wei has her ways of doing things. I often don't find out what she does until it's too late and they're already done. It means that I must plan for contingencies within contingencies, to be alert to any little morsel she thinks to throw my way." Kat sighed deeply. "Though I wonder..." Kat trailed off, pensive. "If Johnson's trying to right her final case—the one that didn't work out—wouldn't she be more interested in finding a way to implicate..." Kat's breath caught. "Oh," she said. "Bugger."

"That's all you have to say? Fucking 'bugger'?"

"Quiet," Kat hissed. There was more rustling, like she was digging through a huge pile of papers. "There's something we're missing. Something I'm not seeing... I need to..." She paused for a moment, inhaling sharply before speaking again. "I'm coming. With the painting. I'll see you shortly and I promise I'll tell you everything once I confirm. This...this could get messy, Marcey." And then she was gone again, her voice fading out into nothingness.

The weight of the world settled onto Marcey's shoulders, heavy and unyielding.

In her mind's eye, as she plugged the auxiliary cord back into her phone and navigated back to her music app, Marcey saw how this would end. It was a twisted web that Kat wove, and Marcey still wasn't sure what was on the other side. The problem was that she had to know. Getting Kat to admit her end game was the only way this would ever work. Marcey was the one who should have been holding all the cards. She couldn't catch herself waiting for Kat to deal her pocket ace into a round.

She was missing something. There was more to this. The pieces weren't slotting into place. Kat's sudden panic and change of plans; why Linda Johnson wanted the book. Nothing made sense, but it carried the thread of what could be the weight of it. It was not a matter, now, of getting Kat to tell the truth.

"What the hell are you hiding?" Marcey asked the empty car.

Kat wanted more from this heist than anyone else, and Marcey couldn't put her finger on *what* it was that Kat wanted. It bothered her more and more with every passing moment. There was something *more* going on here, she knew that much. However, it couldn't be about some deal struck in Barcelona. No, there was something more complicated at work.

She swallowed, thinking of Kat. Marcey wanted—no, she needed—to see Kat pay for what she'd bargained away that wasn't hers. The urge was strong. She didn't know why though. What was it about Kat in that moment of weakness when she was caught that made Marcey so angry? What could she possibly have offered Topeté that the woman wasn't already getting?

Marcey threw the car into gear. She had to get back to her own turf. Her expression was dark as she got back onto the southbound highway, mulling over everything Kat said. Marcey's scowl deepened, her focus on the road.

Twenty minutes later, she reached for her phone and dialed Shelly's number. "Hey."

"How is your friend?"

"Couldn't see him."

"Why not?"

"Kat's Interpol agent."

Shelly laughed. "I told you it was a bad idea to sleep with her, Marcey."

"I get it, okay. I gotta deal with this. It sucks." She bit her lip. "I'm sorry. I'm pissed at Kat, not you. I actually didn't call you to talk about it either."

"Well, so long as I don't have to add relationship counselor to my resume..." Shelly laughed again, only this time it was with genuine amusement. "What did you need?"

"How do I tell Kim and Gwen that Kat's inserting herself into this heist and wants to meet up with us once she's got the painting stateside?"

"Well, first, you should get back from Siberia or wherever the hell it is you went."

"I'm on my way back. I'm about an hour and change away now."

"I'd imagine." Shelly paused, as though thinking. "You sound sad, Marcey. It can't just be because you couldn't get in. That anger is understandable. The sadness, though..."

"Kat called me, on the way up. She didn't think to mention that this ten-hour round trip would be worthless. It was all a game to her, I think, to see if I'd catch her in the lie."

"Oh, Marcey..." Shelly sighed deeply, and Marcey prepared herself for a lecture on her choices. It came as a surprise when Shelly simply added, "Perhaps she didn't know until it was too late."

Marcey wasn't inclined to think so, but she kept it to herself. "Maybe. That's what she said...but I'm not sure I believe her."

They lapsed into silence for a moment before Shelly spoke again. "Drive safely. Go see Kim and Gwen. Tell them why you have to do this. They'll understand."

Will they, though? Marcey thought darkly as she hung up. Nothing was certain in this business.

CHAPTER 22

Wei, Fretting

THERE'D BEEN MANY MOMENTS IN Wei's life she'd later come to regret. For every action taken there was a trail of hurt behind it. To hurt had become her nature. It had become habit, cutting deeply into her psyche and hardening her soul. In time, she came to view her ability to absorb and inflict personal pain as an asset. She was a trained investigator. She spent hours poring over documents, looking for threads and connections. Finding patterns of terrorism and the easy way money, people, and goods slipped around the world when no one thought to look for them.

Those patterns had drawn Wei into their fold, making a career out of tracking them, pulling little threads of information apart and sewing them into larger canvases of conspiracy. She'd taken what little she could, ferreting her way into a murky underworld with the intent of blowing it wide open, only to find herself face-to-face with a man with dark, curly hair and a slightly crooked nose. He'd offered her assistance, taken a priceless sketch off her hands for her trouble, and thus began a relationship Wei had spent half of her career trying to forget about.

Now though, the chance to be rid of that monkey on her back was too strong. It was time to stop letting a ghost and a wish for different life choices rule her life.

Two problems stood in her way: the book and Kat.

Kat was not, in fact, a true problem, as much as Wei sometimes wished she could be labeled as such. Love, twisted though it was, lingered in the heavy silences of their relationship. They were two people crashing together, remembering their dirty secrets and airing out who they truly were only to each other. Kat knew Wei's secrets, and Wei knew Kat's secrets.

It was why they worked.

Sometimes though, Kat used this secret. She used it to remind Wei that despite everything she did, the passive-aggressive nods in her direction by some of her peers in Lyon were entirely earned. Wei hated lying about this to them, to Johnson, hell, even to LePage—though she was fairly certain he had worked out the details on his own and was simply waiting for the appropriate moment to broadcast his knowledge. She hated lying to Kat that there was nothing to their relationship either.

This was another lie, but this one, at least, was built on some modicum of good intentions.

Much could be said about the disinterested look on her face as she sat smoking her cigarette on bench in a small park not far from her hotel, intent on meeting a criminal. She didn't know the park's name— it was unimportant to Wei. Going into a situation uninformed like this was not what a good agent of an international organization tasked with counterterrorism did. She had to be aware of herself, of her choices. Did she regret this choice? The nicotine hit did little to quell her anxiety over this meeting. She wasn't sure what to expect from it, and already she was certain she would come to regret it.

She was sitting in a sunbeam, soaking in the weak spring warmth that broke through the patchy clouds and gray-blue sky above. The shadow of a tall woman fell across Wei's face. She squinted, and then a slow smile pulled at her lips. "It's a bit cold for this," she said.

"Maybe, but it's finally warm enough to be outside." Shelly Orietti was wearing a gray wool coat, unbuckled at the waist with a tunic and thick leggings tucked into boots underneath. She sat down next to Wei. Her hair—an Indian weave Wei was envious of—fell over one shoulder. "Topeté."

"Shelly." Wei nodded coolly. She stubbed out her cigarette. "I heard there's a crew together now. And that you're on it."

"I heard that you're walking a fine line between legal and illegal these days. Wonder if we've been talkin' to the same people." Shelly met Wei's gaze evenly. "You want something that I don't think you know how to get without breaking the law."

"Oh? And what is that?"

"You want to catch lightning in a bottle and turn it to do your bidding. Or to do something that could be considered your bidding, in a perfect world. It won't work. Freedom doesn't come that cheap these days."

"You're rather sure of that."

"Let's just say that we've known each other a long time and if she gets involved in this directly, it'll be all you can do to keep her name clear long enough to execute your endgame."

Wei itched for another cigarette. "Then you've guessed the play."

"Figured it out when you called me about the girl and Charlie's book. You're a fool for trying it again after Barcelona. Rio was dangerous enough. Johnson almost caught you in your lie once—who's to say she won't catch ya at the game this time? LePage is sharp enough to put it together and you're saddled with him for better or for worse." Shelly reached over and touched Wei's forearm. "You need to think about why you're doing this and if you want to tell her why you're doing this. She's gonna want to know. Sooner rather than later. If she doesn't already suspect. In which case you're fucked anyway because she'll cut her losses at the soonest sign of engagement..."

"I can't tell her. She'll never let me—"

"No. She wouldn't. That's why you have to." Shelly stared up at the shifting clouds overhead. Her eyes fluttered closed. "This is a mess."

"I just want her safe." Wei's hands clenched into fists. They were shaking. She dug in her pocket for another cigarette. "That's...the right thing to do. Free us all from the yoke that Charlie Mock's put around our necks. He saw so much he never talked about. Sometimes I think Rio was his greatest act of mercy. Like God himself came down and wrecked that job before it could get off the ground and we could all end up in jail. Noble, isn't it?" She lit the cigarette and sat back, waiting for Shelly to pass judgment on her.

"Nobility in this line of work is decidedly overrated. As is honor amongst thieves." Shelly's expression was open, kind as she angled herself to face Wei. It was the most open Wei could ever remember seeing her face. "But I'm feeling charitable and you look like a sad sack of lovesick bones. The plan's moving forward. Kat's inserted herself into the play. She's going to put it all together and see your long game, Wei."

"Why?" They weren't on the same side. Or rather, their loyalties were not, but Wei would always go to Kat, no matter what anyone else said. Kat was her whole world, twisted as it was. She wouldn't let anyone take Kat from her. "Why tell me, Shelly? There's no love between us. I took the man you loved away from you, let him die alone in jail."

"Because I believe in a level playing field, Topeté. The girl is young, but she's sharp. She'll pick up on what you're doing soon enough. It's all there in the book, after all. And Kat's pushing her toward an inevitable conclusion, as I'm sure you know." Shelly shook her head. "That was a cruel trick you played on the girl, taking away her best friend. Crueler and more foolish even than what you did to Charlie and me. Might have overplayed your hand. She's ticked." Getting to her feet, Shelly stared down at Wei for a moment longer, fiddling with her purse strap. "You should talk to her."

Wei sucked on her cigarette and shook her head. "That defeats the purpose. I need her ignorant, as I needed you to be as well."

"Shame I'm so observant, then." Shelly's expression was wry. "Or maybe's more of a shame that you're in every damn book in the city as an investigator willin' to look the other way. Being thirsty for a cushy job isn't a good look, Wei. That's marked you since before you sold your soul to Interpol. Now you've got that and you're facin' down another one. Gettin' what you want by sleeping with the opposition won't get you anywhere. Shame that Johnson's probably aware of it already and is playin' you."

Wei took another drag. "Shame indeed." She exhaled. Smoke curled in the air for a moment before it dissipated. She had to let herself be played, because it was in the moment when the game ended that Wei would strike. She tilted her head, looking at Shelly. "We're all in the same boat, then. I trust you will keep this to yourself, for the time being?"

Shelly nodded. "I won't be around if Johnson comes calling for you."

"Then I don't want to see you again until this is over."

"Consider me gone."

And she was gone, in a swirl of gray coat and pale leggings. Wei watched her retreating until she cut down a block, heading south toward the subway station. She sat on her park bench, immobile in the ray of sunshine. It was foolish to think she could play Shelly. The woman saw much. She was a formidable foe. There was a reason Charlie Mock had loved her.

Charlie Mock's book was Linda Johnson's white whale. Johnson didn't know what was in it, only that the criminals documented on the pages would be enough to solve most, if not all, of the white-collar crime she'd encountered during her career. Johnson wanted that and she wanted petty revenge on the girl. Not for reasons that made sense to Wei. The connection between the girl and Charlie was lost on Johnson still. She didn't think about the relationships that existed behind the pages of Charlie's book, the ways in which the world would be altered if those names were ever to get out. Johnson didn't know that Wei would be ruined should the contents of that book ever leak. That LePage would be no better off. Charlie Mock had kept careful records for a reason: mutually assured destruction.

Wei sucked on her cigarette and thought of Kat. Johnson knew about Kat only in the loosest sense. She knew of her in the way that LePage knew of Kat: the art thief, the bored rich girl turned criminal because there was nothing else going for her in her life; the woman who got caught in Barcelona. What Johnson didn't know about Kat, about Wei and Kat's relationship, could fill Charlie's book five times over. Kat was so much more than some debutante gone bad.

Wei pulled her phone from her pocket and navigated to an app she rarely used. Guilt ate at her, but Kat was cagey at the best of times and sometimes, only sometimes, Wei really needed to know where she was. It was a violation, a breaking of trust, and something Wei did not use lightly.

But there, clear as day, was all the proof she needed that Shelly wasn't fucking with her. Kat Barber's phone, flashing a location in the city. She flicked her cigarette away and got to her feet. She walked north, past dull office buildings, for a long time. The shade was cold, and the breeze off the river wasn't warm. Wei cut over a subway vent and wrinkled her nose. The smell was awful, warm garbage mixed with sewage. People cluttered the sidewalks, heads down and walking briskly.

After close to fifteen blocks, Wei checked her phone again and cut east, going up three blocks before she found herself looking up at a boutique hotel entryway. A short laugh escaped Wei's lips. Of *course*. She pushed the door open and walked up a flight of stairs into the lobby.

Inside it was warm, and the air was still. Most of the hotel's patrons were either asleep or had already left for a day of tourism. The guy at the front desk gave her a disinterested look and returned to his newspaper. Wei spared him a thin smile before pushing open the fire door to the stairs. Wei climbed to the third floor and walked to the room at the back of the building.

Kat was a creature of habit. She liked everything in her life to be just so. Wei was accustomed to hotels like this—small, posh, and hard to find if one didn't know where to look. She took rooms on the third floor, as far to the back of the building as possible. There was only one door this far back. Wei knocked on it, stood back, fidgeted. Wanted another cigarette.

When the door opened, Kat stood there for a moment, sleep-tousled and confused. "What are you doing here?" She sounded accusatory, but she stood aside to let Wei inside.

The curtains were drawn and the room smelled of hotel chemicals and Kat. The smell of her shampoo and her perfume mixed into a heady combination that had Wei inhaling deeply, calming with each pull of air. Kat bent and switched on a lamp, eyeing Wei with a curious expression. The question still dangled, heavy in the air.

Wei shrugged off her coat, draped it over a chair. "I wanted to see you."

"I didn't tell you where I was." Kat sat on the bed, drawing the throw over her legs. She looked small, her hair frizzing a blonde halo in the lamplight. A surge of affection shot through Wei, and she stepped closer, sitting down beside Kat on the bed and letting Kat curl into her. "How did you find me?"

"You're predictable," Wei said. A small huff of laughter escaped Kat's lips before she hummed, curling her arms around Wei's waist and snuggling closer. "Wasn't hard to pick out which hotel you'd go to, what floor you'd be on."

"You're lying," Kat answered. "Someone's told you I was in town."

Wei wasn't about to correct her. Kat was, after all, very good at lying. Kat's fingers tugged on the soft material of Wei's sweater. Wei saw it for what it was, saw the pout in Kat's lips and the clever manipulation of Wei's emotions in the way Kat's fingers danced over her body. This was all a game to Kat, and this was the next step in the game. "You're still cross with me."

Making no effort to push Kat away was hard, far harder than Wei had ever thought possible. She was here for a reason, with Kat for a reason. Shelly's words were a warning. This was escalating, and quickly. "I'm sorry. It's easier to do this over video chat…" Wei trailed off, looked down at her hands, fidgeted. She hated the indecisiveness of this. There was no reason she should be like this. She and Kat had made their peace with what Kat did. It was for a good reason. A justified cause.

But it still hurt so much.

"I'm sorry too," Kat said. Her fingers were gentle, brushing the hair away from Wei's forehead, tucking it behind Wei's ear. "For what I did. I thought it was the right move... It seemed to be the sort of thing that would keep her guessing...keep her coming back."

"We never agreed to that." She'd never been bothered by Kat's games with other women. Wei wanted to know and wanted to consent. With this girl, Kat hadn't been forthcoming, and Wei's anger at Kat—at the girl—had only grown in the time since she'd seen them together.

Kat rolled onto her back, staring up at the painted ceiling of the hotel room. "We never agreed to anything. We don't talk about anything. We just *are*, Wei. And because of that sometimes sacrifices must be made for the good of the end goal."

I saw you, she did not say. *In Nev's apartment, watching like some Peeping Tom. Did you enjoy it, love of mine?* Wei's stomach clenched. She focused on the wall, the swirling patterns reminding her of a time when they could look up at the sky together and not see two different things, clad in easy lies and the good-natured acceptance that came with understanding that so much of who they were was lies.

And worse still, Wei did not feel anything at all when Kat sat back up, her lips twisted into a grimace of concern. She tugged at Wei's shoulder, fingers brushing against Wei's cheek. "Look at me," she said.

Wei met her green-eyed gaze and felt only regret. "Will you do it again?" she asked, not for the first time.

Kat kissed her, rolling on top of Wei and pushing her down into the soft mattress. It was a drowning kiss, the sort that choked away all of Wei's fears and set them to rest. Wei let it happen, her eyes fluttering closed as Kat tugged at her sweater and pushed it up enough to touch smooth skin.

In the darkness of this hotel room, in the darkness of the unspoken agreement between them, Wei splintered into a million tiny pieces. Pieces that could only be reassembled at the hands of Kat Barber. Over and over again. Fuck, fight, fuck, fight. Everything would be good for a month or two and something would happen. Without Kat there was nothing for

Wei, nothing but the void that could not even be filled by her lingering presence. Kat was everything to Wei—breath, the heart beating in her chest. Wei loved her desperately, and without her there were just fragments of memories half-forgotten.

Who even was she, before Kat Barber made and then unmade her? Kat had taken her heart and cast it in gold. Rendering Wei incapable of wanting anything more. They belonged together, and they were nothing apart.

And when Kat unmade Wei that night, it was a lie Wei could almost believe.

CHAPTER 23

Marcey, Making Friends

"THAT IS A SPECTACULARLY BAD idea." Kim smacked her lips around a fry and gesticulated wildly with another. Perched on the stool in the far corner of Shelly's kitchen, Kim looked all angles, her small frame condensed into an even smaller space of knees, elbows, and a McDonald's Happy Meal. "Like, I'm pretty sure the only worse idea would be her trying to bring in Topeté."

Kat's painting had arrived that morning. Kim had skipped out on Hon-Ya and Gwen had showed up from wherever she stayed when she was in New York to open the crate. Marcey was sweaty and exhausted, chewing pensively on a chicken nugget. They'd gone to the McDonald's around the corner from Shelly's apartment for milkshakes and dinner for Marcey and Kim. Shelly was cooking something vegetarian for herself and Gwen; it smelled of curry and the nutty whiff of lentils.

"That ship's sailed, sweetie." Shelly tapped the spoon against the side of the pan and turned the burner off.

Gwen frowned, passing Shelly a bowl. "What do you mean?"

"Exactly what I said," Shelly answered. She filled the bowl with lentils and onions and turned to the rice maker. "If Kat is involved, Topeté is involved. They're a package deal, for better or for worse. I don't know if she'll try and directly involve Topeté, but I wouldn't put anything past Kat Barber."

"I don't like that." Gwen took the bowl from Shelly and retreated to her stool. "I don't like being beholden to the whims of someone who makes getting caught her damn MO."

"Then why stick around?" Marcey demanded. "No one is keeping you here."

Gwen leveled her spoon at Marcey. "That's where you're wrong. You have the book, Marcey. You have the book and any mistake you make has the potential to cost me my freedom. So forgive me if I want to keep track of you and the book to make sure you don't fuck me and everyone else here."

The room grew colder, Gwen's expression hardening and Marcey's anger rising with each passing second. This was *her* job. Gwen couldn't dictate the terms to her like that. No one could. Marcey lowered the french fry she had in her hand and set it down beside the pool of ketchup she and Kim were sharing.

"That isn't how this is going to work." Marcey's voice was barely over a croak. She was holding back so much. All the emotion over Darius and being barred from seeing him, they were threatening to bubble over. The terrifying fact that his release might get pushed back because of Charlie Mock hung heavy around her. "I have the book, yes. Which means that I can end you, Gwen. I can end you and not even worry about it." She exhaled. "We will do this my way. Not Kat Barber's way, not your way, and certainly not any way that's going to involve goddamn Interpol."

"Her way is Charlie's way, Gwen," Shelly clarified. She glanced sympathetically over at Marcey before continuing. "Charlie wanted this job done because it was meant to be his legacy, his final fuck you to Linda Johnson and your ex. Why are you still worried? We're going to get the bastard for what he did to you and to Charlie."

Gwen frowned. Marcey scowled at her. Gwen turned away. "Look, it isn't that I don't love this idea. Screwing Linda Johnson? That's fucking beautiful. I just don't understand why the fuck Kat Barber has to be involved at all."

"Because she has the goddamn painting."

"She's sent us the painting, Marcey. We have it. She isn't fucking here. Why not take it and ditch her? We'll give her her cut, which is what she deserves, but why not just take it and bail?" Gwen gestured with her spoon. "Look, I know that you've got some sort of emotional bullshit going on with Kat or whatever, but she's bad fucking news and if she stays I walk."

"We *all* should walk if Kat sticks around." Kim scowled down into her pool of ketchup, got up, and went to the refrigerator to get the bottle. She squirted more onto her plate. "Marcey is too new to this to be effective. She might have Charlie's plans, but she's also done something Charlie never did—"

"Which is?" Marcey growled, kicking Kim under the table.

"You got in with Kat Barber."

"Kim, I hate to break it to you, but Charlie was also in deep with Kat Barber. Everything about this job screams her, even if she can't claim direct involvement." Shelly sighed. "We've all made mistakes in our past. But it's done. The past is the past. We need to talk about the job. Kat's inserting herself into it adds a wrinkle, and *we* need to consider, *together,* what she's after, in wanting to come along." She leveled a stern gaze at Marcey. "Which means no more threatening people with their freedoms if they're exposed. It means being goddamn honest about what's goin' on for you so that we can communicate and determine how best to move forward."

"Nothing is going on with me." Marcey set her chicken nugget aside, suddenly not hungry. Leaning forward, she wrapped her hands around the torn knees of her jeans.

Gwen rolled her eyes. "Sure there isn't."

"You have been pretty bitchy since you got back from upstate," Kim added.

The idea of telling this room full of relative strangers what she felt was revolting to Marcey. No one needed to know what she was feeling, or how deeply confused she was about the myriad of emotions racing through her. She swallowed, biting at her lip, and looked down at her hands. Her fingers picked at the fraying edges of her jeans. She didn't dare let them see her face, because if they saw her face, if they saw the pained look she knew she couldn't keep from her eyes, she would lose it.

"I went to see my friend up at Clinton," Marcey began. "You all know about him. Kim, I think probably best. He and I were tight, you know. Like brother and sister. He took the fall for everything we did in high school, everything that went wrong with Becca, Johnson's daughter. Becca and I dated for a while."

"More like had half the school in fits trying to figure out what was actually going on between you two," Kim muttered, stealing one of Marcey's fries. "And then half the school fighting over you both. And he just laughed and laughed."

"Shut up," Marcey ground out. "He went to prison, I got off. Devon Austin Jackson was his lawyer. Pro-bono. I think at Charlie's behest." Marcey exhaled shakily. "That's how I knew him, and why he was left in charge of Charlie's estate. Because Charlie knew that Devon would get me the book and the details of the job. He knew that I'd speak to him about it and get Shelly's name. He's planned this from the start. We're playing out his final game, guys. You were both named as potential people to be involved, and I took Shelly and Kat at their word that you'd be willing to engage. So fucking engage. Stop telling me that this is a bad idea. Stealing anything is a bad idea. My friend has been locked up for eight years because of a bad idea. I want this to be a crowning glory and *ruin* for Linda Johnson. I think we can do it. No, I know we can."

For a moment, no one said anything at all. Gwen set down her bowl on the counter and started a slow clap. "That's some speech, but it doesn't say shit about what Kat Barber's doing trying to fuck this up."

"I think there's something she isn't telling us. Something big. It probably doesn't have much to do with the technical execution of this job, but there's been too many moments when we've spoken—"

"When you've *fucked*."

"Okay, Kim, we get it," Marcey snapped. "It was a stupid fucking thing I did, pissing off Wei Topeté, but I think that might have been the point. Kat's got this…thing with Topeté." Marcey exhaled. "I know that you think they're like star-crossed lovers or whatever, forever doomed be on opposite sides of the same conflict, but there's something off about the way Kat talks about her. I can't put my finger on it; they're working against each other but I think toward the same goal. Pretty much all anyone's told me from jump is that Kat should have gotten Charlie's book. Don't you think it's strange that it ended up with me, rather than her?"

"You think Charlie knew about whatever is going on between them." Gwen was leaning against the counter, having picked her bowl back up and holding it under her chin. Her eyes narrowed, scrutinizing Marcey. "You think this is part of some longer game." Turning to Shelly, Gwen asked, "Something to punish her for Rio?"

"Not sure. It could be. The signs are definitely there. In giving you the book, Marcey, Charlie took away a bargaining chip both Kat and Topeté have been fighting over since Charlie got arrested." Shelly drummed her fingers thoughtfully against the counter.

"Fighting over?" Marcey frowned, and they looked at her expectantly. Wiping her hands left greasy marks on the edges of her paper napkin. "I guess it doesn't really matter. Kat's been caught a fair bit. Do you think some of that might be more to do with the fact that she's turned evidence or something for Topeté?"

"That seems a bit farfetched, even for Barber." Kim shook her head. "She's not the type to work without an agenda, and wanting the book is a good one. She can't get it, obviously, but if that's what we know she's really after, then maybe we keep it at arm's length."

"Kim?" Shelly asked. "Are you saying that you'll be okay with her coming in?"

"Whatever. Just don't expect me to be *nice.*"

"Wouldn't dream of it," Marcey replied. It didn't feel like much of a consolation. Both Kim and Gwen were as reluctant as Shelly to trust any involvement by Kat in Charlie's game, but Charlie had wanted her, and Marcey was inclined to agree. Everyone's fear of what Kat Barber could do was justified. Hadn't Marcey seen it herself in what they'd done upstate? That was Topeté though, it wasn't Kat. Kat didn't have that kind of power.

Would Kat ask Topeté to do something like that?

Would Topeté do something like that if Kat asked?

"I'll work with her, provided she pulls her own weight and doesn't try to freestyle." Gwen set her bowl down in the sink and ran the tap to cover the smeary orange on it with water. "I don't want her to take control of this job... You never know quite what she's planning. Her and Topeté are like onions, layered. If they're after the book, it's probably not to hand it over to Johnson."

A small detail, half-forgotten in the sheer casualness of its mention, drifted like a mirage in Marcey's mind. Something Kat mentioned, back in London...something about bookbinding supplies and taking that out of her cut. Marcey shook her head, trying to make the memory clearer. "I think the book has always been in play," Marcey said. "It's obvious she wants it, so why not see what she does? It isn't a good idea for her to have it, Charlie must have known that. So he took it out of the game to what... let Kat fix whatever was holding her back before she got her hands on it?"

Shelly said nothing. Marcey watched her robotically spoon curry and lentils into her mouth. "Maybe this isn't what we think it is," Shelly said at length.

"How so?" Gwen asked, spoon caught in her mouth.

"Kat wouldn't...want the book to give it to Johnson, and Topeté, well, you've seen it yourself. She's *in* the book too. Maybe this is a play by Topeté to get it out of our hands to destroy it, because it can destroy her." Shelly hummed.

"But she—" Marcey shook her head. "I know it's stupid to dismiss it, but nothing about the entry on Topeté indicates she was anything other than a passing involvement when it suited her ends. So maybe..." Marcey shrugged. "It just seems a little outlandish that she's...I don't know... directly involved? Maybe passively, or through Kat..."

Shelly nodded. "Probably."

"I think we should still treat this whole thing with some very serious caution," Kim said. "Because even if Topeté isn't involved directly, she and Kat are a package deal, and one's bullshit comes with the other."

"That's noted and accounted for." It wasn't. Marcey would have to have a think on that later, when she was away from people who were depending on her ability to make and stick to a plan. Marcey glanced around. "Then we're agreed?"

"I think so," Shelly answered. "You'll lay out terms for her?"

"I will." Marcey gathered her trash. The trash can was over by Shelly's door. Marcey stood there, awkwardly, looking at the three women before her. "I should go."

"We were going to watch a movie," Shelly said. "Team bonding or whatever. It's been years since we've all worked together. Why don't you stay?"

Marcey's gaze slid from Gwen who shrugged, to Kim, who held up some movie Marcey had never heard of. "All right," she said. "I'll stay."

The film was mostly drowned out by stories and reminiscence. The warm feeling of gratitude and companionship settled comfortably in the pit of Marcey's stomach as she sat, tucked between Shelly and Kim, half paying attention to the old movie, half listening to the conversation. She felt like an intruder, but the cracking thaw came quickly when Shelly offered a story about Charlie and a man he'd met in Spain who'd tried to sell him an antique Persian rug. Soon Marcey was laughing along with the memories of Kim, Gwen, and Shelly of the man they'd all known far better than Marcey had ever had a chance to.

It was a welcoming moment, a way of pulling Marcey into this world of women and crime in a way that Marcey hadn't ever thought possible. Here she was accepted; her checkered past was not an elephant in the room, but rather a set of victories to be celebrated.

Marcey shared a few stories about the crew she'd run with in college. Darius's cousins were good people. Kim actually knew a few of them from high school, and sharing the details of the work Marcey had done with them to do the books for their sports betting circle made Kim's eyes go wide and Shelly grin. "So that's how you learned to gamble. You were skimming."

"I was getting paid for what they expected me to do for free," Marcey answered curtly. "No harm in that."

They all shook their heads. Marcey caught herself torn between feeling comfortable and wondering why they wanted her around after what she'd said.

Gwen clarified that later, when they were leaving. She grabbed Marcey's elbow and jerked her away from Shelly's door. "I'm watching you." Her voice was steely. "You might have Kim going along with you for the trip down memory lane, but you don't fool me, Daniels. I know what you're about. You're a walking arrest warrant and I don't trust you further than I can throw you."

"I thought we were past this," Marcey shot back.

"They might be. I'm not. You're going to get caught, Marcey. I hope you have a plan on how to get out of that that doesn't involve running to Kat Barber, because she'll leave you high and fucking dry."

"Then why stay?"

"You have something I want."

"The...book?"

Gwen quirked an eyebrow. "I'll stay on one condition. I want you to destroy the book. Shelly's doing this because she's still in love with Charlie and Kim's in it because she's bored out of her skull, trapped in the city. I want you to destroy the book, burn it in front of me. Do that at the end of this, and I'll crack whatever safe you need."

It was something Marcey hadn't considered, but she stared at Gwen hard for a long moment before she was forced to look away from Gwen's intense eyes, so brown in the low light that they were almost black. Doing that wasn't something she'd ever considered, but Gwen had a point. "It's in everyone's best interest that the book be destroyed, I think." She held out her hand, knowing that she needed Gwen more than Gwen needed her at the moment. This act, she could go back on it if she had to, but she was inclined to agree with Gwen. If the book was gone, no one won.

Gwen took her hand firmly. "Don't fuck me," she hissed.

"I wouldn't..." Marcey began, all wide eyes and perfectly put-on innocence.

"You don't belong in this world, Marcey Daniels," Gwen said as she turned to go. Marcey felt a small surge of victory at Gwen buying her act. She kept her face still, watching Gwen's retreating back.

When she returned home, the apartment was quiet. Marcey settled at the kitchen counter, setting up her laptop to go through the files Kim had gathered on Johnson's past trials. Marcey couldn't let go of the feeling that there was something she was missing about Johnson's motivations beyond the unspoken angle of still being pissed off about Rebecca's continued drug use and the public humiliation of having to have a daughter graduate high school in absentia because of rehab.

In every spreadsheet, the funding of Johnson's campaign was carefully documented down to the final dollar spent on things like toilet paper for the campaign office. Marcey was surprised at how much money they spent on things like morale building. Perhaps the campaign wasn't going as well as Johnson's advertisements would lead people to believe. Still, the money was sound. There wasn't anything that looked like dirty dealings, at least on the surface.

The second set of documents was connected to the political action committee working in Johnson's name. The Super PAC wasn't connected to Johnson directly, as far as Marcey could tell, but it was the Super PAC that this whole job would rest upon. Marcey did the math in her head, calculating how much of the PAC's funds she could funnel into a fraudulent purchase of a piece of art.

Marcey chewed on a fingernail. What was it about Charlie Mock that had Johnson so invested in getting the book? Was that just Topeté's influence and presence in the investigation? Johnson was petty, certainly, but she was pragmatic to a fault. Charlie was a white whale sort of criminal. To run an international investigation and to send her best investigator undercover to seduce a safe cracker like Gwen seemed...excessive. Marcey wondered if she'd missed something in the book, some clue. Marcey stood at the kitchen sink and filled a cup at the tap. Her papers spilled out over the counter, slipping out of her bag and over her laptop keyboard.

"I didn't realize you were back."

Marcey started. She hadn't heard her mother come in. "Yeah," she said. "Sorry. I'll be quiet."

"Don't worry, I was awake anyway." Her mother walked into the kitchen. There was a glass in her hand. Marcey turned and dumped out the rest of her water.

The sound of the glass slipping from her mother's fingers cut through the room like a gunshot. Marcey's mother was staring at the laptop screen. The files had loaded on the screen, and the first document, filling the entire screen, was a write-up of the Mock trial, Charlie Mock's face staring out at her mother, eyes sunken and accusatory. Marcey tore her gaze away from the screen, her eyes wide with horror. A piece of glass stuck out of her mother's foot, bleeding and forgotten.

"Shit." Marcey grabbed a paper towel and fell to her knees amid the broken glass. She yanked the shard from her mother's foot. "Are you okay?" Her mother nodded. Marcey pressed the towel to the wound and helped her mother over to the chair. "Put pressure on it." Marcey went and got the broom, then swept up the remnants.

"How did you find that man?" She looked haunted.

"He died," Marcey said in a low voice. There was no reason left to lie. She got to her feet and threw out the broken glass, returning to her mother's side to inspect the wound. The bleeding seemed to have slowed. There was a Band-Aid in her bag. She reached for it, spilling more papers over the desk. She wiped the blood away with the towel and waited for her mother to look down at her once more. "A lawyer called me." She passed her mother the Band-Aid.

"He wasn't supposed to know you existed." Her mother looked down at the Band-Aid in her hand and then set it aside. "I arranged everything. H-he couldn't've known..."

"He found out," Marcey answered shortly. "He found out and he waited until he was dead to drop this knowledge in my lap. Knowledge you could have told me about yourself, ages ago. You didn't need to lie to me."

"I did." Her mother shook her head. "When you fell in with that awful boy, I knew there maybe wasn't any escaping it, but I'd hoped—with time and distance—that I'd prove it was not your nature to be like *him*." She turned back to the picture. "I sacrificed so much, I gave that…that horrible woman everything I could."

A strange echoing filled Marcey's ears. "You what?"

Her mother set the bloody paper towel on the countertop, crumpled it, smoothed it flat. Her whole body was shaking. "I never told you about Charlie for the same reason. Johnson came by, you were at school. I offered her a chance to look around, through your bedroom. I never thought anything—"

Marcey closed her laptop with a snap and started shoving it into her bag. That was how Johnson had known. That was how she'd known all Marcey's secrets. How she'd been able to broadcast them while Marcey was sitting on the stand, reciting back all her failings, every dark thought she'd ever had. The humiliation of that moment played over and over in her mind. She shoved her papers in on top of her laptop. "You know what." Anger blurred with tears and stars. "You gave that woman everything she needed to humiliate me. You made what she's doing now, with her ad campaign, okay. She's looking for *any* reason to fuck with me."

"I think she feels sorry for you, Marcey, because of those pictures. She's seen what these past few weeks have been like for you. She sent around her investigator to check up on you. I thought it was sweet."

"Her investigator?" Marcey's blood ran cold.

"Yes. I think his name was William. He wanted to know about your trip to London and all those dusty papers you've been looking over recently."

"You told him—you told her? You implied to *them* that I was up to something?" She stared at her mother, baffled. "She knows, then? About everything?"

"About Charlie? I don't know if she knows about him… William did ask… I didn't deny it. So I suppose she must."

"She knows then. About the connection between Charlie Mock and me?"

Her mother shook her head. "No, she's known about that for years. I told her about it during the trial because I was hoping that I knew something about Mock that would help her to attempt a second trial of him. I told her everything."

Marcey stopped herself. She slung her bag over her shoulder. "You met him, what, on a whim? Slept with him on a whim? Told Johnson about him on a whim because you thought it'd get me out of jail time? You've got to be kidding me!"

"Marcey, be reasonable. You were facing ruin. I was facing my career ending because my daughter was all over the papers and it'd look bad for the firm."

"I don't give a fuck about the firm! That was my life you played with!" Marcey spluttered. "And you care about the firm? The *firm?*" Marcey took a step toward her mother. "What did you tell LePage?"

Her mother stared at her, her eyes wide but narrowing in judgment quickly. She saw through Marcey's lie, through to the truth, so easily. Marcey couldn't swallow it. "Why was he here, Marcey?"

"What did you tell him? What did you say to Linda Johnson to make her come here in the first place? You know she hates me. She hates me because of what happened with Becca senior year and because I got away. She hates me because I'm a failure to convict. Because I got away and she didn't get to rest her laurels on me. So what. The hell. Did you tell him?"

Her mother said nothing.

She couldn't stay here. She couldn't be around her mother. She'd told. The violation was too cutting, too miserable. Her mother wouldn't answer her. She stared at Marcey like Marcey was some alien child, not her own flesh and blood.

"You're no better than him, Marcey. If you know about him you already know that's true. You're no better than his sorry excuse for romance. He stole my purse, you know, put his number in it and ran after me like I'd left it behind on a park bench." Her mother stood in the doorway. "The bastard thought it was romantic. Maybe I did too, until he left me pregnant and alone, running off with some half-male floozy."

Marcey worked her jaw, biting back words. She'd go sleep at Shelly's. Or maybe Kim knew a place where she could crash. Marcey threw clothing into her bag haphazardly. "I don't care." Marcey zipped her duffle and threw it over her shoulder. She pushed past her mother, grabbing her thick winter coat and tugging it on over her leather jacket.

"Where are you going?"

"Out."

"Don't walk away from me."

Marcey jammed her hand into her pocket and pulled out her keys. She twisted the key to the apartment from the ring and threw it on the floor. "I won't be back."

CHAPTER 24

Kat, Being There

OUTSIDE IT WAS COLD; HER breath fogged in the chilly air. Marcey stood on the corner and considered calling a cab for a moment before she began to walk. Blocks fell away beneath her feet, taking her over the bridge and into Manhattan. She wasn't cold. She wasn't anything. Numb, she wandered, her feet taking her down the avenue and north, through a small park where two kids shivered while their dog raced the length of a basketball court, back and forth, back and forth. Marcey laced her fingers through the chain link of the fence and watched the dog run. It ran how she felt: in a scattered pattern, not quite able to decide where it wanted to go.

When the kids left, she turned and left with them, trudging through the icy night with no destination in mind. Calling Shelly seemed like admitting failure, and Marcey didn't want that. She exhaled, her mind racing. There was one other name, one other number she could think to try.

It took her nearly an hour to come to a decision. Finally, freezing cold and shaking slightly, she pulled her phone out of her pocket and dialed the number from memory. "I need to see you," she said. "Are you in the city?"

"Yes."

The confirmation came not as a surprise but as almost an absolution. Marcey shivered, her breath fogging before her. The immeasurable, dwarfed feeling that came with living in the city was overwhelming. She curled her hand around the subway railing.

"Where?"

Kat said an address twenty blocks south. A place she'd heard of in passing, a place people like Marcey weren't always welcome. She didn't make enough money. Didn't have a place in that circle. "Are you coming?"

"Give me twenty minutes," Marcey answered. It was late, far too late to wait around for the infrequent train. A girl alone at night? That was a disaster waiting to happen. "I'm taking an Uber." She hung up and called the car, waiting on the curb and trying to figure out what she was going to say to Kat.

This was not what she'd intended, running to Kat Barber. The inherent danger in it was not lost on Marcey. She climbed into the Uber when it arrived and didn't really talk to the driver. She had too much on her mind. Had she finally, finally, been dealt the last straw? Was that okay? The hollow, empty feeling that came with the realization of all she had left behind ached in her in like a hunger pang. She couldn't do this. She couldn't just *walk away*. Could she?

The clouds were cast low against the glow of the city and reflected luster back down upon Marcey. The Uber driver wished her a nice night and drove off. Marcey stared up at the hotel. It was small, boutique. Not the sort of place she'd expect for Kat. Her phone buzzed. A new text from a blocked phone number. Inside there was only three digits: a room number.

No one paid her any mind as she cut through the hotel lobby and turned around to go up the stairs. The lobby was on the second floor; the room Kat was staying in was a floor above. She climbed and walked down a long corridor, trying to swallow back the emotions she didn't want Kat Barber to see.

But Kat Barber would see them. Kat Barber saw everything.

Marcey drifted down the hallway, stopping at the door at the far end. The last one. It seemed almost fitting. Fitting Kat at any rate. Marcey knocked and stepped back. This was awkward.

The door opened and Marcey was barely able to step inside before her bags were pulled from her hands and tossed aside. Kat's hands moved on her, feather light, yet forceful touches reminding Marcey that this was not a situation she could ever hope to control. Kat steered her up against the door, kissing her hard, open mouthed. Marcey's breath left her. Kat took this moment to push Marcey's two jackets off her shoulders. She hesitated then, fingers twisted in Marcey's hair.

"Why are you wearing two coats?" Her breath was hot on Marcey's cheek.

Marcey didn't move. Her fingers were on Kat's hips, her breath coming in shallow pants. "My mother told me what she did. What she told LePage and I couldn't…"

Kat's fingers were warm. They cupped Marcey's cheeks, peppering her face with gentle kisses. "What did she do to you?" Kat's eyes were dark, when Marcey was able to bring her eyes up to meet Kat's gaze. There was desire there, marked with a tenderness that felt to Marcey as though it were genuine. Unforced. The beautiful feeling that came from being *wanted* despite not being perfect. And she wasn't perfect. Not for Kat Barber. Marcey wasn't about to delude herself there but the kissing, the kissing was nice. "What did she do?"

"She knew... I think she's been speaking to Johnson's people. She implied that they came by the apartment while I was with you. And then again, not a week ago. That she'd talked to them about what we were up to."

All color drained from Kat's face. She pulled Marcey to her, arms wrapped tight around Marcey's shoulders. The hug was dangerous, suffocating. Marcey didn't struggle. Maybe this was a better way to go out. She spoke into Kat's shoulder:

"She saw a picture of Charlie on my laptop, Kat. She saw it and she asked about it and I—I couldn't lie to her. I told her the truth and she told me that she'd tried to breed Charlie's nature out of me with good schools and expensive friends as a kid. She told me that LePage had come by recently, asking questions. She said she told them the whole truth. About who I'd gone to see and *Christ*... I've ruined this whole thing, Kat."

Kat's fingers dug into Marcey's shoulders. "Has she seen the book?"

Marcey shook her head. "No, it's..." She gestured to her discarded bag. "It's always been with me." She sighed. "But that's probably what she was looking for, in my papers, isn't it? That's probably what LePage asked her to look for." Even in her distress, Marcey searched Kat's face. She wanted to see Kat's reaction. "Why else would she want it?"

"I'm not sure." Kat's expression was carefully unreadable.

Pushing Kat away, Marcey moved to pace the length of the tiny room. She ran her hands though her hair. Panic was setting in, tight, painful, fearful. It felt good to project such a broad emotion outward, when she was actually feeling it to some extent. Kat had to buy this. The panic had to seem real. "What the hell do I do, Kat? This book is my doom. I never wanted it, but now I have to keep it safe because with it...everyone I've met these past six weeks, you, Shelly, Gwen, you could all go to jail. I should just destroy it."

"Honestly, Marcey. There's no need to be dramatic." Kat took Marcey's flailing hands and pulled her forward, kissing her as if to drown the panic spewing forth from Marcey's lips. She spun them. Marcey's back hit the wall. The breath was ripped from Marcey, replaced with Kat Barber.

Whatever happened to "this was a mistake, Marcey?" Marcey wondered. *What are you trying to distract me from?*

Her fingers were leaden. She tried to tangle them in Kat's soft hair only to feel the desperation make them slip down to cling to Kat's back. She hated how much she wanted this. Wanted to forget her anger, no matter how temporarily. But this place, with Kat's lips slowly spelling her undoing, this wasn't her place. It belonged to someone else, someone with the power to destroy Marcey with one simple word.

And yet when Marcey called, Kat was there, holding court over something trapped deep in Marcey's heart that threatened to spill forth with each passing moment. Marcey wanted Kat, wanted her badly, and Kat knew it as sure as she knew her own name. This was Kat's spell on Marcey, the spell that led to Marcey's bag and Charlie's book falling to the floor and Kat biting at Marcey's lower lip and tugging her shirt from her shoulders. Kat's hands were rough, forceful, pressing flat against Marcey's breasts and tugging at her bra.

Marcey gasped, back arching into Kat as she lowered her head to bite at Marcey's collarbone. They moved from to the wall to the comfortable softness of the bed. Kat's fingers were quick and moved with an intensity Marcey couldn't keep up with. She was feeling too much, words babbling past her lips. This, at least, this was real. This wasn't an act or put-on because she felt like she needed to broadcast an emotion. This was real.

And there was too much. Marcey was drowning.

This was Kat using her emotions as a weapon. The rational part of Marcey's brain that was not utterly distracted by the feeling of Kat's lips on her skin and the pounding of her heartbeat knew that Kat was trying to make a play here. But to what end? Was there even a reason? She could do anything to Marcey now, anything at all, and Marcey would have to accept it. She was homeless—she had nothing.

Kat's nimble fingers divested Marcey of her bra and then her pants. Her body slid down easily. Her lips pressed hot and wet to Marcey's hipbone, to her inner thigh. Marcey's fingers closed, fisting in Kat's hair, and she couldn't think of anything but the feel of Kat's tongue curling against her.

For a long time, there was no reason to talk at all.

Some indeterminate amount of time later, Marcey woke up alone in Kat's very expensive hotel room. She was used to this part—the waking up and wondering why after sex. It wasn't as though she didn't care for the act itself, but rather the awkwardness that came afterward. She liked to have her fun, and then she liked to leave.

She couldn't linger. This was Kat's place, even if it smelled like their shared sex and sin. Marcey didn't belong. She didn't know where she'd go; the conversation with her mother still rang in her ears. Gingerly, Marcey pushed the covers away and sat up. There were bruises on her hips, deep purple and still tender. She winced, bending over and grabbing for her jeans. Kat was not a gentle lover. She tugged them on before rummaging in the tangle of bed sheets for her shirt. The whole thing seemed like a dream.

"Where—" Hoarse, the words didn't come out right. Marcey cleared her throat and tried again. "Where're my…" She spotted her shoes and socks at the foot of the bed. She put them on and grabbed her things, checking to make sure that Charlie's book was still tucked inside her messenger bag. It still being there seemed contradictory proof to Shelly's allegation that Kat and Topeté were playing a long game and were after the book. Maybe doing what Gwen wanted wouldn't have to be Marcey's endgame. She stared down at it for a moment before shaking her head and bending to tie her boots.

She left the room as she found it, no trace of herself save the rumpled sheets of Kat's indiscretion. It was the best she could do for Kat, given the circumstances. What they had done was wrong. And they'd done it twice now. Guilt ate at Marcey, but she wasn't about to get caught in the middle of some tiff between Kat and her lover.

The lobby of the hotel was small, a narrow space that afforded a small kitchenette and the front desk. Marcey paused on the stairs, hearing voices. A voice she recognized. Kat was standing on the landing of the stairs, her back facing Marcey, speaking to a woman with dark hair. The same woman Marcey'd seen at the Perôt. A low curse filled her mouth, but Marcey dove back over the landing and contemplated her options. She could go out the window to the fire escape, or she could wait and see if Kat came up. Marcey didn't think that'd happen as Kat had left Marcey in the room.

"—promised, Kat," the dark-haired woman was saying. Marcey crept closer, straining to hear. She had never heard Wei Topeté speak, but Marcey was certain this was her. Topeté's accent was more pronounced as she ducked her head closer to Kat, fingers brushing hair from Kat's forehead. "We had an agreement. This is how we win it all back. If you keep going off script, I can't promise that people aren't going to start noticing." The pain was evident in her voice.

From the landing, Marcey could only see bits of what was happening. She didn't dare move, afraid she'd attract attention and cause the conversation to move elsewhere. Wei Topeté was older, Asian, with a pretty face and smattering of freckles across her nose. Dressed in a very professional-looking suit that made Kat's trench and early spring sundress look exceptionally feminine, she had a strong presence. Marcey bit back a scowl. She couldn't be jealous, not of the woman Kat claimed to love with all her heart. She was just a distraction; Marcey'd always been dimly aware of that, but now it tasted sour. A bitter pill she was forced to swallow.

"I know," Kat replied. She stepped closer to Topeté and her voice dropped lower. "She's so scared. How could I not offer comfort, especially when it comes with the confirmation of what you've been fearing?"

Topeté let out a long-suffering sigh. "Kat." Her fingers curled around Kat's chin. "My heart can only break so many times. We're supposed to talk about these things before we do them."

"I'm sorry," Kat whispered. "I'm so sorry."

The stood there in silence for a moment, before Kat offered Topeté her hand and the two of them retreated into the hotel lobby.

Marcey's hands were shaking. She stood there, before creeping closer to the landing. She didn't dare go down, not yet, not until she was sure. Motionless, she waited, battered by the conversation she'd just overheard.

The truth ate at her, chewing her up from within. She hadn't considered that Topeté and Kat were in love. That she was playing a homewrecker to their relationship because Kat wanted to manipulate Topeté...and possibly Marcey too. It seemed unfair, cruel even. Marcey wasn't either of those things.

CHAPTER 25

A Heist, at Its Beginning

THE DRIVE TO THE MOUNTAINS was done in mostly a stony silence. Marcey spent the morning running around, gathering the final supplies, and loading the painting into their transport. Kat came along willingly, after an initial false start of Kim sliding into the seat next to her in the rented van and scowling at her. "Barber."

"Montou." Kat sniffed. "I trust that you'll find my suggestions acceptable."

"Never." Kim rolled her eyes. "But I don't have much of a choice."

Marcey gripped the steering wheel and concentrated on driving. Shelly and Gwen met them at a gas station on the way out of the city. Shelly wasn't coming, and Marcey was all right with that. Her part of the plan came later, when they moved to sell the artwork. Shelly was right: New Hampshire was a very different place than the city. She would stick out like a sore thumb. Gwen though, far darker than even Shelly's warm brown, somehow glided right into that New England prep-school accent and appearance, wrapped in a North Face jacket over a sweater and polo shirt and carefully pressed chinos.

"You're going to be cold." Kim wrinkled her nose at Gwen's attire when Gwen climbed into the van next to Marcey.

"Leggings, Kim, thermal leggings." Gwen shook her head. "You know I don't mess with outside much."

"That's a lie, you ran a damn marathon last year," Kim protested.

Marcey was again reminded that these women, who were so standoffish and cagey about everything, kept careful tabs on each other. It didn't make her feel uncomfortable, but rather unsettled. Because they would keep the same tabs on her.

Kat, for her part, said nothing at all. Marcey glanced at her in the rearview mirror and saw she was lost in thought, chewing on her fingernail and staring out the window. Marcey was content with that. If Kat wasn't going to make an issue out of her presence, far be it from Marcey to attempt to do the same.

The drive was long; they stuck to back roads once they reached Vermont, cutting through Keene and driving north and east along Route 9. Marcey wanted to avoid Boston and Providence, and the payoff was driving through snowy towns, the landscape dotted with red barns—picturesque as postcards against the bright blue sky of the mid-April morning.

"It snowed last night?" Gwen leaned forward, peering out the windshield. "Damn. I could never live up here. It's fucking April. Cherry blossom time, none of this lingering winter bullshit."

"Same," Kim agreed.

"I quite like the snow." Kat leaned against the window. "It's beautiful, isn't it? It makes everything clean."

"A shiny white exterior doesn't hide the ugliness underneath," Gwen answered. "Snow melts."

Kat turned away, staring out onto the blanket of fresh snow fallen on the little village they were passing through. Marcey stopped at the single, flashing stoplight at the center of town: a confluence of two roads where the town seemed more like a town and less like a loose collection of houses arranged in a snarl in a snow-filled valley. There was a bakery open on one corner, and a bookseller shuttered against the cold. A church bell rang in the distance. Towns like this made Marcey claustrophobic. There was so little around that what was there clung to the air of suffocation.

They drove north, through countless small towns, each with its own version of the bakery and church. Some had Shaw's or Hannaford's shunted to the outside of town; others still had smaller, independent grocers Marcey had never heard of. She kept her eyes on the road, coasting at two miles under the speed limit through the snowy back roads, past the sign declaring that they were entering the White Mountain National Forest.

"Looks like it's out of the sixties." Gwen gestured to the sign. The car slipped a little on the snowy road. Marcey was grateful for the four-wheel drive.

"National Park shit always looks like that," Kim answered from the back seat. "When I was a kid my mom sent me up to summer camp in Maine. I had the odious pleasure of being the only non-white kid at Camp Downer for two years."

"Downer?" Kat raised an eyebrow. Marcey met her eyes in the rearview mirror. "That sounds...well..."

Gwen giggled. Marcey rolled her eyes at Kat. Kim just fumed. "It was actually really nice. They just had piss-awful naming conventions for things. But I suppose it's better than some tribal name used incorrectly."

"Always true," Marcey agreed. "My mom wanted to send me to sailing camp when I was a kid, but it didn't happen for some reason... Maybe money? It was a while ago."

"Sailing camp is the whitest fucking thing." Gwen laughed.

"True." Marcey inclined her head.

They all laughed then. Marcey imagined what it might have been like, sailing around a lake somewhere surrounded by nature. To be surrounded by all those trees conveyed a feeling of loneliness that Marcey didn't need reminding of. It fit like an old glove. That feeling she could never escape. She drove on, knowing it was only a matter of time before the easy companionship of this car ride would feel like loneliness.

<hr/>

The resort hotel was mostly empty this time of year—the strange, muddy transitional time between winter and summer that plagued the North East. The snowfall of the night before was on top of that mud, and it would make skiing challenging. The resorts were mostly closed, fearing the damage to their slopes should skis and snowboards cut too deeply into the ground cover. With the muddy spring thaw came the constant sound of rushing water.

Marcey stood in the rutted gravel parking lot with her hands in her pockets, staring up at the cloud-shrouded peak of Mount Washington. It wasn't a particularly high mountain, but its prominence dominated the horizon, looming large behind the hotel. There was always snow on the top of that mountain, even in the summer, when the rest of the mountains were long-thawed.

Her boots were covered in mud, splattering up her jeans as she picked her way across the parking lot. The anxious feeling in her stomach mounted as she opened the door to the hotel.

The room key was in her pocket, rented by Kim. Marcey had followed her into the lobby and watched her put on a comically large pair of sunglasses and Kat's winter anorak. She had ambled up to the desk with an air of superiority that fell about her like a perfect mask as she approached. She'd tapped her fingers on the desk, her eyes narrowing and her hip jutting out at an absurd angle. Marcey had stood back, hands in her pockets as though she were with Kim but not involved in the rental.

Kim had begun to speak in halting English, slipping into Japanese here and there when she lost the thread of English. Marcey'd winced as the desk clerk leaned forward and listened to Kim's reservation and made her room keys. The whole thing had been so absurd that Marcey was shocked when Kim came by and looped her arm through Marcey's and led them back out of the lobby and into the slushy mud of the parking lot.

"How did you do that?" Marcey had asked.

"Do what?"

"Just walk up and make yourself so ridiculous that no one would ever think you were American?"

"Well, my parents aren't American," Kim had said. "And it's better to be foreign because it leads people away from the actual truth which is that you're a dirty awful American who's out to rob them. Or involve them in a crime." She'd tossed Marcey a key. "Move the car? This act requires a little more massaging."

Marcey had caught it. "Sure." She'd hesitated for a moment. "What are you gonna do?"

"Feign ignorance and try to ski in that muddy soup."

"Yikes. Good luck."

That was days ago now.

The hotel was done up in a Swiss style, meant to resemble an alpine ski lodge. It looked tacky but was charming in a rustic sort of way: raw wood painted to look blackened with age, with old wooden skis on the wall and antlers from gigantic bucks dominating the rafters. It was unsettling, all that death looking down at her. She slid the keycard into a doorway off the main lobby and slipped inside. Looking first one way, and then the other, Marcey hurried up the hallway.

They'd taken a room on the first floor, ostensibly to do some late-season hiking on snowshoes. Gwen had even bothered to rent some from the hotel to make it look extra legitimate on top of Kim's idiot tourist ploy. They sat stacked up in a corner of their shared hotel room. On the books, the entire thing looked legit, save for the constant back and forth from the city. In the middle of the night two nights ago now, they'd delivered Kat's horrible painting to the room to await the job.

The theft itself was going to be complicated. Marcey was relishing the final planning stages, finding them exhilarating. Never before had she taken to something so quickly, fitting easily into the role of planner with the team's help.

Gwen spent the better part of the last few days clad in camouflage, traipsing around the snowy mountainside, inspecting from every side the house where their mark lived. The snow hindered her progress, and the mud, which started to appear as the fresh snow melted on a warm, sunny day, was even worse. She came back to the room mud splattered, her teeth chattering with the cold. Kat would make her tea, and Marcey would watch them eye each other warily over their hotel-issued mugs as Gwen relayed what she'd seen.

"He keeps dogs." Gwen sipped her tea. She'd thrown her jacket, streaked with mud, into the base of the closet. Kim picked it up gingerly and moved to hang it in the en suite. She reappeared just as Gwen rolled up her sleeve to reveal two long scratches, raised and bloody against her dark skin. Kat tutted, reaching for her arm. Gwen flinched away from her. It would take a lot more than tenderness and tea to heal that relationship. "Big, vicious dogs."

"So, eliminate them," Kat said. She got to her feet, smoothing her sweater flat and bending to rummage in her purse for a bottle of hand sanitizer and small box of Band-Aids. She tossed both to Gwen. "They're just animals."

Marcey opened her mouth to reply that this was supposed to be a simple in and out, a walk away nothing more, but Kim beat her to the punch. "We can't just go and fucking off his dogs. The whole point is that nothing's amiss and that he doesn't realize we've done the switch." She rolled her eyes in exasperation. "Wasn't this your plan?"

"No," Kat replied snippily, shooting a dark look at Kim. "It was Charlie's."

"Charlie wouldn't fuck with dogs like that. He loved dogs." Kim scowled.

Gwen nodded grimly. "I don't mind dogs, but guard dogs? I don't mess with those."

Kat folded her arms smugly across her chest. "So, what do we do?"

Marcey smiled. "I knew about the dogs. It, er…was in Charlie's notes, actually." She crossed the room to the closet. Her duffle was streaked with mud, thanks to Gwen's jacket. She wrinkled her nose before unzipping it. "We'll need to get some hamburger or raw meat of some kind, but I picked these up before I left, figured they'd be useful." She turned, holding up a small baggie with four pills inside it. "Now, this is provided they're not the annoying sort of dog that knows how to eat around a pill, but we should be able to knock them out with these."

"Never out of the drug trade, were you, Mar?" Kim joked.

Rolling her eyes, Marcey tossed her the pills. "Don't work on humans. Strictly for animals. I saw on the schematics that there was a doghouse and made a point of picking these up a few weeks ago from a buddy after I confirmed that Charlie's notes indicated that there'd be two."

"And you never thought to mention it?" Gwen scowled. "Like, I'd like a damn heads-up before I go down into a place like that to potentially get my throat ripped out."

"They'll be knocked out. If not from the pills then I have a backup tranq gun." Marcey pulled the darts and gun from her bag. Gwen took half a step back as Marcey waved the gun in a broad arc. "They're meant for bears. They won't kill the dogs but knock 'em out for a long while. I'm a good shot. That was the summer camp I did go to, and I've kept up with it. Needed it in college."

"We never use guns," Kat said quietly. "Never."

"Well, the dogs threw a wrench into things. Sorry I didn't say anything about them directly. I figured just removing them from the equation was a better option."

Gwen stared down at her muddy boots and toed them off gingerly. She got up, moving them to the tile floor by the door. "I'm fine with it. But they'd better be out cold before you expect me to go in there."

"I'll go see about some meat." Marcey headed back to the door.

When she returned nearly three hours later, having had to drive practically out of the forest to find a grocery store that was still open, a quarter pound of ground chuck and a Coke on the seat beside her, Marcey found Gwen freshly showered, and Kat, stopwatch in hand, perched on the end of the bed they'd shoved into the corner for more space. Gwen's breath came in slow gasps. Her fingers flew, piecing together worn, ancient panes of wood with nails rusted over. The hammer she used was padded with leather, so as not to disturb the rust patterns.

"Twenty seconds," Kat called when Gwen put down the bar and held up her hands. "That's not terrible."

"It should only take fifteen," Gwen replied. She glanced at Marcey before moving to disassemble the frame once more. "Especially since the wood we will be using will be a lot older and stiffer."

Marcey leaned against the door, bag from the grocery store resting heavily against her leg. "What if you were to use the ground to hammer it together?"

"Oh, you're back," Kat said. She smiled at Marcey, but it was entirely put-on. "I would have thought you'd be gone longer."

She noticed Marcey from the moment Marcey walked in. She just hadn't let on. Marcey was almost weary of Kat Barber's games, over the past few days, finding them circular and yet unable to pull herself away. Kat wanted Marcey drawn in, unable to extricate herself and more than willing to linger at the periphery. Marcey didn't know what was right and what was wrong anymore when it came to Kat. Whatever was happening between them seemed genuine. Kat liked Marcey; Marcey liked Kat. That was where it had to end. It couldn't continue past that. Marcey wouldn't do that to anyone. Not after she'd already fucked it up twice.

Marcey glanced at her watch. "It's been more than two hours. You guys lose track of time?"

They glanced at each other before shrugging almost in unison. Marcey was glad they were working together, and so well. It meant that the heist itself would come easier.

"I suppose we must have," Gwen answered. "I think we have this close to down. Why don't you get Kim and we can get dinner? I want to try this one or two more times."

"Where is she?"

"Roof." Kat grunted. Getting to her feet, she took the frame from Gwen and disassembled it in what had to have only been about ten seconds. Marcey frowned. Should Kat be the one to go and do the exchange? Would Gwen go for that?

Crossing to the mini-fridge, Marcey put away the ground chuck and the Coke. She tucked a lock of hair behind her ear and glanced sideways at Kat. Despite the games and the stolen kisses of the past few days, Marcey could not shake the feeling of guilt every time Kat's fingers lingered too long or her lips brushed against Marcey's neck or cheek in passing. There was something so visceral, so painfully awful about the fact that she was ruining something so tender and pure between Topeté and Kat. Marcey was the homewrecker and she didn't want to be, but Kat was like a drug she couldn't refuse. All through high school, and into college, Marcey had wondered how Rebecca could have fallen into drugs like that. She knew now. Kat's smile warmed her soul.

It felt like cheating. It was cheating, and Marcey hated how good it made her feel, how powerful. She had no reason to hate Topeté, when everything about her seemed like a woman possessed of similar values to the rest of them, albeit on the other side of legality. But even that seemed in question after what Marcey'd read in Charlie's book. She hated that there didn't seem to be anything wrong with Topeté. That she was just someone Kat loved and who loved Kat.

Secrets had a way of ruining everything,

And Kat? Kat was hiding far more than one secret. A team on a job like this needed complete trust, and they already didn't have it because Kat wasn't as welcome in the group as Marcey would have liked. Still, the dynamic was relaxing. Everyone was calming down and falling into the job as they prepped.

Marcey slipped out the door. Kat was speaking to Gwen: "Try for seventeen seconds this time?"

"Can do."

Worry over what they were about to do and Gwen's apparent inability to complete the task ached in Marcey's stomach. It was the ache of winter, the brisk cold outside that still clung to her bones despite being inside and warm for some time. Nervousness walked hand in hand, and the other contingency, the one that she would never mention to anyone, was squirreled away at the bottom of her duffle bag—where hopefully no one would think to use it. The gun belonged to her mother, unregistered on account of the city's laws. Her mother was a single woman living with a young daughter in New York City. She'd learned to shoot in college out of necessity. She'd taught Marcey when Marcey was younger, driving long hours up out of the city and into northwestern Connecticut to go to ranges where no one would look twice. Marcey never blamed her mother. She'd grown up during the worst time in the city's history, when crime and drugs and poverty threatened to overwhelm the five boroughs and transform the city Marcey knew and loved into something else entirely. Perhaps that was why she had reacted so poorly to Darius, and to Marcey's arrest. She remembered what it was like before. Or she was just fucking racist. Either way, Marcey had borrowed the gun when this whole business started up, and she'd had it with her when she left.

She didn't know how she was going to process *that*. Avoiding it seemed the best option.

The roof was empty save for a multi-tool-wielding Kim crouched behind the hotel's satellite dish, her laptop set up on a dry patch of roof beside her. The fuse box behind the satellite was broken open, and Kim clenched a zip tie in her teeth as she sorted through wires. She looked up, eyes narrowed and halfway into a crouch to flee, when Marcey pushed the door open.

"How's it going up here?"

"Better than downstairs." Kim spat out the zip tie. It landed at her foot. She twisted her multi-tool and cut two wires, taking the zip tie and lashing their exposed ends together. "Anything is better than sitting down there watching Gwen and Kat try very hard to be *nice* to each other when you just know they fucking hate each other's guts. I don't blame Gwen either. I wouldn't trust Kat Barber if she offered me the world on a silver platter."

The desire to tell Kim about what she overheard before they left was overwhelming. Marcey bit her lip, fighting against the urge. Sometimes sharing was too much, and people were better off if they didn't know the truth. It was the only way they could stay sane and work could be cohesive. "Really, the whole world?"

She said it like it was a joke, but the truth of the matter bit at Marcey's stomach and sent it plummeting. Kat had Marcey. Her fingers hooked like the still-healing bruises on Marcey's hips and thighs, rubbing away the concealer at her neck. Marcey was ensnared; Kat had her tethers in Marcey's soul. Pieces of a game where Marcey didn't know the rules.

It was a game, Marcey thought, which was setting up to where she was the perfect fall guy.

"—something." Kim waved her multi-tool in Marcey's face. "Are you even listening to me?"

Marcey shook her head. "Sorry, what?"

"I just said that we have to be careful if the build is still messing Gwen up. I can only buy us so much time."

"They've got their build down to twenty seconds."

"That's something." Kim spat on the ground. "But it needs to be shorter. We don't know how long the door'll take."

"They wanted to get food."

"Then they should get it," Kim replied. She gestured toward her laptop and the mess of wires. "I need to finish this."

"Okay."

"Did you want anything in particular, or did you just come up here to bother me?" Kim asked, turning her attention back to the tangle of wires in her lap.

"Maybe I thought you were hungry and would want to eat with everyone else."

Something flashed across Kim's face. Something that made her look very young and very vulnerable. Marcey wanted to reach out, to take her hand and promise her that this was a good idea. That everything would be fine; they'd all get very rich, no one would get hurt. She wanted to tell her she knew everything was going to be fine. But that was a lie, and Marcey wasn't about to lie to anyone just yet. Not if she could help it.

There were enough liars around, after all.

CHAPTER 26

Wei, Watching the Unraveling

WEI HAD NEVER LIKED LINDA Johnson. She was too sharp, too quick to judge, and too aware of all the small details that had led to Wei working with her for Wei to ever feel comfortable around her. She saw too much to ever allow Wei to relax around her. She saw too much without ever giving anything away about her agenda.

Johnson's office was as cluttered as ever. The campaign posters were removed, probably a conflict of interest, and replaced with the telltale smell of mold and cats. Wei wrinkled her nose, sitting opposite Johnson. The smell was the worst part of being called in to speak to her knowledge of the case. The smell and being in Johnson's presence in the first place. Wei was well aware of how petty she was and how deep her hatred could run. She wanted nothing more than to avoid Johnson's bad side.

She sat fidgeting, annoyed that it fell to her to break the silence Johnson certainly would not be breaking. Johnson liked that, the surrender of the upper hand before the conversation began. But there was no helping it.

"You wanted to see me?"

Johnson glanced up from her paperwork and smiled, the pretty, petty smile of a career politician. Wei clenched her teeth. She had to be careful; so much of the plan was hanging on this moment. Shelly had warned her of the additional emotional baggage Johnson carried when it came to the Daniels girl, and Wei was inclined to believe it. The woman had a weak point in her diamond-hard persona, and it came in the shape of her daughter. It was something Wei intended to exploit. When the time was right.

"I did, thank you for coming." Johnson made another note, her handwriting slashing and masculine. "I wanted to talk to you about Kathryn Barber."

Her face had to be perfectly still. Wei bit the inside of her cheek and met Johnson's gaze evenly. "What about her?" Wei forced her tone to stay light, gentle. The casualness of it set her on edge. This was serious.

"William came to me this morning and told me that he needed to go to New Hampshire to follow up on a lead. A lead that you failed to mention." Johnson glared. "Marcey Daniels."

The absence of Marcey Daniels from anywhere in the city stuck out like a sore thumb. Johnson's ire at losing track of her was evident in the way her nostrils flared and her gnarled hands gripped her pen. But this was an old hurt, the kind that was never truly forgiven. Wei knew it well. It was the sting of personal humiliation.

She had to play it off though, pretend like she wasn't smarting from what Kat had done, what she continued to do, with Marcey Daniels. "She's no one," Wei answered. "A potential lead, perhaps, someone Barber is interested in for reasons I've yet to discern." Wei paused, as though thinking. "Wait, didn't William arrest her for being at the Perôt when someone attempted to break into it a few weeks ago? Didn't he let her walk?"

The *why are you blaming me then?* hung heavy in the rank air of Johnson's office.

"He had no reason to keep her," Johnson said dismissively. "She hadn't done anything wrong."

"Then why accuse me of being neglectful? I'm here to ensure that the book is found. I don't care about some kid running around with people who could get her sent to jail." Johnson exhausted Wei. Pushing back against the woman's iron will was draining. "William is free to go running off to New Hampshire if he wants, but I'd rather focus on the city, on Devon Austin Jackson, and the actual truth of this investigation, rather than rumor and hearsay."

Johnson pulled a file from underneath her legal pad and passed it over to Wei. "I think you'll find, Agent Topeté, that you're the one chasing shadows."

Inside was a series of photographs taken at a nondescript office building. Marcey Daniels was shorter than Wei expected, standing beside Shelly as she bent over a locked door in an alcove just off a fairly busy atrium. Wei flipped through them, before glancing up at Johnson. "So she's stealing things?"

"Breaking and entering secure facilities at the least. And interacting with three, maybe four, of Charlie Mock's known associates. Logic says she has his book." Johnson sniffed. "Honestly, Wei, I thought you were sharper than this. I know that your…entanglement with Barber is good for Interpol, but you have to consider that she's blinded you to what's right in front of your nose. I can't stand deliberate ignorance. And if you're looking the other way for Barber…"

"I'm not."

"Then go to New Hampshire with LePage and fetch me back that book. The girl has it. I want it." Johnson waved her hand, effectively ending the conversation.

Wei got to her feet but paused. "Can I ask you something, ma'am?"

Johnson's stony silence was permission enough.

"Why go to all this trouble? Charlie Mock is dead. His legacy doesn't mean much to you here in America. He operated mostly overseas. Most of his associates aren't American. You'd have very little ability to prosecute them." The question was a gambit, one that Wei wasn't sure she really could ask without giving herself away. Johnson's motivations had always been something of a mystery to Wei; she never could quite put her finger on what Johnson wanted. "And Marcey Daniels? Isn't that Super PAC supporting your campaign using her as a poster child for how you're tough on crime? Isn't that illegal?"

"Anything that the PAC does has nothing to do with me, Wei, you know that. I don't sign off, I do not approve. I simply enjoy the publicity." It was clear that Wei was overstaying her welcome, but Johnson kept speaking. "It's all political in the end. I doubt you'd be able to understand the nuances of American politics. I hardly understand them and I've lived here my entire life. The people want a candidate that's strong on crime. I'm behind in the polls. I want to give them something that they can really sink their teeth into. A meaty story like Charlie Mock and his legacy will keep me in good press for months. I have a few things I still need to prosecute before I accept the DA's office."

"You say this like you've already won." Wei's eyes narrowed. "Isn't that up to the voters in November?"

"No," Johnson answered with a wicked smile. "That's up to you and William."

Wei turned to leave, knowing a dismissal when she heard one.

"Oh, and Agent Topeté?" Johnson had gotten to her feet as well. She opened a drawer in the filing cabinet behind her. She pulled a file out. "I was trying to figure out why you were so reluctant in this case, but then this landed in my lap and it all made sense."

Wei flexed her fingers. Her palms were damp, she was nervous, but she couldn't show it. She wanted to leave. "What is it?"

Johnson let the file fall, open onto her desk. Inside were photographs of Wei sitting, smoking on a park bench, staring up at the sky. These were taken…oh, *Christ*. Wei leaned forward, feigning interest. "Are you having me followed, Linda?" she asked, her tone deliberately mild. "Because as I'm sure William has reminded you many times, I don't work for you. My investigative work here is purely in an advisory capacity until the matter with Barber is sorted."

The series of pictures showed her sitting next to Shelly Orietti, their heads bowed in conversation. She wasn't an idiot; there was no way to get away from this in Johnson's eyes. The proof was right there, damning and brought to light. It was all about how she played the next few moments that would determine the success of this enterprise. That was what Shelly wanted, that was what Wei wanted. They had a plan also.

"Yes, but don't you see, Agent Topeté? This is proof that you are not doing what you are reporting to me that you are doing. You are not reporting this to your superiors either, are you?" Johnson sat down heavily on her chair and pulled herself up to the desk. She surveyed Wei with the look that a cat gives a particularly delicious looking mouse before pouncing. Wei braced herself. "So tell me, Agent Topeté, what are you doing?"

Wei stayed silent.

A clock ticked loudly on the wall.

Johnson examined her fingernails and reached for a nail file from her pencil jar. "If you don't tell me, I'll ask Kat Barber. Or even our dear Ms. Daniels. William's gone up to New Hampshire to bring them back from their little escapade. He's been liaising with municipal police for the past week. For a child of a very good thief, Marcey Daniels isn't very good."

"Child?"

"Oh…" Johnson moved in for the kill. Wei's mind was racing. "You didn't know."

"How could I possibly have known that?"

"It didn't take William much digging at all. I was aware, or at least I suspected, when Charlie Mock's pet lawyer showed up to defend them both upon their arrest. I sent William along to confirm it with the girl's mother. She owes me a favor or two as it is, after the humiliation that the lawyer she hired to replace Mock's goon got her daughter off on an airtight case. She's not a very good liar when she's in front of a true diviner of truth like William. Neither are you."

Wei had some protections; Interpol wasn't an ADA's personal sandbox. If Johnson wanted to get her into trouble, she'd have to take time away from the campaign and trying to build up her record to ensure Wei's sanction. Wei was counting on this, counting on Johnson's still preferring William do her dirty work, to see this plan through. But they were going to need to be quick about it.

"Do you want me to go New Hampshire? Go with William and make sure that this is done?" Wei pulled the pictures toward herself, concentrating on the affected nonchalance of the action. She was right: there were a few of her with Shelly. Which begged the question, who was following her?

It couldn't have been William. He'd been on assignment—

She remembered then, remembered the old woman sitting at the corner, a scarf bundled up to her neck and a large wool hat on her head. She'd been distracted, thinking about Kat and that girl, thinking about how Kat had told her everything afterward, like she was sitting in confession begging for forgiveness for her sins. Wei wasn't the bearer of absolution, and the hurt of it, the hurt of Kat, must have blinded her to what was happening. How could she not have seen it? It was clear as day. That woman.

Wei hadn't gotten a good look at her, but she remembered finding her hair, blonde and poufy, surprisingly well styled for a little old woman snapping photographs of the park. *Christ,* Kat was destroying everything around Wei, pulling Wei into her head and distracting her from the fact that she looked like a goddamn idiot who was awful at her job.

Merde. She glanced up at Johnson. The woman's slow, smug smile, and the way she looked so utterly pleased with herself had Wei's heart hammering... But Linda had done it herself? Linda mustn't be certain of the information she had then. That boded well for Wei.

"William is more than capable of doing this without your assistance, however helpful it might prove to be. I, however, am not so certain of your loyalties. He's got a nice, neat little theory about you, one I'm inclined to believe. Would you like to hear it?"

"Not particularly." Wei got to her feet. "I think you're sorely mistaken. You took those photographs yourself, didn't you, Linda? Are you really that worried that the ghost of Charlie Mock is going to come back to haunt you? The man is dead. As you said, his child—if she even is—isn't particularly clever or sneaky. Why not just let her hang herself? Why waste mine and William's time when we could actually be working on closing the Mock matter for you? If she has the book, we'll find out when she inevitably gets herself caught." Wei glared. "I am here to solve the other problem. Nothing more. The fact that these two cases have become married to each other does not surprise me. You want what I want. Let's not antagonize each other by accusing each other of crimes where no criminal activity exists." That part would come later, when all the players were set up and the game could move smoothly.

"Association with criminals might as well be a crime," Johnson said.

"Do you forget all the help Kat Barber's given you in cases over the years? All the little tidbits of information passed on to me? Do you forget how she handed you Charlie Mock when William got himself found out?" Wei shook her head, not interested in what Johnson was trying to push onto her. "Sometimes the marriages we have are convenient."

"You'd do well to keep your nose free of whatever it is that Kat Barber is up to in New Hampshire. Go. Meet up with William and get me that book."

Wei turned and left without another word. She stalked over to her desk and called LePage, demanding to know where he was. He gave her an address, and she wrote it down. She stared at it for a minute and then reached for her phone.

The phone rang twice. "Tom Yelnan."

"Tom, it's Wei Topeté." Wei spoke quickly. While LePage could run off and do whatever he wanted with only the feeblest of blessings from Linda

Johnson, Wei had to plow through more red tape. Her work with Johnson's office was overseen by the Justice Department, and Wei still marginally reported to Tom, rather than Johnson. She hadn't checked in for some time, and now that she was going to be moving into another jurisdiction, she was going to have to get clearance.

"Wei!" Wei could picture him leaning back at his desk, throwing a ball up into the air, paperwork strewn around. He was young. Wei liked working with him. "How are you?" He segued neatly into French. "I heard you were sticking your nose into things all over New York."

"I was. The Mock case is turning out to be far more complicated than I'd ever anticipated."

"How so? I know that Interpol has wanted him for a while."

"They have, but the trail's been cold since he got locked up. It isn't him so much as his legacy we're after, after all." Wei exhaled. "There's a chance that his book is being used to conduct an art heist. Can you put a call into the New Hampshire state's attorney?"

"And what?"

"Let them know I'm going to be up there." Wei hated this, hated the lack of autonomy that this Interpol assignment gave her. She was used to roaming, to liaising where she wanted, and pushing herself through the worst of the weeds alone. Working with Johnson and LePage, feeling like a kept animal, was never going to lead to victory, no matter how pyrrhic it would be in the end. "I'll be going to Lincoln, in the mountains."

"Will you be with anyone?"

"William LePage. Possibly a defense attorney."

"A defense attorney?" Tom sounded intrigued. "What are you doing, Wei?"

"I've found a thread, Tom. I'm pulling at it to see what unravels."

He hummed. "I'll make a call."

"Thanks," Wei said, and hung up. She turned to leave, and then hesitated. She picked up the phone once more.

The number was one she had dialed many times before, when she was actively looking for the book, not trying to avoid thinking about where it was in order to undercut Kat's proposed endgame. The secretary who answered was nice enough, putting her call through with only a few moments of resistance.

"Devon," Wei said when he answered. "Do you fancy a weekend in the mountains?"

CHAPTER 27

A Heist, at Its Ending

LATER THAT NIGHT, KIM RETURNED with a half-eaten box of vending-machine Pop-Tarts and a triumphant smile. "You needed a secure connection, you've got one. Now, what do you need to use it for?"

"I need to call Shelly," Marcey said. Gwen and Kat glanced at her with equally bewildered expressions. "One of the things I asked her to keep an eye on while we were out of reception range—thank you, Kim"—Kim gave a little salute and sat down with her box of Pop-Tarts—"was the chatter around this particular piece of artwork. She's been monitoring the security company from the inside for the entire time we've been up here. Turns out her pretend job at their information storage facility has paid off."

Marcey clicked a few keys on her computer after Kim obligingly plugged her into the Ethernet cable protruding from her laptop. The call rang and Shelly's face swam into view. Her eyes were drawn down, her lips pursed. She sat at her desk in the library, which served as a TOR relay, so it was guaranteed to be far more secure than their connection at the hotel, hacked though it was. Marcey stared at her, and realized, quite suddenly, that she was *fidgeting*.

"Is everything all right?" Marcey asked.

"You need to do it tonight."

Marcey swallowed. She was afraid of that.

Kat leaned forward, past Marcey. She smelled good, like summer and winter snowmelts. If that even was a thing. Marcey wasn't sure it was. "Shelly?" she asked. Her eyebrows furrowed. "This isn't about—"

"No, you fool girl, of course it isn't." Shelly shook her head. Marcey glanced from Gwen to Kim and then back to Kat, absolutely lost. "The owner of the painting's been floating transporting it to the city for storage until the auction next month, wants to get it cleaned or some bullshit. I intercepted one of the calls and was able to delay him until tomorrow. He's going to be out of the country and wants this taken care of before he leaves."

"Oh." Kat's lips smacked shut.

"What did you think it was about?" Marcey's question only drove home the truth: that Kat was worried about Topeté and would not openly admit it.

Kat waved her hand dismissively. Marcey scowled. "The plan was for two days from now. We aren't prepared." The anger behind Kat's pretty, blank expression made Marcey draw away. It was drawn up around her eyes and it curled with the twist of her lip. Kat's teeth were clenched, her jaw a tight line.

"This is Marcey's job, Kathryn," Shelly answered, her voice barely above a whisper. "Mar, what do you think?"

"We need more time," Marcey said automatically, because they did. Gwen wasn't ready. Her fingers were still clumsy with the final forging work. Getting the painting stretched on the stretcher bar and into the frame took far too long and her canvases were never quite straight. Marcey exhaled, a headache building behind her eyes. "Kat would have to go along if we were to do it tonight. Gwen, I know that you've been practicing for a one-man job, but we may need to make it two. Kat can still stretch a canvas and make it look authentic faster than you can."

Gwen nodded her agreement. Marcey was grateful that she didn't argue the point. Theirs was a business arrangement, four pieces working toward a whole, complete job. Sometimes improvisations had to be made, even though Marcey's every instinct was screaming at her to scrub this whole thing. This was a part of the plan too, after all, the part they weren't privy to. "She knows the plan as well as I do." She fixed Kat with an inquisitive gaze. "You're not going to wander off, are you?"

The smile that drifted across Kat Barber's face was slow and predatory. "I make no promises." There was a smugness in her voice that made Marcey want to scream. She winked at Marcey, her smile contorting to something more sly and playful. "I like beautiful things, what can I say? That picture is dreadfully ugly."

"Damn straight," Kim muttered.

Shelly gave them a hard look. "Be careful." She reached up and ended the connection before they could talk more.

Gwen folded her arms over her chest and surveyed the room. Kim fiddled with her laptop. "Changing the plan is a great way to get people arrested," she said. "Are you going to be able to do this, Barber?"

Kat's expression and tone were bitter. "I would've liked more time."

"Well, you don't have it," Kim pointed out.

Marcey exhaled, rubbing at the back of her neck. The headache was getting worse. She ran her hand through her hair. She was stretched, worn. If they could just get through tonight...maybe then Marcey could find the words to ask Kat what the hell she was planning. Right now, Marcey just wanted her to say yes.

"I'll do it," Kat said eventually.

"Right," Marcey said. "We'll be on the clock in six hours. Let's work Kat into the plan."

The adjustments were fairly rudimentary. Gwen would get Kat into the building, open up the safe, and keep time while Kat disassembled and reassembled the canvas inside. Kim would hopefully be able to hold off the security system long enough that the alarm wouldn't have to be disabled, but if it needed to be turned off, Marcey would cut the power, as well as take care of the dogs. It felt...messy. Marcey didn't like it. There were too many chances for error, but this was their *only* chance. They had to do it tonight.

Marcey's heart felt like it was beating somewhere around her navel.

She sent Gwen and Kim out to take care of their getaway cars, carrying their things. The plan was to leave the hotel and go in four different directions, rendezvousing in four days at Charlie's storage unit. Getting away from them was the best Marcey could do for her fraying nerves. Panic tasted acidic. She'd never known that before.

Kat stood by the window, her back to Marcey as Marcey dumped out their trash into a single trash can and checked under the beds for any lost receipts. They would take it with them, throw it away at a gas station in Bow. Better to be safe than sorry.

"You overheard the conversation I had with Wei," Kat said, not turning around. She held herself perfectly still, her back ramrod straight and her arms wrapped around her sweater-clad torso. Her hair fell down her back in waves, a beautiful splash of yellow against the blackness of the nighttime forest outside. "Didn't you?"

"I don't kn—"

"Save it, Marcey." Kat turned around. "You're a terrible liar."

That was where she was wrong. Marcey stuck her chin out defiantly. Kat was taller than her and loomed over her effortlessly. A wild light took to her eyes, making them sparkle low and dark and ominous in the dim hotel room light. She put her hands on Marcey's shoulders, on her neck, smearing away the concealer.

"What if I did?" Marcey asked. *What if this was the plan all along?*

"Then you know that I am on borrowed time and I have very little patience for"—she paused, gestured to the room at large, fingers of her other hand twitching against Marcey's jaw—"all of this. Marcey, you must understand why I did what I did."

But Marcey didn't understand it at all. She didn't want to understand Kat with her beauty and her twisted doomsday smile and her ability to make Marcey make the stupidest decisions of her life. "What did you do then?"

The grip Kat had on her neck tightened. "This isn't the time for this."

"There is no good time for this," Marcey pointed out. "And you brought it up. Yes, I overheard you and Topeté talking. Yes, I know you're on borrowed time. What the hell did you do?"

Kat pursed her lips into a thin line until her red lipstick was all but obscured. She stared down her nose at Marcey, her nostrils flaring out slightly, her expression utterly unreadable. "I was in Barcelona. It wasn't meant to be a job."

The realization dawned on Marcey effortlessly and she flinched away from Kat's grip. It was the worst possible outcome, the one that they were speeding toward in just *having* this conversation. To have it spelled out into truth. Marcey swallowed, spoke the truth: "You got caught."

"Wei couldn't protect me forever. I knew it was coming. I hadn't... expected it so soon."

"What did you promise them?"

"Something I shouldn't have. Something I thought I was about to come into. You, my dear, were quite the unexpected turn of events."

Marcey looked down at her hands.

"I hadn't anticipated liking you," Kat continued. She seemed undeterred by Marcey's nervousness. "Or finding your naïveté so charming. Either way, I did not anticipate that I wouldn't want to go through with Wei's plan. You remind me a lot of Charlie, Marcey."

This whole thing was Topeté's idea?

"Wei's plan?"

Kat's face contorted, first in surprise and then in realization of what she'd let slip. She sat down on the edge of the bed, not looking at Marcey. "I never meant—I'm sorry. I just never meant to like you, Marcey."

"You can't play both sides!" Marcey threw her hands up in the air. "You can't bargain with our lives like that."

Kat was quiet for a moment before she looked up. Her eyes were still the same, bright green and intense beyond any measure. "I'm not," she said. "Not yet."

The door banged open. Kim and Gwen stuck their heads inside. "We ready to go?" Kim asked. Gwen was silent, but worry was evident in her eyes. She hated Kat but had buried the hatchet for the good of this job. They all knew what might happen, should this go south. Changing the plan usually spelled disaster, but they were committed now, and there would be no other opportunity for them to all meet their goals if they didn't even try. Four individual goals, and one chance to make it work. "The cars are all prepped."

If we can. "Okay." Marcey glanced at the window. At Kat. They would talk about this later. They had to talk about this later. "Are you ready?"

Kat's expression was perfectly blank when she turned around to face the room, face their little band of criminals. "Let's do this."

<hr />

They didn't have even well-established cell connections. Kim was a wizard, but she wasn't *that* much of one. There simply wasn't the infrastructure, or any locals willing to create the infrastructure, so they could speak to each other. Instead they were huddled in the cold beside the northwesternmost corner of the property, running over the plan one last time. Marcey checked her pocket for the wire cutters and the video relay feeds she was to place to enable Kim to hack into the security system's internal workings. That would at least get them eyes. The initial thought was to use their cellphones to communicate, but Kim distributed earpieces to everyone and had them scatter and test them for reception before coming back into where they were huddling.

"Are we all right?" Marcey asked in a low voice.

Kim nodded. She turned her tablet so they could see them. "There are cameras in the headlamps you and Gwen will be using, Kat, so Marcey and I can see what you're doing. I've got that scrambler up too, the one that disrupts cell conversations and Bluetooth hacking. I'll stay out here and drug the dogs. You three go over the wall at my signal."

They nodded, all clad in black and their faces grim. Gwen trailed her fingers over the bark of a nearby tree. "Never wish a thief luck."

"And never tell them happy trails," Kat said. She tucked her hair, braided down her back, into the neck of her shirt and stepped forward. "You'll cut the power and get Kim in?" she asked Marcey.

Marcey nodded. "I've got this."

This was something she could do in her sleep. It was a simple beginning of a standard smash-and-grab. The sort of thing Marcey'd done before with Darius's cousins, and with Darius himself that one memorable time. She knew a bit about wiring from when she was a kid and had taken a class on it after school, and she'd learned more since then. She could get Kim into the system, no problem.

The idea was that Gwen and Kat would go in, do their thing, and come back out. Marcey would stay outside with the relays so that they could put everything back the way they'd found it once they got out.

Kat hitched the two long tubes of materials, one of the painting and the other of a deconstructed stretcher bar for the canvas, up on her shoulders and adjusted the straps. Her lips were pursed as though she was thinking hard. She glanced at Gwen as Kim faded into the darkness of the growing night.

No one spoke. They all were preparing, mentally, for the coming moment. Marcey inhaled and exhaled slowly, counting. Twenty, forty, sixty, eighty. She'd reached two hundred when Kim's voice came over the comline. "Go," she said.

They went. Stealing through the night like shadows caught on a strong breath of wintery wind down the mountain, they ran through the woods and onto the property. The house itself was dark, shuttered against the cold, and massive. Marcey moved cautiously through the damp, still mostly dead grass, avoiding the lingering patchy snow. The last thing they wanted was to leave footprints.

At the corner of the house they paused, before Marcey oriented herself to find the outdoor electrical relay. She cracked it open with a screwdriver and worked by touch rather than sight, because they didn't dare use their headlamps outside. The relay here was simple, just a quick splicing in of two wires and tucking the entire bundle back into the box and closing it up.

"Alarm's out," she said. "Go."

Kat and Gwen disappeared back up the side of the house and Marcey exhaled slowly. She pulled a small flashlight out of her pocket and bent down to a second box, half-obscured by snowfall from the roof. Down there, the air was still cold and the ice grated at her fingertips as she dug for the cable wire she knew would be running down from the electrical relay. She twisted her fingers, and there it was. Marcey tugged it out and shook the ice and dirt from her fingers.

"Video feed's about to go live," Marcey said.

"Nice," Kim answered.

Marcey stripped the wire quickly, clipped the splicer device to it, and fidgeted with the antenna before tucking the whole thing back down into the dirt. "Feed live?"

"Feed is live. There are eyes in the sky, ladies."

"Excellent, we're on the move."

Marcey sat back on her heels and glanced at her watch. Five minutes. That was all the time they had to be out of here. But things never went as planned, did they?

"Shit," Marcey muttered. Her jeans were smeared with dirt. She crouched low, pulled out her phone, and shook it. She didn't want to tell Gwen and Kat that a pair of headlights had pulled into the long driveway of the property and was now sitting, bathing the far side of the house where the safe was located, in bright light. Any movement would be detected. Gwen and Kat were already inside the safe. "Do you see the light?" she asked.

"What is it?" Kat's voice cracked a bit.

"I see it, Marcey," Kim answered. "Do you have it?"

"I got it," Marcey said. She had to get the guy to follow her somehow. She could just pretend to be lost; she was, after all, still wearing the hiking boots, and there was a flannel in her pack she'd been wearing all week. She had a pack of gear with her: it was their go bag for the trip back, containing a change of clothes and a few toiletries. Marcey looked down at her muddy knees and cursed again. Who the fuck was she going to fool?

There was no helping it.

Staying purposefully low, Marcey inched her way around the periphery of the fence and waited until she got to the gap in the back. She threw herself across the gap into the woods and circled back. Her phone signal came through the moment she was back in the woods—*of course*—and Marcey hurriedly sent Kim a series of texts explaining what she was about to do.

> **MD>KM** *going to circle around and approach house from front. Pretend lost hiker.*

> **MD>KM** *switching SIM cards so call the other number. Taking out Com.*

She didn't wait for Kim to reply. She had to do this quickly. She would get out and rendezvous back with them somehow, in the city, on the set date. She'd make it.

Marcey pulled the back off her phone and pulled the SIM card out, switching back to her actual card, not the pay-as-you-go version she'd been using since they got to New Hampshire. She plucked the earpiece from her ear and threw it as far away from her as she could. Her fingers shook with cold. She left the phone turned off and shoved it into her backpack, breaking the other SIM into tiny pieces as she stomped through snow and muck circling around to the car and bursting through the woods, forcing herself to look elated. This she could do. This she could fake.

"Hey! Hey!" she shouted. Her breath fogged in the air before her. There were leaves in her hair. "Hey, mister!"

The car window rolled down. It was an older guy with sandy blond hair that Marcey recognized dimly. "What are you doing here?"

Marcey's teeth, as if on cue, though it was entirely unintentional, started to chatter. "L-l-ost," she said. "I was hiking down from the Omni.

Parked my car up there. Where is here?" Marcey glanced around, eyed the house. "I fell and then I got all turned around and couldn't find the path."

The guy narrowed his eyes before switching off his headlights and getting out of the car. "Christ, you're soaking wet." He moved to the trunk and pulled out a blanket. "Here, use this. I work security for this house. I can give you a lift back to the police station. I'm sure if your car was left abandoned and you signed the log, they're out looking for you."

"There was a log? I just started from the parking lot."

Shaking his head, the guy gestured for Marcey to get into the car. Marcey hesitated. Strange men and strange cars, while a worthy distraction to a far larger crime, was not worth the risk of being a young woman alone in the woods at night. But she didn't see another way to get him to leave.

"Well, get in. You need to get warm, you'll freeze."

Fuck it, there was no helping the situation. Kim had her number, and she was good enough to hack into any phone with battery life even if it was off, so long as they went toward Lincoln, and not further into the mountains, they could track the phone. She hurried around the car and got in gingerly, tapping as much mud out of her boots as she could before getting in.

The car smelled of wet socks. There was a pair of Nordic skis in the back seat. "Been skiing?" she asked.

"Nah." The guy put the car in gear and performed a neat K-turn. "It's too sticky for that."

They drove in silence for a few minutes, the heating on full blast. It took a few minutes more before Marcey stopped shivering. She hunkered down in the blanket and pulled a leaf from her hair. She hoped to *God* that he would take her back to the hotel and her car. She glanced over her shoulder, at the well of darkness where the house was. "What's so special about that place?"

"Why were you over there?" the guy countered. "Don't give me that bullshit about hiking. You were casing the joint, clear as day. You're not a good liar." Marcey opened her mouth to reply, but he kept on. "There's a cop here, investigator up from New York City. Looking for a girl about your age and height. I'm taking you to him."

Marcey's jaw clicked shut. The door handle was right there. She could fling herself from the car, but the woods were dense and close to the road.

She'd get pulverized by a tree. Her fingers twitched. "What's the guy's name?" she asked, just a little weakly.

"LePage. Will LePage."

Marcey couldn't quite manage the smile it took to laugh at herself. Instead she tugged the blanket close. This was going to get messy, but this was what she'd wanted.

CHAPTER 28

Marcey, Playing a Hand

THE HARSH FLUORESCENT OVERHEAD LIGHT burned Marcey's eyes after hours in the dark. Her hands were shaking. She jammed them into her pockets and her fingers twisted around the extra set of wire cutters she hadn't thrown into the woods. *Shit.* It was close to four in the morning and the Lincoln police department was abandoned.

Marcey glanced around, desperate for somewhere to ditch the tool. The guy, Officer Chris Raker, paused at the front desk. Marcey leaned against the counter, carefully feeling along the edge of the raised lip of the front desk. There was a gap there. She exhaled and took her chance as Raker rummaged in the drawer for something. Marcey moved quickly, feeling for the space in the gap of the lip of the table where it was supported by three support beams, spaced evenly apart. There was just enough space to wedge the wire cutters into one of the small pockets created by the beam before Raker surfaced with a ring of keys. "Found 'em," he said.

Marcey smiled weakly at him. "Good for you."

Raker took her to a small interview room behind the desk. The town was so small that the police office doubled as city hall and the local court. He instructed her to change out of her wet clothes, pulling out dry ones from Marcey's bag before taking it and her cellphone away with him. Marcey knew asking for a lawyer was a bad idea and would give Raker more reason to be suspicious of her, so she did what she was told, shucking off her wet clothes and leaving them in a pile on the floor. The clothes from her bag were stone cold, and Marcey shivered when she pulled them on. She left her sopping wet boots off and sat cross-legged in the chair, waiting for the moment when LePage walked through the door, smug and smiling. Would Topeté be with him? Would she have some final trump card to play?

Time passed slowly. There was no clock on the wall, and Marcey didn't regularly wear a watch. She had no idea how long she sat there, her wet jeans dripping from where she'd hung them over the back of an empty chair in the corner—for observation, probably.

Marcey was never good at waiting, but this was a game she could play for as long as they wanted her playing it. She ran through the previous few hours in her head, marking the ticks in the progression of the job and how smoothly everything had gone. They'd carry on without her—that was the plan, the goal. There had always been a risk that this would happen, and Marcey had a plan.

The table she sat at was old, made of plastic and cheap metal. It was rusting at the bottom of one of the legs, making it wobbly. Marcey let it wobble, back and forth, back and forth, to pass the time.

She thought about Darius. Wondered if this was his experience too, sitting alone in a room, waiting for someone to come in and accuse you of crimes you hadn't committed. She thought about how that wasn't her experience. How there'd been a lawyer present with her from the beginning, and how, not even for a moment, had she felt as though she were going to get railroaded into a confession. Was she any better than the people who had done all that to Darius now, willingly committing a crime just for the hell of it?

No, not for the hell of it.

Marcey wanted it to be LePage to walk through the door, because she wanted it to be LePage she got away from.

When Devon Austin Jackson had showed up to Darius's hearing, he'd been calm, suave, confident, the sort of guy anyone would want fighting for their cause. But he was young and inexperienced against the much more formidable Linda Johnson. He'd lost, but not for lack of trying. And he'd gained Marcey's friendship for life.

From what her mother had said, it was LePage who was skulking around asking questions. Topeté hadn't so much as breathed the same air as Marcey before that chance meeting in the hotel lobby. Christ, Marcey didn't know what to feel about that, other than that both she and Kat seemed to be struggling with the same problem: they both needed to continue this farce of an attraction—and there was considerable attraction between the two of them—to keep Topeté off her game. Marcey was using Kat just as much as Kat was using Marcey right now. It was just a matter of applying the right pressure at the right time to ensure everything went according to Marcey's plan.

And she worried. Worried that it wouldn't be enough. That Gwen or Kim would see through it and tip Kat off somehow. That LePage wouldn't buy the story.

It was LePage that Marcey wanted to screw over, after all; he was the one who'd cajoled his way into Marcey's home. LePage and Johnson seemed like a match made in heaven. He was her perfect little lapdog. They were both willing to use personal understandings of Marcey to get at her. Marcey hated them both on principle.

Topeté was another story. Topeté scared Marcey because of the hold she had over Kat. Kat was a force to be reckoned with on a good day, but Topeté had a way in to Kat that Marcey could not understand. Maybe it was love, that bitter disease that had landed Marcey in this situation in the first place. Love was a problem. It clouded judgment and made one weak. Marcey did not want to be weak. She did not want to be like Topeté when it came to Kat, or Kat when it came to Topeté.

Topeté was too smart and saw too much, yet she seemed to have fallen right into that insipid trap. Time was not on Topeté's side, and irrational behavior came with love. Still, Marcey had to give the woman credit. She played the game like she was born to do it, and she had Kat wrapped around her finger in a way that made Marcey's heart clench uncomfortably. When the time came, Marcey wasn't sure Kat could do what she had to do. Or, in her moments of stark honesty, that she was willing to do what had to be done if Kat would not.

Topeté was there, and Topeté would never go away. She was the sign that all this was never meant to be how Marcey had imagined it, but rather the omen of how horribly sideways it could all go.

A confrontation with Topeté was out of the question. Marcey knew that holding her own in such a situation would only end badly for her. But the position was as intriguing as this move toward martyrdom was. She didn't know enough about Topeté's endgame, or about how she would handle the fact that Topeté *knew* that she and Kat had done what they had. She knew and she was going along with it.

Marcey didn't understand. Her hands were shaking. She had done something horrible to Topeté in London. Given in to temptation and allowed a moment to develop organically then, and then allowed it to happen again. She'd let Kat pull her in, enticing her into the darkness of whatever fucked-up game she and Topeté were playing. And why? Why let this manipulation happen?

Did Kat want her freedom from Topeté?

Marcey tilted her chair back and stared at the ceiling.

The table rocked.

It was LePage who came in first, some time later, bringing with him a steaming cup of coffee and eyes ringed with circles so dark he looked like a raccoon. He looked worn out, as though the investigation was slowly eating him alive from the inside. His shirt hung thinly at his neck and his tan skin looked sallow in the harsh light of the fluorescent overheads.

Marcey sat up straighter as he came in, eyeing him as he sat down across from her. She was glad he was alone. She guessed that the case was getting to him, and that he was struggling. She wondered if he'd caught wind that Gwen was involved, because that would change how she engaged. How could she find out? Marcey thought hard, fast. She saw the file in LePage's hands, thick and intimidating. If it was that thick, it couldn't just be for Marcey. Not for just this case. There was no way.

"So," he began. "We meet again, Marcey Daniels."

"I wasn't aware the NYPD had jurisdiction this far north."

LePage ignored the comment and took a sip of his coffee. "Officer Raker says you got lost in the woods." He set the cup down on the table and set the file beside it.

Marcey wished, oh how she wished, to see inside it, but it remained resolutely closed. Instead she nodded. Her expression had to be kept neutral. This was what she'd learned in school, when they'd all found out about her. This was what she had learned to suppress. The panic, the feeling of exposure, all of that was weakness that could not be shown to this man. That was what he wanted. And Marcey refused to give it to him. "Figured

I could get one last good hike in before the trails were closed for mud season."

LePage blinked wearily at Marcey and settled himself into the chair opposite Marcey. "Cut the crap, Daniels."

Marcey shrugged, looking at her fingernails. She picked at the dirt caked under them. "It was what I was doing."

"No, you were casing that place, looking to rob it. For what I have no fucking clue, but it doesn't matter. We have you dead to rights trespassing."

"We?" Marcey asked.

LePage glanced over his shoulder at the door. Marcey watched as it pushed open, her stomach sinking. The panic she'd managed to quell when it was just LePage mounted once more. Marcey's heart raced, and she found she couldn't swallow. This was different—this was a game changer. Wei Topeté stepped into the room with a tight-lipped smile and an appraising glance at Marcey.

"My partner and I—well, temporary partner. I don't know if you've met. Marcey, this is Wei Topeté, of Interpol." LePage gestured to Topeté. "Wei, this is Marcey Daniels."

"Interpol?" Marcey's eyes went wide, almost comically so. It was all fake, but the reaction would cover her calming down enough to not give herself away. Christ, she was fucked. "What's Interpol care about my getting lost while hiking?"

Topeté raised an eyebrow at LePage, who picked up his coffee and shrugged. "That's your story?" Her voice was accented, but not unpleasantly so, this close. Marcey watched her with narrowed eyes. "It's not a very good one, don't you think, Ms. Daniels?"

"That's what happened." Marcey tried to keep her tone even and not flippant. If she wanted to pull this off, she was going to have to tread lightly. "If you're really that concerned about it, I'll pay the trespass fine. I believe it's about two hundred bucks." She leaned over and tapped LePage's folder, watching as the cover shifted to reveal the first line of handwritten notes. Marcey kept her eyes on Topeté; stealing a glance would be too much, but the folder remained propped partly opened as she retreated. A little triumphant thrill shot through Marcey, but she pressed her lips together for a moment, as though thoughtful, before turning to LePage. "You can't hold me. I wasn't doing anything illegal."

There, on the first page of the file, was Gwen's name.

Bingo.

Marcey glanced over at Topeté. Resting her chin on her hand, Topeté surveyed Marcey with the sort of look that made Marcey want to crawl into herself and never come back out. It was the look of a woman betrayed, a woman unable to speak to the hurt she was going through. But at the same time, it was appraising. She was sizing Marcey up, and Marcey didn't particularly like it.

The guilt ate at her, despite the put-upon feeling of Topeté's eyes on her. Marcey swallowed. She'd done this to Topeté. She'd allowed Kat to go through with what she was doing, with whatever the game was that Kat was playing with Topeté. It took two to tango, and Marcey had never once said no. The hurt Topeté hid behind disinterest and her appraising look was well concealed, but Marcey was good at reading people, and it was plain as day.

When Topeté finally spoke, it was slow, drawn out. The sort of accusation that was leveled with a great deal of gravity. Marcey didn't dare interrupt her. "Taking things that don't belong to you is illegal, yes. And you haven't done any of that just yet." Topeté paused, as if for effect. "Have you ever heard of a man named Charlie Mock?"

Feigning confusion was harder than Marcey imagined it would be. "I'm sorry? Who?"

If they knew to ask about Charlie, then they were after the book. Marcey's mother had spilled her guts to LePage when he'd visited her. None of this was about the painting or Marcey's revenge. This was about the book and freedom—all of their freedom. That book could send everyone in this room to jail.

"Charlie Mock. He was a figure in the lives of several of your new friends." LePage opened the file. He ran his finger down a set of dates. Marcey struggled to read them upside down. They knew a *lot* about her movements in the past month. How had they been able to put all this together?

Someone told them.

Marcey thought of Kat, thought of how easily she drifted between two worlds. Kat wanted to drive this job, despite Marcey running it. Would she have betrayed their trust like that? Kat wanted Charlie's book. That much was plain in the ways she spoke of it, the way she knew its contents backward and forward.

Heartsick, Marcey stared at Wei Topeté. This was the woman Kat loved. Marcey was just the girl she'd fucked. That was obvious in the way that Topeté was eyeing her. This was betrayal. Cheating was a choice and Kat was doing it. Marcey had let it happen. The guilt chewed at the back of Marcey's throat, threating to pull the words from her lips.

"I still have no idea who that is." Marcey spoke quickly, afraid the words would be smothered if she didn't.

LePage hummed and seemed to ignore her. Marcey swallowed. She couldn't look away from Topeté. Kat wouldn't have told her. There was no way. Kat stood to lose as much as the rest of them did.

LePage sucked on his teeth, pensive. "I see here that you went to London recently. Why was that?"

Distracted, Marcey turned to face LePage. She couldn't follow his line of questioning. Why did it matter? "I was, um, visiting a friend," Marcey answered. "Why? What did I do wrong?"

"Oh, nothing," LePage said. "Just trying to establish a timeline. When did that trip happen?"

"About three weeks ago. Again. Why?" Marcey's fingers twitched. She couldn't look at LePage and his folder of damnation. Topeté kept staring at her, channeling hurt and anger into her steely glare. Marcey wanted to hide.

"What was the name of the friend?" Topeté asked mildly.

Marcey clammed up. If she said Kat's name, they'd know. But she couldn't lie, because they already knew who she went to go see. She could say nothing, she supposed, but that was as good as an admission of guilt. She exhaled shakily. The truth would set her free. Or at least throw them for something of a loop. "Her name is Kathryn. But seriously, *what did I do wrong?*"

"Did you know," LePage continued mildly, "That Kathryn Barber authenticated the painting that was housed in the Perôt Gallery the day it was broken into?" He was deliberately ignoring her! Marcey felt the indignation rise like a red flush to her cheeks. That…that *ass.*

"No," Marcey said flatly. She never said Kat's last name. Topeté's face was expressionless. They already knew all of this.

"Did you know that that same painting belongs to the man who lives at the residence where Officer Raker picked you up?"

"What painting?" Marcey demanded. "I don't know about any painting."

"Really?" Topeté's tone was mild, the killer sort of quiet that came before the storm hit. "Ms. Daniels, you need to stop jerking us around. We know you're not the big fish here."

"I—"

There was a knock on the door. Marcey closed her mouth. Officer Raker stepped into the room and bent to whisper in Topeté's ear. She glanced at LePage before bending to speak to him in a low voice. "Johnson's on the phone. Wants a status."

"Wait." Marcey felt confidence surge within her. This was where she could make her move. "This is all about Linda Johnson?"

"It could be," Topeté answered. She leaned forward, her elbows on the table. "The assistant district attorney has some thoughts about you that seem to be driving how you are behaving right now, Ms. Daniels. If she weren't on the phone, she'd be here, looking you up and down, trying to figure out how someone so small and insignificant could cause so many problems."

Marcey glared.

Officer Raker looked between Topeté and LePage. "One of you needs to take the call."

"I'll go," LePage said quietly. He got up and followed Raker out of the interview room.

Topeté pulled a small device from her pocket and set it on the table. Marcey stared at it, watching as the blue LED light on it pulsed three times before glowing a solid red. It was the same device that Kim had brought out during the job—the signal scrambler. "I believe we should talk."

There was no way she could know what that device was. She had to play dumb. "I'm sorry?"

"This will scramble the video camera for the next five minutes. Johnson likes to go on, yes, but we don't have much time, Ms. Daniels." Topeté leaned across the table, tapping the device. "You're about to be arrested, but I can help."

Marcey kept her expression natural. "All right," she said. "Talk."

PART THREE

The Jailer's Gambit

CHAPTER 29

Wei, Bargaining

STARING OUT INTO THE EARLY spring night, Wei shivered. Her breath fogged, mingling with cigarette smoke. William stood beside her, hands jammed in his pockets, staring up at the stars. "It's beautiful here," she said. "You can see so much of the sky." She glanced at William, putting her cigarette to her lips. "Are you angry?"

He shook his head. "No," he answered. "You did what you had to do. Not your fault the lawyer showed up when he did."

"And if your ex is involved?"

"What happened between Gwen and me is in the past. We've both moved past it."

Wei flicked ash away from the end of her cigarette and brought it back to her lips. Her expression was pensive; she was lost in the romantic notion of what William and Gwen Lane-Wright had once had. How she'd wanted them to succeed, how ultimately they'd never had a chance.

"Have you really though?"

It was a nasty business, this game they were playing. Wei sucked down smoke tinged with air still tainted with winter's chill. The lawyer had arrived right on cue, right when Marcey Daniels was about to crack. It would keep Johnson guessing, and keep LePage thinking he was about to come out victorious, even if there were names said, names that should have been left silent. Wei hadn't wanted to engage on that level, but her hand was forced. Marcey Daniels was a wild card, a variable that Wei hadn't anticipated when she and Kat had hatched this plan years ago.

Now, with the new hurt of Kat's manipulation, of her betrayal, ringing so acutely in her ears, and the look of pity that Marcey hadn't quite been able to keep from her eyes, Wei wanted nothing more than to walk away from everything. She did not want to be *pitied*. Not by someone like Marcey Daniels who had no frame of reference for what she'd stepped into. Wei kept her hurt contained, kept it close to her chest. The hurt belonged to Kat, not the child sitting in the interview room with Devon Austin Jackson. Kat played manipulation like it was her right, and this was just another wrinkle.

She'd done it again. Fallen into the trap again. Allowed Kat to choose what would hurt her the most and allowed it to happen. *I'm a fool.*

"I could ask you the same about Barber. The edge she wants you to walk is getting narrower by the day. How soon until you fall off?"

The barb was wrapped up in William's sly smile. Wei looked over at him, wishing the nicotine would kick in faster. She didn't want to look at him anymore.

"I'll stay until it comes time to bring her in, and then I'll walk away," Wei answered. Her gaze was straight ahead.

He sighed and changed the subject. "What did you find out in there?"

Once, Wei would have debated telling him the truth, that Marcey Daniels was working on something bigger. But her action against Johnson was in Wei's best interest as well, because the book could never fall into Johnson's hands. The intent was there, carefully exposed, if only Wei was willing to piece it together. It was held out like an olive branch, a peace offering wrapped in the put-on innocence of Marcey Daniels.

William could never know and would probably never see the larger picture. He was focused on the *crime* rather than the action behind it. Wei flicked her cigarette away and reached for another. "Do you want one?" she asked William.

He shook his head.

Wei shrugged and lit it. She couldn't debate for too long. The question of the cigarette would only stall a moment. The bone she threw out, a hurt she couldn't hide, cut into her deeply in the exposure. But eventually it was going to come out. "She's sleeping with Kat Barber, which I thought was particularly interesting."

"I wasn't aware Barber was the type to cheat," William said. "That seems out of character." He glanced at Wei sideways, his face a mask of shadows. "How does that make you feel?"

"Like this isn't a time for you to be my psychiatrist, William," Wei said. Irritation crept into her voice. *Honestly.* "It intrigues me because it implies that she's at least somewhat aware of Barber's agenda. Whatever she was doing up here wasn't connected to Charlie Mock, at least not in any way that carries meaning. Kat is involved, yet her agenda in this is the wild card, I think. She wants something and I don't think Marcey Daniels knows what it is."

"What does Daniels want then?"

Wei shrugged. "Far as I can tell, she wants to make a name for herself using Charlie Mock's legacy as a jettison point. It's foolish, yes, but she's young. Her brush with Johnson when she was a teenager stung."

"Johnson's vendetta against her is something else." William scratched his growing beard. He'd been up for close to thirty-six hours at this point, if Wei's math was correct. His mind was sluggish. "Never got a straight answer outta her about what that was about."

"Marcey Daniels supplied the pills the first time Johnson's daughter nearly overdosed." Wei sighed heavily. "She doesn't broadcast it because she should have recused herself from the case because of the obvious conflict of interest but instead chose not to prosecute based on that set of charges. I have no idea how your American legal system allowed her to stay on the case."

LePage frowned. "She would have been removed. No DA is going to allow something like that. The mere *implication* of a personal vendetta or a conflict like that and the entire case could get thrown out."

"And yet it wasn't. Think about it, William. Think about *why* it didn't get thrown out. Think about how much Johnson stands to lose if that whole story ever comes out. That's why she wants Mock's book. Because the bastard documented the whole thing in there. He was the one who paid for that defense."

"Really?"

"Not Daniels's defense. Her mother handled that. But her friend, the one that's up for parole in May."

"Is that why she didn't ask for a lawyer until he walked into the room?" William rubbed at the back of his neck and shivered, flipping his collar up against the stiff breeze. "She wants to get caught? That seems foolish, but it would explain why she just walked out there for Raker to find."

"You don't think she's after something more than just the painting?" The painting was still there. "Maybe something that would make her want to get caught?"

The call that had drawn William from the room and allowed Wei to speak to Marcey alone and unmonitored had been from Johnson. She'd had people back in the city track down the homeowner and obtain permission to enter the home and check the contents of the vault. Officer Raker drove back up to check, finding the place abandoned. With the painting still there, there was no cause to arrest Marcey Daniels. Wei couldn't figure it out. Why not just walk away? There was no sign of intrusion at the house, so why would Marcey go to all the trouble of coming up here only to get caught?

Wei thought back over the conversation she'd had with her. Behind the veiled threats and barbs they'd shared, there'd been an understanding of their mutually assured destruction. They both knew that if the book were to fall into the wrong hands, it was on both their heads.

"I want it gone," Marcey had said.

"How?" Wei had asked.

"Burn it, I don't know."

"People won't take kindly to that," Wei had answered. "I wouldn't. I couldn't."

"Your cases will fall apart, right? And you won't be able to protect her anymore?" Marcey had tilted her head to one side. "Isn't that why you're doing all of this? To keep her, and your own ass, I suppose, safe?"

A terrible thought drifted across Wei's mind and the cigarette hung limply from her lips. Kat wouldn't have been so stupid as to fake the painting, would she? She wouldn't try to fake the damn book.

Would she?

"What? Like she's going after Johnson?" William shook his head. "There's no way. She's just a kid. Nah, bet you a million bucks she's just in over her head with Kat Barber and doesn't know how to get away. Maybe this was her trying to get caught so we'd separate them."

"Perhaps," she said. She needed to speak to Kat. "That seems a bit weak, though, don't you think?"

Shrugging, William moved back toward the door. "It's cold as fuck out here. I'm going inside."

"Suit yourself."

The door opened, casting the back steps in the warm glow of yellow light before slamming shut to leave Wei alone in the darkness. She stared up at the stars, watching the clouds shift across the face of the moon. It was five in the morning. She was exhausted.

From her pocket, her phone rang once, then twice. Wei tugged it free, looking at the blocked number on the screen and resigning herself before she answered the call. "What?"

"You have my mastermind." Kat's voice was full of triumph, cocky and smug. It was all the confirmation Wei needed. "I'd like her back."

"You did it again, Kathryn," Wei hissed. Glancing to the door, she switched to French, knowing Kat would have no trouble following. "You *promised* me you wouldn't do this to me." Even as a child, Wei had never been any good at hiding her hurt. Not now, when Kat had shattered the fragile trust they'd built in each other. Not when she was going for all of their destruction through her own hubris. "I want to know why you did it."

"Because I love you," Kat answered in sullen French. "Because there's only one way to make sure that this ends in our favor, and that is to *control* any possible outcome. You're doing the same, aren't you, with your little liaisons with Shelly when you think no one's looking? She's not stupid, and neither am I."

"I won't be played," Wei retorted. "If you love me, prove it. Tell me what the fuck this is."

Kat chuckled. "It's a heist, darling. These things go in stages."

"You haven't stolen anything."

"Haven't I, darling?" Kat's tone was deliberately mild. "Perhaps this isn't about the act of stealing itself, but what comes after. You want what I promised to your bosses back in Lyon. I want my freedom. I'm getting both."

"I want to protect you," Wei said testily. "Even if it's from yourself."

"I'm not a child," Kat said, equally annoyed.

Wei pinched the bridge of her nose, cigarette smoking between two fingers. She couldn't do this. This was insane. Kat wanted her to play some sort of twisted game that represented something far more complicated than anything Wei could ever possibly want.

"And neither are you my protector, Wei. We're here for each other because that is what people who love each other do."

"You keep telling me you love me, but I've yet to see you do anything that convinces me that this isn't all just a show for your criminal friends." Wei put the cigarette to her lips and sucked in smoke. "I want to believe you, I truly do."

"Then meet me," Kat said. "At the airport, tomorrow morning."

"What about your *mastermind*?" Wei asked sarcastically. "Shouldn't you be concerned that she's arrested, locked away when you need her most?"

"Oh, I have no doubt you'll be letting her go. Nothing was stolen, after all."

Wei ground her teeth. "What time?"

"Eleven o'clock at LaGuardia, darling. On Wednesday."

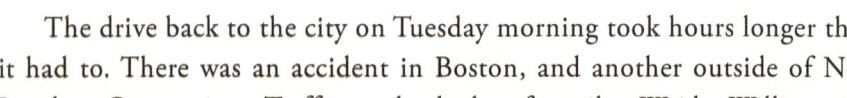

The drive back to the city on Tuesday morning took hours longer than it had to. There was an accident in Boston, and another outside of New London, Connecticut. Traffic was backed up for miles. Wei let William sing tunelessly along to the radio and ignored her itch to call Kat. Reaching out was surrender.

So Wei maintained her silence.

She let William drop her off at her hotel and collapsed into sleep. She dreamed of nothing, the twisted, empty blank dreams of an exhausted mind. They'd spent hours on Monday combing through the woods around the property, looking for signs of any intrusion. There were none. The melting snow and mud made it impossible to tell if anyone had disturbed the ground around the house, and the painting was still there. Wei had seen it with her own eyes, supervised the transfer to the courier that was taking it to the auction house in the city, vetted him against every agency she could think of.

It was odd; there was nothing to indicate that Marcey Daniels was in those woods for any reason other than her flimsy hiking excuse.

On Wednesday, Wei rose early and took the train out to Queens before hopping a cab to the airport. She paid in cash with her own money. The last thing Wei wanted was for Johnson to catch her using investigation funds to pay for a rendezvous with Kat Barber.

Still, she thought they'd take public transportation back to Midtown and walk from there. She didn't think it was wise to be alone with Kat just yet, in the back of a cab whose driver and onboard camera could damn them both to years in prison if they weren't careful. Wei waited just inside the terminal doors, leaning against a pillar by baggage claim, watching the tourists collect their baggage, dark circles under eyes the common denominator in this mass of cultural variation.

Pulling out her phone, Wei sent Kat a text explaining where she was waiting. She wondered if she should wait outside, if that was more dramatic, more in keeping with Kat's flair for such things. Wei's thoughts spun, wondering if getting involved in Kat's dramatics was worth the heartache or the anxious churning at the pit of her stomach.

So much depended on the détente she'd formed with Marcey Daniels. So much depended on Kat being able to walk away from the girl and not allow herself to be drawn into this cheating game that Wei hated so much. Maybe all it would take was Wei being able to press Kat, to force her to acknowledge that what she'd done was wrong.

Never admit you're wrong, darling.

Wei clenched her hand into a fist and looked away from the doorway where Kat was set to emerge. Her phone beeped. Kat was on her way, having deplaned successfully. Wei bit her lip, steeling herself for the conversation that was to follow. She could do this. She could get Kat to tell her the truth about Marcey Daniels's part of this plan.

Kat emerged from the terminal some ten minutes later with her hair caught up in a messy bun and her anorak slung over one arm. It was warm outside; Wei hadn't brought a jacket with her. She pushed herself away from the support column to greet Kat, taking in her faded jeans and worn sweater with the little hole at the elbow.

Wei loved that sweater. Kat had had it for years. It made Kat seem softer somehow, less brittle around the edges. Wei wasn't sure what to say, seeing Kat in a garment so clearly meant for comfort. Was she frightened too?

"Hello," Kat said, guarded. It made Wei nervous because it was that guarded tone that always gave Kat away. No one else knew how to look for it, how to pull it out of the seeming nothing of Kat's serene expression and slightly smudged makeup. This was just another mask, or rather one in the process of falling into nothingness.

Knowing why Kat was projecting that guarded nature was enough to make Wei want to turn and walk away. It came from Marcey Daniels, from the girl Kat saw no easy way to control other than to offer up her body. Wei's fingers twitched.

"*Salut*," Wei answered. She shoved her hands into her pockets to keep herself from reaching out. The gesture was empty when Kat set down her jacket and carry-on and pulled Wei close. She smelled of airplane-stale air and cheap coffee. Her perfume was gone, but she was warm and soft. Her fingers curled at Wei's jaw, cupped her cheeks, and she met Wei's gaze evenly.

"This feels as though there should be tears."

Wei rolled her eyes, not quite able to keep the little hiccup of a desperate, awkward giggle from her voice. "Tears of heartbreak, perhaps."

"I said I was sorry." Kat laughed and shook her head. She kissed Wei continental style, first on one cheek and then the other. She paused, just for a moment, before leaning in. Her lips were warm, sweet, hesitant. Wei hated this play at faux-innocence. This, too, was a manipulation. "And I truly am, Wei."

It was all a show. An opening volley at Wei's defenses. Yet Wei couldn't help herself. She pulled her hands from her pockets and wrapped them around Kat, holding her tight and kissing her like she was salvation. She loved this woman, loved her with all her might, and Kat...well, Wei never knew how she felt. This was the only time Wei could convey to her all that was being dashed upon the ground when Kat did what she'd convinced herself she had to do in order to control this situation.

"Promise me something," Wei whispered, her forehead bumping against Kat's. "This has to play out to the end, play out to whatever conclusion we're all building toward...but promise me you won't... Not again... Not with her."

Kat's smile was gentle, kind. Her lips were flushed with Wei's kisses, her lipstick smudged a little at the corner of her mouth. Wei swiped her thumb over the smear, wiping it away. "Of course," she said. Her eyes shone bright in the spring sunlight. Wei saw no reason to think her dishonest. "I only did it to—"

"*Don't.*" Wei pulled away from Kat. "Don't try and justify it to me. I understand why, I don't agree with it, and it hurts, Kat. It hurts so much to know that what we have doesn't matter enough to you to consider how I might feel when you go and do these things."

Standing stock still in the middle of a sunbeam, Kat frowned. "Do you know what she wants, Wei?"

"What?"

"The same thing we do. To see that Johnson never gets her hands on that book."

CHAPTER 30

Marcey, Regrouping

THE TRAIN ARRIVED AT GRAND Central a little before ten o'clock in the evening. The cars were packed by the time it rolled into the station. Marcey stood, having given up her seat for a mother and her baby a few stops back, and was now sagging against a posted set of Metro North rules, dirty with graffti, running over the conversations of the past few days.

It had taken three days for her to get out of New Hampshire. Devon Austin Jackson had encouraged her to pay the trespassing fine and get out of Lincoln and the mountains before anyone asked more questions. He hadn't said anything about Wei Topeté or the twenty minutes Marcey had spent in her presence on Sunday night. He hadn't even said how he'd somehow ended up coming to her rescue. He'd just told her what she needed to do to make this whole thing go away and expected Marcey to follow through without question.

And she had. The trumped-up charges were enough to make Marcey *want* to get out of there. William LePage had been more than willing to stick more on her, assuring Marcey that she was being watched and that she should tread carefully.

The next move would require finesse. And a decision Marcey wasn't sure she could make on her own.

Wei Topeté's plan was simple. Marcey just had to agree to it. And she wasn't sure she could. Not willingly, not without fear of reprisal. Her plans were fleeting, leaves on the wind; thoughts slipping easily from her mind, replaced by Topeté's sharp, black eyes. They looked straight past her lies and into the motivations that Marcey kept guarded, secret, and locked away.

During the drive south, and after returning the rental, Marcey had wanted to call Kim and see how the job had gone. But her phone had no SIM in it, and she wasn't sure that calling was a good idea until she bought a new burner phone. There was nothing for her in this city anymore. Nowhere for her to go.

I need you to stay away from her. Topeté's eyes had been pleading. *I know what you're doing.*

You know I can't do that. We're doing this—this thing together.

But you can keep your hands to yourself. If you want my help, you'll do it.

As a rule, Marcey hated cheaters. Kat Barber had told her once that she was a pretty face, and that Kat liked kissing her. Marcey, however, did not think that was fair. Not after talking to Topeté, not after the way Topeté had conveyed her hurt with the look in her eyes, and in the way she'd gripped the edge of the table when Marcey told her what her plan was going to be. She was the interloper, the homewrecker. She'd let Kat pull her into that part of the game wanting it to be okay, yet knowing it wasn't.

Marcey hadn't dared speak. Hadn't dared to say that at the time, she hadn't known about Topeté. At the time, she'd thought it was just Kat trying to be kind in a way that no one had ever been kind to Marcey before. It was a lie. Marcey simply hadn't cared. Wei Topeté hadn't been a real person then. She was just a name. Just a word on her tongue that hadn't represented the hurt that had sat in front of her while they'd talked.

"It's a manipulation," Topeté had answered. "Nothing more. She wants the book. Same as you or I. But what she wants with it…I couldn't say."

"And what do you want?" Marcey had asked.

"I want it gone."

Marcey had bowed her head. "It can't just vanish. Not with Johnson after it like she is. Not with your bosses after it." She'd thought back to what Kat had said. What Shelly had said. "Doesn't Kat owe it to Interpol, to buy her freedom?"

Topeté's smile had been small, tight-lipped and giving nothing away. Marcey hadn't known what to make of that, if anything at all. "We all have bargains, deals that we're letting go to seed. You and I, we understand each other in that sense. There are things that must be done in order to get to the point where that decision can be made."

It had been so *cryptic*. Marcey knew what Topeté was saying, what was written between the lines. Her want to destroy the book, to comply with Gwen and Kim's wishes, would cost Kat her freedom. It was a Catch-22, and not one that Marcey thought she could successfully navigate without some serious contemplation.

But...what about Kat's other plan?

The train doors opened and the pungent smell of garbage, warm and acrid, hit Marcey's nose. She inhaled deeply, lingering on the train. She knew she should lose herself in the crowd, disappear before she was ever missed. There were millions of people in this city; it would be easy to fade away into nothing. Find herself a new identity. A new life.

But there wouldn't be an end then, and it was the end that Marcey sought.

A conductor came by and eyed her. "You gotta get off." His accent was Staten Island thick. Marcey smiled thinly at him. She got off the train and walked up the track.

The concourse was busy, even at the late hour. Marcey stood for a moment in the middle of the wide, open space. She loved moments like this, when she was stopped and everyone else was a blur of motion around her. These moments were safe, when she could not be moved. An idea, half-formed and still raw, swam in her mind's eye. Perhaps she could stay with Shelly. Shelly who was removed from this terrible mess. Shelly who could listen to what Marcey learned from Topeté and tell her what to do with the information.

Marcey glanced at her watch before springing once more into motion. There was a train she could catch that would take her to Penn Station and another from there she could take across the river. But she had to hurry. The express was waiting when she trotted down the stairs, tucking her metro card away in her wallet again. Once on the train, Marcey leaned against the window and dozed, exhaustion threatening to claim her.

An hour later, Marcey was standing in front of Shelly's apartment door, hesitating before knocking. She had come in behind another resident, and now he was lingering at the end of the hallway, watching her, his apartment door half-open. Marcey narrowed her eyes. "What?" she demanded. "Got a problem?"

The guy shrugged and went inside. Marcey knocked on Shelly's door. She came a few minutes later, still dressed for work. Her hair was up in a messy bun and her nametag was crooked on her chest. "Oh, thank God," Shelly said, and pulled Marcey into the apartment.

Kim was sitting on the couch, and she looked up sharply upon seeing Marcey. "You're okay."

Marcey nodded. "Blew through some of Kat's emergency cash, but yeah, here I am."

"When I got your texts, I pulled them out as fast as I could. We saw the cops come back to look the place over. Thank God Gwen and Kat were fast." Kim got to her feet and pulled Marcey into a hug. Shelly clapped Marcey on the shoulder.

"Which one of you called Devon?" Marcey asked. "He showed up just as Topeté was about to start laying into me."

"Topeté was there?" Kim's eyes went wide. She stepped back. "That'd explain this then." From her pocket, she produced a folded-up piece of paper. Wordlessly, she passed it to Marcey, who unfolded it.

Printed on the paper was another of the crude likenesses of Marcey's face, along with Johnson's Super PAC's name. This time the details were more sordid and more closely connected to the job they'd just pulled. "Is she feeding them information?" Marcey asked. Her fingers were shaking. "Johnson, I mean."

Shelly and Kim exchanged a long glance before both their gazes fell on Marcey. "What did you talk to Topeté about?" Shelly's tone was mild. "Beyond the usual threats and subterfuge."

Marcey frowned. "I didn't—Kat, mostly." She sighed, smoothing the creases from the paper. "She laid out her side of things. I told her what happened with Kat, I said I was sorry. Promised I wouldn't do it again." Marcey stared up at Shelly. Kim's expression was stony. Shelly's eyes were unreadable. Marcey swallowed. This was the gamble. The lie she had to tell them in order to feel out what Topeté was doing. Shelly could read people; she read Marcey easily enough. Marcey had to tread carefully or this lie, too, would show. "Was I not supposed to do that? She had me alone in a room and she started telling me things…things about Rio, about Charlie's life going to pieces. About how Kat had sold him out to keep herself safe."

Kim huffed. "Now you know why we don't care for working with her."

"Topeté is in the book, Kim." Marcey closed her eyes. "That was the other thing she told me. She's in the book and she's every bit as screwed as we are if the book gets into Johnson's hands. Charlie documented every time she looked the other way for Kat. Every time she wasn't where the action was happening despite being in the city is documented in here." Marcey pulled the book from her bag. "This is twice now that I've been arrested with it in my bag. And twice now that they haven't lifted a finger to take it from me."

Kim's lips drew into a thin line. "Okay." She nodded. "Okay. So Topeté's not working for Johnson, but to her own ends. Does that help us or hurt us?"

Shelly sighed. She unpinned the name tag from her shirt and set it in a dish by the door. "I think it helps, in a way. The riskiest move of this whole thing was having Topeté out there as a wild card, but if her end goal is the same as ours, then I think we're okay. Her goal's always been the book, after all."

"After all?" Kim's eyes narrowed. "You make it sound like you've got some sort of an inside scoop there, Shelly."

Moving into the kitchen, Shelly ignored Kim. "You know how she was in Rio. Didn't want to ruin Gwen and William's relationship just to save the job."

"No, she left that to Kat." Kim scowled.

"You weren't even there—" Marcey protested.

They ignored her.

"And Gwen had to pay the price." Shelly shook her head. "Topeté has a vested interest in not getting caught up in whatever it is that we're planning, but I also think she won't deliberately try to hinder us."

"She's been in *touch*," Marcey said, the realization dawning on her. "You've talked to her, Shelly."

Shelly set the kettle on the stove, clicked the burner on, and crossed her arms over her chest. "She came to find me at the beginning, not long after the card game. At first, I thought she just wanted to throw her weight around. Threaten a bit and see what I knew."

"What did you tell her?"

"Nothing," Shelly retorted. "What sort of a fool do you think I am?"

"The sort who carries on with Topeté!" Kim spluttered. "You're no better than Marcey, shit."

"Hey," Marcey said. "I don't think that's fair."

"Tough," Kim said. She leveled an accusatory stare at Shelly. "So, she came to see you. Where, the bar?"

"Where else?" Shelly shrugged. "I guess I've gotten complacent with Charlie gone. Going to the same places, seeing the same people. She came to find me a few other times. I guessed at her game...but I wasn't sure. Not until just now." She gestured to the kettle. "Do you want some?"

Marcey nodded. Kim sighed before jerking her head down once. "So Topeté's been trying to make overtures for a while?" Marcey asked.

Shelly got down three mugs. "Seems that way." She set out two boxes of tea. "Take your pick. Sorry to not have a better selection." She stepped back and Marcey leaned forward to inspect the tea. Kim grabbed a black breakfast tea bag and jammed it into the mug she'd claimed. "So, she's spoken to me a few times, mostly threats. I'm sorry I never talked about it. It didn't seem like it was worth it to make anyone worried when we were doing so well." Shelly took the kettle from the burner just as it began to hiss. "I mean, we knew she was sniffing around. And she never told me anything we didn't already know."

Kim frowned. "Still, it's a bit underhanded, Shelly."

"I know," Shelly said.

Marcey took her tea and retreated to the couch. If Shelly was speaking out of turn, they needed to know why. "Why don't you tell us about these encounters and we can see if they keep to the story she told me? If they do, I don't see why we can't use it as an olive branch."

———◆———

They talked long into the night. Kim went home a little after 3:00 a.m. Shelly retreated into her bedroom only to come out with a blanket and a pillow for Marcey. She'd never asked to stay, but the implication hung heavy in the air.

"The couch isn't much," she said, "but at least it's a place to rest." Marcey thanked her and curled up to sleep. She didn't feel better about their proposed plan, so much of it relied on the idea of keeping secrets from everyone. She wasn't sure she could keep them all straight. Or if she wanted

257

to. What could be done about the book? Destroy it and many lives were saved; keep it around and there was always the risk of Johnson or Interpol getting a hold of it. Topeté couldn't have that, and Kat was fucked either way.

Shelly, Kim, and Gwen all thought the book should be destroyed at the end of the job, to keep Topeté from getting her hands on it. Marcey wasn't sure. She liked the leverage it gave her over Topeté, over Kat. She liked how powerful it made her feel.

Sleep wouldn't come. At close to four, Marcey pulled out her laptop and opened a spreadsheet.

It took hours, but Marcey painstakingly copied each entry from Charlie's book into a spreadsheet, saving it into an untraceable private document backed up into an anonymous e-mail account's cloud storage drive. Hidden behind layers upon layers of the banalities of everyday life.

You can't trust the internet. Kim's voice rattled around in Marcey's head. *Anyone can find anything on there.*

It wasn't that Marcey didn't believe Kim, but rather that this was part of the other plan, the plan she hadn't mentioned to Shelly or Kim. The private deal between herself and Kat, and by extension, Topeté.

Marcey ran her hand over the book. It was a work of art. Charlie's handwriting was a complex web of years of work, put together, torn out and taped back into place. It was a lifetime of contacts, the perfect key to a world she could only dream of just a few months ago. This was a future and a past all at once. And Charlie had given it to Marcey—not to Kat, as everyone thought—but to Marcey. It was up to Marcey to figure out how to save everyone in this book from Johnson.

He had given it to her because she would have never wanted it, had she known it existed. She'd talked a big game about wanting to know more, but it wasn't until Shelly had drawn her into the game that Marcey wanted more. The book sat heavy in her hand, its leather cover worn smooth with age. It was beautiful.

Marcey wanted nothing more than to keep it around forever, but the book, in this form, could never survive. The backup was the first step.

The next...

Marcey leaned over, pulled her phone from its charger, and dialed a number from memory. The burner phone was awkward and cumbersome in her hands. She waited once, twice, three times as the phone rang. "I need to destroy Charlie's book," she said when the voice on the other end of the line picked up. "That was what you wanted, right?"

"Not quite." Kat Barber's voice was smooth as butter. "Are you back in the city?"

"Are you?"

"Tell me where you are, Marcey Daniels, and I'll come to you."

This was the beginning of the end for Kat Barber.

This was the promise Marcey had made to Topeté. The promise that this was *done* between Kat and herself.

CHAPTER 31

Kat, Creating

MARCEY SAT ON THE EDGE of the bed in Kat's hotel room. It was midday. The blinds were flung open and light poured in from outside. Kat was at the desk, supplies scattered around her. She hummed as she worked, exhaling, writing, exhaling again.

"Why do you do that?"

"Do what?" Kat reached for her mug of tea.

"Breathe like that when you're writing."

"If you hesitate when you're forging someone's handwriting, even for a second, it starts to look fake. Half of what I do is confidence. The other is breath control. Here, I'll show you." Kat grabbed a notepad and tossed it to Marcey. "Sign that."

Marcey pulled a pen from her purse and scrawled her signature. Kat took it back and stared at the mess of letters for a moment before exhaling and duplicating Marcey's signature perfectly below it. Marcey stared, awed by this display of skill. "Wow," she said, adding quickly, "please don't steal my identity."

Kat laughed. "Never, darling."

They weren't supposed to meet. Both of them, in their own way, had promised Topeté that they'd avoid each other. This was part of Marcey's plan, to some extent, but meeting like this, drawing each other into the same games as before, wasn't meant to happen. This companionable silence, while Kat worked and Marcey observed, was comfortable.

Did Kat feel guilty about this? Did she want to crawl into some dark place and hide from the revelation that Marcey's presence in Kat's life was destroying something beautiful? Marcey did. She wanted to curl into the darkness and hate herself for what she'd done, for what she'd allowed to happen. Cheating was a two-way street, and it wasn't as though Marcey hadn't known Kat was seeing someone. Maybe she'd thought the relationship was different, a picture of convenience, open, but she had been wrong. This was real, growing, changing. Kat wanted it; Topeté wanted it.

The game now was in playing that she didn't care, that Kat's hands on her didn't make her burn with shame. The game now was about making Topeté think Marcey was every bit as much of a horrible person as her actions indicated. Marcey had to shoulder the force of this, the force of the speeding train that was about to slam into the cold, cold wall of Marcey's bad intentions.

She sat back, leaning on her elbows, her feet kicked out in front of her. The bed smelled like Kat, like her hair and perfume, mixed together with the stiff, stale scent of starch and hotel cleaning products. It was a safe smell, a place where Marcey could relax enough to ask what came next.

"Does she know what you plan to do with the book?"

Kat frowned. "I don't think so, not quite in the terms I have planned for it. You want to use the painting to eliminate Johnson from your life and draw out her humiliation of you and your friend. I want to use the book to illustrate the hypocrisy of this whole endeavor." Kat reached for a ruler and drew a perfectly straight line before switching from blue to black ink. "The dates and places in this book are in a code. A code that anyone could figure out given the barest knowledge of Charlie, I might add. And all it takes is careful manipulation of the facts to remove the guilty parties."

"So you're just going to what, tell Topeté you weren't in the places where you so clearly were?" Marcey sighed. That made the whole effort seem pointless, shortsighted even, especially on Kat's part. "It isn't going to work."

"It doesn't have to work, Marcey. It merely needs to be *present* and I'll be free." Kat clicked her tongue. "Wei wants more from the book than I can give. I promised Charlie's book, his contacts."

Ah, Marcey thought, *so that's her game.*

"What happened? How did you get caught?"

Kat sniffed. "That was a nasty business." She tilted her head to one side. "I'd love to paint you. The small girl in over her head." Her eyes were alight with the childish sort of glee that one saw when the impossible was realized. Her face transformed. She was beautiful, completely and utterly beautiful. Marcey swallowed, wanting. "You'd be like a nymph, all the great forces surrounding you, wanting you for a myriad of different reasons… conveying that in brush strokes would take a loving touch."

"That doesn't answer my question." Marcey looked away. She couldn't look at Kat; the gravity between them was just so strong. So intensely married to the charade, if she stayed there too long, she'd have to kiss Kat.

And if she kissed her…well…

"You got caught. What happened?"

The look that drew across Kat's face was pained. "People like me, we don't get caught. We negotiate, charm, bargain our way out of things. Even if they're not our things to give away." Kat got to her feet, almost prowling toward Marcey on the bed. "I was in Brussels. Too close to home for Wei, I suppose. There was a series of bonds—hand-painted, exquisite. I wanted to have a look at them, see their craftsmanship. I may have let myself into the Spanish Consulate and caused an international incident. Next thing I know there's a gun in my face and I'm sitting in a basement room face-to-face with my lover, trying to pretend I don't know her to save both our skins." Kat sat down next to Marcey. "I do love her, you know. You—you're a pretty face, one I happen to rather enjoy kissing—but what Wei and I share isn't like that."

Marcey stuck her chin out, her bangs falling into her eyes, a play at defiant and hurt. "There's no need to rub it in, Kat. There's no future here, I get it."

Kat bought it.

"Oh, but darling, look at us. You've made quite the splash already, haven't you? Allies and partners from all walks of life, places that don't belong to you, people you should never have met." Kat's fingers tangled in Marcey's hair, jerking her face around, forward. Marcey swallowed and forced herself to meet Kat's expectant gaze. "I offered Wei Charlie's book because it was all I had that she knew I would never willingly part with. Everything else I give to her freely, as I give to you." She leaned forward, kissing Marcey with fierce desperation. She was a woman drowning, desperate to cling to anything that would keep her afloat.

Worse was that Marcey let it happen. She made no move to stop Kat from kissing her, from pushing her back. She let it happen, let Kat have her because that was what Kat wanted. It was all a game, the careful manipulation of emotions and feelings, betrayal and hurt barely kept contained. What Kat wanted, Marcey still wasn't sure. The biting guilt was tempered by Kat's fingers, pushing Marcey's shirt from her shoulders, her jeans from her legs. This was a promise and a rebuke all at once; this was everything Marcey did not want.

And yet she drowned.

Kissing Kat was easier than trying to understand her. Fucking her was easier still. She smelled of summer and best-laid plans gone awry time and time again. Marcey's fingers scrambled across Kat's back, through the soft fabric of her worn sweater, across the places she kept hidden, the long scars on her back and neck.

"Where did these come from?" Marcey asked. Her lips smeared kisses on Kat's skin.

Pausing, Kat pulled Marcey upward, her lips seeking, yearning. Marcey kissed her, let herself be rolled onto her back. Kat's fingers splayed across the thin raised white line at her neck. "My mother, before they locked her up. She was mad, you see. My father didn't get there in time. She nearly killed me before he pulled her off."

"I'm sorry." Marcey didn't know what else to say.

"Don't be, darling, just let me forget for a while." Kat's hair fell into her eyes, which shone in the mid-morning light. Marcey was halfway in love with her.

And *that* couldn't last.

Kat slept lightly, tossing and turning, caught up in the throes of nightmares. Marcey watched her, cracked open and raw, her knees pulled up to her chest. Her entire body ached from what Kat did to her, what she'd done to herself to fall so low. She hated herself, hated that she'd allowed herself to get this far down.

Stupid, stupid. This is all so stupid, but remember that this is for a reason, Mar.

Yet this was insurance. Protection against the inevitability of where this was going to end. Somewhere, in the in-between space of this encounter, Marcey had figured out the final steps to this plan. The only way she was going to keep everyone safe was to play a game all her own. To sink as low as Kat, as low as Topeté, as low as Johnson… Marcey wasn't sure she could do it.

Beside her, Kat grunted. She slept like she was trying to protect herself from the world around her. The dark, twisted world of dreams haunted her, even in the serene bliss of sleep. Seeing Kat so open was an odd benediction; the woman laid bare without the piles of caked-on bullshit. She was small in sleep.

She was beautiful.

I could get lost in her. It was the last conscious thought Marcey had before she curled into a ball, her back to Kat. She couldn't touch Kat. Never. Not like that, not in the peace of sleep. Was that the only solution to the problem of Topeté and Kat? To end the relationship? It was the right thing to do, to throw herself to her knees before Topeté and beg a forgiveness she didn't deserve.

Marcey dreamt of Darius.

They were seventeen again, laughing, smoking weed at the top of the fire escape of his building. He taught her how to hold a blunt and she taught him how to inhale. Becca had just left and they were alone. She'd gone home because her mother had called her away from this perfect world. She'd left high, her lips catching Marcey's in the hallway outside Darius's mother's apartment.

They made tacos later, flipping bits of hamburger and onion together. Marcey leaned against him, lost in a haze of how amazing everything tasted when she was high. They drank hard cider that tasted like blueberries. It was like an explosion in her mouth.

Later, when he kissed her, she told him she was gay.

He held her then, letting her cry when she told him how she was worried he wasn't going to love her any more.

"How could I not love you?" he asked.

He was her best friend in the entire world. She didn't know where these things started and ended. All she knew was that she couldn't imagine life without him. He had the start of beard; his hair rubbed against her face. It would soon be cut off by the New York Department of Corrections, but it was the memory of how it felt rubbing against her face that Marcey could never shake.

"I'll love you to the end of the earth."

She just never thought the end of the earth would come so quickly. It crumbled around Marcey with Johnson's smiling face staring up at her from the courtroom floor. It stared out at Marcey from the posters. It was a promise Marcey made to herself to make the world whole again.

The buzzing of her phone drew Marcey up from sleep. Kat was curled around her. The light slanting through the window was lazy with late-afternoon warmth. Marcey fumbled for her phone, pushing back the guilt and reminding herself that this was all for the plan. She had to do this to make sure that this ended up how she wanted it to end. And, if she was perfectly honest with herself, it wasn't just that Kat couldn't control herself around Marcey—but rather that Marcey was unable to say no to her.

Marcey fell back onto the pillow. "Hello?"

"Where the hell are you?" Kim demanded.

"Uh...I'm not sure... Where are we?" She hadn't really been paying attention when Kat came to fetch her or on the train over to Kat's new hotel.

"Williamsburg," Kat grunted, rolling over.

"Oh Jesus, you fucked her again." Kim groaned. "What the fuck is wrong with you, Marcey?"

The sting of setting up for the final act bit into Marcey like a slap to the face. This was going to be harder than she thought.

Kat made an annoyed sound, a low growl at the back of her throat. "'Zat Kim?"

"Yeah," Marcey said.

"Bugger." Kat sat up, rubbing at her neck. A bruise was forming there, obvious and stupid for anyone who cared to see it. She looked at the clock on the bedside table. "We need to be at that meeting."

"Tell Kat she's a moron and get your ass over here. I'm not covering for you again if Topeté shows up demanding to know where you are."

"She what?" Marcey hissed. "She's there?"

"She didn't, but she could. You're holding a live grenade. You have to fucking stop doing this. She'll only play nice for so long before she's gonna gun for your throat." Kim hung up before Marcey could respond, and Marcey pulled the phone away from her ear.

"We should go."

"Yes." Marcey bent to pick her shirt up off the floor at the foot of the bed. She looked over her shoulder. Kat's hair hung limply over her face, the blonde curls lifeless. The bones of her spine stood out against the contours of her back, and Marcey's breath caught. There was black ink there, merged with the scars. A vine laced down the skin of her back. "Do you love her, Kat, truly?"

There was an anchor, roots at the small of Kat's back. They splayed out, wrapping around the base of her spine, a warm brown inking into the cream of her skin. That was Topeté, Marcey realized with a shock. They were intertwined in a way Marcey had never realized before. They were connected. The question seemed stupid then. Marcey busied herself with her pants.

"With all my being."

Marcey picked up the fake book from the desk. Her jacket was on the floor by the door, discarded with the brutality of Kat's assault on her being. Marcey picked it up and tugged it on, not looking at Kat.

It was time for the final coup. "We can't keep doing this, then. It isn't fair."

Kat heaved a shuddering sigh, hiding her defeat behind the blank mask of impassivity. "I know."

CHAPTER 32

A Transaction, Completed

THEY ENDED UP MEETING THE next morning. Marcey went back to Shelly's and passed out on the couch without a word. Shelly didn't seem to mind, either. She just shook her head and went back to her preparations. There was an entire dossier spread out across Shelly's kitchen table. Marcey glanced it over before she left to the appointed meeting place: a Starbucks off 42nd near the train station. It was central for everyone. Marcey went alone, as Shelly had to go into work for a few minutes to pick up some documents she'd left behind. She was dressed to the nines, in one of those killer dresses her library salary could scarcely afford, applying fake eyelashes when Marcey slipped out of the apartment and walked up the block to catch the 7 train into Manhattan.

Gwen was the first to arrive, blinking blearily into a coffee and perching on a stool across from Marcey. "I don't know if I can be involved with this part," she confessed, shrugging off her oversized scarf. "Because of Will. Because of how integral a role he's playing in the end game." Gwen's eyes fluttered shut. "I know that it'll rattle him to see me, but it could also tip him off. Or make him think more critically about what we're doing in a way that I think maybe…we don't want."

"Well," Marcey said thoughtfully. This move was expected. After what had happened in New Hampshire, Marcey wanted it to go this way. Gwen's ability to be objective was something that Marcey worried about, and her taking herself out of the equation saved Marcey having to find a reason to ask her to leave. "It's your call in the end."

The silence surrounded Marcey. Gwen sipped her coffee. "I would have married him, you know."

"Really?" Marcey asked. "Even though he's a LEO?"

"Despite that." There was a fond smile at Gwen's lips. Her beanie, crimson red against her dark hair and skin, stood out in the low light of the coffee shop. It was overcast and raining outside; everything was in shadows despite their window seat. "Will was, well, you know how Kat is with Topeté, right? It was like that, only more intoxicating. Like this drug I couldn't quit." She glanced sideways at Marcey. "Kat's always been able to quit Topeté when she needs to or wants to. It's part of what keeps Topeté coming back to her."

"I think they really love each other." The truth of the matter was that Marcey was the one who couldn't stop saying no. She was letting Kat destroy the beautiful, perfect thing they shared. All because what? Marcey wanted to save her? Did she? Could she?

"I'd believe that if she bowed out of the game and went legit." Gwen scoffed and went back to her coffee. "With Will, at least, I knew when Kat told me it was no good, down in Rio, that I had to get out. He was going to turn us all in, you know. That train job of Charlie's went all sideways and we were stuck down there, trapped like rats on a sinking ship. Topeté tipped her off, God only knows why, but she probably saved my ass from jail."

"Do you think he would have arrested you, just like that?"

"Honey," Gwen said, almost sarcastically. "That man doesn't give a damn about anything but himself and his career. If it'll move him forward, he's all over it. He wants to get into the FBI."

"So why's he still working with Johnson? He can just go apply to the academy."

"Can't pass the psych eval. Part of the reason he's so good under pressure is because he doesn't emotionally engage. But his impulse control is really poor. He's like a dog with a bone and I honestly think that it hurts his ability to be objective. He gets fixated...on one thing. It's why he and I had such an intense affair, but it's also why I never went to prison after what happened in Rio. He was so focused on Charlie that he didn't see what anyone else was doing. It was Topeté's saving grace too, with that whole mess, because one word from him, had he noticed, and I don't think he did, and he could have ended her career." Gwen sighed. "Sometimes I wonder if he's got something on her and that's why she keeps working with him. Or if Johnson's pulling that string."

Marcey hummed thoughtfully. "Johnson and Charlie had that in common. She collects names and dates like he did. I wouldn't put it past him."

"Now you're getting it. We loved Charlie, sure, but the reason he worked so well for us all was because of the safety and anonymity he guaranteed all of us. Johnson isn't like that. I don't know what she wants the book for, but it sure as hell isn't to coordinate jobs."

"To send us all to jail, probably." Kim slid into the seat beside Marcey and dropped a tangle of wires and her tablet into the space between Marcey's crumpled napkin and the balled-up Starbucks bag that had held Gwen's breakfast sandwich. "I looked into that Super PAC for you, Mar, and you're right. Once I got past the security it was pretty easy to see the e-mails about you and Darius between Johnson and the head of the PAC." From her bag, Kim produced a sheaf of papers and a flash drive. "This is the documentation we need. A lot of it is pretty damning. The legality of the use of your likeness is pretty dubious and you probably do have grounds to sue for defamation. But you'd never get Johnson on it without this. This is her consenting to what they've done in a way that she can't deny the illegality of. Leak that to anyone and you'll have Johnson ruined."

"She can weather a press storm." Gwen frowned. "God knows she did after the first time she almost had Charlie."

"Which is why"—Marcey flashed Kim a grin—"we're going to make it really obvious she's corrupt."

Gwen followed the logic quickly, her eyes growing wide. She sat back, her smile broadening. "Oh, that's wicked. No one will be able to dispute it then."

"Especially when it turns out to be a fake." Kim shook her head. "Kat may be all kinds of problems, but she's got that stellar reputation for spotting fakes."

"Mostly because I made them."

They turned to see Kat, coffee clutched in one hand, standing a few feet away from their table. Marcey's breath caught in her chest. There was something about a windswept Kat Barber that made her *want* more than was allowable, more than was okay for anyone who knew that there was someone else who was far, far more important. She looked away. They couldn't, she couldn't, fall in love.

She wondered if Kat realized that this was all it was. If she was pulling herself into the situation thinking it was something that it wasn't.

"Well, true." Gwen held out her hand. Kat took it, shaking and grinning warmly, before leaning in to kiss Gwen on both cheeks. Marcey looked away, deliberate and scowling. "Is Shelly with you?"

"At the counter." Kat indicated with her chin. She slid into place next to Marcey, leaning over to peck her on the cheek hello. Marcey's cheeks burned. Kat couldn't keep doing this, not if she wanted this not to end in tears. "So, I heard that you're going to go along, Gwen?"

"That was the idea," Gwen answered. "Shelly thinks it might rattle Will to know that we're there, especially when he can't put together why. It'll keep Marcey out of his crosshairs, as well as yourself and Kim."

"But you and Shelly have had the most time with him out of anyone." Kim reached for the knot of wires and started to untangle them. "You were going to fucking marry him."

Marcey sighed. "That's the idea, Kim. We want him emotionally off-balance. Knowing that Gwen's somewhere... Well, men are awful with emotions. Gwen says he's particularly stunted. It'll give them a chance to... *talk*...while the rest of us do our parts."

"Ah." Kim nodded. She passed Gwen a successfully untangled wire. "Wrap that around your cell phone charger cord and keep it in your pocket."

"What is it?" Gwen took it and pulled her charger cord from her pocket.

"Transmitter." Kim explained. "With the city being how it is, signals can get a little wonky, this will ensure a good connection while looking like just another charger cord." She held up the other one to Shelly when she approached. "Do you have the account and routing numbers?"

Shelly rattled off a collection of numbers and Marcey's eyes went just a little wide. Kat nudged Marcey with her elbow. Marcey's gaze slid from Shelly and her warm smile to Kat, Kat with her quiet, almost sad smile, and the warmth of their legs pressing against each other as they huddled together over the small table.

"Are you ready for this?" Kat asked.

"No," Marcey said truthfully. "It feels too much like an ending."

"That's because it is, darling."

Marcey tilted her head. "Maybe I don't want it to end...just yet."

Kat leaned forward, and it was an almost kiss. Kat's breath was hot on Marcey's lips.

Kim cleared her throat loudly and waved the mess of wires in their faces. "If you are done mooning at each other, we've got work to do."

———◆———

In the wake of everything happening, Marcey went home. Back to her mother's apartment, despite walking out of there what felt like weeks ago. Marcey was a vagabond, surfing from couch to couch to Kat Barber's hotel bed. She needed a few things from home, and she needed to see her mother one last time before the pieces fell into place. It was late enough in the day that her mother answered when Marcey knocked and stepped aside to allow her entry without a word.

Marcey stepped into the apartment, a wash of nostalgia and the uncomfortable feeling of an ill-fitting life hitting with waves of disquiet.

"Why are you here?" her mother demanded. Her mother, who'd started this whole thing without so much as a thought to what it would mean for Marcey's future. Her mother, who'd let herself fall in love with the wrong man and had, despite his failings, never mentioned to that man's child that her entire life was a lie. "I thought we were done."

Sticking her chin out, petulant and defiant, Marcey jammed her hands into her pockets. "I came to get some things." She paused. "And to say I'm sorry."

"Sorry for what, Marcey?"

Her mother's tone was gentle, but it was the implication of it that bit into Marcey's consciousness. In an instant, Marcey went from feeling like an adult about to do a great and terrible thing to a child once more. She bit her lip and looked down at her feet, at her two-day-old dirty socks hidden by scuffed boots. "I was caught up in being angry at you, for Charlie Mock. For not telling me about him. I lashed out."

The warmth of her mother's embrace was enough to make Marcey recoil. She drew back, thinking of other hugs she'd received: Shelly's warmth and the way Kat smelled. This wasn't like that, but rather a Band-Aid on a wound still bleeding. "I'm sorry too. I shouldn't have said all those things about your friend." Her mother exhaled hot breath onto the crown of Marcey's head. "You're right to be angry at me. I never told you that story because I saw how seductive his life would be to you. I didn't want that for you."

Marcey fisted her fingers in the back of her mother's shirt. "Promise me something," she said.

"Anything, honey."

"When I leave here, promise me you won't talk to the police. They're going to come looking for something—a book of Charlie's. I have it with me. After I get what I need I'm going down to ADA Johnson's office and I'm going to give it to her." Marcey stepped back from her mother, looking up to meet her gaze evenly. "I don't want them coming in and trashing the apartment looking for something they won't find."

"What is the book?"

"Something that ADA Johnson wants very badly." Marcey reached into her bag and pulled out the book, flipping it open to the photograph of Kat, Charlie, and Shelly. Her mother reached out to take it with shaking fingers.

"Chuck..." she whispered. "Christ, I never thought I'd see him again." She flipped the picture over. "Rio, huh?"

"Yeah." Marcey shook her head. "Things went south for him in a hurry there, far as I can tell. ADA Johnson worked with Interpol and the Brazilian authorities to bring him in. I think giving her this will be the sort of a peace offering she'll want to drop her resistance to Darius's parole hearing, but also maybe to get that Super PAC to back off." She took the photograph from her mother and tucked it away.

She was getting better at lying.

"That seems like a good idea, a peace offering." Her mother squeezed her shoulder. "I'm proud of you."

"Thanks, Mom." Marcey ducked away, down the hallway to her closed bedroom door. Kat's work on the book was flawless, she knew that, but there were two touches she had to add in order to make it convincing. From her desk drawer, she pulled out the original packaging that the courier had left the book in, as well as Charlie's letter. There would be questions about why she was in New Hampshire, but as far as the cops were concerned, the painting was still there. What would come later, the threading of the pieces to knit into the fabric of this plot, all of it would hinge on how convincing this lie was.

She buried the original book deep under a stack of her journals; each worn black leather book was just like Charlie's journal. She didn't think it would come to that, with Kat's fake, but it had to be kept safe, hidden.

"Will you be coming back?" Her mother leaned against the doorframe as Marcey slipped the book into the packaging and made sure the letter from Devon Austin Jackson was fully enclosed in the envelope. "Or is this another good-bye? Where have you been staying?"

"With friends. And I'll be back, but it won't be for a while, Mom. I think it's time I got myself a place. I'm twenty-five."

"You quit your job."

Marcey shoved the package into her bag and checked her pocket for the flash drive. It was quarter to three. The auction started in fifteen minutes. She had to get downtown. "I'll figure it out, okay? I needed a change of scenery after work started making the connection between those pictures and me. It was only a matter of time before I got fired."

Her mother reached out, pulled her hand back. Marcey tugged her jacket up her shoulders. There wasn't much more that could be said. "Just trust me, okay?" Marcey exhaled. "I'll be all right."

CHAPTER 33

Wei, Baffled

AT TWENTY AFTER THREE, MARCEY Daniels walked into Linda Johnson's office. She paused, just for a moment, beside Wei's borrowed desk. Wei stared at her, confused, as Marcey pulled a package from her bag and set it neatly on top of Wei's copy of the *Times*. She smiled at Wei before her expression turned almost sad. Wei opened her mouth to speak, but no words came out. Marcey stood there a moment longer before she walked straight to Johnson's office and waited to be admitted.

Wei took the package and pulled out the contents. The letter she set aside; it was covered with recognizable handwriting—Charlie Mock's handwriting—but it was the larger object that drew Wei in. The book. A peace offering if ever Wei saw one. Wei's fingers trailed over the names and dates on the pages. She flipped back, looking for her own entry, and then to Kat's. Everything was exactly the same, except for one small, glaring omission. Wei searched back across the span of her memory and drew a shuddering breath.

None of the dates were correct.

"A fake," she breathed. "*Merde.*" Glancing over her shoulder at Johnson's office door, Wei reached for the desk phone and punched in a number, messed up in forgetting to dial nine first, and tried again. After two rings LePage picked up, gruff and flustered.

"What?"

"We have a problem, William." Wei spoke in a low voice. No one here was directly assigned to the case, but Johnson was an advocate of vigilance, and she was also an advocate of competition. She liked it when people pushed against each other and when the competition created synergy in the office. That was when everyone was cracking at the highest levels. That was when cases got solved.

Wei did not want to be overheard. Not because she didn't trust that the others wouldn't respect her wish to keep this private and quiet, but because she didn't want to jump the gun. The game was slowly swimming into focus, and the more Wei saw of the plot, the heavier the blanket of despair felt as it draped around her shoulders. This was the moment, this was the end.

No one looked at Wei as she bent her head and cupped her hand around the phone mouthpiece. No one looked at her when she pitched her voice low and said, "Marcey Daniels has just walked into the bullpen and handed me Charlie Mock's book."

"But..." LePage drew breath sharply. "There's no way. Why would she do that?" He was babbling, speaking quickly now. "Look, we've got a bigger problem. Gwen Lane-Wright is probably here. I saw Shelly Orietti. If Shelly's here, Gwen is here. They're probably bidding on that damn painting."

"What?" Wei echoed. That didn't make sense. Why would they be bidding on the painting that Marcey Daniels had failed to steal...unless... *Kat.*

Son of a bitch.

Wei's blood ran cold.

Kat... Kat had authenticated that painting. Kat had appraised that painting. Kat had confessed her fascination with the painting from the first moment Wei had been in its presence at that gallery in SoHo. Wei racked her brain, trying to remember. What had Kat said? Something about how it was a shame no one knew its value? Or how it was an inspirational work for some great piece that Wei could scarcely recall? There was a missing piece, unseen. It was vital.

Kat wanted that painting.

Kat wanted the painting because it was connected to this damn book and her scheme. All of this went back to Charlie Mock. That was what Marcey Daniels had said, and that was what Wei believed. The puzzle felt incomplete. There was still something missing, still something Wei didn't see. She exhaled, inhaled, and got to her feet.

"William, I need you to stop that auction."

"I can't just do that," LePage retorted. "I need to see them *sell* the piece in order to have any grounds to move against them. Wei, we need to catch them at something or else we're fucked in court and we both know it. Whatever they're planning with this painting, I need to see it trade hands before I can do anything at all." He paused, humming at the back of his throat. "I suppose I could try and make an argument that we already know the painting is fake. We do know it's fake if they're trying to sell it, right?"

Wei didn't know. She thought back to Kat's flat, to the paintings leaning against the wall on top of that drop canvas. She couldn't remember seeing anything like the painting at the Perôt in Kat's flat. She couldn't remember seeing much of anything at all in Kat's flat besides Kat herself.

Kat, who had betrayed Wei's trust. Kat, who was setting up some final coup, and with whom Marcey Daniels was clearly colluding.

"I don't know," Wei said honestly. "And frankly, I don't care. They're up to something. Something big, I think. We need to stop the auction before that painting changes hands, because Marcey Daniels would not be here *while* they were trying to sell the painting if this wasn't a double move." Wei glanced at her watch. "Call me back in ten minutes; I need to speak to Marcey Daniels."

"I'm not gonna be able to stop the auction, Wei."

"I know, William, I'm just asking you to try." She exhaled. "I'm sorry she's there." Her voice softened when she spoke. From before, when she had been only somewhat aware of what was happening within Charlie's circle, she knew the undercover work William did for Linda Johnson during the Rio job. He'd gotten too close to Gwen Lane-Wright. He'd fallen in love with her and put the entire operation at risk because he was so blinded by his feelings. It was stupid, foolish for both of them. Wei had done the only thing she could think of: she'd told Kat who LePage was and let Kat break that news to Gwen.

He's like you now, with Kathryn.

Wei pushed the thought away, shaking her head violently to clear it from her mind. Now was not the time to get caught up in her own hypocrisy. She closed her eyes, exhaled, and then waited for William's response. His heavy breathing came over the line. Seeing Gwen was hurtful for him, and he expected her to bear the brunt of it.

Wei hated men. Hated how William clammed up his emotions and refused to see anything beyond humor in the knife to her gut each time

Wei found evidence of Marcey Daniels in Kat's hotel room. Kat plunged the knife into Wei, over and over again. Kat took, and took, and took. To him, it was all just a big joke, something to laugh about with Johnson's investigative team over beers. But this was Wei's life. Or more specifically, its destruction.

Over and over, Kat did little things that cut into Wei, but in Marcey Daniels she'd handed Wei the answers, carefully written down and made right.

"She's here because your fucking girlfriend knows that it's the only way to make sure that I'm off my game." LePage growled into the phone. "I don't want to see her, Wei. When it all ended in Brazil I swore I'd never see her again."

"And yet here we are."

"Yeah." He paused. "Okay, you figure out what the hell's going on. I'm going to stop this auction, if I can."

Wei hummed her agreement and hung up. She took the book and ran her fingers along the edges of it. "What are you up to, Kat?"

There were so many options. Each stripped Wei bare, built her up again. This was a peace offering and an exoneration of all of Wei's past sins. This girl, who had taken everything from Wei without thought and yet gave it all back to her without a thought. Wei didn't understand it. That was not the game Kat played.

Kat was cruel; she was selfish; she was Wei unmade in the quietest parts of the night. She pushed Wei past her comfort zone, and she held Wei closer with the selfish grip of a child. This girl was just a pawn.

But was she?

Wei turned the pages, glancing over the entries, trying to make sense of them. Things had been moved around in Charlie's flawless script. Dates were changed, contradicting, providing alibis that could be checked and rechecked, places she knew she'd been, the dates crossed with other, less damning ones that still aligned with her passport. Wei frowned, turned another page, and found the most damning evidence of all. There, between two Kenyan antiquities traders, was Marcey Daniels. A picture was clipped to the page, from a few years ago, when she was still wearing a high school uniform. Wei tugged it loose, flipped it over.

On the back was a circle and a date. A date that meant nothing to anyone other than Wei.

"Kathryn," Wei whispered. "Fuck." This was Kat's endgame. Wei doubted Marcey even knew it was in here. She couldn't know. This date, the day they'd completed their circuit of that wide table mountain in Nepal, it meant nothing to anyone but Kat and Wei. For it to be here—to be written so clearly was a promise. This was the freedom Wei had bargained for with her bosses in Lyon, freedom for Kat, freedom for herself.

Marcey Daniels was a patsy for Kat.

And she'd walked right into it.

Wei slammed the book shut and shoved it into her desk drawer. Her heart raced; she had to hurry. There was no time—no time to call Kat and confirm—no time to decide anything other than that Kat was *wrong*. This wasn't what they'd agreed to at all. Wei swallowed down her dignity and strode purposefully over to Johnson's door just as it opened.

Linda Johnson stood in the doorway, her reading glasses slipping down her nose and her piled-up hair wispy around her face. Wei's stomach turned. The girl was sitting, her hands clearly visible on the desk, watching them with some interest.

"Can I help you, Agent Topeté?" Johnson's tone was curt, but there was an underlying exhaustion to it. The same exhaustion Wei felt in her bones, weary and creaking with the weight of all that was slowly descending upon her shoulders. She had to make this right, and there was only one way to do it, and the knot of emotions at her throat threatened to choke the breath from her lungs and the light from her eyes.

"Could I speak to you for a moment?" Wei jerked her chin toward Marcey. "Alone."

Johnson glanced back at the girl and then stepped from the room. In the hallway, her voice dropped lower as her presence seemed to grow larger. Wei swallowed, took a step back. Johnson folded her arms over her chest. "Well?" she demanded.

And in that moment, confronted with the truth of what Kat planned to do, Wei's tongue turned to rubber. She couldn't speak. She couldn't even move. There were too many maybes running through her mind. Kat, sun-kissed in the sand, hiding beneath a wide, floppy hat. Kat kissing Wei at the airport like she was salvation. Kat…Kat…Kat.

The lie, the realization of the endgame, slipped off her tongue like a benediction.

"She left..." Wei pointed to her desk. To where the book was hidden. "Before she went in to see you."

Tilting her head to one side, Johnson glanced back toward her door. "She left you the book?"

"Yes."

"Why?"

Wei swallowed down the rebuke. "I'm not sure. Perhaps she wanted to make sure that she'd have a minute alone in your office when I realized what she'd handed me."

"She wouldn't *dare*." Johnson turned her attention back to her closed office door. "Get the book and get in my office." She wrenched the door open only to find Marcey Daniels sitting exactly where she was before. Johnson raised an eyebrow at Wei before stepping back into the office. The door was still ajar. Wei swallowed.

A long, shuddering breath escaped Wei's lips. She closed her eyes and hurried back to her desk, collecting the fake book and hurrying back into Johnson's office. Inside, Marcey Daniels was staring at Wei and Johnson as though they'd both sprouted extra limbs.

"What's this about?" she asked. Her eyes were wide and unblinking— the picture of affected innocence. Wei saw through her, Johnson probably did too, but she had to continue on and they all knew it. Whatever Marcey's plan was, she was playing right into their hands. "If it's about that book, it arrived weeks ago. I never did anything with it."

Wei wanted to shake her. How could she not see how clearly this was playing into Wei's hands? It was so obvious: all she had to do was look though the book first before waltzing in here like she owned the place.

"I heard from LePage," Wei said to Johnson, holding out the book like a peace offering. "He's down at the auction. So far nothing seems amiss." The lie was slight, but it was the sort that would tell two tales, depending on what the listener wanted to hear. Wei liked lies like that, the sort of lies where she could challenge the people around her to think more critically. Judging by the way Marcey's brow furrowed, she sensed that same connection.

"Good, good," Johnson muttered. "Ms. Daniels, I believe you wanted to speak to me regarding this book. Tell me, why did you leave it on Agent Topeté's desk?"

The girl shrugged. "I met Agent Topeté in New Hampshire. I thought she seemed like a good person to trust with something like this. Plus, from what my mother told me about Charles Mock, he was quite the art thief. Agent Topeté works for Interpol, right? Isn't catching people like him a big part of her job?" Marcey bit her lip, her cheeks coloring slightly. "Or do I have that all wrong?"

"No, no, no, you're right." Wei sat down, following the line of logic and realizing how this was meant to play out. She tried not to think of this girl willingly sleeping with Kat, or Kat wanting this girl. That had never been the goal, she realized. It was always about Johnson. Instead, she focused on the game Marcey Daniels was playing, and how best to beat her at it. "Tell me more about the book."

"Well, as I was saying. It arrived by courier a couple months ago." She sat forward, her fingers curling around the edge of Johnson's cluttered desk. Wei was struck by how small she looked. "I didn't think much of it at first, but the letter in there, it's a little damning. I spent a lot of time digging through my mom's old pictures, trying to figure out if it was true. Eventually I had to go see his lawyer, that's why he came to New Hampshire, I think, because he knew me from—"

"He was hired by Charles Mock to defend your best friend and Charles Mock has been footing the bill for that boy's defense ever since." The malice in Johnson's tone surprised Wei.

Marcey flinched and her expression went steely. "He isn't a boy."

"Well, you certainly let him take the fall like one." Johnson's voice was cruel and biting. "Isn't that just what you do, you, the little white girl in over her head lead the young black boy astray and then feel so guilty about it you do everything you can to make sure that he's taken care of. That he's *cared* for. You keep paying his attorney bills—"

"I never—"

From her desk, Johnson produced a folder and flipped it open. "We've had a subpoena for your bank records for some time. Once we started to dig into your finances, it was amazing how many little accounts you had open. A few hundred dollars here, a few there. And then this one." She plucked a piece of paper from the stack and turned it around with a flourish that Wei thought overly theatrical for an office meeting. It made her jaw clench and her eyes flutter shut, annoyance threatening to bring on a headache. "This one is special. It came into your possession about five years ago."

Marcey took the paper. "I don't know what this is—"

"Your lawyer certainly did. He's been drawing a salary from it for some time. As has someone else. Someone I think Agent Topeté here might be more equipped to explain than I. All of these funds for art supplies, to rent an industrial-grade oven for two weeks, to buy paper at estate auctions—this is damning stuff, Ms. Daniels."

"Devon isn't like that. He's not going to just take money. Not without asking."

"He certainly would." Johnson's tone was curt, cutting Marcey off. Her gaze slid to Wei, and her lip curled. "Perhaps you should have pressed him harder on *why* he was so keen to help your friend out. Surely you know no one does anything without having some stake in the process."

Wei scowled, looked away. This conversation was as much directed at her as it was at Marcey. This was a condemnation of Kat's forging the book, forging the painting, without actually saying it. This was the proof and the manipulation that Kat had taken Marcey's trust and had used her to get exactly what she wanted. The money from the painting and, Wei could only assume, Charlie's real book.

"And you, Agent Topeté. When you went to interview Mr. Austin Jackson, why didn't you press him harder about where his funding was coming from?"

She had to keep her face perfectly still. She couldn't rise to Johnson's bait. Johnson wanted an admission of guilt from someone and at this point it didn't matter who. And Wei was walking a fine line, knowing what Marcey Daniels stood to lose.

"I didn't press him because your country has laws that shroud him in privilege and privacy." Wei turned up her nose. "Does it matter, really, in the end? Ms. Daniels can tell us what we want to know. You have her finances. We can only hope that Ms. Daniels is aware of the fortune that's been left to her, even if it appears that she's misusing the funds." Wei sank into the chair beside Marcey, catching her eye and shaking her head, just a little, imperceptible. The girl's eyes grew wide, and Wei felt a little surge of triumph. This was not what she'd planned. Excellent. Now was the time to press. "Can you tell us a little bit more about how you fell into associating with certain people in the book and why you're buying some of these things?"

"Certain people?" Marcey was smart then, avoiding discussing the financial element of it, because that would get her caught.

Johnson passed Wei the file, speaking over Wei's prepared remark, derailing the direction Wei was attempting to steer the conversation in. "We have record of you spending time in the presence of known criminal associates of Charles Mock. Shelly Orietti and Kathryn Barber. I want to know why you were interacting with them."

"I know this is going to sound strange to you both..." Marcey bent and from the bag at her feet she produced a file of her own. Inside were photographs and handwritten notes in what Wei had come to recognize as Charlie Mock's handwriting, as well as pages and pages of another's hand, probably Marcey's. "My mom never married Charlie. I think she was already pregnant when Charlie disappeared from her life. That letter dropped a big bomb in the middle of my life. I took some time to try and piece together who Charlie was. I wanted to know who the man my mother fell in love with was. I spoke to Kat and Shelly because they were in the photograph Devon Austin Jackson gave me with the book. It was taken five years ago in Rio."

Johnson's brow furrowed. "And you being in New Hampshire?"

Wei closed her eyes. There was no lie that could cover this, and they all knew it.

"You've got me there. I came here to turn myself in, because I'm clearly the cause of all this confusion. With my giving you the book and with me removed from the board, I figured that this would be easier to sort out." Marcey Daniels looked up and met Wei's gaze, her eyes shining, begging for the understanding that Wei did not possess. She was baffled.

"Turn...yourself in?" Johnson's nostrils flared. "Have you committed a crime, Marcey Daniels?"

Marcey turned and smiled sweetly at her. "Why, Ms. Johnson, if I had, do you think I would come right out and tell you?"

Wei stared at the two of them, at this silent war of attrition. The circle on the back of that photograph made more sense now, a promise from Kat that Wei had never thought possible. This whole time she'd been caught up in the hurt of what Kat was doing to her, but she'd never thought about the reason *why*. This girl, this perfect patsy, was sitting here willing to give herself up for something she did not fully understand.

Or perhaps that was the problem: she understood too well.

The insult of it was almost perfect. Kat played the victim as only the best could. The girl must think Wei heartless, to see this as the only way out. Why hadn't Kat reassured her that this was the always the plan?

Perhaps it was that Kat and Marcey were working in concert, each playing their part toward a common goal. If that was the case, what was Marcey's goal in all this? Kat's was as transparent as the sky was blue, but Marcey? Wei's brow furrowed. To see a future with Kat? It couldn't be that. Kat had been clear enough, and Wei had seen the honesty in Marcey's eyes back in Lincoln. Why would she think this was the only way for this to end unless Kat—

Kat *wouldn't*.

"Should I call in an officer?" she asked. Wei kept her face perfectly straight.

"Yes, if you don't mind." Johnson leaned forward, almost greedily, wanting to get a look at the papers in Marcey's hands. The papers, the papers! *Fuck*. "What did you discover, Ms. Daniels, when you started digging into your mother's past?"

Wei retreated out the door, her head swimming. She moved quickly, sending the first duty officer into Johnson's office and retreating to her desk. She sat, knee bouncing, fingers drumming on the desk for five minutes—ten minutes—until she couldn't take it anymore. She got to her feet, pushing the chair away from the desk and grabbing her jacket and purse. Kat wouldn't be acting, not with the sale going on. She'd be in her hotel room, watching the slow destruction of this girl's life.

The sacrifice was almost perfect, whittling away this girl until there was nothing left. Johnson's hubris would stop her from seeing the truth—seeing Kat's game. The game Wei'd played right into, the game where Marcey Daniels was nothing more than fodder to prove Kat's point to Wei.

The city was alight in spring, the temperature rising throughout the day to push the warmth of the forgotten sun into Wei's bones, seeping into her skin and reminding her of better times: a beach, a forgotten dream, a carefully hidden promise. People who loved each other hurt each other more than anyone else. Wei knew this. This was Kat's endgame: the final act of defiance. The refusal of everything Wei offered her.

Once, Wei would have simply asked why, but now, her face turned up to the sun as it hung heavy in the sky above the aching fingers of the skyscrapers of Lower Manhattan, she knew that the why was unimportant. Kat was a cornered animal, trapped and unable to break free. This book, the perfect forgery that saved all their skins at the expense of this girl who was playing her own game, it wasn't good enough. Johnson wouldn't see through it, but Wei's bosses at Interpol certainly would. Wei lit a cigarette, watched the smoke curl around her hand, sucking cancer into her lungs.

Kat's hotel was ten blocks north and seven blocks east. The walk took twenty minutes. Wei went in, climbed the stairs, and knocked on the door of the last room at the end of the hall. Kat answered, her eyes sunken, her face scrubbed free of makeup. "Wei." Her voice was full of trepidation. "What are you doing here?"

"What did you do, Kathryn?" She didn't want to push into the hotel room. Didn't want to see the evidence of Kat's creation that was certain still to be scattered about. She could barely hide the hurt, the insult. Kat had *refused* her. Kat had gone and made a contingency plan because she didn't believe that Wei could fix this when Wei was on the cusp of doing just that. How could she? Wei wasn't some damn puppet.

Her hands were shaking, staring at Kat. Wei couldn't look at her—couldn't keep her hands steady.

"Do?" Kat reached out, grabbed Wei's wrist, and pulled her into the hotel room. Wei resisted, only just, just enough to give the pretense of the semblance of dignity to be there, before allowing herself to be led inside. "I have no idea what you're talking about."

From her pocket, Wei produced the photograph, the perfect circle and the façade of the mountain sketched onto the back. "Everything comes full circle, Kat."

When Kat was angry, her eyes became like emeralds, hard and unbreakable. There was none of the storm that a woman with blue eyes could manifest, but rather a shocking, vibrant green that set Wei's stomach churning. Kat wasn't a violent person, but it did not mean she was incapable of the act. Kat was angry now, her nostrils flaring and her eyes like grass after a rainstorm were electric.

"She was always meant to fall. Into my lap, into yours, a perfect patsy for our freedom." Kat reached for Wei, her fingers scrabbling on the fabric of Wei's jacket. Wei didn't pull away, but she hated herself for following the line of logic through. "She gives the book to your boss, and then we're free. Don't you want that? Don't you want to be free of all of these petty, miserable obligations?"

"What about the real one?" Wei asked. "The book you promised was not that fake. It'll fool Johnson, but it didn't fool me."

Kat looked away, seeming to settle herself, but then pulling on the fraying thread of what they had together. "I did it *for* you, for us. The real book is safe. It can't hurt us anymore."

"You don't have it."

The mood in the room turned sour, icy. Kat looked back at Wei sharply. "I never wanted it."

"Don't lie. You bargained with it like it was always yours to have. I remember you sitting in that interrogation room in Barcelona plain as day, Kat. I watched you sell my bosses on this plan of yours to rid yourself of the guilt of that forgery."

"It was just a shame I got caught." Kat's eyes flashed dangerously. Wei wanted to take a step back. "What's the life of some ignorant babe if we can be free of all of this? We can go away somewhere. We could be anything, Wei. Anything at all."

Wei reached out on instinct, grabbing Kat's shoulders and drawing her close. She shuddered in Wei's arms. It was all Wei had ever wanted, but she couldn't. Not at the expense of another, even one who'd been so cruel. Her mind had been halfway to made up when Marcey Daniels had looked up at her from that interview room up in the mountains, but now, seeing Kat and Kat's game laid bare before her, Wei knew what she had to do. There was no way around it, the crumbling of a great love. What Kat wanted to destroy without so much as a second thought. Wei couldn't stomach that. Not so flippantly. Never like this. She exhaled, then drew a shaky breath, staring at Kat. There was no way that this could work without Kat, no way that this was viable. She had to be firm; she had to be ready.

"I had a plan. I had a plan, Kat, and you didn't trust me. You didn't let me execute it. I'm not some puppet. I don't do as you tell me. I never have. We had an agreement. An *arrangement* about how this was going to go."

Kat stared hard, her expression steely. Wei met her gaze evenly. "I love you."

Wei wanted to vomit. She swallowed down the bile and forced her expression to soften. "I will not allow you to throw that girl's life away for your freedom, Kat. Our freedom. I won't let you make me dance this time. I can't. Not like this, not for this cost. We can save her and ourselves without losing our integrity." Earnestness crept into her voice. Wei wanted to hate it, but found, in the moment, she couldn't. This was their truth, after all.

Kat looked up, pulling her arms from where they were trapped between the crush of their bodies. She hesitated, as though at war with herself over the act of charity. "You don't have the stomach for this."

"I think you'll find that I do. When I need to. When I'm *asked* before I'm forced to act."

Kat cupped Wei's face, wonderment on her face. "How?" she asked.

Wei smiled. She bent, kissing Kat gently. "I'll show you," she promised as she pulled away. What Linda Johnson had done to that girl was enough to destroy her. Kat was willing to do the same.

It was time someone threw her a lifeline.

CHAPTER 34

Marcey, Stewing

MARCEY SLEPT POORLY IN LOCKUP. The other women in her cell were nice enough. One was coming off a heroin high that had her shaking and sweating, muttering to herself and crying. Marcey gave her the blanket from her bunk and sat, her knees drawn up to her chest, on the hard steel, her pillow forgotten beside her. She'd known this was going to happen when she walked into the DA's office. That was part of the problem. Johnson had reacted exactly as anticipated, and Topeté had fulfilled her part of the bargain once she threaded the plan together. It was up to Marcey to keep up appearances now. Until the final act.

Johnson had sent her to the local precinct for processing. The staff wasn't on hand, so late in the day, to book her at the DA's office, and the seven o'clock shift change happened in the middle of her booking. There hadn't been enough time for her arresting officer to take her to Central Booking without clocking in overtime that the city, apparently, wasn't that keen on paying out to some meter-minder who happened to be on desk duty when Johnson's people delivered Marcey.

"She gotta sit overnight," the woman had explained. "Bus's already left and I don't have an officer free to drive her. She'll stew with the drunks for the night."

The court officer—Marcey's escort—had been all right with that. He left her to get her pictures taken and her body roughly searched before she was pushed unceremoniously into a women's holding cell.

It was loud; the whole block echoed. Marcey wasn't intending on sleeping much anyway. She was too busy thinking through Topeté's next move. The woman had disappeared after sending in the duty officer, never reappearing in Johnson's office. Johnson hadn't commented on it, but Marcey was sure she'd noticed Topeté's absence as well. Marcey guessed what she was up to, running to Kat to demand how she could let Marcey take the fall for this job just to get the book. That was part of the act too, because Kat had to believe she'd won. Marcey thought about Topeté, pushing away the surge of jealousy and the want, no matter how selfish, to sell out their ticket to freedom for one more chance with Kat Barber.

The woman was like a drug, distracting, intoxicating. Marcey wanted her, even when she knew it was all a lie. A carefully wrought manipulation to ensure Marcey's compliance in Kat's foolish plan. Sex was like that, she supposed—a drug that she could go without, but that, when she had it, she wanted more and more of it.

And she wanted Kat Barber.

Not because of some sort of desire that would allow her to feel love for Kat Barber, but because they were fucking and the sex was amazing. Feelings didn't factor into it. It couldn't. Topeté was the one who felt for Kat. She was the one Kat went back to. Marcey couldn't be that person and she didn't want to be. Leave that for Topeté, for her twisted mass of emotions when it came to Kat.

Marcey tilted her head back. It was encouraging that LePage had never resurfaced either. It made this next step, the next act, so much more exciting.

A slow, almost smug smile drifted across Marcey's face. In the two minutes Topeté had allowed her alone in Johnson's office, she'd removed the flash drive from her pocket and set it into the back of Johnson's computer. It was small, designed to look like a transmitter for a wireless mouse. Getting it back would be tricky, but Kim knew a guy who could slip in and out of such spaces looking like an IT technician. After it had done its job, it would mimic a bluescreen error and force Johnson to call for assistance. The drive would be in Kim's hands soon enough, as she had to check in with her parole officer two floors down anyway.

The whole thing was genius, really. On that flash drive was the evidence, the authorization of the transfer of funds directly from Johnson's campaign to the Super PAC. From there, Kim would do the rest remotely.

Marcey rested her forehead against her arms, curled around her knees. She was exhausted. She wanted to get out. The plan was starting to come together, but she was troubled by Topeté's disappearance. She'd anticipated Topeté being there, shepherding Johnson through the interview process. Johnson did not know as much as Topeté about what the book contained. She'd flipped through it, demanding details, answers. Marcey had none to give her. She didn't know how much Kat had changed the information in the book about herself and Topeté, her real reason for doing all of this.

It wasn't until Johnson had turned the page to reveal a short entry about Marcey herself that the lie started to crumble. Kat had done that too. Marcey had known because it was the only way to make this believable for Johnson. She had to pull off the confusion without giving anything away. She didn't know if she was that good, especially in the face of someone like Johnson, someone who'd torn Marcey's entire life to shreds because of what had happened to Rebecca. Marcey's hands had shaken; she'd buried them in her lap. She wouldn't allow Johnson to see her fear. She'd kept her chin up, her jaw clenched. When Johnson had asked why Charlie would damn his child in his petty little paper trail, all Marcey could do was shrug. She had no idea why Charlie had done it, she'd said. There was no other lie to tell.

But now, surrounded by the quiet din and bright fluorescent lights of the drunk tank, the agreement fell short. The agreement they'd come to, back in London, lying sweaty and sated in Kat's bed, wasn't meant to feel like this. Marcey wasn't supposed to fear what might come next. *Believe me,* Kat had promised. *Wei's too much of a do-gooder to allow herself to not do the right thing in the end. When the time comes for her to act, she'll do what's necessary.*

Destroying Johnson had never been Kat's goal. She wanted the book. Marcey had wanted Johnson destroyed, and Kat had promised that. Kat had wanted the book—not to keep, she'd assured Marcey, but rather to duplicate. If she duplicated it and exonerated herself in the process, she could rid herself of the yoke of Interpol around her neck.

"And Topeté?" Marcey had asked, feeling guilty, mentioning Kat's lover having just fucked Kat. "Will you be free of her too?"

"No," Kat had said. "What I want is unimportant when it comes to Wei; it has nothing to do with you or what we did here."

"Doesn't it though?"

"As I said, it's none of your business, Marcey." Kat had pulled her shirt over her head, hiding small breasts and freckled skin. Marcey had looked away, down at her hands, at the bruises purpling at her hips. "What Wei has to do with the book should be apparent, you've read it."

Marcey had thought about it. Thought about Shelly flipping easily to a page and showing her details about Topeté; about how easily Shelly found the information. "She's in it."

Kat had bent and picked up her pants. "So, you see why she's interested in getting it."

"But what about me? What about us?"

"There is no us, Marcey. This is fun. But don't get attached, darling. You won't do well in the end."

Marcey sat back, her head resting against the concrete wall of the drunk tank. Kat was setting her up. Kat was setting her up to take the fall so that Kat could walk free of everything because Topeté would ensure her protection. Kat wanted to be rid of Charlie's insurance and rid of Interpol. Marcey getting caught took care of both. Kat had delivered what she promised. "That bitch," she breathed.

The woman beside her blinked drunkenly at her. "What bitch?"

"No one," Marcey said, curling back into herself and chewing on her lip. Kat had used her, fucked her over and over, let it fester like an open wound peppered with the guilt of this great love she shared with Wei Topeté. Why? Why let that happen? Marcey would have gotten involved with Kat and her plot anyway. Their two goals were intertwined. So why bring sex into it? "Some girl I was involved with."

"She hot?" the woman asked.

"Yes," Marcey said. "But she's in love with someone else."

"Don't be a homewrecker, kid, it isn't worth it. Everyone gets hurt in the end." The woman smiled, glassy-eyed and drooping, at Marcey. "And besides, don't you have scruples?" she slurred.

"Do you know where we are?" Marcey raised a wry eyebrow. "Ain't nobody here got scruples."

The woman waved a hand at Marcey, opening her mouth to speak. But the wave of detoxifying nausea struck her hard and she lunged for the toilet in the corner of the room. Marcey forced herself to breathe through her mouth to push away the smell and looked toward the door. A uniformed officer was approaching keys in hand.

"Daniels?" he called.

Marcey got to her feet. She crossed to the door. "I'm Marcey Daniels." She tried to put Kat's face and her gentle kiss outside the building out of her mind. It couldn't happen again. It could never happen again.

"Hands." The guard gestured to the gap in the cell door. Marcey balled her fists and presented them, trying not to gag over the smell of sick and the feel of metal encircling her wrists. "Fucking stop vomiting, Amerson. I don't have time to clean up after your drunk ass every damn night."

The woman waved from the toilet. "This isn't urp—drunk. This is some stomach thing. Bad sushi."

"Sure it is." When the handcuffs were locked in place, the guard indicated for Marcey to back up. She stepped back. The officer opened the door and Marcey stepped out. "You've got a visitor," he explained. "Two, actually."

"Did I make bail?" She was eager. She wanted to go home, to scrub the filth of this place from her skin.

"You can't make bail until you go down to Central Booking, kid." The officer gave her funny look. "This isn't your first time in. You know this."

"Maybe I got hopeful," Marcey shot back. "Maybe I thought Johnson grew a conscience and was just going to throw out the charges because I did the goddamn right thing."

"That'll be the day." The officer laughed. "I saw your poster up in her office."

Marcey scowled.

"Did you do what it says?"

"I was a minor. And I was *acquitted.*" Marcey let the officer lead her into an interview room. "What she's doing is illegal."

"I think you'd need to guess again, kid," the officer said. "She wouldn't ever condone it if it wasn't legal. She ain't stupid." He settled her into a chair across from a concerned-looking Devon Austin Jackson and his companion. The officer removed her handcuffs and pocketed them. He turned to leave.

Marcey's eyes slid over the careful updo and the extremely professional suit Kat was wearing. Her eyes were hooded, cast in dark eye shadow and an air of mystery. Marcey wanted to slap her. "What are you doing here?"

Kat had the nerve to look wounded. It seemed they were both far better actresses than they gave themselves credit for. "I was concerned about you, darling."

Devon shot Kat a weary look. He rolled his eyes when Marcey caught his gaze. Marcey closed her eyes, revulsion leaping forward. She felt dirty, playing this game, like the deck was already stacked against her and she was set to be screwed over by Kat just because that was the game Kat wanted to play. That was the game she and Topeté were playing.

"You landed my ass in here."

"That was entirely your doing, actually," Kat shot back. "One does not simply waltz into the dragon's lair and expect to come away…*unscorched*." She quirked an eyebrow. Marcey glared.

Ever the peacemaker, Devon put up his hands. "Ladies, please."

Marcey sat back, her arms folded across her chest. "You can't get me out of this, Devon. I have to get taken down to Central Booking before you can bail me out."

Nodding, Devon slipped a piece of paper across the table at Marcey. Marcey picked it up, reading carefully. The penmanship was messy, clearly not Kat or Shelly's. "We thought we'd communicate to you what the next steps were to get out once booked, since you were…waylaid," Devon explained. Marcey read quickly, following the innuendo without prompting.

Devon clicked his pen and drew a line across the bottom of the document. "This is what has already happened. The below is what is going to happen, should you give the word."

The plan was simple: they would walk out of here right now. The paperwork had already been filed with the courts last night. Marcey would never be booked, and therefore would be free of the blemish on her record. Kat didn't know about that part of the deal Marcey and Topeté had struck. Topeté had sorted all of it out, initialed each page as though to assure Marcey that her hands had been all in this ruse.

But the next steps were complicated. Marcey had to play along perfectly. Marcey scowled, wondering if the messiness of this was Kat, or if this was some sort of backhanded revenge for going to Topeté with the book before it was time. She was playing both sides now, in the complicated little war that was transpiring between Kat and Topeté; if she had to be sick, so be it. She could be sick.

But what good would it do?

Humiliation burned at Marcey's cheeks. She didn't understand and didn't want to ask.

A little vial pressed into her waiting palm wasn't enough to make her want to ask, but it wasn't enough to make her take anything either. She stared at Devon across the table. "Why do it this way?" she asked.

Devon grinned at her. "I would think it obvious. You want to fuck up someone's day, don't you?"

"That's bullshit and you know it."

"I don't think you realize what you're compromising by not going along with this," he answered. "Your paperwork's already been filed. I don't know who did it, Mar, but they've hooked you up. All we need to do is get you checked out." He glared at her pointedly. Marcey tilted her nose up and tried not to look indignant. She'd figured this out. This was just an added humiliation. Kat wanted her departure memorable, but not in a way that would make the paperwork seem oddly timed.

That bitch.

"You say you've been feeling ill since you had to spend time in the cell? Why didn't you say something?" Kat's expression was kind, but her eyes were flinty. *Do it,* they said, *or else we'll leave you in here to fend for yourself.*

Marcey raised a hand to scratch her cheek. She swallowed the vial in the same motion. This was Shelly's game, the distraction and the redirect, but with Kat's twist on it. Kat's humiliating twist. Kat's lips twitched. Marcey furrowed her brow and lurched forward. In the years since the one time her mother had forced her to take it after eating a tube of lipstick as a child, she'd forgotten just how unpleasant the sensation was of her entire body revolting against the slippery substance in her throat.

"Ms. Daniels!" Devon jumped to his feet, his expression serene and his tone panicked, but only just. The histrionics came from Kat as Marcey lost the dinner she'd picked at last night, all over the table. "Officer?" He ran to the door. "Officer, we're having an…incident. I need you to open the door."

The officer came, a different one from the one who'd escorted Marcey up to the interview room. He pushed the door open and took one look at the mess. Kat was supporting Marcey, trying to get her to throw up into the trash can from the corner of the room. It was no good though; it was going everywhere. She cringed, looking up at the officer, her forehead stinging with sweat. "Mr. Austin Jackson just said my bail was posted—urp." Marcey threw her head forward, this time actually succeeding in getting most of the vomit in the trash can. Kat's fingers were warm on Marcey's back, gentle.

"Fucking hell. Don't come near me." The officer took a step back and held out his hand to Devon. "Let me see the documentation. She's still gotta go to Central Booking."

"Apparently Johnson fucked up. She put the paperwork in even though Daniels never made it there. It means we were able to post before Central Booking closed."

Kat raised an eyebrow at Marcey. That was a mighty breech of protocol.

"Does ADA Johnson know?" the officer demanded.

"She signed off on it too," Devon answered. "Now, I probably should get Ms. Daniels out of here before she makes an even bigger mess."

"I'm going to need to clear it with the DA's office."

"Look," Devon said. He got up and moved to stand beside the officer. "See here, and here? That's Johnson's signature. She signed this authorization herself when she realized that Ms. Daniels couldn't have possibly done what she'd turned herself in for."

"Fine, then. Let me get her things."

"I hate you," Marcey said to her as Devon put his papers back into his bag and settled it across his chest. She tilted her head forward once more and threw up bile. "I hate you so fucking much."

The room blurred when Marcey's things where shoved into her hands and the three of them were shooed back out onto the street. Marcey felt a smug little surge of triumph, as though knowing they'd gotten away with something so daring was somehow vindication. She knew it wasn't. She knew the whole thing was a mess, but she walked out of there content all the same.

Kat led them up the street, passing Marcey a bottle of Pepto and a package of makeup remover wipes. Devon hailed them a cab. And then, just like that, they were gone. There was no Marcey sitting waiting for Linda Johnson's judgment now. There was just the thrill of it all.

"Where are we going?" Marcey asked. She gulped down a few minty mouthfuls of the Pepto and put it into her purse. Her stomach was still churning, but she was focused enough to push forward now. "I mean, they're going to start looking for me soon enough."

Devon shook his head. "Probably not, actually. Johnson will, sure, but she'll find that all the paperwork is kosher. She signed it. She'll have to find a justifiable reason for you to have never made it to Central Booking. And any way she does it'll make her look bad."

Marcey nodded. "So we've got some time there. Has the transaction gone through?"

Kat flipped her phone over and unlocked it. There was a text from Kim. "See for yourself, Marcey, and watch your empire grow."

"There's no need to be dramatic." Marcey scowled. She read the e-mail quickly. "So a rendezvous at the storage unit?"

"Given what we're up against, it needs to be empty as soon as possible," Kat said. "And then we'll figure out how to break the story."

"Wouldn't…"

"Let's not talk about her, Marcey, all right?"

"Why not?" Marcey demanded. "She's your fucking girlfriend, Kat. If she's the one pulling the trigger on this, as we agreed, then I need her to buy in like, yesterday."

Kat looked down at her fingernails. The cab filled with an uncomfortable silence. Marcey swallowed down another mouthful of bile.

"She'll do it," Kat promised.

"You don't sound so certain," Marcey shot back. "Is she pissed at you because you're fucking around on her? Because I know I am."

"I like you, Marcey. You're a pretty face, but you're playing with forces you couldn't possibly hope to understand. And until you realize just how doomed you are, you'd best let the big girls manipulate the board."

"This is *my* heist, Kat."

"Your part is done, Marcey. This is about Wei and me now. How this plays out will determine our future."

Devon, beside them, was silent, and the city fell away and rose up and then fell away again, the wave of business transitioning to residential and then back to business. Marcey met Kat's gaze evenly until Kat looked away.

CHAPTER 35

The Walk Away

SHELLY, GWEN, AND KIM WERE already at the unit when Kat and Marcey got there. They lingered outside for a moment while the cabbie sorted out the fare. Marcey pulled on a clean shirt and flicked some sick from her jeans. Devon grabbed her arm and pulled her aside. He'd gotten out of the car with them, but he wasn't planning on staying. "Don't stay with Kat tonight," he hissed.

"I was going to go to Shelly's." Marcey kept her voice low. Kat was on the phone, presumably with Topeté. Marcey wasn't that keen on overhearing what was being said. Not after the day she'd had. Her stomach lurched. Marcey pulled away from Devon, afraid she was going to be sick again. "Why?"

"I've known Kat Barber a long time, kid. This is the moment when she truly shines. She'll need the time tonight to make sure that Topeté does what she wants. So stay out of her hair." Just then, Kat turned and the mid-morning sunlight caught her hair and made it shine the color of straw, warm and welcoming. It reminded Marcey of happier times—Thanksgiving, autumns in full fall colors back in college—and her fingers twitched. She wanted to be free to reach out and touch it, free enough for Kat to say she was more than a pretty face. "She's using you," Devon added. "She knows that sleeping with you will make you controllable, like some sort of sick puppy. That's what she wants. Because you and your plan were never part of her endgame."

"Does everyone have to know my fucking business?" Marcey's lips pitched downward, but then Kat smiled a serene, gentle smile, and Marcey felt herself returning it effortlessly. She was already too far gone. This was a disaster in the making. "I'm fine. I know what I'm doing. This isn't about her and Topeté."

"You're in love with her, Marcey. That's the problem. Shelly's worried. She sees the signs."

"So she sent you, the big scary lawyer, to set me straight? Devon, no offense, but you're not exactly the most intimidating guy on the planet. Plus, we both know that Charlie owned your ass." Marcey tilted her head. "What were you in with him for? Don't you stand to lose if the book ever goes public?"

Devon opened his mouth. Closed it. Opened it again, his brown eyes almost black and flinty with annoyance. "If you pursue this any further, she's only going to hurt you."

"Devon, I'm not going to. I never planned to. It was never about her like that." She touched her cheek, the back of her neck, looked down at her feet. Everything seemed ill-fitting. "This is a *game*. We all have our roles to play. If I needed to set up something that ensured I got the outcome I wanted, then so be it."

He didn't seem convinced. Marcey wondered if her face was giving something away, if she was projecting some emotion that she wasn't aware she was showing. She was always better than that. Everyone said so. Her poker face was unreadable, even if she made dumb decisions in the process of playing sometimes.

Marcey tried again. "Look, I get it. It looks bad. All of this looks bad, but I'm not a goddamn idiot, okay? I know that getting in between them was stupid, but it bought me the time and trust I needed from Kat, and it got this job done. We're all about to get what we want. Why not just let it lie? Why lecture me?"

"Because you're still that same kid who sat next to Darius and cried when he got convicted. You're still that same kid who fell in love with Linda Johnson's daughter and brought all this hurt upon yourself. You're human, Marcey. Sex? Manipulation? That's one thing in theory, but it's another thing entirely in practice. You're not that person. I worry about you."

Because this is the end and you could never see her again. The thought came unbidden. *And it'll hurt far more than you know.* Marcey bit her lip and looked down, away from Devon. "Thanks," she said, not feeling thankful at all. "I'll be careful. No feelings, right?"

"Better to avoid them all together." He pressed a Zippo lighter into her hands. "Don't burn it anywhere too exciting, okay? I've canceled the contract on this place. So, once you're out, you're done here."

Marcey nodded. "Okay."

"Good luck."

He climbed back into the cab just as Kat hung up the phone. The lighter was warm from Devon's pocket. She flicked it open, and the flame blew out in the wind. Marcey closed the lighter and looked up to meet Kat's gaze. She shifted, uncomfortable. There was nothing safe about this moment of freedom. "Where are we burning this?" Marcey asked, just as the cab sped away into the busy lunchtime traffic.

"I was thinking the parking lot across the street." Kat gestured to the empty lot across the street. "The chain on the fence shouldn't be an issue. I know how good you are with locks."

Marcey's cheeks burned and she couldn't meet Kat's smirking face. She turned and stalked into the storage locker, pushing past the guy at the guard station as it was business hours and there was staff on hand. She didn't need to sign in.

The unit was already open when she approached the door. The lighter grew warm in her pocket, warmer still when she caught sight of Shelly and Kim shoving armfuls of paper into a metal wastebasket. Gwen was sitting at the workbench, flipping through notebooks, probably checking for important details they'd missed. There was a pile of things—a deck of cards and a few other mementos—set aside on the workbench. Marcey slipped in and stood next to Gwen, running her fingers over them while Kat lingered in the doorway.

"Good, you're all right," Gwen said.

"Yeah." Marcey glanced over her shoulder. "Turns out you were right. Giving Johnson the book would ensure that she was distracted during the time that LePage was trying to get a hold of her while the action was taking place. And Topeté stalled her just long enough. Her face when he finally called back was impressive."

"You were with her?" Gwen raised an eyebrow. She ran a hand over her close-cropped hair. "Was she livid?"

"You have *no* idea," Marcey said. "I got grilled for another few hours on the auction after that. I didn't tell her anything, but I think she thinks I'm involved. She just can't figure out why I'd give her what she wanted."

"Because it's an obvious fake," Kat cut in.

"Kat," Kim said shortly. "So nice of you to join us."

"Things to do, Kimiko, you know how it goes," Kat replied airily. She swept into the room, a whirlwind of rolling up her sleeves and depositing her jacket on the workbench. "I do miss this space though. Charlie wrote half his legacy in here. It's a shame we had to give a fake away without discussing what we were doing." Her tone was icy.

The tension in the room was palpable. Marcey took the lead. It had to be her. It couldn't be anyone else. She ripped down a schematic from the wall and balled it up. "We couldn't tell you, Kat."

"Why not?" Kat's gaze was starkly accusatory. "We're all on the same team here, Marcey."

"Are we, though?" Marcey asked. "I took your lead on this, I followed you because it got me what I wanted, but what I wanted was not what you wanted, was it? You were perfectly content to let me fumble around your plan without ever telling me the whole thing." She glared. Kat huffed. "We might all be on the same team here, but at least the others, even your girlfriend, were honest with me about what was happening."

All the air left the room. Marcey ripped down the original picture of the ugly painting and balled that up too, throwing it into the trash can. Gwen glanced at her sideways, her eyebrows climbing up her forehead.

"You've spoken to Topeté?" Kat's voice was breathy with surprise.

"In New Hampshire." Marcey nodded. "She was the one who interrogated me, not LePage."

"But you said—" Kim gestured to Gwen and then to Shelly. That wasn't what Marcey had told them. Or even what she wanted to be believed in the end.

"It wasn't worth the risk. LePage was a wildcard she couldn't predict or control. She wanted the book. I told her I'd get it to her if she left me out of things. Guess she couldn't control Johnson either."

Kat's lips were a thin line. "No, that was her. She put the paperwork in for you last night."

"Oh?"

"Don't you see, Marcey? Honesty wouldn't kill you." Kat stalked closer. "Even if we don't trust each other—"

"Fat chance," Gwen grunted.

"—it's always better to be honest."

"Kathryn, you have a terrible record with honesty," Shelly said in her quiet way. She stepped forward, looming over all of them in her heels and with her height. Marcey was grateful; the conversation was a private one being had in front of a collection of criminals. It didn't need to be had here. She and Kat could fight about this some other time.

If there ever was another time.

"Why did you lie to me?" Kat demanded.

"Think about it, Kat. We needed to have Johnson be *absolutely* convinced that you and Topeté were on opposite sides in all this. We all knew about your arrangement. Hell, I'm sure even Johnson does." Shelly laughed. "Marcey came up with it when you sent her back from London and she found she couldn't go visit her friend anymore. Your girlfriend's emotional, invested." Shelly leaned against the workbench. "I've been talking to her since she came back to New York."

"You—you—"

Kim laughed at Kat's spluttering and nudged Gwen with her elbow. The two of them started to gather things into neat stacks that would, by Marcey's estimation, burn quickly.

"It's amazing, really, what lengths Topeté will go to in order to ensure that you both are free to fuck up your lives some more at the end of this. Romantic if it wasn't so doomed." Shelly leveled an accusatory gaze at Kat. "She cut a deal with Marcey up in the mountains and never looked back."

While Shelly admonished Kat and brought the two plans together, Marcey's stomach was roiling once more. This time the sick was not from the syrup, or even an overdose on Pepto, but from the chilling, aching feeling of heartache. Whatever foolish dreams she'd allowed herself, whatever lovelorn ideals she'd slotted Kat Barber into, Kat was not that person. This was the end. This was where they parted.

The notebook in Marcey's hands held diagrams of some bank vault in Dubai. Marcey closed it, her eyes fluttering shut. This was a good-bye in so many ways. It was cathartic, to know that it was the end of the job, this final moment of denouement before the leveling out of life once more. The weight on Marcey's shoulders was lessening, transitioning to the dull ache that came with success.

She'd succeeded, hadn't she? They were all about to get paid.

Why did she feel so awful?

"—could have just told me, Shelly. I'm not the enemy here."

Gwen cut in, her voice softer than Marcey could ever remember hearing it before. "No one is saying that you're the enemy, Kat. Not even me, and I have every reason to hate you for what you did back in Rio. But in order for Marcey to step into Charlie's shoes, she's the only one who can know the full plan. That's her role: she's the mastermind."

Marcey's cheeks burned. It was high praise from the usually quiet Gwen. "Thanks," she whispered. Gwen winked at her.

Kat looked around the locker. "This feels like a death, then. We're burning Charlie's funeral pyre."

Thoughts of gratitude and relief filled Marcey. Kat was letting the subject drop. *Thank God.*

"In a way, it is." Marcey looked down at the mess of papers in her hands. She straightened them, yellow and wrinkled as they were with age. "This was the last of Charlie's legacy—the last that we control, at any rate. And we're going to burn it."

"That's it then." Shelly put her hands into the back pockets of her jeans. "We come together this last time, Kim distributes the funds, and then what? We rely on Topeté to break the news of Johnson's demise?"

Marcey nodded. "Got it in one."

"You sure relying on her is a good idea?" Kim glanced over at Kat, who was still stewing in the corner of the storage unit. "Like, I know you've got her pussy whipped or whatever, Kat, but that's an awful lot to ask a LEO who maybe isn't too keen on this anyway."

"I think you'll find," Kat said shortly, "that the feeling of distaste is entirely mutual. Wei does not want this any more than we do, but she also is required to do her job. Interpol works to expose things like this, illegal art sales and the like. While it's bothersome for her to destroy so close an ally, for the book, she'll do pretty much anything." She cocked an eyebrow at Marcey. "And she knows it's a fake, before you start thinking you've won."

"Guess you can't fool everyone, huh?" Marcey bit her lip. That was the hold out, the part of the plan Marcey wasn't going to tell *anyone*. Topeté had agreed to it, and with it she'd promised something to Marcey far more precious than any book of names Topeté had no intention of ever turning in anyway: she was going to make sure Darius got his parole and got out, by the end of the month. "Topeté will get it."

"This was just supposed to be a walk away," Gwen said, her voice low in her throat. "You told us this would end. If Topeté has the book, there's no way she'll ever go away. She'll have dirt on us, evidence. We won't be free to move. You fucked us, Daniels. Fucked us good."

"I don't think so," Shelly answered. "Because she's done things documented in that book too. That's why Charlie kept it up to date. It's a document that's damning to all parties. Knowing she has it, has it and can never use it, that's good enough for me."

"That isn't good enough," Gwen said. "It's a fine plan for now. We get paid, take on new identities as was part of the deal, but what happens when Topeté finds a way to get herself immunity and starts going through the book?"

"She won't," Kat answered. "I'll destroy it before it ever comes to that."

"Your word is no better than dirt." Gwen's frown was deep now. Marcey watched helplessly, not quite knowing what to do or what to say. "Send it back to Marcey if it ever comes to that."

Marcey shoved the stack of journals she was holding into the metal trash barrel and put up her hands. "And my word is any better?"

"You're a kid, Mar," Shelly said quietly. "You can keep it safe, or destroy it."

"I could just do that now," Marcey pointed out.

Kim opened her laptop. "Yes, but we won't get Johnson without the book."

"I'll give it to you once we know Johnson's going down." Marcey turned to Gwen. "Is that good enough for you, Gwen?"

Gwen nodded. "It'll have to be."

"Good." The hair on the back of Marcey's neck stood up; the chill that ran through her at the icy tone in Kat's voice was enough to make the involuntary shiver of fear she felt seem more pronounced, more real. This was the woman they'd all warned her about, her expression a black and stormy sea. "Then this can be the walk away we all wanted it to be."

From her bag, Kim tugged her tablet and a Bluetooth keyboard. "Shall we then? So we can get out of here before this all comes to blows?"

"It won't, Kim, stop being dramatic." But Gwen's voice was tight, her expression pained and annoyed. This was hard for her. Marcey hated it for her.

Marcey glanced over her shoulder, trying to catch Kat's eye, trying to figure out if this was the end, but Kat was not looking at her. Kat's expression was eerily blank as she stood before the metal drum, her hands plunged into her pockets.

"Okay. This is a program I've built, you input your account and routing numbers into it, it disperses money. It's auto refreshing—the cache deletes every three minutes, privacy and security, whatever, anyway, so you have to go quick, but once you punch in the numbers, your allocated amount will transfer from the shell we set up for the auction house to pay. They'll be deleted once the money transfers, or three minutes, whichever comes first." Kim held out the tablet to Gwen.

"How do we know you don't keep a cache?" Gwen muttered, keying in numbers. Marcey looked away.

Kim shrugged. "Suppose you'll just have to trust me."

"That'll be the day." Kat's smile was without mirth.

Gwen passed the tablet back to Kim and flipped her wrist over to watch the time. The silence drew out. Gwen's phone chimed. She pulled it out and nodded to Kim, who held the tablet back out to her.

"See, history erased." Kim sounded almost smug.

Gwen flashed a thin smile at Kim. "Okay, I believe you."

It was as though the ice had melted. Victory churned, uncomfortable and unrelenting, in Marcey's stomach. They passed around the tablet, and after Kat had put in her final series of complicated account numbers and pins, Kim took the tablet back. She heaved a great sigh and swiped her finger over the screen in a zig-zag pattern. The screen went dark. Smoke started to emanate from the headphone port. Kim threw it into the trash can with the rest of Charlie's papers. "That was my only copy of that program."

"Shame," Kat said airily. "That could have earned you some good money."

"Sometimes personal safety and preserving professional relationships is worth more than two hours of coding, Barber." Kim rolled her eyes and slung her bag over her shoulder. "You need help with the burn?"

"Nah, I got it covered." Marcey shook her head.

Kim grabbed Gwen's elbow and drew her to her feet. "Come on, I have to show you something about that thing you asked about last week."

"What—*oh*." Gwen got hurriedly to her feet. "It was nice knowing y'all."

"Same to you," Shelly said, a weak smile on her face. "Shame I've already forgotten your name."

"I'll call you, Mar," Kim called over her shoulder as she and Gwen hurried away.

Marcey watched them go, full of a hollow ache, wondering if she'd ever see either of them again. Her fingers flexed, twitched. She looked to Kat, staring down at the papers and broken tablet in the trash can.

Kat turned to Shelly, her face oddly open. "Are you all right with this plan?"

"I don't have much of a choice, do I, Kathryn? You have what you want, Topeté gets her due, and you'll get your freedom?"

"There's always a choice," Kat replied. She moved the workbench before taking a handful of papers and crossing back to the trash can. "It's just a matter of making sure that the one you make is the correct one."

Shelly watched Kat like a shark evaluating her next meal. Her expression was closed off. Marcey could not read it at all. "I understand that. Do you, Kathryn?"

Kat's reply came breathily, as though she was exhilarated at the mere prospect of it. "You've no idea what it's like, having something like this hanging over your head, Shelly."

"It's a noose we've all willingly slipped out necks into," Shelly said. She swept large armfuls of the paperwork into the trash can. "Getting involved with Charlie was a risk. You knew it, I knew it. Hell, even Topeté knew it. This is just the end game of that. You have to own the ending or else the beginning is nothing."

Kat nodded. Shelly dusted off her hands. "You're done in here?" she asked Marcey.

Marcey nodded.

"I'll take this out then, burn it. Will you wipe down the place?"

Marcey held out the lighter from Devon. "Devon said to use this."

A smile curled at Shelly's lips. "Charlie's lighter. That's fitting." She tossed it up, caught it, and put it in her pocket. "I guess this is it for us, then, isn't it Marcey?"

"I suppose so," Marcey said. Her promise to Devon was forgotten. She would go home tonight, beg her mother's forgiveness, find a place for her and Darius to live when Topeté came through with her final piece of the puzzle.

"It's been nice knowing you," Shelly said. And then she was gone.

And Kat lingered, like a moth to the flame. Her eyes tracked Marcey as she scrubbed down the unit, wiping away any evidence of themselves. The space was gaunt, the echoing crusting remains of a place forgotten, Charlie's legacy stripped away from the walls and burning. The lights illuminated the dark hollows under Kat's eyes, making her look skeletal. She hadn't slept last night either, then.

"Is this going to work?" Marcey asked.

"I don't know." Kat wrapped her arms around herself. "Wei's connection to the Justice Department should be enough to get them in the door. Especially if we can couple it with Kim's leak to the press." Kat sucked her lip into her mouth. "This is the end for us too, Marcey."

Marcey turned, rag in hand, and stared at Kat. It was the truth she had known was coming, but they were the words Marcey refused to accept. Even in her moments of clarity the night before, knowing that Kat was using her, positioning her in the perfect place to take the fall, Marcey had still wanted this, had still been most of the way to loving her. "I don't want you to walk away."

Somewhere in the distance, there was the slam of a unit door being closed. Kat cast her eyes down and looked away from Marcey. As the words tumbled from Marcey's mouth, Kat's nostrils flared and her posture went rigid. Her gaze was icy. "You don't control me, Marcey."

"That doesn't change that I don't want you to leave when this job is finished!" Marcey threw the rag down and raked her fingers through her hair. Her mind racing, mouth outpacing her logical thoughts. She stared down at her feet, shoulders quaking with the humiliating tears that stung at the corners of her eyes.

Marcey wanted to hate her.

Kat's shoes, expensive with the red bottoms, swam into her blurry vision, and Kat's fingers brushed her cheeks. Her thumbs smoothed the tears away from Marcey's skin and tilted her chin upward to meet Kat's green-eyed gaze. "You knew how this was going to end the moment you got on that plane. The moment you called me." Her lips were warm, sweet, good-bye. "You are a wonderful girl. You will make someone very happy one day." Kat shook her head sadly. "But it can't be me, darling. As much as I'd like it, we're no good for each other."

"It's because of her, isn't it?"

"Wei?" Kat laughed bitterly. "This has nothing to do with her."

"You're lying."

Kat leaned in, her lips brushed against Marcey's bottom lip. "Of course I am," she whispered. Kat's fingers tangled in Marcey's hair. Marcey wanted her to let go, to walk away, not make her feel this pain again. Marcey bit down on Kat's lip. Kat pulled away and Marcey tasted copper with the stars in her vision. Kat's tongue was relentless, taking, taking, and taking again.

Marcey pushed, aggressive. Her fingers tugged at Kat's blouse, at the buttons of her suit pants. Kat pulled harder still, spinning Marcey around and forcing her up onto the bare workbench. It bit into Marcey's ass, and Marcey hissed in pain. Kat hummed into the kiss, her eyes glistening with tears all her own.

The workbench was low, and their hips bumped against each other. Marcey's hand trapped between them. She kissed Kat back, her other hand wrapping around Kat's neck and refusing to let her break the kiss. Marcey twisted her wrist in quick, erratic circles, pushing past until she felt slick wetness. She pressed into that wetness, marveling at how Kat shuddered against her.

When they broke apart, Kat's eyes were blown and a trickle of blood trailed down the corner of her mouth. "Inside," Kat urged, lowering her lips to Marcey's neck, one hand splayed out across Marcey's breast. Her other still tangled in Marcey's hair and she pulled so hard the pain shot through the back of Marcey's skull. Her finger slipped inside and she had Kat. Had her exactly how Marcey always wanted her: wanting, willing, and utterly captive.

Kat didn't last long. Marcey rocked into her and Kat came, cresting on Marcey's fingers. Her breath was sticky, wet on Marcey's neck.

Breathless, Marcey drew back. "Come back to my place," she said, even though she had no place to go. "We'll do this properly."

Kat bent, buttoned her pants and straightened her shirt, pocketing a busted button. "No," she said. "We won't."

"But—"

"I'll be in touch, once Wei's part is done. Good-bye, Marcey."

CHAPTER 36

Wei, at a Moment of Decision

"MY NAME IS WEI LIN Topeté. I work for Interpol and am currently liaising with the New York Assistant District Attorney for Manhattan." William scowled at her, but Wei forced a tight-lipped smile onto her face. She'd been on the phone half the morning with the police in Lincoln, New Hampshire. Apparently, a painting had been delivered to the eccentric collector who lived up in the woods, with a very polite note attached thanking him for the loan. William hadn't understood it, and Wei hadn't either, until they looked at the manifest for the shipping company. The package had been sent from the auction house where the painting was sold, but this was a second copy, as the purchaser of the painting had yet to collect it from the auction house.

William came back from the auction house looking haunted, one of Linda Johnson's campaign posters in his hand. "Look at this."

Wei hung up the phone. She could call back. "What?"

"You were right. They were up to something." He smoothed a sales receipt down on the table and set it next to the campaign poster. "Look at these." He indicated the names. "They're the same. Johnson's PAC bought this painting."

"Why would she do that?" Wei's brow furrowed. "Especially if the painting is back in New Hampshire?"

"You're the one dating Kat Barber," William answered. "If I had to hazard a guess, she's fucking with you."

Wei shook her head. "No, that isn't what this is. This is too targeted, too calculated." She flipped the receipt over.

"Hey, do we have a Topeté in here?" The desk sergeant from the front of the bullpen called across the room. A few eyes slid around, looking for Wei. A few more wore expressions of confusion. A courier clad in a bike helmet and leggings stood at the desk, a small package in his hands.

Wei got to her feet and crossed the room in five quick steps. "I'm Topeté," she said.

"Gotta sign." The courier smacked some gum and passed her a form. Wei scribbled her signature and took the package. She ripped it open and a thumb drive fell into her hand, nondescript and black. Wei poked her fingers into the package and looked into it. There was nothing else.

She made her way back to her desk. "Maybe this is your answer," she said to William. He was poring over the documents, rubbing his temples, trying to make sense of them. "Special delivery." She held up the flash drive.

He looked up at her with weary eyes. "I don't want to play any more of Kat Barber's games." But he tugged his laptop toward himself and plugged the flash drive into it. "Let me scan this first."

"Oh, come on, they wouldn't put a virus on it."

"Are you joking?" William snorted. "Of course they would. The breed of asshole you're fucking would totally try and bring down our entire computer system just as a final middle finger to this goddamn mess." He exhaled and narrowed his eyes. "But it seems you're right. No viruses."

The smug thrill of triumph shot though Wei like lightning until she saw the files contained within the flash drive. There were hundreds of them: a series of payments, all small, all from different accounts funneling into a two-million-dollar payment from one account to another and then to a third. And there, at the bottom of each transaction was a memo. Indicating a donation to a political action committee.

"No," Wei breathed.

All the color drained from LePage's face. "They didn't."

"They did."

"This is...this is... Johnson used her campaign funds to pay for this painting. She authorized the transaction while the auction was going on. She paid for this out of the public money she took to fund her campaign." William's voice was no more than a whisper. "Fuck me..."

"We have to keep this quiet," Wei said in a low voice. "No one can know about this."

"Fuck, Wei, we have to *report it*. This is damning. It could get her sent to jail." William tugged his awful hair out of his eyes and tucked it behind his ear. "We need to be really careful about what our next move is."

"But is this information true?" Wei whispered. "Shouldn't we verify it?"

"Where's Marcey Daniels?" William asked. "Didn't Johnson have her sent to Central Booking?"

"She should still be there." Wei tugged the flash drive from the computer and tucked it into her pocket. "If we hurry…"

"What do you mean, if we hurry?"

Wei tugged her jacket on, flipping her hair out from under the collar. "She's got a damn good lawyer, William. It's only a matter of time until they let her out."

Marcey Daniels wasn't in lock up. She wasn't anywhere. The paperwork had all been filed. Wei's eyes went wide, staring down at one particular document. Her signature stared up at her, plain as day.

"Did you sign that?" William asked.

"No, but I know who did." There was only one person who could fake something so convincingly.

"You're…you're *joking*." William looked disgusted. "Topeté, she's a loose cannon. We can't allow this to continue."

Wei handed the clipboard back to the booking clerk, her expression hard. She tugged William away from the busy atrium of the station where she was sure no one would overhear. "I need you to stall Johnson. Just for a few hours."

"What are you going to do?" Wei froze, wondering if this was the moment when William revealed that his loyalty was not to the law and his career, as Wei had initially thought, but rather to Johnson. She didn't think she was wrong about him, not after Rio, not after watching him throw away a marriage and the love of his life for the sake of his career. William sucked in a huge, heavy breath. "Evidence like this will get found sooner rather than later. All she has to do is get a whisper of it and she'll hide everything."

"I need to see someone." Wei didn't elaborate. "Just stall her."

He put up his hands. "I hope you know what you're doing, Wei."

Wei's expression was tight-lipped. "Me too." She turned and left, walking out into the cool day. She hesitated only for a moment before she raised a hand and hailed a cab, rattling off the address of Kat's hotel without a second thought. She had to know what the hell Kat was thinking, doing this. This didn't feel like Kat; none of this felt like Kat.

And Wei's deal with Marcey Daniels wasn't enough to get her this sort of sway.

No, there was some bigger shift happening here, and Wei didn't know what it was.

The hotel was empty. It was just after check-out time. Wei made her way up to the third floor and let herself inside. Kat started, as though surprised. Her pants were unbuttoned and she was just in her bra. "What did you do?" Wei demanded, closing the door with a snap.

Kat turned, her eyes going wide. Her hand scrabbled for her purse, for something hidden there. Wei crossed the room and grabbed her hand, wrenching it away and pressing her up against the wall. Her fingers closed around Kat's throat. "What the hell did you do?" Her voice was cracking now, bitter. Her accent grew more pronounced. "You ruined this. You ruined our chances, Kat."

"Have I?" Kat asked. Wei wanted to squeeze, but Kat's pupils were already wide and her breathing labored. She pushed Kat against the wall. "I thought I'd all but assured victory."

"How can this be a victory? How can this be anything other than the end of my career?"

"Isn't—" Choking, Kat pushed Wei away. She ran a hand over her neck, gasping for air. She looked at Wei like a caged animal, poised to lash out. Her lips curled away from her teeth, her voice a snarl. "Isn't that what you wanted? A chance to walk away? With that book out there and your stupid American friends aware of its existence, we had no hope. Now we control it."

"Because you're fucking her."

"No," Kat said. "Not anymore. She has what she wanted. I'm done."

Wei's hand clenched into a fist. She couldn't accept this. This manipulation that was as clever as it was hurtful. Kat knew how to push Wei into saying yes to things, but this time, this time it would not be enough.

The wounds of this relationship, of the woman caged before her, were aching and deep. Wei clutched her chest, her eyes glassy with the onset of tears. Love was a death meant to be died a thousand times over the course of a lifetime; each blow, each careful cut from Kat, severed years from her life. "I'm nothing anymore. You've torn everything out of me and settled yourself against my heart, Kat."

Kat's gaze softened, a single tear rolled down her cheek. "Yes, darling," she said.

"So why does it feel as though you've ripped my heart out to make room for yourself?" She said nothing, turning away from Wei, from the tears that now flowed freely. "Answer me!" Wei begged, words in English all but forgotten. "Please."

Her back ramrod straight, Kat turned back to face Wei. "I promised you that I would find a way to get Charlie's book, long before Interpol ever caught wind of me. Long before I ever got caught. Long before Charlie ever did either. That was the first promise I made to you, Wei. How could you have forgotten it?"

"Because you couldn't do those things, Kat! You could pretend to be something you're not. You like the game, the manipulation of people and feelings to get what you want." Wei looked down at her hands. "Now you have me right where you wanted me, don't you? Where you can watch as I betray the profession I've given my life to, just to run away with you. That's what really makes you tick, doesn't it?"

Kat was a ship in the sea of Wei's anger. Good. Let her see how she'd broken Wei for her own amusement. Kat's face was no longer blank, her expression no longer serene. She was outraged.

"Everything I did, every time I slept with that awful girl, that was for you." She turned, grabbing a shirt and pulling it on over her head. "I did it so you could get out from under the thumb of Johnson and her idiot assistant. They were going to find your name as soon as they got the book. They were going to find out what you did for Charlie and they were going to destroy you for it. I saw it coming, Wei. I saw it and I did everything I could to stop it. If you do this, if you tell your handler at Justice what you know about Johnson, Marcey will give us the book. The original. No forgery made to throw Johnson off the scent." Kat stepped forward, grabbing at the lapels of Wei's jacket. "It's just a little thing, Wei. You don't even have to worry about Marcey after this. She's got her revenge and her friend's getting out. She won't be a problem."

So, the eleventh hour was upon them. "I can't do it, Kat."

"What?"

"I can't lie. Not when I have just as much evidence to show that you deliberately framed Linda Johnson for corruption." Wei grabbed Kat's hands and pushed Kat away gently. Her hands shook. Kat had gone about it all wrong. Wei could get the book from Marcey Daniels so long as her friend was granted parole. With the book, Wei could find a way to clear her name without having to do this, to play into Kat's fantasy.

She drew a shaky breath. Tears stung at the corners of her eyes. Maybe, in the end, all of this would be for nothing, but this was her freedom. She leaned down, kissing Kat gently on the mouth. "When William called me and told me Charlie was dead, I wondered if this would be the end of us."

"No—" Kat's breath hitched. "No, Wei." The tears at the corners of her eyes were real now. "We can be free, we can be together. Happy. In love."

"Maybe one day, we'll meet again, Kat, but I think…for now, that this should be good-bye." Wei kissed her once more, turned and walked out of the hotel room and into the growing night.

POST

Services, Rendered—

THE ARTICLE IN THE PAPER some three weeks later was bombastic to say the least. Marcey read greedily, sitting on the appointed bench, a little before the appointed time. William LePage, it read, ace investigator for the New York District Attorney, had found another way to demonstrate his innate understanding of crime. He'd found a trend in the campaign donations of his boss, ADA Linda Johnson, and brought it to the attention of the Department of Justice.

"The man always was career oriented."

Marcey jumped and lowered the paper. Kat Barber stood before her holding a bag from a bakery Marcey knew well. It wasn't close. Marcey was almost flattered. "You scared me," she confessed. "Who's career oriented?"

"LePage." Kat wrinkled her nose. "I hadn't considered him, not in depth, as an option for the end game." She shrugged. "Shame though, as Wei backed out." Kat sat down beside Marcey. Her leather boots were splattered with paint and her jeans were old; the knee on one of the legs was a giant hole. "I got you a scone."

"You're so English." Marcey rolled her eyes. "Thanks."

Her nose wrinkled. "Everyone appreciates a good scone, Marcey."

"I suppose you're right."

"So, your friend gets out today."

"He does." Marcey nodded. "I hadn't expected you to stick around to see it happen."

"It wasn't by design, I assure you. The book never made it into my hands, as per our deal." Kat waved her hand dismissively, as though she wasn't speaking a threat. "I came to collect."

"I told you to be here." Marcey put a corner of the scone into her mouth. It was still warm. "So, is this really a conversation where you hold any of the cards?"

"My, my." Kat raised an eyebrow. "Aren't you big for your boots, Ms. Daniels." She looked down at her nails. "If this isn't a friendly exchange, then why am I here?"

From her bag, Marcey produced a thin Moleskine journal, filled with pages upon pages of her own notes. The spreadsheet on the anonymous cloud drive was gone. Instead, all that remained was this. The book. A code, written in dashes and notes. She tore a page from the back of the book and flipped to an entry designated with only the number three. She wrote down the address carefully, her tongue caught between her teeth.

"A little bird told me you might want to know where this was." She got to her feet, her smile blossoming. It was on the other side of the world. Kim had taken it there doing some charity work. It would keep Kat guessing, keep her busy until Marcey could figure out how to deal with the myriad of emotions that still came up when she looked at the woman. "I've got to get down to the bus station. Darius is going to be arriving soon." She paused, the early June sunlight warming her cheeks, before she added, "Be seeing you, Kat Barber."

"I'm sure, Marcey Daniels. I'm sure you will."

CODA

Wei, at a New Beginning

SHE STANDS AT THE BASE of a mountain, this one far shorter than the last. It juts straight out of the sea, the city crawling up around it, as though it will protect it from the angry ocean. This peninsula and this bay, the point where two great forces meet, feels old to Wei. Old as she crawls through streets lined with wire, old as she passes vibrant houses and colorful people.

But it is here, tucked away at the end of the world, that she finds a woman sitting on a patio, her face turned toward the sea. Coffee in her hand, a flower in her hair. Wei reaches out, but does not touch. Not just yet.

"I never thought you'd find me." She doesn't turn around.

A smile tugs at Wei's lips, it's small and wry. Shy. In the shadow of another flat-topped mountain, they meet again. It's almost fitting.

"Maybe I wanted to see what came next."

Kat turns, her eyes warm and her body wrapped in a blanket against the cold ocean air. "Hello," she says. "I've missed you."

"Hello," Wei answers. "It's been a while."

ABOUT ELLEN SIMPSON

Ellen graduated from the University of Vermont in 2010, majoring in political science with an emphasis on media and its effects on society.

She served as social media writer and story editor for *Carmilla: The Series* before becoming creative consultant on *Carmilla: The Movie*.

A love of running, watercolor painting, the mountains and the ocean fill her downtime.

Ellen Simpson's first book with Ylva is *The Light of the World*.

CONNECT WITH AUTHOR

Website: www.ellenannes.com
Tumblr: anamatics.tumblr.com
Twitter: @anamatics

OTHER BOOKS FROM
YLVA PUBLISHING

www.ylva-publishing.com

THE LIGHT OF THE WORLD
Ellen Simpson

ISBN: 978-3-95533-507-6
Length: 357 pages (107,000 words)

Confronted with a mystery upon her grandmother's death, Eva delves into the rich and complicated history of a woman who hid far more than a long-lost-love from the world. Darkness is lurking behind every corner, and someone is looking for the key to her grandmother's secrets; the light of the world.

COLLIDE-O-SCOPE
(Norfolk Coast Investigation Story – Book 1)
Andrea Bramhall

ISBN: 978-3-95533-849-7
Length: 291 pages (90,000 words)

One unidentified dead body. One tiny fishing village. Forty residents and everyone's a suspect. Where do you start? Newly promoted Detective Sergeant Kate Brannon and King's Lynn CID have to answer that question and more as they untangle the web of lies wrapped around the tiny village of Brandale Stiathe Harbour to capture the killer of Connie Wells.

REQUIEM FOR IMMORTALS
Lee Winter

ISBN: 978-3-95533-710-0
Length: 263 pages (86,000 words)

Requiem is a brilliant cellist with a secret. The dispassionate assassin has made an art form out of killing Australia's underworld figures without a thought. One day she's hired to kill a sweet and unassuming innocent. Requiem can't work out why anyone would want her dead—and why she should even care.

THE LAVENDER LIST
Meg Harrington

ISBN: 978-3-95533-623-3
Length: 249 pages (62,000 words)

After the Second World War, Amelia Maldonado opts to live a quiet life bussing tables at a diner during the day and going out for auditions at night. The one bright spot is her friendship with the charming Laura Wright, a well-heeled woman with a mysterious war-related past.

When Laura shows up outside the diner, barely conscious and spitting lousy lies, Amelia takes it upon herself to figure out the truth. From mobsters to spies, Amelia quickly finds herself forced back into a world of shadows she thought she'd escaped long ago and thrust into partnership with the one person she's sure can ruin her—the enigmatic Laura Wright.

A Heist Story
© 2018 by Ellen Simpson

ISBN: 978-3-95533-958-6

Also available as e-book.

Published by Ylva Publishing, legal entity of Ylva Verlag, e.Kfr.

Ylva Verlag, e.Kfr.
Owner: Astrid Ohletz
Am Kirschgarten 2
65830 Kriftel
Germany

www.ylva-publishing.com

First edition: 2018

Credits
Edited by Andrea Bramhall & Robin J Samuels
Proofread by Paulette Callen
Cover Design by Adam Lloyd
Print Layout by Streetlight Graphics

www.ingramcontent.com/pod-product-compliance
Lightning Source LLC
Chambersburg PA
CBHW031333020726
47499CB00005B/1247